DI MORRISSEY is one of Australia's bestselling international novelists. She trained as a journalist with Australian Consolidated Press and became Women's Editor for the Daily Mail Group in London and worked as a creative copywriter for Ogilvy and Mather Advertising. She had her own television program in the United States on CBS and was a regular presenter on Network 10 Australia. In addition to radio broadcasting, she has written for TV, film and theatre. Di has also directed and produced films, TV programs and commercials. She recently published her first children's book, *Buster and the Queen Bee*, and is completing another. *The Bay* is her tenth adult novel.

Di lives and works in Byron Bay, in New South Wales, in between travelling to research her books.

Di Morrissey can be visited at her website:
www.dimorrissey.com

Also by Di Morrissey

Heart of the Dreaming
The Last Rose of Summer
Follow the Morning Star
The Last Mile Home
Tears of the Moon
When the Singing Stops
The Songmaster
Scatter the Stars
Blaze

DI MORRISSEY

The BAY

PAN

Pan Macmillan Australia

First published 2001 in Macmillan by Pan Macmillan Australia Pty Limited
This edition published 2002 in Pan by Pan Macmillan Australia Pty Limited
St Martins Tower, 31 Market Street, Sydney

National Library of Australia
cataloguing-in-publication data:

Morrissey, Di.
The bay.

ISBN 0 330 36344 1.

1. Women – Fiction. 2. Lifestyles – Fiction. 3. Interpersonal relations – Fiction.
4. Real estate development – Fiction. I. Title.

A823.3

Typeset in 11/13pt Sabon by Post Pre-press Group
Printed in Australia by McPherson's Printing Group

Cover and text design: Deborah Parry Graphics
Cover photograph: Tom Keating/Wildlight
Author photograph: Stuart Owen Fox

The Bay is a work of fiction. The story, events and most of the characters in it are
fictitious, although some people have kindly allowed their names to be used in the book.

Acknowledgments

JIM REVITT . . . who has always watched over me and with his brilliant wordsmith skills, improves every book I write by making me think harder, do better and reach higher.

MY FAMILY . . . my mother Kay Warbrook, who cares and fights for her coastal community; my children Gabrielle and Nick Morrissey, whose love, support, advice and humour make every day worthwhile.

BORIS JANJIC for his devotion and for smoothing the wrinkles out of every day starting with a morning flower.

IAN ROBERTSON, loyal legal friend, for soothing the scratchy bits of life.

JAMES FRASER and all my family at Pan Macmillan – thanks for all the love and encouragement over the past decade.

RON REVITT for his delightful sketches and being, along with Jim, a 'Big Brother' uncle.

Special thanks to my friends and the community of Byron Bay.

Along with all those other special bays around Australia – like Lovett Bay where I grew up – I hope they will always remain treasured and protected places.

Prologue

The Southern Ocean of Australia, 1878

THE OCEAN SLEPT. ITS SUNSET-MIRRORED SURFACE
rising and falling in a gentle swell. The men in
the small boat were silent. Smoothly, quietly,
the long wooden oars stroked into the golden
sea.

The man in the bow stood, legs planted apart,
knees flexed to maintain his balance as he
searched the water for some indication of their
prey. The six other men, some mere boys, also
studied the glistening ocean, knowing that somewhere beneath them slid the mighty leviathan,
which they had glimpsed what now seemed like
aeons ago. It was a rogue individual.

On the steam barque *Orion*, anchored to the
south, the crew remained hopeful that their men in

the small whaleboat would capture the humpback that was cruising steadily north.

Jergen Strom, the harpooner, was among the best – fearless like his Norse ancestors, strong, swift and deadly accurate. He had an instinct; they said he could think like a whale, knowing where the giant creature might rise up and blow. And it was this intuition that made him now turn and look around.

'Ahoy, blow astern. Come about, pull to the port.' The men had the double-ended boat retracing its wake in seconds, surging forward to meet the oncoming shape that was cleaving the ocean just below the surface.

They charged towards each other, the boat suddenly seeming so fragile, the massive bulk of the lone bull whale looking so formidable.

The man in the bow was poised, his thigh braced in a niche cut in the decking. The headsman grasped the twenty-foot steering oar and stood ready for 'the change'.

'It's sounding!' A young seaman shouted what all hands knew. But in the instant that the whale arched its back, elevating the big tail flukes to throw itself sideways and plunge to the depths, Jergen lunged and released the harpoon. It flew in a low arc, its tail of rope spinning behind it, then fell as the whale dived. The steel fluke thrust into the back of the beast, searing into the soft layers of blubber.

Then, according to ancient custom, the steersman moved from the bow oar to the aft and the headsman, in command of the craft, exchanged places with the harpooner. To the headsman fell the honour of the kill. Picking up the lance he waited for the whale to surface.

The maddened creature rose, shuddered, then disappeared beneath the churning sea, the thread that joined it to the boat whirring so fast around the loggerhead it began to smoke. The men waited, their oars resting horizontally above the water. The rope played out then stopped. They tensed and watched the sea.

It was an explosion of many sounds – the great gasping breath from the blowhole, the eerie high-pitched call, the crunching of oars, the splintering of wood, the shouts of the crew. It was the night-mare they all feared most.

The whale rose under the boat, its angry bulk lifting the wooden peanut out of the water before the vessel tilted to one side and began to slide down its body. But in those seconds the steersman threw his weight behind the lance, sinking it into a vital section of the spine. One of the men, frantically grasping for some support, felt his hand graze over the thick rubbery hide before he was in the foaming water with the other men and the upturned boat.

With a mighty flick the whale's flukes came down, splintering the small boat, dangerously close to the men doing their best to swim away from the monster. The young seaman, afraid this was the end of him, turned to see the whale blow once more – a gushing of spluttering air. But this time the milky vapour rushed red. And the whale began its agonising flurry, shuddering, shaking, shivering in bewildered pain, a prelude to death.

As it slowly rolled onto its back, breathing its last, each man was fighting to save himself – from sharks, from drowning, from his companions struggling to hang onto any debris from the shattered boat. None had noticed that Strom had caught his leg in a loop of the rope and been ripped into the sea, tangled beneath the dying hulk where his drowned body now floated, trapped.

By the time a rescue boat launched from the *Orion* had recovered the shocked survivors, the whale carcass had sunk into the deep reaches of the ocean, towing with it the umbilical cord that joined the hunted and the hunter.

As night fell on the silent sea and drifting debris, darkness softened the floating red mantle of death.

The Bay. Dawn, New Year's Day

The moon and sun blended, their paths overlapping in the rising of a new day and the relinquishing of the night hours. The gold and silver sisters glided past each other in a pearly sky, and in that moment worlds and time briefly touched.

From the gleaming white lighthouse adorning the headland like a spun-sugar decoration atop a wedding cake, another light signalled mechanically from prismatic crystals, winking seaward to the dawn and misty horizon.

And in that distant mist there suddenly appeared a shimmering boat of another age. It had two masts, square-rigged, and six whaleboats suspended from davits. On the deck were two glowing brick fireplaces, each supporting a huge black metal cauldron of whale blubber and boiling oil.

On the heavy wooden stem beneath the bowsprit was the carving of a woman, full breasted and proud faced, with waves of flowing hair painted gold. Behind the figurehead and on port and starboard bow planks, red letters proclaimed this brigantine to be the *Lady Richmond*.

When the light next winked at the eastern horizon, the vision had disappeared.

Chapter One

Dawn, New Year's Day

HOLLY STIRRED IN THE PASSENGER SEAT, GLANCING at her husband who was driving with his usual grim concentration. His profile lit by the dawn light showed a faint shadow of stubble and the beginning of a slackening of his jawline. But Andrew was still a handsome man in his late forties. Holly was forty-five. Did he think she was still as attractive as she had been when they'd met? She had been pretty enough at twenty-two to be offered a modelling contract overseas. Andrew had proposed when she told him about it. So she'd chosen Andrew. It was many years before she realised he had given her no choice.

She'd dabbled at things, but two children quickly came along and there had never been time for her to consider a career. A devoted mother and the wife of a successful architect, she had spent her days running a beautiful home and garden, and smoothing out the wrinkles in her family's lives.

Now it was time for a change – a decision she had made and gently orchestrated. She was still amazed Andrew had agreed to the whole Bay idea. Although, he had made vague remarks about 'perhaps doing some business with people from up that way'. She knew Beacon Bay was regarded as a gem for anyone in the building, design and development arena. Just as it was for those dedicated to preserving its tranquillity and natural beauty.

'Happy New Year. Where were we at midnight?' Holly stretched as best she could.

'No idea. I didn't bother to wake you, seemed a bit pointless. We must have been around Kempsey. Saw a few fireworks in the distance. We're nearly there, I might stop and stretch my legs soon.' Andrew yawned.

'It's been a long drive for you,' she said, 'but I think it was best to drive through the New Year's Eve madness and leave them to their parties. Much traffic?'

'Um, some in local pockets, but the freeway has been pretty clear. I'm ready for breakfast though. Not that I've seen much in the way of places to eat. Petrol stations are about it. Last McDonald's was at Grafton, must be due to hit another.'

'Not in The Bay. They stopped the fast food

people and the big hotels.' Holly sounded approving.

'Bloody madness. The place is taking off, that's what tourists want. You'd be better opening a smart takeaway food joint than a dinky B & B.'

Holly was calm. 'It's not a dinky bed and brekkie, it's a guesthouse. And it's going to be charming when I'm done. Now, find a place to stop, I have a surprise in the back.'

'Yeah? Well, there's one in the seat behind you. The dog threw up some time ago.'

'Oh, poor Curly.'

'It didn't sound too horrendous. But she probably wants to pee. What's the surprise?'

'Pull off the road somewhere pretty. I have a New Year's picnic in the Esky. I thought we could start the new year with champagne and orange juice, smoked salmon and cheese on pita followed by sliced mango. And there's coffee in the Thermos.'

'Sounds good,' Andrew said, trying to be enthusiastic. Typical of Holly – always the nurturer, full of thoughtful gestures. A cutesy picnic was so her; never mind that it had been raining and was a grey dawn. After eight hours driving all Andrew wanted was a feed, a cold swim, a hot shower and a soft bed. He hoped this homespun, rustic, back to nature trend that Holly seemed bent on was only a phase. How long was she going to last in some rundown old house on two overgrown acres, even if it was near the beach? Soon enough she'd be glad to get back to their mansion on Sydney's North Shore with its luxury and convenience. But he'd agreed to this plan of hers of starting up a guesthouse. It suited him very well, in fact. Not that he could ever imagine seeing out his days in some small beach resort. He had a business in Sydney that was expanding into Asia and taking up all his time. But property values were going through the roof in The Bay so it would be a good investment and give Holly an interest. They both knew their marriage had hit a stale patch, and he wanted to show his wife of twenty-three years that he was supportive and prepared to make an effort – though he considered it more like indulging her whim. She'd put up all of her inheritance and what she'd saved for her 'old age' to buy the place, so it was her money she was playing with, not his.

It was ironic that he, too, was quietly embarking on a new project that was linked to The Bay. But Holly was completely unaware of this. He'd let her continue to think their involvement in the area was all her idea.

'There, look, isn't that lovely?' said Holly.

Andrew pulled over and parked in a cleared area with a small shelter that faced the distant ocean. It was the turn-off to a scenic drive that skirted the hills above The Bay. 'Come on, Curly,' he said, trying to make amends with the dog. 'Stretch the old legs and take a look at your new home.' He clipped the leash on her collar as Holly pulled sheets off a roll of paper towels to mop up the dog's blanket.

Andrew stared at the few twinkling lights that

were shining in the small town which clung to the fringe of the crescent-shaped bay. The moon was still visible as the first dawn streaks lit the clouds. Suddenly a flash of light pierced the sky. The lighthouse. The beam swung around, and in its wake Andrew felt his spirits lift. He turned to Holly. 'So here we are, kid. The world is at your feet.'

'Bit late for me to conquer the world. And I smell burning bridges somewhere back there.' She gave him a faint wry grin. 'It will be all right, won't it?'

Andrew dropped his arm awkwardly around her shoulder; affectionate gestures did not come easily. 'Let's hope so. Happy New Year.'

She leaned against his chest, feeling a rush of love for him. This had been her idea, she knew she'd never get him to slow down and make time for her, for them, unless there was a good financial reason. She hated to admit it, but unless there was a profit in something Andrew didn't see any sense in being involved. Ever since she'd turned forty, her frustration at having never done anything on her own, to be someone, had grown till she was at a point where she felt she had ceased to exist. The children were at university and out of the nest, Andrew had become more involved with expanding the business and spent even less time at home or with her, and when he did he was tired and not interested in what she had to say. And Holly had realised she had little to say. She went to lunch with her friends, who always seemed to talk about the same things. And she had taken to going on her own to the movies during the day several times a week, and found herself telling the plots to Curly. She fretted about her looks, her stagnant marriage, her future. Then, leafing through a lifestyle magazine she'd come across an article about The Bay.

Not quite in Queensland, the subtropical paradise was on a peninsula with a sweeping protected bay, surrounded by lush rolling hills that rose gradually to become a steep volcanic range. Everyone had heard of The Bay – its beauty, its tranquillity, its laid-back, alternative population. It had been through many phases. When she mentioned it to Andrew he'd immediately summed it up: 'Hippies, protestors, beach bums, backpackers. Not my idea of a holiday.'

'I wasn't thinking of a holiday. It's becoming very trendy, not too yuppie like Noosa, but interesting. I've done some research on the net and got some stats through the real estate agencies, the tourist boards, the newspapers –'

'What on earth for?' Andrew had cut in.

Holly continued as if he hadn't spoken. 'I became interested in the history of The Bay and started reading about one of the original companies, the Richmond Whaling Company, which the district was named after. I was put in touch with an old fellow, a local historian, and he told me that one of the original homes was going on the market. There'd been a bit of a fuss as developers wanted to knock it down and put up apartments.'

'That's life these days.'

'There speaks an architect,' Holly said, and smiled gently. 'Anyway, I rang Trudy James, the local real estate agent, and she filled me in on what had happened. So I said I'd buy it.'

'You did what?' His eyes were suddenly less glazed and he'd started to pay attention to what Holly was saying. She had a folder in her lap. This was most unusual.

'The land and environment people have upheld the heritage value of the old home and it can't be pulled down, so that's put paid to the big developers wanting it. We talked quite a bit and I asked about restoration, which Trudy said few people would want to take on.'

'That'd be right. Cost a fortune, never get your money back.'

Holly took a breath and continued speaking, opening the folder and shuffling papers, avoiding Andrew's eyes. 'I had her send me some photos. I thought we could revamp the home into a guesthouse that kept the Richmond name alive, which is what the locals want. So I told Trudy we'd go up and have a look and make an offer.'

Andrew had gasped at his wife, who had never made any decisions on her own in their entire marriage. 'What the hell for? It's a mad idea.'

Patiently, Holly had run through the reasons why she thought the potential investment was good, the amount of money she would put in from her savings, that it would give her a sense of satisfaction to be in charge of something, and why it would be wonderful for the kids. It would give them a long-term investment and a place they could stay for summer holidays, bring their friends.

Marcus, their 22-year-old son, was a keen surfer and Melanie, their twenty-year-old daughter, would appreciate the walks in the rainforest. She might even dabble in painting again. She was unsure what she planned to do with her fine arts degree when she graduated, perhaps spending holidays in The Bay would inspire her. And deep down Holly hoped that they could share more family time together, as a group of adults. Since her son and daughter had left home they'd all been leading very separate lives. Holly was the one who'd felt left out – until she'd found the old house in The Bay.

She'd rushed on, 'Andrew, I know you can't put in a lot of time but you'll be available to back me up. If they accept my offer, I think it could really be something special. I'll need your advice, of course, but I don't expect you to move there, just come up every other weekend or something. Here, look at the photos . . .'

Andrew had ignored the pictures and stared at her. 'Are you mad, Holly? You're moving up there? And I'm expected to zip up and down over 700 ks a weekend to help you out of some crazy scheme. You know nothing about renovating, running a business. It's sheer madness. Nice idea, honey, but, *sheesh* . . .' He'd tried to laugh it off but was not prepared for Holly's steely persistence.

'I had the bank manager look at the deal. He thinks it's a good idea. They'd give us a loan to lock it in place.'

'You spoke to the bank? Of course they're going to give you money. They know I'm around to bail you out.'

'I'll do the work, well, get the right people. At least come and see it.'

When Andrew hadn't been able to dampen this fire Holly was fanning, he agreed to fly up with her and look at the house, crazy as it sounded. But when he'd arrived at The Bay, he had been intrigued. It was as beautiful as he'd been told – by someone in Bangkok of all places, only a few months before. The setting was magical, the weather perfect, they stayed in an elegant unit across from the beach, ate a delicious seafood meal at one of the better restaurants, swam in crystal-clear water and made love like they hadn't in years. A proposal that had been dangled in front of Andrew in Bangkok now assumed more interesting possibilities.

Back in Sydney he'd rationalised that it had been a nice weekend, they'd flown up with no hassle, rented a car to explore the environs and hinterland and, yes, the old house had potential – if one wanted to get into the nightmare of starting a business from scratch. Gradually, the idea of being a bachelor a couple of weeks a month began to appeal, especially when he worked out that he could play golf on weekends and tennis two nights a week. Things he'd let go because

Holly didn't play and he was always too tired. Andrew decided to get fit again.

So here they were, sitting at a scenic lookout above The Bay at the start of a new year which was going to bring many changes. Where would they be twelve months from now? he wondered.

Holly was having similar thoughts. She patted the dog and gave her a slice of salmon then topped up their glasses. 'Here's to the best New Year ever.'

Andrew clinked glasses and leaned over and kissed her lightly. 'Here's to you, Holly. And to your big venture.'

'Our adventure, you mean. I think it's going to be the most important thing we've done, Andy . . . apart from having the kids of course.'

'This might turn out to be far more expensive than putting Marcus and Melanie through university,' he joked. But Holly didn't look amused, the worry about what she'd undertaken had descended. 'Hey, come on, don't fret. You know I'll rescue you if it falls in a heap.'

'It's not going to fall over,' she said crossly.

Andrew let it go. 'What are you going to call it?'

Holly's face cleared and she took a sip of champagne. 'I'm going to keep the old name, Richmond House, that was part of the deal – after the whaling company. There's a remnant of rainforest at the back of the property where a special butterfly still breeds because of the trees and vines. I thought I'd use the butterfly as my logo.'

'Sounds like you've thought a lot about all this,' he said quietly.

'I have, Andrew. You might be surprised. I'm going to make this work.'

She lifted her chin and he was struck by her almost youthful determination. In the soft light she looked a very young woman. How different would their lives have been if Holly had been this strong minded and independent in the early days of their marriage? He raised his glass and downed it. 'I think I believe you.'

They both looked at the dog, one of the few things they had in common these days.

Curly glanced from one to the other and gave a hopeful wag of her tail, her eyes seeming to say, 'Tell me we're not getting back in that car.'

Andrew read the signal and laughed. 'Nearly there, old girl. You're going to like it up here any-way – a whole beach on your doorstep. Scruffy real dogs to play with. None of those poncy clipped and pouffed-up poodlely things like in the old neighbourhood.'

Holly smiled at her dog. Lazy and fat Curly may be, but when Andrew went back to Sydney she'd feel safer having a dog around. Thinking over Andrew's comment she said, 'I wonder if the neighbours are going to be scruffy real people too.'

'You chose The Bay knowing some weird people live there. Attracting up-market visitors to Richmond House might be a challenge.'

Holly began gathering their picnic things together. 'Andrew, I don't want to hear negatives now. We're here, we've made the commitment. It's up to me to make it work.'

Andrew stared at his wife. Why was she suddenly seeing herself as a businesswoman, a proprietor of an elegant, successful beach B & B? He shrugged. He had his own reasons for agreeing to this mad scheme. It would be a tax loss and keep Holly occupied and far from Sydney, which suited him just fine.

The sunrise was filtered by fingers of milky cloud, like a coy young woman peeping through her hands, half masking her face. The quiet sea was streaked with splashes of pale gold sunlight. Nola Florens glanced down at her matching gold chiffon caftan, now wet and sandy and clinging to her legs. Sitting in a golden sea in a golden dress, she mused, rather pleased with the image. Then she stretched her arm and the light caught the gold bracelets and gold rings. She raised a crystal champagne glass to toast the dawn of the New Year. It was empty.

She waved it behind her head and heard the clink as the bottle was lifted from the ice bucket by the boy.

Andre had been nodding off at the picnic table near the sand. It had been a long night. By now he was utterly bored with the antics of Miss Florens, who was capping off the partying with what she cheerfully described as a 'sit-in with Mother Nature, darling'. It involved enjoying the caressing wash of the incoming tide while sipping a fine French champagne.

As he walked barefoot in his tuxedo to refill the glass, pants carefully rolled above his ankles, he studied the sea. Might be worth a surf later in the day. A few breaks getting up. How much longer was he on call for? he wondered. Not that he really cared, he was being paid by the hour. Easiest money he'd ever made – after he'd paid for the hire of the penguin suit. He'd driven Nola Florens to a few of the parties given by out-of-towners, posh people from Sydney and Melbourne, and followed her around topping up her glass from her own vintage champagne. He'd then driven her back in her Daimler at dawn to her penthouse overlooking Mighty Beach, thinking that was it. But no, she wanted to 'soak up the sunrise'. He hoped none of his surfing mates would see him in this gear playing flunky to The Bay's rich and reclusive Nola Florens. She made curtains or something. What a waste of money. He silently poured the pale gold liquid into the glass and retreated to his seat under the pandanus palms to daydream about how he'd spend such a fortune as this woman possessed.

Nola Florens took a sip and raised her glass to the sun.

It was a cruel light that showed the relentless march of time. But this woman in her seventies looked remarkably youthful. Surgery, money, careful living or all three had preserved her well. Her lips carried the remains of bright lipstick, which had been applied with a shaking hand, and like a child's casually coloured picture, it had gone 'outside the lines'. This was not the result of the champagne but arthritic hands.

It had surprised the social world when Nola Florens had retired to this remote coastal town where she knew no one. She had created a business and an image for herself, not only in Australia but overseas as well, and she had ruled the social scene in Sydney for many years. Yet no one suspected that behind the glamorous queen of design there was a lonely and sometimes frightened woman.

But all that had changed when she moved to The Bay – its lifestyle, the gentle landscape, the live and let live attitude of the locals. She had a good feeling about this year. Ly the clairvoyant had told her she wouldn't be on her own. Good friends were coming her way. Nola smiled as another little wave slapped over her feet.

The lights of the Holden station wagon wavered over the dirt road in a valley behind The Bay. The beam was watery in the pearly dawn. The man behind the wheel nodded for a moment, swiftly caught himself and reached for the can of beer between his legs. But his concentration had gone and the car took over, trundling across the road. And while he wasn't driving more than 50 ks, Eddie was unprepared for the rather graceful nosedive the car took off the dirt and into a shallow canal.

There was a choking kind of protest from the

engine, as the car settled in the mud. Eddie looked down, amazed he was wearing his seatbelt; definitely must be running on auto. He had no recollection of buckling up. Too often he didn't bother with his seatbelt as he cruised through the back roads around the banana and sugarcane plantations. He turned off the ignition and groped for the can of beer that was now somewhere on the floor of the tilted car. He had trouble opening the door, so wound down the window and thrust his legs through it, congratulating himself on his great foresight in driving an old manual. He would never have got out this easily in a modern car with electronic windows.

Actually this was all he could afford. A documentary filmmaker didn't make a fortune trying to raise awareness of the plight of refugees or Aboriginal reconciliation, especially when he lived away from the mainstream. Eddie was also broke because his ex-wife had emptied their savings account and wiped him out with alimony and child maintenance. The demands for money for Alice's singing and ballet lessons, horse riding and school skiing trips – for God's sake at ten years old – had run over him in an avalanche of incomprehensible paper. And while he adored Alice and had regarded her as his own for the past seven years, the fact was, she wasn't his child. She was part of the package – or should it be 'baggage' – that he'd acquired when he'd impulsively married Laura.

Laughing-eyed Laura, who'd swung into his

life in Melbourne, motivating and pushing him to give up the photographic studio and get out there and make films as he really wanted to do. She'd pushed him to fill in forms, hassle for funding, persuade a corporate bigwig to back his first project. And it had paid off. He'd won awards, had lots of pats on the back, the documentary was screened on public television and it felt great. Except he hadn't made a red cent. He was offered a job with one of the networks to work with their investigative affairs unit – regular pay, travel, interesting work. Laura, however, who'd only ever dabbled at jobs, was convinced one day he'd go to Hollywood. He'd told her that was the last thing he wanted, but Laura only seemed to hear what spun around in her own pretty – he didn't say 'empty' – head. She had sulked, withheld herself and looked so hurt that Eddie asked her to marry him. She said yes, but knocked the job on the head. He'd be selling out, he was just starting to follow his dream, she didn't want to live in the suburbs.

It had been her idea to move to The Bay . . . creative atmosphere, cheaper living, healthy lifestyle, Alice could go to the Steiner school, they could set up their own mini production company. Eddie had been reluctant, but gave in when Laura had pointed out that here he was, yet again, staying in his comfort zone, afraid to take a gamble. Where was his faith in his abilities, his vision? He could give her no coherent argument that sounded strong enough, and when they drove up and Laura took him to the hills and showed him the farm she'd seen advertised in *The Beacon Bugle*, he'd had even less reason to protest. She had it all worked out. The property was big enough for Alice to have a horse, they could turn the barn into a studio for him, grow their own vegetables, even revive the neglected avocado plantation. Laura could take a course in ceramics, or spinning – something rustic and rural. What she'd always wanted.

Eddie had gazed in amazement at his trendy urban wife. It seemed a big jump from caffe lattes with her girlfriends in South Yarra to the green tea and brown rice set scattered in the hills above The Bay.

Laura had insisted on handling the paperwork of the purchase in case Eddie got cold feet. It was only later they discovered that the creek had been diverted and they'd lost access to 'natural spring water on the property'. Other nightmares emerged over the following eighteen months.

Two years later Laura was 'sick and tired of being stuck in never-never land'. She wanted out – of the hills and the marriage. She was bored, he hadn't made a successful film again and she had lost patience with the endless waiting involved in getting up a film. So Laura and Alice had moved down to the beach. She'd found a small unit, Alice went to the public school and took surfing lessons instead of horse riding. Occasionally Eddie brought her back to see her pony at the farm, but Alice announced she didn't like horse riding any more.

Far from getting into a small business as she'd planned, Laura drifted around The Bay, having vegetarian lunches with friends – a bunch of women who all seemed to Eddie to be on the dole or living on their ex-husbands' money. They spent hours prattling over where they were going in life while never moving from the cafe. Or else she talked of 'finding herself' by taking courses in healing, weird health practices or spiritual enrichment.

Eddie sank to his knees in squelchy water and gazed at the wall of green sugarcane on both sides of the road. He got back onto the verge, sat down and reached for a joint in the old tobacco tin in his shirt pocket. Inhaling deeply, he decided this was not an auspicious start to the New Year. Then he reconsidered. No, this was possibly a very good start to the year. He wasn't dead. He thought back over the evening. Who was the girl he'd been kissing in the laundry up against the washing machine? Did she ever tell him her name? Doesn't matter, he probably wouldn't recognise her if he saw her again anyway. Nose ring, green hair with feathers in it. Nothing unusual. He wondered how Laura had spent the evening. He'd collected Alice from school a few weeks back and she'd said that her mother had some nice smart friends visiting from Melbourne to 'play with'. She'd taken Alice shopping for new clothes.

Eddie was feeling quite calm now. He knew everyone who lived along this road. Since Laura had moved out he'd become even better friends with the neighbours. They had adopted him and took turns sending over home-grown food and home-made jams and pickles. Eddie figured somebody would come by eventually. He curled up on the damp grass, pillowed his head on his arms and began to drift off to sleep. A last thought came to him – snakes; the cane fields were full of them. Then he recalled they wouldn't come out till the sun warmed up; late morning. Hours away, it was just past dawn. He dozed off.

Amber slithered down the sand dune at the far end of Mighty Beach to the north of The Bay. A rocky point divided it from the bay itself and Mighty Beach seemingly stretched into infinity, almost to the Queensland border. It was protected by a kilo-metre of native bushland, though small tracks made by fishermen, beach walkers and nudists were known to all the locals.

She glanced at the sky. The sunrise was going to be a washout, clouds everywhere. Hadn't stopped the crowd assembling, by the look of it, though. Must be close to three hundred people – upright and moving people. In the dim light she could make out prone bodies rolled in blankets or flat out on the rain-soaked sand – nowhere to crash, no money, or merely unconscious. She'd lost touch with her girlfriends from the party. Maybe they'd decided not to come down to Drew's dawn celebration, Salute to the Sun, a group yoga and spiritual 'awakening of the spirit' to a new dawn, a new year. It was to be followed by a cleansing plunge in the sea and a shared breakfast under the marquee erected at the top end of the beach near the sea wall.

The rolling waves were sludgy; it was too overcast. Great shark-feeding conditions. Amber decided she would have to see in the year uncleansed until she hit the shower back at the beach house. She fell into the last of three lines of casually dressed people of all ages – visitors and locals mingled. She hoped she didn't look as bad as some of the jaded partygoers; she had grabbed a couple of hours sleep around 2 am. The healthy self-righteous types who'd spent the night drinking wheat grass juice or had seven hours sleep were in the front row.

Drew, the yoga master and well-known local identity, was sparkling with silver and gold glitter in his hair, over his shoulders and across his smooth bare chest. Had a devotee flung it or had he assiduously placed it himself? Amber decided Drew was always too perfect to allow himself to be randomly decorated. The shining shoulder-length curls, the perfect teeth, the fine features, high cheekbones and smooth eyebrows, and the always freshly washed look of him reminded Amber of a TV ad for some cosmic cosmetic. Ooh, she liked that. File that away under brand slogans.

Drew lifted his arms to gain the crowd's attention. Yes, she could easily see him running along a beach towards the camera, spinning and tossing his hair. All in rippling slo-mo. She refocused and stretched out her arms as Drew called for them to embrace the air and take a deep breath.

'Oh, 'scuse me.' Amber had flung her arm into the person next to her.

'No problem.' The man beside her gave her a friendly grin and the little girl with him smiled up at her. 'We just got up, I'm not very co-ordinated this early but young Hope, here, is full of energy.'

'You letting Mum sleep in, eh?' laughed Amber.

'You got it. We drew straws. I lost. Though I shouldn't complain, this is a pretty good way to start a new year. My name's Billy, by the way.'

'You run the hair salon in the arcade, don't you?' asked Amber. She'd passed by and seen him smoking and reading the racing guide. He'd always struck her as being different from the few hairdressers she'd met. 'I'm afraid I rarely go to hair salons.'

'Doesn't look like you need to.' He'd taken in the mass of wavy auburn hair, her tilted nose, large green eyes and a great smile. Probably early twenties, he thought.

'I'll give you more room.' She stepped a pace to the side. 'I'm not an expert at this. Drew persuaded me to start classes a couple of weeks ago, but I think I prefer swimming.' She turned her attention back to the yoga instructor, following the movements of the line in front of them.

'My wife is really good at it,' said Billy. 'Personally, I don't think God meant us to sit on our heads.'

21

Amber laughed. 'It's all part of The Bay experience. Along with float tanks, Reiki, kinesiology, tarot and tantric breath classes.'

He looked at her. 'Are you a local?'

'Since a kid. But I left years ago and just came back.'

'Did you come back to be with your family?' He spoke quietly, the group was settling into a concentrated silence. They were at the back and felt less obvious.

'No, to start a business. My mother lives here though.'

'What kind of business?'

She smiled. 'You're not a local, are you?'

'Came from Melbourne eighteen months ago. How could you tell?'

'A local would've asked my family name rather than what sort of business. Starting a business in The Bay is regarded as vaguely heretical, well, pretty desperate.'

He smiled. 'Yep, people just seem to hang, they avoid doing. So what kind of business – seeing as we're of the same heretical ilk?'

'Oh, natural beauty products. A Bay kind of business.' She leaned down to grasp her ankle as the crowd let out a singular breath with a moan reverberating from deep in the collective diaphragm.

'Sounds like a Tibetan monk's chant,' whispered Billy.

Hope broke the spell by asking loudly, 'Where are we going for breakfast, Daddy?'

Amber laughed with them as Billy straightened up. 'I think I'll pass on the soul food the yoga people are offering. Want to join Hope and me for something rich and unhealthy down at the Beach Café?'

'Sounds great.'

They unobtrusively left the group and began walking along the beach.

'So tell me about your natural products. I've been experimenting with a few things for the hair.'

Amber found herself chatting about what she'd been doing and what she hoped to do. It was true what they said about hairdressers being easy to talk to. Hope took her hand as she skipped along. Suddenly Amber felt glad to be back at The Bay, even if unhappy circumstances had forced her to come home. Maybe this year was going to turn out all right after all.

The sound of the taxi reversing from her front yard seemed too loud in the stillness of the neighbourhood dawn. The parties were over. Kimberley glanced up at the lightening sky, it was going to rain again. The wet weather had dampened many New Year parties.

She thought back over the night. She'd lost track of a chunk of the evening, although she thought she'd had a good time. As good as it gets when you're in your mid thirties and a single mother – because your husband spends most of the year somewhere else. It's not a lot of fun watching the younger chicks duck upstairs, out-side, anywhere, with the pick of the men, leaving the dregs looking hopefully in your direction. She'd danced though, non stop between many drinks and a few joints. She could still dance up a storm.

Midnight came and went. A rustle of rain, scudding clouds, a new year, a new age. So what? She had nothing new to look forward to this year any more than last year. Well, one could always hope.

Kimberley had turned away from the mob in the main room of the house and wandered along the verandah where people were comfortably sprawled, sitting on the railing, chatting, coming down from the midnight frenzy. She found an old sofa at the far end facing the dripping garden and settled into it. She pulled her cigarettes from her pocket and lit up, then contemplated the glowing end of the cigarette. Maybe that was something she could do – make a resolution to give up the fags.

'Is someone sharing that seat?' A woman sud-denly appeared beside the sofa, holding a drink and a cigarette.

'No, help yourself. Smoke away.'

'Did you make a resolution to give these up?' The woman twirled her cigarette.

'It crossed my mind. Didn't seem particularly original as a resolution, though.'

'Maybe we should make a resolution to take something up rather than give up something,' the woman said.

Kimberley smiled in the dark. 'I wish.'

'You've just got to do it.'

'So what have you taken up lately?' Kimberley glanced at the woman beside her trying to place her. She seemed older than Kimberley, well spoken.

'Me? I've embraced life. Eat, drink and be merry . . . for tomorrow we die.' Her tone was bitter.

'Doesn't sound like embracing life to me, more a case of drowning not waving.'

'You might be right there. Ever since I came to The Bay I have plunged into whatever was going. My husband and my parents would say I was out of my depth.'

'Is he here too?'

'God no. I'm divorced. He's off with the secretary and I couldn't rattle around in the house any more.' She took a large swallow from her glass. 'My life turned upside down and I never saw it coming. Not a clue. What about you? Oh, I'm Bonnie, by the way. Bonnie Bitternden.'

'Kimberley. I've been here fifteen years. Came up with a man trying to relive the sixties and seventies. I got pregnant, we got married and suddenly living in the hills in a mud house with a colicky baby lost its appeal. By the time I'd persuaded Colin to move into town he'd become Ashok and went on a pilgrimage to India.'

'Ashok. Asshole. Lot of people up here have weird names. Orange people, Sannyassins, Miracle mob, Raelians, whatever. People I never knew existed when I lived in Melbourne. Maybe changing your identity is the way to go.'

Kimberley began to sense the loss and desperation of the woman beside her. Well-to-do middle class with the Persian rug pulled out from under her. 'Changing your name and mumbling mantras doesn't really change your life. It has to be more fundamental than that. You have to change yourself first. Or get to know yourself perhaps. But you've come to the right place. This has always been a healing place for women,' said Kimberley quietly.

'Yeah, well for the moment I'm making up for lost time. How old is your child?'

'Matilda? She's fourteen.'

'My daughter is the same age. Erica. I s'pose they know each other,' said Bonnie rather bleakly. 'I don't do the school scene any more. Had enough of being the proper rah rah, pooh bah mother.' She rose to her feet, swaying slightly. 'Well, happy New Year. Talked more to you than I have to anyone since I've been here.'

As she turned away Kimberley had the impression that the woman regretted talking about herself. She called after her, 'Bonnie, when you're ready for friends, look me up.'

'I'm better off on my own, thanks. Nice to meet you.'

She was gone. A sad woman, aged around forty, Kimberley guessed. She had seen others like her and she wondered what the New Year would bring her. Now Kimberley decided to go home, her own life didn't seem quite so bad. To quote the classics, life is what you make it. I'd better have a stab at this year then, she thought. At least now she had a goal.

Kimberley opened the front door to her house. A light burned in the sitting room where Mac was sleeping. Normally Matty didn't need a sitter, but New Year's Eve, when Kimberley planned to see in the dawn, was another matter.

She stared at the sleeping woman. Thank heavens for Mac.

Tilly MacDonald, almost grandmotherly – if you overlooked the henna-streaked braids, her 'hippy dippy jewellery' of silver bangles, feathers and beads, and the fact she was always dressed in layers of purple. Satin embroidered bolero on top of a blouse over harem pants, a chiffon shawl draped over one shoulder and glittery mules, now threadbare, all in purple hues, on the floor by the couch, cast her as fairy godmother or possibly a benevolent feminist witch. In her sixties, she was hearty, practical, silly and described herself as 'mad as a cut snake', which endeared her to practically everyone who met her.

Mac's wardrobe might be thought eccentric in a capital city or country town, but in the main street of The Bay she wasn't given a second glance. She was into her third Saturn return and had taken up ceramics. She was reliable and welcomed the few dollars she earned for spending time with Matilda. Sometimes she read tarot cards for extra cash. She and Matty got on famously, watching

TV while Matty painted Mac's toenails with her favourite purple polish.

Mac was sleeping on the couch, the silent, flickering TV screen replaying the New Year's Eve celebrations over Sydney Harbour. A bottle of Pimm's sat on the coffee table with the remains of a plate of cheese and biscuits. Mac's little celebration. Kimberley kicked off her shoes and dropped her handbag on a shredding cane chair, wondering who on earth but Mac drank Pimm's Number One Cup any more. But then everything from the 1950s and sixties was so *in*, Matty had told her. She hoped Matty hadn't drunk the stuff.

She headed for the second bedroom in their small rented house and quietly opened the door. The room was in its usual state of teenage clutter. The ceiling fan churned slowly and Matty was sleeping on her back, one long brown leg thrust from beneath the sheet. Tiredness, a sense of relief all was calm in the sleeping house, made Kimberley's shoulders sag. Why did she always succumb to desperate parties that she didn't enjoy? Why couldn't she make some decision, one way or another, about Matty's father? This was half a life for her, though it suited him.

She thought back to the woman she'd met briefly on the verandah. Did she want to be like Bonnie – bitter, frantic, playing fast and loose in a world she didn't understand and one that could possibly destroy her? Kimberley had seen it happen. She sighed. At breakfast she'd get Mac to read her cards. Just for fun. Now she'd decided to make a stab at something this year, perhaps Mac could point her in the right direction.

Kimberley tiptoed across the room and closed the screen door that Matty had left open, allowing moths, mosquitoes, cane toads, maybe a snake to get in. She glanced down at her sleeping daughter and smiled with contentment. No matter what happened between Ashok and herself, they had created and shared a wonderful girl. 'Happy New Year, Matty,' she whispered. And suddenly, it was.

Chapter Two

ANDREW STOOD IN THE FRONT GARDEN OF THE proposed Richmond Guesthouse. Or was it the back garden? This was debatable. The driveway led into overgrown gardens which surrounded an old stone swimming pool, and from the broad verandah, through Bangalow palms, wattle and tropical vegetation, there was a view of the sea.

And what a view. The house sat on a low headland, with views of the Cape to one end and out to the ocean and the raw rough rocks of the marine reserve island, Brierly Rocks, straight ahead. A track ran down from the garden, and in two minutes you could be walking on the fine gold sand of Tiny Bay Beach. The property was at one end of the beach, angled away from the promontory which gave the home a sense of privacy and proprietorial claim to Tiny Bay Beach.

Traditionally, the people of the town had been hardworking, many with chequered family histories that went back to the mingled marriages of Kanaka canecutters, local tribespeople, white women of dubious repute and adventurers from across the seven seas. Like the fusion of elements, the town forged families of great strength. They frequently faced hardship and tragedy, but more often there was laughter, hope and success, the occasional disagreement, and the wisdom of the old-timers to chart their course. They had struggled and they had prospered. Many families had settled along the river, lured by the 'red gold' – cedar. But the majority had clung to the sea. It was their lifeline.

Those hearty souls – including ladies, suitably attired in neck-to-knee costumes – who indulged in swimming sometimes trekked or rode over the headland to dip into the sheltered waters of Tiny Bay. Others swam in the inland lagoons and swimming holes in the rivers or at the base of waterfalls, deep in the rainforest.

Much of the area was still being opened up in the early 1900s when travelling photographer Tolston Beckheath, visiting from Sydney, became fascinated with the scenery and the people. His black-and-white prints from big glass-plate negatives brought him a measure of fame and prosperity, not only among the locals but in the city where there was increasing curiosity about life in the countryside.

The area now attracted camera-carrying visitors in their thousands. For the past forty years the town, the beaches and the lush hinterland had been shot in colour and with increasing frequency as the tourist industry put The Bay firmly on the map. With each generation and as each new cult came and went, more and more photographs were taken of the people who helped give this unconventional community its growing reputation for offering a good time and good value. The modern record of The Bay and its people was captured on postcards, calendars, posters, and proudly framed in the community hall. A local artist had taken it upon himself to paint a colourful mural on the outside walls of the dilapidated hall, portraying characters and scenes from life in The Bay.

Inside the community hall there were shots of early surfers on their long boards including one of the local boys alongside the famed Duke Kahanamoku. The King had spent some time at The Bay enjoying the surf and teaching the locals the art of riding the waves on a plank. The Flower Power People, the hippies, the Aquarians and New Agers had all made postcard fame at some stage.

Each group that settled at The Bay had brought their own music, which reached new levels of excellence in the creative environment. From country and rock to om and hip hop, the music added to the tourist boom and the district's reputation.

Street musicians, buskers, players in pub bands, all went from amateurs looking for a few bob to professionals with a string of dedicated followers. The annual Blues Music Festival brought performers and fans from all over the world. It all seemed far removed from what the early families had seen and heard when they arrived at The Bay.

Indeed, what would they have made of the Aquarius Festival, which for four days in the mid 1960s put The Bay on the front page of almost every major newspaper in the country? The sound was loud enough to waken the dead, so maybe their spirits did tune in when a bunch of long-haired, pot-smoking refugees from the cities staged a local version of America's Woodstock. The festival, held in fields near the town, was billed as a musical fanfare to a new age of liberated souls who rejected most material possessions in favour of free love, improvised dancing, experimenting with drugs, and the consumption of massive quantities of booze.

The conservative locals tried to ignore the invasion but wondered at the stories of wild music and crazy behaviour that filtered back to town. But it wasn't long before they were looking in awe at the massive cash flow the young people generated, and complaints faded, as did demands that the authorities do something to stop such an event happening again. They assumed that after the long weekend of excesses, the worn-out revellers would disappear back to the cities. But the hard-core hippies had found the area as intoxicating as the pot and grog they consumed, and decided to stay.

There were periodic skirmishes with the local police, the council, the town fathers, and a war of words hurled in public forums and in the pages of the press. Generally, though, the local populace retreated in the face of these odd-looking, articulate, educated, self-supporting free thinkers. Some of the locals began to realise that these tribes that were now living among them wanted to co-exist, to raise and educate their children under new rules, and to create a better world.

For many of the new arrivals, cash and credit ratings weren't a big problem. They were well educated, had good career skills, healthy bank accounts, and they happily pooled their resources to buy up practically every failing dairy farm in the hinterland and establish what they called communes.

'Communes, bloody hell, this is a communist invasion,' growled a retired dairy farmer, who was drinking in the pub.

The manager of the new RSL club agreed. 'Doubt they'll be darkening our doors. They know they're not welcome in town.'

'Maybe, but their money is,' said Reg, the local real estate agent. 'They've got money to spend and so have their friends. If they make a go of this it's going to change the whole district. We won't know ourselves in ten years. There'll be people moving here and coming to see what it's all about. That means new money in town. Because let's face it, there ain't much else happening.'

As if to back up his words, two of the long-haired, colourfully dressed intruders wandered into the bar and ordered beers. The locals ignored them but the two men were unfazed. They settled themselves at a corner table and one of them pulled the guitar off his shoulder and began idly to strum. It was low key and the bartender glanced at the RSL manager, who waited to see what would develop to give him fair grounds to challenge the interlopers. But strangely the mood in the bar calmed, voices normally raucous with booze quietened and despite themselves the drinkers all had one ear tuned to the popular folk song.

When the man put the guitar to one side and ordered a second beer, the bartender gave a cheerful grin and asked, 'You blokes know "The Pub With No Beer"?'

'Don't tell me you've run out?' answered the hippy, and the rest of the bar laughed as the bartender pushed the beers across the counter and the tension in the room melted. It was like that in The Bay for years to come – humour and music generally defused an argument.

But in the late 1970s and early eighties, violence crept into the idyll. The pushing of hard drugs, the operation of large marijuana plantations by international 'businessmen' and the rising use of guns changed the peaceful paradise. And while this was not unique to the area, the drug culture became associated with The Bay.

This was the sketchy backdrop Andrew had absorbed. He'd even studied 'hippy hinterland housing' in first year architecture; the early freeform, experimental and environmental homes in the hills had become icons.

Richmond House, though, had no such claims. It was solid, conventional, but built to suit the climate and lifestyle. It was raised on sandstone foundations to allow airflow beneath the floors and to keep water out during the severe tropical rains and the occasional cyclone. The steeply sloped roof acted as a sail, funnelling the wind over and away, rather than presenting a barrier to be beaten down. The rooms were large and airy, opening onto the verandah in the traditional style, but particular to this house was an attic bedroom that opened onto a widow's walk – a small railed platform on the roof – where the mistress of the home could watch the horizon for the return of her menfolk. Or it was a place of peace and privacy to watch the sunrise over the sea or the sunset behind the peak of Chinamans Hat, or to gaze at the dolphins leaping in the line of crystal breakers.

Andrew had seen a lot of good ideas in the old home, and there was no doubt it had some potential, even though it was very rundown and little had been done to it since it was built. He didn't believe it was significant enough architecturally to be saved, but it had an old-fashioned charm – if you liked that sort of thing. He imagined that it had been built by nouveau-riche settlers with memories of grand homes in the old country. As he studied the building, his architect's eye began to discern other influences: England via empire outposts, touches of Penang, perhaps. The traveller's palms in the garden were the same as those outside the entrance to Raffles Hotel in Singapore. The fans along the verandah, the use of marble tiles and a courtyard with a well that had been made into a fountain smacked of the Raj. Initially he hadn't looked at the house other than as a bricks and mortar investment. Now he could see that thought had been given to the place. And best of all, its gardens hadn't been altered in a century. He assumed there must have been vegetable gardens, some fruit trees, and Holly had mentioned stables or a barn.

He had raised a concern over the wooden structure of the house but it was declared termite free. It had been built of cedar and ironbark, which had been treated well and would no doubt last. When Andrew had pointed out the cost of restoration and maintenance to Holly, she had brushed it aside. She'd had more immediate concerns on this, their first morning of official occupation.

They had picked up the keys from the real estate agent's office as arranged, and driven to the house for morning tea – another Holly picnic. Within minutes of going into the house, as Andrew stood gazing at the shambles of the garden, Holly had rushed out screeching.

'Andrew, we've been robbed! Everything's gone!'

'What do you mean? We haven't moved in yet, what's gone?'

'I had an agreement with Trudy from the real estate place that they'd leave the old furniture, the knick-knacks, the china, all the old stuff. Andrew, some of that stuff was valuable. The antique cedar furniture —'

'Maybe the agent or the estate of the previous owners found out it was valuable and sold it.'

Holly shook her head. 'No. There aren't relatives. The house has been empty for years. Some old lady had been renting it with all the original stuff in it. She went into a home. When the council decided it should be preserved, that included the fittings and fixtures.' She was close to tears.

'Ring up the agent, for God's sake, and sort it out. Here's your first problem,' Andrew said unhelpfully.

Holly glared at him and returned to the house, only to discover that the phone had not yet been connected as she had been promised. She searched for her mobile.

Her anger turned to disbelief and then outrage as Trudy casually told her, 'Ah, some people came round and wanted to take a few pieces, and we figured you wouldn't want so much old stuff. It's not a big deal, is it?' The sale was complete, Trudy's friendly warmth had evaporated.

Holly struggled to hold her temper. 'The fact is, we had an agreement, I paid for the contents. You knew I wanted to keep the original pieces together in the house. I think it's outrageous you didn't ask me. Who are these people? They have taken virtually everything. Only the furniture that's too heavy to carry away is left.'

'Look, it's not really my concern. The couple are Lynn and Stolle, they buy and sell a lot of stuff from deceased estates. If you want any of it, you can probably pick it up in the Sunday markets for a song –'

'The markets! You mean buy back stuff that belongs to me? I should get the police. They're selling stolen property.' Holly's voice was rising and Andrew decided to take a walk around the grounds. He didn't want to know about bloody china and old chairs.

'I wouldn't do that, it's a small community. You're a newcomer and if you want to start a business you'll need the locals on side,' said Trudy.

Holly was getting the picture. 'Okay, where are the markets?'

'Let's see, the first Sunday of the month, that'd be Brigalow markets. They rotate around the district every Sunday. Briggy is a big one. In the footy field as you go into the village. Yep, sure to find some of the gear on their stall.' Trudy felt she was being more than helpful.

'We're talking large household items and lots of them,' said Holly through gritted teeth. 'Markets tend to be fruit and vegies, knick-knacks. I mean, what sort of a market is this?'

'You have a lot to learn about the area. Do yourself a favour and check it out. Stolle and Lynn are reasonable people. Listen, I have to go now.'

Trudy had initially been so helpful, especially

39

when Andrew had stepped in and handled all the paperwork for the purchase. He probably hadn't insisted on keeping the contents. Holly wished she'd followed the contractual dealings more carefully. But she wasn't going to make a scene over it.

Andrew was reluctant to leave the waves at Tiny Bay. It was a glorious sparkling morning, the water was refreshing, dolphins were cruising past the breakers and the waves were great for body-surfing. He was just starting to feel alive. It had been a dreadful night, sleeping on a futon on the floor of the main bedroom, being eaten alive by mosquitoes, kept awake by the croaking of cane toads and the sound of possums or rats in the roof. What a disaster the place was. Give him the sculptured clean lines of modern architecture and minimalist decor any day. Holly loved clutter, bits of this and bits of that, flowers in jugs on every surface vying with photographs and old books. She said she was sentimental. Andrew thought she was a pack rat. Well, she could fill this old joint with all the junk she wanted, he wasn't going to live in it. Nor was anyone for some time to come; it needed a complete overhaul. Or better still, pull it down and put something contemporary on the site. It was a great location, but heritage laws and council regulations were a major irritant.

He rolled onto his back, bobbing in the water, and gazed up at the rambling house almost hidden among the palms and wattle trees on the headland above the beach. Holly would be doing it piece-meal, she didn't have the funds to rip the guts out of the place and rebuild, and she had this idea in her head of reclaiming its past glory. He wasn't going to be involved in its future. It was bad enough that he had to get out of the surf and drive her to some damned market out in the hills to look for the house contents. And it was not even eight in the morning.

'We have to be there early. This kind of stuff gets snapped up quickly by the professionals,' Holly said as she tried to follow their route on the basic map she'd picked up at the garage.

'You don't even know if it's going to be there. Sounds a long shot to me. God, these roads are shocking.'

'That's why I have a four-wheel drive,' said Holly in some delight. She'd always laughed at her friends who drove around Sydney in immaculate tank-like four-wheel drives to collect the kids from school and fight for slots in the supermarket carpark. Now she had a legitimate reason to own a practical and reliable vehicle and had bought herself a Forester. Andrew thought it a great car and was impressed that she'd made the decision on her own. As they hit another pothole he was glad they hadn't driven the BMW.

'How much further? We're in the middle of nowhere, for God's sake, and we've been driving for forty-five minutes,' he muttered.

'I'm not sure, this is only a tourist guide not a proper map.' She turned the brochure upside down.

Andrew sighed. He should have known better than to ask. Holly was hopeless at directions. 'How the heck are you going to find your way around when I'm not here?'

'Get lost a few times, I suppose. I feel happier on these back roads than on the freeways and traffic in the city,' she said cheerfully.

Again she surprised him. She hated driving, her biggest dream had been to have a chauffeur. Or unlimited taxi dockets. 'Then why aren't you driving and leaving me to surf?'

'Because this sounds fun. And I might need help bargaining over our stuff.'

'My famed negotiating skills to the rescue, eh?' Holly was right, he wouldn't take any nonsense from a couple of down and outs scrounging for other people's possessions to flog in a market. Druggies probably.

'There's the turn-off. See the sign, "Market Today". Oh, Andrew, look, they must be going there too.' Holly craned forward as they caught up with a string of vehicles meandering down the twisting road. They followed gaily painted Kombi vans, trucks piled high with all manner of things tied under billowing rugs, and immediately in front of them was a lorry overflowing with pot plants and tubs of trees. From the cabin flew a large green flag but Holly couldn't make out the writing on it.

The convoy wound along the gravel road and below them they could see the broad expanse of the football field. Cars ringed the white fence while in the centre the grass was smothered with circles of small camps. Stalls and tents and open-air displays all sat cheek by jowl. At one end was a row of mini caravans with umbrellas and tables and chairs set up outside each one and big illustrated boards advertising food and drinks for sale.

'It looks like a massive gypsy camp,' Andrew exclaimed. 'There must be several hundred sellers there.'

'Judging by the cars and stream of people going in we're not too early, either.'

'How are we going to find your people in all that?'

'We'll just have to look at everything. We'll do it in a sequence.'

As they got closer Andrew began to study the people walking along the roadside to the main entrance. They all looked like they were going to a fancy dress party. Men wore multi-coloured leggings, tie-dyed shirts, painted T-shirts, Indian-style pants and long flowing shirts. Both men and women wore feathers or decorations, many had dreadlocks and beads or shaved heads like runaway monks. Children skipped along in strange outfits, but it seemed that more than the kids it was the adults who were wearing such magical accessories as crowns and fairy wings.

'This is a bloody circus. I'm not getting into this. They all look filthy.'

'They all look happy, like they're having a good time,' Holly said. 'It's a party.'

'A hippy dippy madhouse,' muttered Andrew as he slowed the car to walking pace while people meandered among the cars queuing to get in. 'Are those people charging money for parking? What the hell, this is outrageous.'

A girl in a sparkly Indian outfit and a man in bright pink pants tucked into gumboots, a pink shirt with lots of bead necklaces and a battered Akubra hat over shoulder-length hair, waved a plastic bucket. Andrew pressed the button and his window glided down. Before he could speak Holly leaned across him. 'How much?'

'Two dollars. Dollar for parking, dollar for the charity of the day.'

'And what might that be?' asked Andrew with an edge to his voice. He was thinking Protecta-Plantation, or bail for some dealer, maybe save the tree huggers.

'Helicopter Rescue Service. We need a chopper for this part of the coast. Good men can't fly without machines, right?'

'Don't they have helicopters to patrol the coast?' Holly asked, somewhat alarmed.

'The men in blue have something of a flying wreck. We need to be able to pull people out of the sea, that kind of thing. You look like a surfer, you know what it's like, eh?' He gave Andrew a wonderful smile and Holly realised the pink man had a hint of shrewdness behind the grin.

'Yeah, yeah.' Andrew fumbled and pulled five

dollars from his wallet and dropped it in the bucket.

'Good one, man. Round to the right. Have a cool day.'

Holly glanced at Andrew in his board shorts, T-shirt and tanned face. 'There, isn't it nice to be recognised as a surfie and not a city slicker?'

They parked on the grass at the edge of an adjoining paddock, locked the car and followed others across to the centre of the field. There was a definite order to the snail coils of stalls. Holly stood beneath some bamboo poles strung with long, coloured triangular silk flags and huge painted three-dimensional stars. 'Left or right? Food that way, crafty things that way. What do you think?'

'Clockwise. Just get on with it. We don't want food, walking this way could take ages, everyone is wandering like Brown's cows and it's going to get damn hot.'

'Told you to bring a hat.' Holly jammed down her own hat. It was a chic lady's panama from Sydney and she felt it looked very out of place.

They began walking past the rows of stalls that lined the path. Andrew kept striding ahead paying little attention as Holly hung back, fascinated by all there was for sale. He was feeling uncomfortable. These people unnerved him, and someone was always bumping into him. Why didn't they walk on the same side? Everyone was smiling, stopping to hug and chat. Even men hugged each other. He supposed they only came out of the hills every so often. Kids were scampering everywhere and it was mostly fathers who were carrying babies in backpacks and cloth slings as women congregated in clusters like chattering birds. Andrew was hot and while he could see the appeal of the market, they had come for a reason. He hoped the old furniture and junk – if they found it – was worth all this.

Holly's fury at the loss of the house contents seemed to have dissipated with her enthralment at the markets. She was hovering at another stall. It sold hand-made cosmetics and Holly was opening jars and rubbing lotion on her hands and exclaiming in delight. The stallholder, an attractive young woman with auburn hair and flawless skin, explained to her, 'These products are all made with natural ingredients – you can even eat them. I have done a lot of research with a pharmacist friend into retail cosmetics and you'd be horrified if you knew what they were made of.'

Holly had looked at similar products when shopping in the city, tried a couple of them once but didn't persist and eventually threw them out on the grounds that they were beyond their use-by date. Up here, though, the products seemed to demand more serious consideration. Why was this? Holly wondered.

'They really work?' she asked, as if struggling for an opening line.

The woman smiled. 'Of course. It's the only way to stay in business, particularly up here.'

'You study botany at uni?' Andrew asked, barely masking his scepticism.

'Nope. But I've got a couple of friends clued up on all of that. As I mentioned, one's a pharmacist and she's brilliant at analysing what's in some of the big name commercial products. Horrifying stuff really. And then there's a mate who's a botanist. Spends most of his time hunting around the forests here trying to find something new in the way of herbs and other plants. He reckons we are only just beginning to learn the value of plants for health and beauty. He's been given a grant by the uni here.'

'First steps in a long journey,' commented Andrew as he sniffed a bottle of tea tree oil-based aftershave lotion.

'Hey, you're talking like a local,' laughed the girl.

Andrew grimaced. 'The labelling isn't very good,' he said in a bid to regain the high ground.

'Prefer to put the money into the contents,' she responded a little sharply.

Holly stepped in to the conversation. 'I'll take these, thanks,' and handed over several jars and a bottle. 'Are you at all the markets?'

'Every Sunday, just like a churchgoer. I've moved back from Sydney and one day I'd like to open a shop, but for the time being it's strictly only on Sunday.' She reached into a bag. 'Here's my card. And a sheet you can fill in, personal details, and then I can make up things specially for your skin.'

'Thanks a lot. I'll give it some thought,' said Holly glancing at the card. 'Oh, that's a lovely name – Amber. You said you've just come back, so I assume this is home.'

The girl's expression faded for a moment then she forced back the bright smile. 'Yes. Born here, but had to go south to the big smoke just to see what it's like; now I'm back for good. I'm working at it, damned hard. As you probably know, this area is at the cutting edge of holistic health and lifestyle changes. Not to mention all the other things that ruffle the conservative traditionalists.' She grinned, giving Andrew a sideways glance. 'This is the place to start a business that is grounded in a caring belief system.'

'That's nice to hear. Good luck, Amber, I'll let you know how I find these,' said Holly.

'Please do,' she said before turning to serve another customer.

'Idealism of youth,' said Andrew with a slight smirk. 'She'd go broke in a proper shop in a month.'

As they turned into the next avenue of stalls, Holly stopped and dug her elbow into Andrew's ribs. 'Look there.'

At the end of the row a man was sitting in a polished wooden squatter's chair under a fringed Indonesian paper umbrella, his legs slung over the arms, an embroidered footstool and coal shuttle beside him. Three card tables were covered with an assortment of crockery, ornaments and silverware. On an old Persian rug on the ground were piled lace doilies, crochet rugs and damask cloths, cushions and patchwork quilts. Several paintings and prints of old boats were stacked against one of the tables. A tall thin woman wearing a top made of what was once a brocade curtain over a silver and red Indian sari skirt was showing a couple a large silver teapot.

Holly rushed forward. 'Excuse me,' she said and she tugged at the teapot. 'I believe that came from Richmond House. It belongs to me.' She turned to the suburban looking couple who were dressed in unflattering baggy shorts and golf shirts. 'It's not for sale, I'm sorry.'

'Yes it is,' protested the woman running the stall, whom Holly assumed must be Lynn.

'There's been a misunderstanding. We bought the house and everything in it. The estate agent had no right to let you have these things.' Holly appealed to Andrew who had caught up with her. 'Look, it's everything from the house. Where's the rest of it, the furniture?' she demanded.

The potential buyers edged away as the woman called to the man in the chair. 'Stolle, get over here . . . we got a small problem.'

He unfolded his lanky body with a nonchalant air. 'What's up?'

Holly nudged Andrew who didn't waste time with preliminaries. 'You're selling property that doesn't belong to you. We purchased Richmond House and paid for the contents – we can produce an itemised inventory which includes all this,' he lied easily.

'We really want our things back, to keep all the original pieces in the old house,' added Holly, trying to balance Andrew's aggressiveness.

'So buy them,' Stolle said. 'Everything is for sale.'

'Would you rather we called the police to settle this?' asked Andrew.

'Be a big hassle for you, man. How you going to call them? No mobiles work out here, the boys are up dealing with a grader in a flooded creek anyway. And we have a bit of paper too, telling us we can clear the house.'

Andrew glanced at Holly. He knew she was ready to pay for the lot.

'Is there a problem?' The woman at the next stall came over to them.

Holly did a double take when she saw the older woman dressed all in purple, even down to purple ribbons threaded through her dyed red braids. But she had a friendly face.

'Couldn't help hearing. So you've bought old Richmond House . . . great home. Going to live in it?'

'Keep your nose out, Mac,' said Lynn without rancour.

Mac was unoffended and continued, 'Sounds to me like you both believe you have a case here. What's the bottom line?' She looked at Holly. 'You want the gear, Stolle and Lynn want a donation, to save all the hassle, right?' The woman eased herself into a position between the two couples and all eyes were on her as she gently took control.

'Yeah, make us an offer for a job lot.'

'But that's not fair, or right,' protested Holly.

'What were you going to do with the money you cleared today, Stolle?' asked Mac.

He shrugged. 'Have a good feed, and give Eddie a hand.'

'Plus pay the market fee,' added Lynn.

'Fifteen bucks. Now, let's ask this good lady and gentleman – by the way I'm Tilly MacDonald but everyone calls me Mac, and you are?'

'Holly. Holly Jamieson. My husband Andrew.'

'G'day. Lynn and Stolle.' She waved a hand at the two stallholders. 'Now, let's ask you what you wanted from today?'

'We came here to get our stuff back.'

'How long you been living in The Bay?'

'We just arrived, but I don't see what that has to do –'

'Ah, newcomers, rush, rush. As you are new arrivals, you'll need to get to know the area, the ins and outs of the place, where to find people, things you'll need. Maybe someone to give you a hand . . .'

Holly and Andrew didn't answer. They'd had this discussion in the car on the way to the markets, wondering how they'd find appropriate workers, for a start.

The purple lady continued, 'I would say it would be a small price to pay to have Lynn and Stolle – old, old hands in The Bay – become your mentors, so to speak. Stolle can fix anything, knows where to find anything and Lynn, she knows everyone and gives great massages. Now wouldn't their expertise be of value to you?'

'I'm not about to do business with people who flog stolen property,' snapped Andrew.

'Not stolen, given, in their minds,' said Mac. 'And I can vouch for them. Very handy people to know. They'll save you months of mistakes, paying through the nose for the wrong stuff and the wrong people.'

'And what do you do, Mac? Who are you?' asked Holly turning to look at her stall, which seemed rather empty except for a few blue bottles, some oils, soaps and candleburners and a pile of coloured cards.

'Like most people here, I do a bit of everything. I'm best known for reading the cards. Tarot,' she added as Holly and Andrew looked blank.

'Oh, great!' Andrew threw back his head, laughing. 'What a reference.'

'Take it or leave it, your loss,' said Stolle.

'I wouldn't mind helping you guys out down at the old house. Bit of a mess, isn't it?' said Lynn. She gave Holly a big smile and Holly found herself smiling back. Her instinct – long dormant – told her this wildly dressed woman was a friend. She knew Andrew wouldn't understand why she was suddenly prepared to trust her gut feelings, but she plunged in anyway. 'Andrew, let's do it. Trade off ... buy the stuff and we get the services of Stolle and Lynn.' She turned to Lynn with a smile. 'We can work something out, can't we?'

'Of course.'

'Holly, you're not taking this crystal ball gazer, whatever she calls herself ... Mac, her word as a reference for these people?'

Mac didn't look the least insulted. 'Tell you

what, Mrs Holly. Come and sit down and let me do your cards, then you can decide if I'm genuine enough for you.'

'Ooh, I don't think I want my cards read. I don't want to know if there's any . . . bad news.'

'It's nothing like that. Sometimes one's life follows a pattern. Knowing when you are falling into bad habits, or making an incautious decision might help you re-adjust your thinking. Understanding what has happened in your past can help with the present.' She paused, then added, 'Arriving at a new place can be a sensible time to clear your mind and know what to focus on, what not to waste energy on –'

'Holly . . .' Andrew sounded concerned.

'No, Andrew. I'm going to do it. You work out the deal with Stolle and Lynn. Mac, how much do I owe you for this . . . reading?'

'You decide. See if you feel I am helpful.' She took Holly's hand and led her to a chair opposite her table.

'I'm going to get a coffee. I'll be back,' said Andrew to Stolle. 'Don't sell anything of ours.'

'No worries, mate.' Stolle settled back into the chair.

Holding his coffee – in a china cup which he'd promised to return to the stall which only used crockery or recyclable cups – Andrew wandered along a row of stalls, pausing to rummage through old tools and second-hand books.

'Looking for anything in particular?' asked the man running the stall.

'No, unless you have any books on architecture. I collect them.'

'Got an interesting one on Gaudi's work.'

Andrew flicked through the glossy hardback. 'How much?'

'Let's see, it's a good quality coffee-table book, old edition, in good nick, sell for sixty bucks in Sydney. How about ten?'

'Done,' said Andrew, pleased at his buy.

The man put the book in a bag, pocketed Andrew's ten-dollar bill and smiled. 'Nice to know it's going to someone who appreciates it.'

Andrew glanced at the other boxes of books, noticing that many of them were related to alternative lifestyles, from herbal medicine and natural therapies, to an incredible selection of spiritual texts, overwhelmingly on Eastern religions.

The bookseller was dressed in what Andrew assessed as 'normal' clothes: jeans and a plain open-necked shirt. 'You into this scene?' he asked, then added quickly in explanation, 'I mean into this therapy and spiritual business.'

'Up here everyone is at some stage. Helping others or trying to save ourselves.' The bookseller gave Andrew a gentle smile. There was no hint of cynicism or fanaticism in his manner. 'This is a place people come to change their lives.'

Andrew nodded awkwardly, picked up his coffee and moved away.

In front of him a man had set up a tripod and

was video-taping several buskers. One was a handsome tall Caribbean man singing a calypso as he tapped out a rhythm on the sliced-off top of a silver forty-four gallon drum. He was wearing red boxing boots, yellow satin shorts and a full-sleeved frilled shirt. The calypso song he was singing in his rich baritone voice seemed to be slinging off at the local council over some issue. Beside him a pretty teenager was mimicking a calypso rumba dancer. Her mother, an attractive woman, clapped her hands in time, singing out, 'Yo, Matty.' The small crowd laughed and applauded as the song came to an end, some throwing coins into the steel drum with a clatter.

The man filming turned around with a grin and said, 'Now what I need is to film that when he sings it in the next council meeting!'

'Are you chronicling the local colour?' asked Andrew.

'In a way. I make documentaries,' he said, taking the camera off its tripod.

'What sort of documentary are you making here?'

'There's a bit of a stoush on over a whole lot of issues. This song is about a big supermarket chain trying to stop the markets.'

'Doesn't like the competition from the cash economy, eh?'

'That and a whole range of issues – the region around The Bay is getting to crisis point. We need a vision for the future.'

'I've heard that before –' They were interrupted as the teenage girl came dancing up to the cameraman.

'Hi, am I going to be on the news tonight?'

'Sorry, sweets, this is for a little TV thing, don't know where it will end up.'

She looked crestfallen but the man with the camera reached into his back pocket. 'Listen, if you want to come and have a look at it sometime, get your mum to ring me up. I'm Eddie. I live out at Spring Hill.'

'We're in The Bay, I'll ask her. I'm Matty and my mum is Kimberley. See ya then.'

'Cheers, kid.' He picked up the camera and tucked his tripod under his arm. 'I'd better see if there's anything else around,' he said to Andrew. 'Interview one of the organic growers maybe. Enjoy your visit.'

'I look like a tourist?'

'It's the vibes, man. You just don't look at home,' Eddie said and smiled.

'It's not my home. You're right. Good luck with your film.'

'Thanks.' He wandered off but his comments about the area being at a turning point stuck with Andrew as he began to walk back towards Stolle and Lynn's stall.

After speaking to them Andrew looked across to Mac's area. She was sitting across from a man at her table, dealing oversize coloured cards. Holly was nowhere to be seen, and Andrew wanted to go home. He headed for the car hoping she was waiting for him.

Holly was doing the circuit of the stalls in a daze. All she could see were the medieval cards falling in slow motion onto the table. She was trying to remember everything that Mac had said. So many strange associations, so many things rang true – things she hadn't fully acknowledged herself. She wished she'd taped it all . . . Mac spoke so quickly, so much information, so much to take in. She tried to distil the points that had made the biggest impact: that she was led here as an inevitability, she was following a path, Mac said, that was leading backwards. There would be some severance, some loss, possibly financial, but she would gain in other ways. New people would give her what she'd been lacking in her life. And when she asked Mac what that meant, the older woman had merely replied, 'Look at your life.'

As Mac had read the cards, she seemed to become a different person, one in a trance, as if she were drawing these things from somewhere else.

What else was there . . . Oh yes, the hangman. That card had frightened Holly. But Mac had been calm. 'Yes, there are factors working against you, but the noose need not strangle. It is up to you not to keep waiting as you have been.'

'Waiting? For what?'

'That is for you to discover. This card also represents sacrifice. You have sacrificed yourself to others. It is time for you to take control.'

'I've never been one to take control, that's Andrew's role.'

Mac had lifted her eyes from the cards and asked, 'Why?'

Holly had no answer. She tried to dismiss this. All she was doing was trying to establish a business for herself. For her family. To prove to them she was capable of doing something this ambitious.

It seemed Mac had read her thoughts. She tapped a card. 'The Fool, the destiny card. This journey, the fact you are in this place is for a reason. There is unfinished business and only you can help. You have taken on a bigger task than you think. Continue to follow your instincts . . . that is what they're for. To guide you, not your husband.'

Holly glanced around and saw their car across the grass with Andrew standing by it, shading his eyes, searching the crowd for her. She headed towards him, pushing down feelings of guilt, knowing she couldn't tell him anything of what had transpired, knowing he wouldn't understand. And for the moment, nor did she. But strangely, she felt a small sense of triumph. There was a reason she was here. Eventually it would become clear.

Chapter Three

KIMBERLEY BOUGHT A LIME GELATO FROM THE ICEE
stand across from the Big Pub and trailed back to
the row of beach shops with sarongs, Indian shirts
and skirts festooned around their doorways. She
leaned against a cocos palm and waited for Matty.

Kimberley was tall, her tightly curled brown
hair tumbled below her shoulders. She rarely wore
make-up, favouring a sporty outdoors look. While
she dressed casually she would have liked to own
a few smart clothes similar to those she saw on
city visitors strolling round The Bay, but money
was tight. She had a deserted wife's pension and a
little in the joint bank account which her husband
had left when he went to chase dreams in India.

Occasionally he sent them money earned from

casual teaching jobs he picked up, but mostly he mailed his wife and daughter embroidered tops and cushions from Rajasthan or miniature pictures painted on silk and canvas, or small brass ornaments. Matty loved them and Kimberley didn't have the heart to tell him you could buy the same things at the Indian import shops in The Bay. Kimberley hated being dependent on the part-time job she had at the glass studio packing hand-blown glass creations to be shipped to stores around Australia and overseas. She'd watched the artisans at work over the searing fire deftly blowing and twirling the glass pipes to produce the distinctive, wildly coloured vases and ornaments that were a trademark of the local crafts people.

She wished she had developed a skill when she was younger instead of being a rebel who drifted around on the dole or in low paid jobs. When she met Colin, a schoolteacher, they lived together, and when Kimberley became pregnant they bowed to parental pressure from both families and got married. The pregnancy and marriage coincided with Colin discovering New Age philosophies. He became fanatical about yoga and meditation, began exploring Eastern religions and took the family to live on a rural commune.

His obsession with Buddhism led him to adopt the Indian name Ashok, and one day he simply packed his bag and went to India, promising to come back soon, when he had completed his studies, whatever they might be. They were still waiting.

When he did make fleeting visits, Kimberley knew she'd never settle for any other man. Infuriatingly, despite his absence she loved him. Had she found someone else she was sure he'd let her go, wanting her to be happy. Sadly, he was the only man who made her feel fulfilled – when he was around.

She now lived in a rented house in The Bay and concentrated on giving all the support she could to her daughter. Above all else she wanted Matty to avoid the mistakes she had made, mainly as a result of conflict with her parents. In an odd way Kimberley felt that Ashok was still a part of the family, even though they had seen little of him since he moved to India. Matty adored her father, but as she grew older she was becoming aware of the difficulties he had inflicted on her mother. She lived in hope that one day they would all be together again. Life in The Bay was so relaxed, the weather so beautiful, that it was easy to lose focus and just drift along, day after day, year after year. However, Kimberley increasingly pondered just where her life was going.

When her teenage daughter appeared Kimberley gave a shout. 'Here, Matty . . . any luck?' Matty had been searching for the 'right' pink bikini for weeks now.

She shook her head and looked morose. 'Can we go up the coast, Mum? There's nothing in this dump.'

'Now, Matts, we've looked in at least a dozen shops. People come here to buy swimsuits because it's a holiday town. You're just being too hard to please. It's impossible to believe that you can't find a nice bikini.'

'I am not being hard to please. And you know it has to match my shirt and sarong. I did see one . . . but it was nearly two hundred dollars –'

'Forget that!'

'I know, I know,' Matty sighed wearily. There was never anything left over in their budget for even the smallest luxury.

Kimberley was determined not to make a scene over her daughter's petulance. She knew Matty was not alone, it seemed part of the early teens syndrome. She thought back to her fourteenth year. Yes, she'd been interested in boys and clothes. But she and her girlfriends and their mums had sewn their own clothes and made do with daggy swimsuits. They didn't want to draw attention to their newly developing bodies in a two-piece. But she wasn't going to drag up what Matty called 'boring ancient history'.

'So what's next on our Saturday list?'

'The record shop, I want to listen to the new CDs. What are you going to do while I'm there?'

Kimberley smiled. 'I'll go and play at the beach. Bit of role reversal, huh? Or maybe I'll see if Billy can give my hair a quick trim.'

'I'll meet you at the Caffe Latte then?'

'Okay. I'll treat you to a Ginger Nektar.' Kimberley headed to the hair salon.

The Teepee had been created by ex-Melbourne hairdresser Billy Bowditch, known in The Bay as Billy Blue Bear.

About eighteen months ago he'd arrived in his 'Toorak clobber' of navy Armani pants, white silk shirt, his sleek pepper and salt hair trimmed close to his head and a silver moustache. He knew The Bay well from many holidays over the years and decided to quit Melbourne and resettle there after hearing so many of his clients lamenting how hard it was to get a decent haircut whenever they visited Beacon Bay. He saw the opportunity to set up as a sophisticated stylist, convinced his wife Paula to sell their slender holding in Melbourne, and they headed north chasing their dream.

Billy opened his shop in a smart new arcade. Initially, though, he was rejected by the locals as too posh, too Melbourne. When the holiday season dwindled, the salon was empty. He had a younger wife and a five-year-old daughter and he began to question what he was doing in this 'backwater'. When the rainy season hit, Paula became hysterical at being trapped indoors with a small bored child and closets sprouting green mould on clothes, shoes and bags.

With time on his hands Billy began to indulge his interest in Native American history. So when a Sioux Indian elder came to The Bay to run a series of sweat lodges, Billy signed up and before it was over found himself on a vision quest. After it he'd changed his whole approach to life.

The elegant salon became The Teepee, redolent of the inside of a tribal tent – weavings and totems on the walls, traditional emblems painted on the floor, sepia photographs of Indian elders and framed sayings of Little Big Chief. Billy shaved his moustache and let his hair grow. Blue jeans and simple plaid or Hawaiian print shirts became his uniform, and he began collecting silver and turquoise jewellery and wore a particularly ornate buckle on his belt. While he didn't elaborate on his experiences, it became known that he'd gone through a rebirthing and had been given his totem name of Blue Bear. A discreet logo of an entwined BBB appeared on the door of the renamed salon. Arrangements of feathers, dried twigs and smudge sticks replaced the angular glass vase with its spiky heliconia bloom. Subdued hypnotic, rhythmic music with drumming and chanting replaced the movie soundtracks and jazz CDs. The locals wandered in and stayed as clients. Tourists thought it all very quaint. But Billy survived because he was a good hairdresser.

Kimberley pushed the tribal rug to one side and stuck her head into the salon. She was pleased to find him alone, hunched over the form guide, the radio tuned to the Brisbane races.

'You going home to tell Paula it was another wild Saturday in the salon?' she asked with a grin.

'Hey, Kim, come in. Everyone's watching the dragon boat races across the bay. Want a coffee? I was looking for an excuse to duck out for a fag.'

'I thought you'd given them away. You were on a health kick two weeks ago.'

'I feel great. Been on the aloe vera juice. No more ciggies, just these.' He picked up a packet of slim cheroots.

'You're impossible. I'll have a cappuccino with you. I was thinking I'd get you to knock off the straggly ends.' She lifted her hair and showed him.

'Yeah, could do with it. Where's Matilda?'

'In the record shop, she's exhausted every store along the coast for a bikini.' Then seeing Billy's raised eyebrow she added, 'Wait till your little princess is fourteen. Obsessed with her body, how she looks, what to wear, what people think of her . . . I'm being very patient.'

They sat down at a table outside the coffee shop in the arcade so Billy could watch his doorway. He'd left the answer machine on.

'Why don't you bring the portable here? You might miss an appointment,' said Kimberley.

'Can't stress out about missing a colour job or whatever. Money isn't where it's at, Kim,' he said.

She eyed his Volvo in The Teepee parking space. 'Easy enough to say when you're comfortable. I have to watch every cent. Matty is costing me a bundle, now she even wants to have her legs waxed!'

'Introduce her to Lady Schick.'

'Oh, they had some beauty consultant come to the school and she put the horrors of razors to them. One of Matty's friends shaved her top lip and that sent them into a frenzy. Still, I'd rather this than drugs.'

Billy lit up his cheroot. 'Your daughter is friends with Erica Bitternden, isn't she?'

'They're in the same class, hang out in the same group. I met her mother, Bonnie, at a New

65

Year's Eve party. She seemed to want to keep to herself. I guess Matty does see quite a lot of her daughter, why?'

Billy turned and glanced down the arcade to the Beach Hut, a small shop filled with swimwear, beach accessories, sunglasses, hats and sandals, run by Bonnie. He lowered his voice. 'Trouble brewing, I predict. I've seen it too often . . . I know the symptoms. I went through it a bit myself,' he said. 'She's not there a lot of the time, sometimes a pal turns up and opens the shop for her, but I've seen her at the Big Pub more than a little merry.'

'Paula doesn't mind you hanging out at the pub?'

'I shut shop at four if there's no one coming in. Pick up my winnings from the TAB, have a few ales and head home in time to walk the dog on the beach with Hope. I don't wipe myself out. I've seen young Erica come looking for her mother after school. It's not the drinking, it's the kid Bonnie's hanging out with.'

'Kid?'

'Young lover boy, early twenties. Nothing wrong with that,' Billy was quick to add, 'but the guy is a loser. A junkie. And have you noticed how Bonnie has changed?'

'Can't say I have. Never seen her at school meetings and I don't spend time in this arcade like you do. Anyway, it's her business.'

'Sure, sure it is. But if my daughter was hanging out at her place I'd be worried. No one at home, mother and boyfriend on dope and whatever else. Bonnie can't handle it. She came up here from Melbourne a few months after me, a straight up and down smart suburban divorcee. Gets bored, buys a business and being lonely she's a target for the likes of lover boy.'

'Umm. So how has she changed? You notice these female things.' Kimberley studied Billy, his rough good looks, heavy shoulders, a nice smile. Never pick him as a hairdresser in a million years. Men liked him too. He had as many male clients as women. Billy was blokey without being butch. Loved the horses, beer and fishing. Idolised his daughter, Hope. He was the sort of man women loved to gossip with and quietly share their feelings. He was known to his men clients as 'The Bear', and they found him a sensitive and comforting ear to bend about their problems. They respected the fact that he'd changed his way of life and was open enough to embrace an old culture that helped him in the present. Wasn't their thing, but if it worked for him, fine.

Kimberley wondered how much Billy really knew about Bonnie and her little shop down the arcade. She felt slightly guilty she didn't know the mothers of Matty's friends very well.

'Bonnie talks to me,' Billy continued. 'She confides a bit. But just look at the way she dresses now. She was always very smart casual, then casual gave way to hippy and then sloppy. The blonde bob has been let go. Now it's mad curls, she covers the grey with henna . . . the natural look, she calls it. Looks like she's wearing a bloody bird's nest. She's trying to be one of the young guns.'

'That's a hairdresser talking. But thanks for the tip, I'll check it out if there's a sleepover at Erica's planned.'

Their coffees arrived and Billy took a sip before asking, 'And what news of your old man?'

Kimberley paused as she thought about Ashok. 'Probably still has dreadlocks, wearing sandals and a *dhoti* and *omming* in some Indian ashram.'

'Is he into dope and stuff?'

Kimberley looked at Billy's earnest face. He could ask those sorts of personal questions without offending.

'Nah, smoked joints when we first got together. He always seemed spaced out but he's just one of those quiet, vague kinda guys. That was when he was called Colin, before becoming a Buddhist.'

'Doesn't he get in touch with Matty? Teenage girls need their dads.'

'Hell, Billy, don't make me feel bad. It's hard enough coping on my own. There's that underlying accusing look in her eyes when I say, no, she can't have a two hundred dollar bikini like . . . well, Dad would say yes.'

'Would he?'

'If he had the money, probably yes. Too easygoing, that's his trouble. A gentle soul. Not the ideal partner to forge ahead with in the real world.'

Kimberley looked into the foamy dregs in her cup. Matty so adored her absent father, that was the trouble. If he was around more than once a year she might see him for the waste of space he was. Mac referred to him as 'the guru' and kept advising Kim to 'move on'.

'We were really happy with our little daughter in those early years,' she said, almost to herself. 'I had to make him see you can't raise a child on lentils and dreams. So off he went to India on his own. He comes and goes, says he's researching some sort of book. He lives on the smell of an oily rag over there and I'm on a deserted wife's pension here in bloody paradise.'

'If he comes and goes you're not deserted, are you?'

'I am as far as the government is concerned, thank you very much.'

'What happens when he comes back?'

Kimberley pushed her cup away. 'Ah, we play happy families for a couple of weeks and then he's off.' She stood up. 'Let's do my hair, Matty will be back soon. She doesn't like to be kept waiting, you know.'

'I'll keep my eyes open for a real bloke for you,' said Billy, dropping a ten-dollar note onto the table.

'You do that,' said Kimberley, smiling.

Holly had no idea what time it was. There was no comforting green glow from a bedside clock. She was sleeping in the annexe attached to the main house while it was being renovated. It still felt strange – being in a narrow bed, alone, with different smells and sounds. The first few nights she'd been nervous, knowing she was in a big empty house on an isolated headland. Curly slept in her basket by the door but the old dog's deep snuffling snore didn't give Holly a huge sense of security. Andrew had told her to book into a motel, he couldn't believe she'd stayed alone in the old house. But Holly wanted to bond with this place that had so much history, that was now such a big chunk of her life.

She was glad she was alone. If her family was there they might think she was slightly mad because of the way she walked through the near empty rooms, running her hands over the old ledges, windowpanes and balustrades. She'd even sat on the floor rubbing her hands over the worn floorboards, exposed beneath frayed modern carpet. They would come up beautifully with a little sanding and polishing. Everywhere she went in the house she wondered about the family that had lived there. She was beginning to feel a responsibility for Richmond House – to restore it, to maintain it, to stay faithful to those who had built it, lived, loved, cried and laughed within it. This place was a tangible link with the history of The Bay. Gradually her fears had subsided and she imagined the house wrapping itself around her, protecting her. She felt she was one of the family who'd always be a part of this home.

Holly pulled the cotton duvet up to her chin. The wind must have woken her; it was howling and thrashing at the windows and in the garden. She saw, as they were lit by a flash of the beam from the lighthouse, the tops of the palm trees whipping and bending. Then came the rain, a solid downpour of wind-driven water. She decided to get up and check that no rain was coming in – a chance to look for leaks. The electric lights were few, high and dim, little changed since the 1950s. The last people here had favoured lamps. Holly made a mental note to talk to an electrician about recessed spot lighting.

One part of the wall of the sitting room in the annexe was trickling water. She turned on the torch, deciding to run along the covered walkway to the main house and inspect it. Curly caught up with her and reluctantly padded behind. But as she rattled the side door of the kitchen, the dog began barking.

Holly looked back, swinging the torch around in the wet blackness. Curly was standing out in the garden, barking wildly into the storm, looking up towards the roof.

She called the old dog, who hated storms, but Curly took no notice. There was a warning sound to her bark that alerted Holly. She ran out onto the lawn, her nightdress soaked through in seconds.

'What is it, old girl? What are you barking at, Curly?'

The dog continued to bark at the upper level. It was in darkness, the outline of the roof barely visible in the storm-blacked sky. But as Holly was about to turn away, the beam from the lighthouse swung again over the trees, showing in dim relief the top of the house. Holly was looking straight at the widow's walk. In the seconds of light she clearly saw a dark figure silhouetted – a figure leaning out scanning the sea. Her instant impression was of a woman, dressed in black, her hair streaming behind her.

Holly grabbed Curly's collar and began stumbling backwards in shock, oblivious to the water plastering her hair, pouring down her neck, her eyes riveted to the top of the house somewhere in the blackness.

By the time the beam swung around again the dark shape had gone. Was it ever there? Had she imagined it through the rain?

She hurried back to the annexe with Curly trotting to keep up with her, slammed the door and went through the rooms, throwing on the lights. She turned on the radio and went into the shower, dropping her soaking nightgown in a corner.

Later, wrapped in her bathrobe, a towel around her head, she put the kettle on in the small sitting room and began to dry Curly's thick wet fur.

'You saw her too, didn't you, Curly? Looking out to sea in the storm. Who is she, Curly, who could she be?'

Holly was not afraid. The shower had helped calm her nerves, and she knew there was no strange woman in the attic. She knew what they'd seen. 'We've seen a ghost,' she said softly to the dog. 'I wonder if she'll come back, Curly. What do you think?'

Holly lifted her head, suddenly aware that the wind and rain had eased, almost stopped. The kettle whistled. The announcer on the local FM station spoke cheerfully. It was 3.15 am.

Holly settled Curly in her basket then went back to bed with a mug of tea. She locked the door, left the light on and, propped up against the pillows, she tried to imagine being a wife watching the storm, waiting for her loved one to return from the sea in those pioneering days. She tried to imagine the deep worry that must always be at the back of the woman's mind, while still having to cope with everyday family life until the wait was over. And how were things then? If it hadn't been a successful voyage there'd be financial worries. Were they thrilled to be together, or had this woman overly romanticised her seafaring husband? Holly thought of all the times Andrew had been away on business trips, how she'd looked forward to his return, planned a romantic evening, only to have him disappear into his office to finish some drawings or plans. Or else he'd complained he was exhausted, he'd eaten on the plane, and gone straight to sleep. How foolish she'd felt at the untouched candlelit dinner, at wearing sexy perfume and nightwear. Maybe Andrew and the children had been right when they told her to find an interest, get involved in something – women's clubs, charities. Well, she'd certainly taken on something with Richmond House. And she knew they thought it was all too much for her. Not physically, for Holly was trim and energetic, but perhaps because she'd never had to deal with a whole range of problems like those that now loomed outside the home, outside the family.

Holly instinctively felt it hadn't been easy for the woman who had lived in this house. That made her determined she wasn't going to let the woman down and see her home become dilapidated or unloved. It was a place to be enjoyed, a place to be at peace, a place linked to the sea.

She finished her tea and lay back on the pillows and fell into a deep sleep. She dreamed of being on a boat, huddled below deck as the wind whipped at straining sails; the low mournful sound from the rigging was like the shriek of a creature in distress.

When she woke the morning was still, sunny and clear. Holly felt refreshed and headed to the beach with Curly for an early swim, which was becoming part of her new routine. She'd never been a morning person, loathed getting out of bed to see the children off to school, and Andrew always joked that he hid behind his newspaper until Holly had drunk her second cup of coffee. Yet here her eyes snapped open, she was alert and ready for the day. Maybe it was sleeping alone, maybe it was not having curtains so the sunrise wakened her early and gently.

After her swim Holly pushed the pace of her climb up from the beach to give herself a workout.

Her heart rate was well up and her breath a little strained when she reached the top and eased down, but self-congratulation was spoiled by the sound of the builder's truck arriving . . . late again. This was the second week of renovation work, and they were taking advantage of sunny dry days to restore the stone walls and tiled pathways in the garden. Andrew had hired the builder soon after he and Holly had made a list of all the obvious things that needed to be done in the first stage of bringing new life back to the old house.

'Mick, just call me Mick, missus,' the burly builder with an impressive beer gut had said when Andrew introduced him.

Her attempt to establish some personal involvement in the work was dismissed with as much subtlety as he could muster. 'No sweat, missus. Have a chat any time you like, but there's no need to hang about every day. The blokes get a bit put off by that sort of thing, ya know. We got Andrew's mobile. Can always give 'im a bell if there's a problem.'

'But I want to be here, and involved,' Holly repeated as firmly as she dared. She didn't like the secret men's business smile that swiftly passed between her husband and this builder from Central Casting – navy singlet, stubby shorts, work boots and football socks.

And how right her instincts had been. Mick had left his two offsiders, Kirk the Scot and Dick the dill, as she privately called the rather slow-moving, silent Queensland boy, to get on with the 'rough stuff'. Straight away Holly disagreed with what they were doing, but she might as well have spoken to a brick wall. They paused, they listened with exaggerated patience, they shrugged, and then continued what they were doing. Now as Holly entered the courtyard she noticed that many of the old Italian ceramic paving tiles had been smashed. Politely she asked Kirk what had happened.

'Mick told us to clear the area.' Kirk's accent was thick and stubborn.

'Maybe, but that doesn't mean cutting down that beautiful frangipani tree, or breaking the tiles.'

'Tree's dead. Tiles are old and lots missing.' He looked at her as if she was the village idiot.

'That tree is not dead, they look like that until they bloom, and those are expensive tiles. I intend to re-use what I can. Please remove them without breaking them.'

'We take our orders from Mick.'

'And I'm telling you, and Mick, I want to keep as much of the old stuff as possible.' Holly suddenly caught sight of a smashed stone figure of a lichen-covered cherub. 'What the hell! How did that happen?' She rushed to the broken statue.

'That's what happens when a hammer hits stone. It was cemented there, had to go,' said Dick.

Holly was furious – not just at the senseless destruction but at their almost mocking attitude towards her. 'Don't you touch another thing until I speak to Mick.'

'Suits us.' Kirk began rolling a cigarette, Dick opened his lunchbox and Thermos flask.

Holly was unable to reach Mick on his mobile for fifteen minutes. She watched the two men stretch out, take off their hats and bask in the sun. When she eventually got hold of him at another building site, Mick was irritated at the interruption. 'Those blokes know what they're doing. It's not up to you to tell them what to do, missus. Your husband gave me very detailed plans.'

'Those plans did not include smashing everything in sight. I'm renovating, not knocking it all down to start again. I want you to come over here, your workmen won't listen to me.' She hoped her voice didn't wobble. While she was angry, she was also feeling intimidated by these oafish men.

'That's because they're under orders from me, and I take orders from Andrew. Sorry, missus, but that's how it is.'

If Andrew had been on hand she would have let him deal with the crisis, but he was in Sydney. She recalled how he had expressed concern at the idea of her getting involved with 'the complicated heavy building stuff' and that made her angrier. 'Leave it all to Mick and his team, darling. Amuse yourself with planning the interior detail that will pretty things up,' was how he'd put it. At the time she had let the arrangement with Mick pass without challenge because the excitement of the occasion was intoxicating. Now in a more emotionally sober situation, his ambivalence about her role in the project – which had been her idea

– seemed monstrous, and the attitude of the workers preposterous. She took a deep breath, turned her back on the men, who immediately exchanged knowing grins, and walked to the verandah and looked out to sea, struggling to calm her rising temper and organise her thoughts.

In the distance she saw a large freighter and suddenly thought again of the woman who'd lived in this house, a woman who must have been on her own for many months while her menfolk were away at sea. She probably had to deal with all manner of problems. No phones, no one close by and no one to make decisions for her.

All the time Mick had been prattling on in reassuring, almost condescending tones on the phone about trusting him to do the right thing, that he would give Andrew a call, and yes he would tell the workmen to be more sensitive about the 'bits and pieces' in the garden. He even suggested that she take a drive into the country since it was 'such a beaut day for getting to know more about the district'.

She glanced back at the two workmen idly passing the time that she was paying for. Suddenly she remembered Mick's surname. 'Well, *Mister* Langdon,' she interrupted firmly and loudly, 'I'm sorry to tell you that my husband takes his orders from me on this job. I am terminating your involvement. I'll tell your men to leave immediately.'

'You can't do that, lady,' said Mick, 'I have a contract.'

Holly hesitated, Andrew had told her he'd hired them on a month to month arrangement. 'I'll pay out the month as agreed.'

'I have an agreement with your old man for six months work. I can sue, you know.'

'So sue me. I'm saving myself money by getting these oafs off my property. They're doing more damage than good.'

'That's not a smart move, lady. You won't get any other tradesmen to work there,' Mick growled.

'I hope you're not threatening me, Mr Langdon. I'll manage, thank you very much.' There was a click at the other end of the line and Holly started to shake. What had she done? How could she do that? Had she really said those things to that man? A small sense of elation stilled her shaky legs and she headed to Kirk and Dick with a determined stride.

'I've just fired your boss. You are free to leave any time in the next few minutes.'

'What for? Why'd you do that? Mick said your old man was the boss.' Kirk was aggressively defensive.

Dick looked worried. 'Not because of us. We haven't done anything.'

'Well, what you have done isn't what I want. Good morning, gentlemen.'

She went to the kitchen and made a strong black coffee then sat on the steps savouring the caffeine kick as the two men loaded up their truck.

Her husband was on the phone an hour later. 'Holly, what the hell is going on? I've just been pulled out of a meeting by your builder saying he's suing. What have you done?'

'I'm sorry Mick felt he had to bother you, Andrew. I wasn't happy with the standard of their work, or the fact that they wouldn't listen to me. So I let them go. You said you had a month by month agreement, didn't you?'

'Are you sure you know what you're doing?' There was a short silence. 'Fortunately I did only agree to a month by month deal. You'll have to pay them out, and then what are you going to do? They could spread the word around their mates not to touch your place.' Andrew sounded exasperated.

Holly worked hard to keep her voice calm and pleasant. 'I'll deal with it, sweetheart, no worries. How's everything down there? Haven't talked to you for two days.'

'Busy. The big project in Thailand looks like coming off. I might be away . . . so you won't be able to reach me at the drop of a hat with any little problem that comes up.'

'I didn't insist you run out of your meeting,' she reminded him sweetly. 'I'm handling things. I'll call you tonight.'

'I'll be late, dinner with the Thai bankers. Gotta run. Let me call you. Bye.'

She looked at the phone feeling suddenly alone. Brave words had fallen so easily from her lips. What the devil was she going to do now? She could feel the shakes returning. She made another cup of coffee, stronger than the earlier one.

Holly was washing up her breakfast plate and cup when an old utility rolled down the driveway with Lynn and Stolle in the front. As they turned to park she was amazed to see all the furniture from Richmond House.

'Got hold of a friend's ute so figured we'd bring your stuff around, seeing you couldn't carry it the other day,' Stolle said, making no reference to money.

'Oh, that's kind of you. I'm afraid it will have to go into storage in the shed, I've started all the renovations . . . well, I had until about an hour ago. What a day. What a night. How did you fare in the storm?'

They both stared at her. 'Storm? What storm?'

Holly laughed, then stopped. 'You mean you didn't get the rain and wind? It was crazy.' She looked around the garden and slowly it dawned on her – how tidy everything looked. No mess, no broken branches or fronds that one would expect to have blown down; it all looked very dry. She shivered and glanced up at the white railing around the widow's walk.

'It was a massive storm . . . pelting rain, and the wind . . .'

Lynn and Stolle exchanged a look. 'Ah, sometimes it rains on one side of town and not on the other. The hill attracts the rain clouds . . .' They changed the subject. 'So how's the building, or rebuilding?'

Holly was glad of the distraction. There was no point in telling them about the dreamlike events of the previous night. And her immediate problem was pressing.

'My husband hired a builder who started two weeks ago and was hardly ever here and his two sidekicks were a disaster . . . I fired them.' She gave a pleased smile. 'Shocked them, and my husband, and me!'

They all laughed.

'So what are you going to do? Got a lead on a good team?' asked Stolle.

'No idea. They gave me dire warnings I'd never get anyone to work up here. I guess I'm blacklisted.'

'Congratulations,' Lynn said, grinning.

'Means you're a thinking person of integrity with standards above the grunge level,' added Stolle.

'Well, thanks . . . I guess. But that doesn't help me, does it?'

'No worries. We know just the person for you. Let's get this stuff unloaded, give us a cuppa and I'll make a phone call,' Stolle said.

Lynn glanced at him as he began untying ropes looped over the furniture. 'Mitchell?'

'Who else?'

Holly set up a small table and chairs on the verandah and poured the tea. 'Sorry, I only have English breakfast. I'll get a selection of herb teas in.' Stolle had asked for green tea, Lynn for peppermint.

'Cleansing, good for the digestive system.' Stolle reached for a shortbread biscuit. 'Haven't had one of these for a long time. Loaded with fat, but what the hell, eh?'

'So tell me about this Mitchell.'

'Nice guy. Very creative, clever with his hands, good with people. Has a great bunch who work with him. There is one problem . . . well, we don't see it as a problem, but your husband might.'

'I'm running this show, not my husband,' said Holly with some bravado. 'So what's the problem? He does sound too good to be true.'

'No piece of paper. Got the okay up here from the bureaucrats and local clients, but he's not, you know, official,' Stolle said.

Holly looked at Lynn who explained, 'Not qualified. Never went to college, no degree in engineering, building whatever. Self-taught, just a natural gift.'

Holly looked worried. 'I'm not sure the wink-wink, nod-nod approach sits too comfortably with me, Stolle. There are building regulations, council inspections, all that sort of stuff.'

'Ah yeah, but don't let it get you down, Holly. You've spent too long in the city where everything needs a bit of paper – degrees, certificates, approvals – and there are enough rules and regs to confuse Confucius.' Stolle grinned, rather pleased with his reference to the Chinese sage. 'Nah, Mitchell knows what's what when it comes to wood and tools. Born with talent, I reckon. Just went into the wrong career. He became a craftsman extraordinaire once he left his desk.'

Lynn nodded. 'Trust us, Holly, he'll do the right thing.'

Stolle ran his eye over the house and scanned the garden. 'Most of what you want done around here is repair stuff, doesn't need mucking about with council. He'll get the right blokes to make sure water doesn't come out of the light fittings and you don't get a jolt every time you turn on a tap.'

Lynn gave him a sharp elbow jab in the ribs. 'Okay, funny man, stop trying to be the new millennium Paul Hogan.'

Stolle doubled up in mock agony. 'Ouch! I'll sue, I'll sue!'

Holly laughed. 'It seems to be a day for legals. That's the second threat of suing I've heard today. Must be the moon phase.'

'Talking about the moon, it's full moon tomorrow night,' said Lynn. 'There's a big women's thing happening, Goddess Night. You must come.'

'Not sure that it's really me,' said Holly, a little embarrassed. 'I've never been a group person. Hardly got past girl guides and parents and citizens.'

'Fair enough, but it's not in the same league. You'll love the sense of community, and you'll make a lot of new friends. Every celebration is a bit different. Depends on who's the energy behind it this year. Come on.'

Holly hesitated, a Goddess Night sounded far

too radical. 'Where is it going to be held? Down at the beach?'

'No. In a little church hall just out of town. Right by an avocado plantation. I'll give you more details later.'

'A church hall!' exclaimed Holly in surprise. But she had already made up her mind to go along. Even though her experience of The Bay was limited, she figured that it was useless trying to cling to what was regarded as the norm by city standards. The Goddess Night wasn't going to be anything like a View Club dinner, that was for sure.

The full moon rose over the sea, fat, cheesy yellow, postcard perfect with the lighthouse silhouetted against it. Holly wondered what on earth one wore to a Goddess Night, and finally opted for white cotton slacks, a loose blue shirt and sandals. Lynn, no surprise, looked goddess-like in a floaty caftan with several rainbow-hued scarves, feathers in her hair and a rope of silver wound up her arm.

'I've got a plate of date slices, some cheese and fruit,' said Holly.

'Great. The food is always delish at this thing. Now just go with the flow, girl, don't worry about it.'

Holly decided to drive in case she wanted to leave early. Lynn had said she could always get a ride home with any number of friends.

They parked the Forester in a grassy patch

under huge Moreton Bay fig trees which formed a leafy arch over the dirt road. Groups of women were already clustered outside the cream-coloured, wooden church hall.

All ages of women were represented, from grannies – hippy to matronly – to young mothers with babies. Some women looked like school-teachers, others were the characters Holly had seen in the markets, body pierced, coloured hair in dreadlocks threaded with beads and feathers. Their babies were often identically dressed in hand-painted clothes. Most of the crowd was wearing elaborate and fanciful gear and looked happy, expectant, and non-threatening. Holly saw Amber, the young woman who made the cosmetics, and she recognised some other women from seeing them around in shops and on the beach and the streets.

Lynn rushed over to a woman handing out leaflets at the steps of the hall and they hugged each other warmly, but Holly hung back.

'We all look like a bunch of extras from a Fellini fantasy,' said a cheerful voice beside her.

Holly turned and saw Mac. Naturally she was in purple with glittery bits. 'Glad to see you're hanging out with Lynn. Listen to what she and Stolle have to say, got their fingers on the pulse of this part of the world.'

'So it seems. Thank you for arbitrating at the markets. We settled on a price and the historic mementos have been returned. I think Lynn and Stolle will be very helpful.' Holly had embraced

Lynn and Stolle while Andrew was still a little suspicious. But so long as Holly was happy with the arrangement he wasn't going to fuss over some old household bits and bobs. She changed the subject. 'So what goes on here exactly?'

'Wait and see. Different people organise this every year so it's never the same. Cynthia is doing this one, she's big on drumming. Runs an interesting workshop to relieve stress by drumming. Frees the inhibitions and you can beat the shit out of a drum instead of your old man,' said Mac with a grin. A young girl dashed up to her and gave her a hug. 'This is Matilda, known as Matty. This is Holly.'

'Hi, Matty.' Holly touched the flower coronet she was wearing on her hair. 'That's pretty.'

'Thanks. Mum and me made it this afternoon. And she did the French braids.' She swung around to show them her hairstyle.

'And this is Matty's stylist . . . her mother, Kimberley,' laughed Mac, introducing the attractive woman who joined them.

She shook Holly's hand. 'Hello, I've heard about you. How are things at Richmond House?'

Holly did a mild double take. 'Oh, you know about my plans?' She glanced at Mac but Kimberley broke in.

'Don't think me nosy. This is a small community so everyone gets to know everyone's business, which can be good and bad. If I can help out in any way, let me know.'

'Why thanks, er, what do you do?' asked Holly.

Mac patted her arm. 'When you say "do", you mean make a living in cityspeak. Here everyone does many things – hanging out at the beach is doing something. Ask people what their interests are and you might get closer to what people do.'

'It's one of the dreams people come here to find,' said Kimberley. 'To do what interests them. Follow their passion, to bliss out.'

Following passions. Blissing out. Finding dreams. Holly suddenly realised with a little shock just how far she'd travelled from Mosman, at least in terms of language and values. She couldn't recall anyone having mentioned share prices since she'd arrived. It was the first thing people asked each other back in Sydney. In Holly's circle what their husbands did immediately established who they were and where they all fitted into the social hierarchy. There were no such ground rules here. She turned to Matty. 'And what's your big interest? Your passion?'

Matty twisted her mouth as she thought about it. 'Singing, designing clothes, dressing up rooms . . . oh, lots of stuff.'

'You might give me some ideas on decorating my new place, when it's ever finished,' said Holly. 'I've had a disaster with the builders, but Stolle is introducing me to a fellow he says is very good.'

Kimberley laughed. 'Stolle and Lynn know everyone all right. But seriously, if you want any design stuff, we have a very famous old bird up here.' She glanced around. 'In fact she should be here. Have you seen Nola?' she asked Matty who was waving to another teenage girl.

'No, Mum. There's Erica, I'm going to sit with her.'

'Yeah, Nola Florens. Made a fortune from fabric and wallpaper designs in the fifties . . . apparently invested shrewdly. She's worth millions, so they say,' said Mac.

'My God, of course I know of her. Practically every house in the Eastern Suburbs of Sydney had Florens wallpaper and fabrics at some time,' exclaimed Holly. This was familiar territory.

'Richest woman in The Bay. Bit eccentric but a good stick. She'll be here, you won't miss her,' said Kimberley. 'If you want an intro, I'll fix it up.'

'I'd really like that. Nola Florens has such a talent for using colour. Maybe we could all get together for a morning tea at the old house . . . well, in the garden perhaps. It's still a shambles inside.'

'I like that idea,' enthused Kimberley. 'I've always wanted to have a good look around Richmond House. And hearing Nola's initial off-the-cuff colour ideas will be as entertaining as it will be inspired.'

'You can be assured Nola won't disappoint, dears,' said Mac. 'I've always wondered why she never became a TV star on a talk show with a decorator theme.'

'The booze, one suspects. You can wobble a bit in The Bay, but not when you've got a million people watching.'

As if on cue a male voice from behind cheerfully greeted them. '*Hari Om*.' Holly turned to see a young man with a video camera and a tripod. Mac gave him a hug.

'*Hari Om* to you too, darling. How timely. We were just talking about what one needed to make the big time on the little screen. Could you make me a TV star, Eddie?'

'I'm not sure you have the magic "it" quality, Mac. But one day we'll do a little screen test, hey?'

'Promises, promises. Eddie, meet Holly. New in town. Doing up Richmond House.'

'Delighted. So you're the face that goes with the gossip.' He grinned at her reaction.

'Gossip?' said a surprised Holly. 'Whatever is being said?'

'That you're easy on the eye and hard on workers who don't toe the line.'

'Oh!'

'And that's just for starters,' he added.

'Take no notice of Eddie, Holly. He has a terrible reputation with women. Beware.'

'Fair go, Mac. You'll ruin my good name.'

'Already ruined, young man, too late for salvation. I suppose you want me to put in a good word for you to video this gala occasion for the masses not lucky enough to be here?'

Eddie smiled in acknowledgment. It was a smile that lit up an open friendly face, and Holly couldn't help but overlook his cheeky demeanour.

While the women worked out how to facilitate Eddie's coverage without it becoming intrusive, he made small talk with Holly about her work at Richmond House. He had a cameraman's eye for an attractive woman and he thought Holly was very beautiful, and certainly had fine photogenic features. There was a softness, a vulnerability to her. She was so simply dressed among the many peacock women that her lovely features and skin, her smooth blonde hair and warm blue eyes were shown to advantage. She must be around forty, he surmised, but could certainly pass for early thirties. He could have guessed she was a new arrival, she had a slightly bewildered, unsure look. Mac had obviously taken her under her wing. Good woman was Mac. He'd had a few heart to heart discussions with her. She didn't know Laura, his ex-wife, for which he was grateful as he thought of Mac as a motherly confidante as well as being very perceptive.

He focused his attention back onto Holly who was giving him a friendly smile. 'So what are you going to do with the old place? Glad to know it's not being bulldozed by developers. I heard a rumour that was in the wind. It's very historic.'

'I'm keen to learn more about the history of this place,' agreed Holly.

'There's a bit in the library, but some of the best of the old photographs are up at the lighthouse apparently. I've been told that their quality is remarkable considering their age. I intend to really dig into that archive for the doco I'm making on The Bay.'

Mac returned from talking with the organisers

for the evening just in time to hear Eddie mentioning the lighthouse and its pictures. 'Don't forget the logbooks they've got up there,' she added. 'Tina, the ranger, is plugged into that stuff.'

'I'd love to take a look at them when I have time,' said Holly.

'After you get the taps and lights working,' Mac added, and Holly laughed.

'Oh jeez, there's my ex,' Eddie said. 'I'll go talk to my daughter. Tell her not to take any notice of this goddess mumbo jumbo.' He grinned and neither woman believed him for a moment. Suddenly Eddie turned back to Holly. 'Look, just a thought. For my doco on The Bay I'd love to include Richmond House, its transformation, its history. Could be a good link to fill in the background to this area.'

'Sounds interesting. Come up and have a chat about it,' said Holly, glad she'd come after all.

The woman at the foot of the steps handed Holly a leaflet and a flower from the basket she was carrying. 'Pause as you get inside the door for the greeting.'

Holly stepped through a curtain into the vestibule – and total blackness. She groped for a door but her hand was taken by a figure standing beside her. Holly recoiled in shock.

'It's all right, sister. Come into the embrace of light and love.' A match flared, a candle was lit and put into her hand by a woman seemingly dressed in veils. The woman laid her hand on Holly's head then touched her forehead with her finger while murmuring, 'We are blessed, we are women, we are one. Go in peace and strength and join your sisters.' She pulled aside a heavy drape and Holly found herself in the hall.

The room brought back images of school concerts, the first time she voted, P&C meetings. She glanced around looking for the traditional portrait of a young Queen Elizabeth II, but instead saw portraits of garlanded Indian gurus. All around the walls and windows temporary swathes of dyed pink muslin were draped to soften the plain white. Several electric fans on the small stage blew over the rows of women already seated on mats on the floor. In front of each of them a candle flickered in a jar next to a paper plate and plastic utensils. A long strip of scarlet carpet ran down the centre of the hall.

Holly hesitated, temporarily frozen by the detail of the room, but was gently edged forward by the women behind her until her elbow was taken by a firm hand and she was propelled across the room by Mac. 'Didn't anyone tell you to bring a cushion? The floor gets damned hard.'

As they sat down the woman beside Holly introduced herself. 'Hi, I'm Laura, and this is Alice, my daughter. You been to one of these before?'

Holly shook her head. 'I just moved here. Ah, do you know Mac?' She gestured to Mac beside her.

'No, I don't. Seen you around, of course. Always been meaning to get my cards done.'

Tinkling music suddenly seemed to rain down on them. Holly turned to see three young girls dressed as cherubs dancing along the carpet. They were followed by six striking bare-breasted women daubed with paint in a tribal pattern on their bodies and faces. They were wearing elaborate strands of beads and feathers and each carried a small drum. An amplified voice from the stage asked everyone to join with the warrior princesses.

Laura leaned towards Holly. 'Looks like Cher's rejects from a seventies video clip.'

Holly couldn't help smiling as the warrior women began drumming and dancing, chanting, clapping, even slapping their bodies as they weaved through the audience before sitting down along one wall. There was silence. After a minute, eerie music wafted from the speakers, the overhead lights were switched off leaving the stage lights on – covered in coloured paper – and the flickering candles cast shadows on the faces of the seated women. Some began to sway as the music tempo and sound level increased. Then it tailed away and a woman's voice came over the PA system.

'Sisters, welcome. I am Cynthia, sister of the sun. I bring my blessings to light this night. Reach out and hold the hands of the sisters beside you as I call upon one of our wise women to give this year's affirmation.'

Holly took the hands of Mac and Laura then leaned forward to study the woman who walked on stage. Tall and solid, she looked to be in her seventies and was outlandishly dressed even in this group – magenta silk robes studded with gold stars, a jewelled embroidered shawl with a long silk fringe. A swathe of chiffon studded with shining sequins was wound around her head, its ends trailing. Dramatic art nouveau earrings swung to her shoulders.

'What a fabulous costume,' breathed Holly.

'It's not a costume, that's just Nola. She'd wear something like that to a barbecue. Makes them herself,' chuckled Mac.

'She's like a 1926 cover of *Harper's Bazaar*,' said Laura.

'Of course, it has to be Nola Florens. I can't wait to meet her.' Holly was recalling how the designer had ruled the social pages in Sydney in the sixties.

'Forget inviting her to tea,' said Mac. 'Make sure you have chilled champagne on hand. Nice of them to ask her to be the representative woman. She's a bit isolated here, hasn't mixed with the locals. They think she's, well, a bit off the planet a lot of the time. You should see her place.'

'I'd love to,' said Holly.

Nola Florens drew a small card from the folds of her gown and stood in front of the microphone and in a strong, clear voice began to read. 'On this night we affirm our womanhood, our femaleness, our being as one. To nurture, to heal, to cherish and to love all those we know, those who are strangers, those who come into our community.

We pledge to care for our world, the land, the water, the air. To support one another in all we do, to share the joy and share the tears. We promise to show our children that in women there is softness, there is strength, that we are thinkers, leaders, teachers. We promise to remind each other that we are here for each one of us. That united we are the power. The power of women!'

She finished on a firm rising note and the women who had been holding hands, clapped, cheered, raised their arms, stamped their feet.

As Nola Florens swept off the stage, from the corners of the room the warrior princesses moved quickly to the carpet, sat cross-legged and began to drum. The background music faded and the heady, heavy, throbbing took over.

Holly had never heard such drumming. Marcus, their son, had flirted briefly with a drum set, but the tinny percussion that had ricocheted around his bedroom was nothing like this. The raw energy of the women, their focus, their concentration ranging from elation to a fierceness made Holly wonder what was going through their minds. They chanted as they beat the drums.

It was fascinating to see the spell it cast over the women and girls in the room. Some threw back their heads, moved, clapped to the beat or joined the throaty chant. It reminded Holly of scenes of Native American dances. But then the beat and sound changed as four more women walked in and sat along the carpet and began playing didgeridoos. The drummers now picked up clap sticks and the song changed again. The haunting thrumming transported them to the red earth of the Australian outback. Holly was swept up in the atmosphere, the sounds, the emotion of the women. She'd never felt anything like it and she too joined in the clapping and swaying.

The song ended on a crescendo and all the women in the room leapt to their feet, joined hands and raised their arms. To the renewed beat of the drums they began stamping, swaying, moving together, forwards and back, to one side and the other. It was a total release of energy, a nurturing of joy and love.

Suddenly it was all over – the hypnotic sounds, the compulsive dancing – and in a surge of emotional relaxation there was much hugging and kissing and laughter. Everyone was sweating from their exertions and the temperature in the crowded hall. But they happily settled back on the floor as the cherubs led in a column of sarong-clad women with jugs of cool juices and great platters of food, mainly vegetarian.

'This is divine.' Holly hadn't tasted such a delicious combination of vegetables. They were crunchy fresh and delicately flavoured with wasabi and an unusual honey on a bed of fregolane.

Laura leaned over to help herself to chunky grain bread and olive tapenade. 'I had a farm here. I wanted to get into Aussie bush cuisine, lemon myrtle, finger limes, rose apples – not just the avocado and macadamias everyone else here grows.'

'Why didn't you?' asked Mac.

'Too long a story. All got too hard. No water. Too far away for Alice to get to school. My ex is living there but he'll never do anything with it. I wanted to sell it, but he screamed he didn't have anywhere to go. You know what men are like. Hate change.'

Holly didn't make any comment, but Mac slowly peeled a mandarine and said, 'Change is good. You can only grow by changing.' She turned to Holly. 'You'll discover that.'

'Look at Bonnie Bitternden.' Laura nodded her head, indicating midway down the hall on the other side of the carpet. 'There's someone who's changed. That woman with the mad red hair, in the shock frock from the op shop. She was a boring, stitched-up Melbourne matron when she came here. Opened a little shop then went feral. The young boyfriend is the worry.'

Mac glanced over to where the woman was sitting with her daughter Erica and Matty. Suddenly she stiffened, her eyes took on a strange expression.

Holly looked at her. 'What is it, Mac? Are you okay?'

'I'm leaving,' Mac whispered tensely.

'Oh, I'll come with you,' said Holly instinctively and she followed Mac's gaze to the hippy looking woman with her teenage daughter.

'Fire,' said Mac in a distracted, trance-like voice.

'What, what are you saying?' asked Holly in some alarm, shaking her arm.

Mac seemed to return to the present and shook

herself. 'Oh, hell. Let's vamoose. I'm not into immolation by fire.' She tried to smile and pointed to the lengths of gauzy muslin blowing over the row of burning candles.

Holly blew out her candle and muttered good-bye to Laura, who was talking intently with the woman on her other side. 'Watch the candles near those curtains,' said Holly and Laura gave her a no-worries shrug.

Outside in the cooler night air and bright moonlight Mac gave Holly a quick hug. 'I'll call you. Let me be, Holly. Goodnight.' She hurried away, still looking distracted.

As Holly got into her car she thought of Mac's uncanny gift of prescience. She recalled the pain she'd seen in Mac's face, and felt a cold shiver run down her spine. What terrible vision had Mac seen?

Chapter Four

THE AUTOMATIC BEAM OF THE LIGHTHOUSE WAS NO longer visible in the bright dawn sky and the slight breeze that usually came with sunrise had eased. An attractive young National Parks ranger, Tina Cook, put on her Akubra, took the keys from her shoulder bag and locked up the old lighthouse keeper's cottage that now served as the Parks office and tourist centre on the lighthouse reserve. Her shift was over. Another ranger would start later in the morning. It had been a quiet night after the moon had gone down and the last of the moon watchers had left. All that remained was a handful of boozy teenagers who had to be urged to find somewhere else to continue their party.

Tina decided to head home for a nap. A

morning surf didn't appeal since the wind was offshore and the swell was down. She strolled over to the cliff-top railing and peered out to sea. Sometimes below Cape Beacon she'd see sharks cruising, but today the seascape belonged to a lazily drifting turtle and a scatter of floating seagulls waiting for something to happen. It wasn't the whale season and the dolphins were probably off Tiny Bay.

She turned and leaned against the railing and ran her eye over the few buildings and parking lot she privately called her own, even though she was well aware everything belonged to the state. Everything that is, except the great love she had for the place and the job. It was a job that fulfilled two of her great passions, a love of the sea and nature, and a fascination with local history, not just the events that made history, but the people who gave it life.

At school and university Tina had agonised about career paths until activities with the uni bushwalking club had made her more aware of national parks and the satisfaction so many of the rangers seemed to get from their work. Then the way ahead was obvious. But she had never dreamed of one day winning a posting to a ranger's dreamland – the Cape at Beacon Bay. At twenty-nine she was pretty happy with her life. She'd been in The Bay for six years, had a small circle of good friends, had been in a couple of relationships but was unfazed at not having a man in her life at present. She'd gone through the mid-twenties panic of 'finding' someone and was now enjoying her job, her life and her surroundings. The right man would come along when the time was right.

The cottage office was dwarfed by the original main house, a classic Australian stone residence with verandahs all around. The lighthouse keepers had lived in it for one hundred years after the tower had been built. It was empty now, but preserved in good condition for its heritage value. Before the existing tower was built, the Cape had been marked with an unsophisticated stone beacon. Despite its size, it gave comfort and direction to the local whalers and fishermen, as well as the trading boats that plied up and down the coast. That's how the township had got its name, Beacon Bay; a detail of the area's history that many locals had told Tina since she'd taken up the post.

The main house was once again in the public spotlight, thanks to the latest wave of economic rationalism to wash through the government. The number crunchers wanted to turn it into an earner: perhaps a backpackers' hostel, a restaurant, or a rentable community venue. A great place for weddings, said some. Tina had her own views on what should be done with the house, and they didn't include hosting fun-and-havoc nights for backpackers or newlyweds.

So much of the town's history was kept in the lighthouse – the old lighthouse keepers' logs and photos, and the furniture, tools and souvenirs that had been salvaged from shipwrecks. For Tina there was also history in the natural world of the

Cape and The Bay. She loved the swooping sea hawks and eagles, the nests of seabirds tucked precariously into the cliff face, the teeming array of creatures, from mice and bush rats to emerald frogs, bandicoots and wallabies. There were the five cows that wandered the plateau on the southern side above the beach. And of course, Ramses, the old ram confined to the backyard of the main house to keep the grass down.

She had mixed feelings about the herd of feral goats that rambled the cliffs through the undergrowth, sometimes appearing on the shrubby dunes to startle a fisherman. Descended from the first goats that were kept to supply milk and meat to the early lighthouse families, they darted all over the headland, eluding capture. They kept to themselves and each dawn several could be found dancing on spindly legs up and down the steps at the base of the lighthouse.

Leaning against the old bolted steel door of the tower was a woman in a swimsuit and sarong, hugging her knees, staring down at the curve of the wide, sheltered bay.

Tina shooed away the two billy goats standing possessively on the bottom step. 'They won't butt you. Watch their poos, though.' She indicated the woman's bare feet and well-manicured red toenails. 'I'm Tina. I'm about to lock this area. Do you want to go through or are you walking back down to the beach?'

'I've just walked up from the beach, I'll go out the main gates. Thanks.' She eyed the healthy looking young ranger in her khaki shorts and matching shirt with the National Parks emblem on the pocket. 'I'm Laura. Thought I'd start the year off by getting fit and walking to the lighthouse every day. I was going for a swim but it doesn't look too appealing. And there's a lot of rubbish along the beach.'

'Weekend revellers,' sighed Tina. 'The council will be along to clean up soon. Any bodies crashed down there?'

'A few.'

'We discourage that,' said Tina firmly. 'You on holidays?' she asked as they walked towards the main entrance.

'Feels like it. No, I've been here about two years. The last couple of months in town. Left my husband in the hills.'

'Ah.' Tina made no comment. She was used to chatting to women newly on their own. It seemed they all headed to the lighthouse early in the morning. Some walked in groups.

As Tina locked the gates across the driveway, Laura gazed at the lush green hillside that rose above Ten Mile Beach. It was pristine, save for a platform that was used as a launching site for the hang gliders.

'Is that Bedford Hill?'

'Sure is. It's home to some amazing plants and animals. And birds.'

'Wasn't there a plan to develop it at one stage?'

'Yes. But it got defeated, thanks to a rare little

endangered orchid that grows there and nowhere else.'

Laura stared at the virgin, green slope facing the sea. 'You can see why they wanted it. Fabulous view.'

'It gets a bit windy sometimes, but the view is great. I'm really grateful to the dedicated locals who were behind preserving it.'

'Some would have called that development,' said Laura mildly.

'If we all thought that, this place would have been overrun like Surfers Paradise. You have to fight. That's one thing The Bay has shown – people power can work.'

Laura didn't look convinced. Or particularly interested.

'I guess you have to be here a while to really understand,' said Tina. She looked at Laura, swiftly assessing her, noting the make-up, the carefully done hair and nails, the expensive swimsuit. 'Are you planning on staying?' Tina had seen these separated and divorced women come and go. Some changed, some grew, some stayed in their same old comfort zone of bitter bitching, others moved on. Some floundered in indecision for years.

'I don't know. I have a young daughter . . . I'm not sure what to do with my life . . .' her voice trailed off. Laura didn't like thinking about this. One day she thought she wanted to dump Alice with Eddie and just travel. Another day she thought she'd be an artist. Or perhaps she wanted to be rich and famous – but how?

'Be careful. This place can trap you. You can lose ten years of your life in a blink. Pleasantly enough, but then what?' Tina unlocked her car and gave a bright smile. 'Don't mind me. I get a lot of ear bashing from the girls around here. Can I give you a lift into town?'

'That would be great,' said Laura. 'I can tell my daughter I lived up to my New Year's resolution – a walk to the lighthouse. Walking down doesn't have to be part of the equation.'

Tina reversed out of the carpark and Laura threw one more look back at Bedford Hill. 'I sure would've liked an apartment on that hill. Maybe I'll win lotto and get a place at the new beach development at Mighty Beach.'

'What new development?' asked Tina with barely concealed surprise.

'Oh, well, nothing's definite. I just met some guys at a party who want to build along that bit of beach in front of the old wharf.'

'They wish. Everyone would like that piece of land,' said Tina. 'No way anyone would build on it, for lots of reasons. Anyway, a cyclone would take it out in a flash.'

'You get cyclones here?'

'Rarely. It's been thirty years since the last decent one. We must be due,' said Tina cheerfully. But Laura's remark had disturbed her. She'd check out if there were developers snooping around. You had to be ever vigilant in paradise.

Lynn had introduced Holly and Curly to Tinder-box Beach, known alternatively as 'Dog Beach' because the walking of dogs was permitted.

'The councillors are taking themselves a bit too seriously,' complained Lynn. 'No dogs on most of the beaches and keep 'em on a leash. It's getting bloody ridiculous. And some poor bugger got fined the other day for skinny-dipping.'

'Is there a law against it?' asked Holly, glancing up and down the near-deserted beach.

'Depends where, when and who. It's coming up before the council. If they crack down there'll be a riot. It's not dirty old men wandering around, it's couples, families, kids, that get their gear off . . . It's healthy. There's the sun cult people who like to dance naked, and Drew's nude dawn yoga class do it at the far end of Mighty Beach. You have to go out of your way to get there.'

'I've never seen anyone naked on the main beach,' said Holly, wondering what it would be like to swim in the ocean without a costume. Wouldn't Andrew be shocked if she suggested it.

So Holly added another routine to her day, Curly's sunset walk. She said she did it for the dog's sake, but she loved the walk along the beach as the sun set over the mountains, the clouds, rosy gold, reflected in the hard wet sand like melted rainbows. Often the dolphins cruised past. Most of the dog walkers had left by this time and she enjoyed having the beach to herself. If they ran into another dog and owner they'd nod or exchange a smile and a few words, depending on the social interaction between the dogs. Holly and Curly usually walked for thirty minutes in one direction, reaching the channel where Tea-tree Creek ran out of the dunes onto the beach, then they turned back as the sky began to dim and the lighthouse switched on its flashing beam.

This afternoon there were three people on the beach but only one other dog. The sleek animal's graceful movements were as smooth as a ballet dancer's. It was energetically dashing into the surf to retrieve a stick thrown by its owner.

As they came closer, Curly paused in her sedate paddling to watch the stick game, then dashed off to join in the fun. On her first competitive plunge into the surf she won the race to the stick and ran triumphantly to Holly and dropped it at her feet.

'Well done, old girl. I really thought you'd out-grown such capers.' She gave a friendly hello to the other dog as it bounded up and sat panting, eyeing the stick in anticipation of Holly throwing it.

The dog's owner, a mature man with longish brown hair and fit build jogged up and nodded towards Curly. 'Not a bad effort there. She's not exactly a youngster by the look of her, but still try-ing to prove she's got what it takes.'

'Aren't we all?' said Holly with a grin that hid the astonishment she felt at coming out with such a flippant, even suggestive, remark to a complete stranger. She instantly changed the subject. 'What kind of dog is she?' Its golden brown coat was like velvet, its face alert and friendly. It seemed heavier than a greyhound, closer to a Weimaraner but had rich toffee-coloured eyes. Against such an elegant dog, Curly, with her muddled genealogy of golden retriever and labrador, looked shaggily disreputable.

'This is Romany, she's a Hungarian vizsla. Still a bit young and dancy.'

'The dancing gypsy. She's lovely.' Holly threw the stick and the dog raced after it, Curly trotting behind at a respectable pace.

The two dogs began a tug of war with the stick, one dropping it, the other picking it up waiting for the other to pull it away. Their owners watched them for a few minutes, then Holly sank onto the sand. 'I'll take a break, it's nice for Curly to play with another dog. She gets a bit lonely up at our place. We're new so she hasn't found many playmates.'

'The beach is the best place to meet pals.'

'Do you walk here every day?' asked Holly.

'Just about. Mind you, we might not have many places left to take our dogs if we don't shake some sense into the council. Most of the locals are responsible pet owners who pick up after their dogs. It's the visiting kids in their vans and trucks who let their dogs run wild. Are you coming to the dog rally?' he asked, turning to look at her.

He was an attractive man, about her own age with a pleasant voice and easy manner. Probably married with kids, she thought, and was surprised that she should consider this. Holly shook her head. 'What rally?'

'You should come. Dog owners in the shire are protesting on Saturday week; the council wants to ban dogs from here. That only leaves two beaches, one some distance and one quite small.'

'Oh, that would be a shame,' said Holly.

'That's why we're marching through town – with our dogs. We're meeting at 9 am in Station Park.'

'I'm not sure I'm ready to go that far,' she said, hesitantly.

'You must come if you can. The more who do, the better we can make our point.'

'I've never actually taken part in a protest,' said Holly with a small smile.

'You *are* new,' he said kindly. 'Well, welcome to the end of the rainbow where good things happen, or people make them happen.' He gave an exaggerated courtly bow then plonked down on the sand next to her. 'You name a cause close to the hearts of the New Age alternative thinkers and you find advocates and followers here. Save the planet from global warming, save the rainforests, organic food is the only food, don't eat anything but veggies, get that compost or worm farm working overtime. Every do-good slogan gets an airing around this patch.'

Holly laughed. 'I'm not sure if you're an advocate, a follower, or sending up the scene.'

'Well, to be honest, I'm not sure either,' he chuckled. 'But I like a lot of what I hear. I like the energy created by some of these causes. Sometimes the ripples of sense and sanity travel a long way.'

Holly enjoyed his easy flow of words and the fact that he wasn't taking himself completely seriously. 'And a dog rally fits in with all that?' she asked.

'I have news for you. This issue is not going to change the world, but finding a practical solution to problems such as dogs on beaches is very much what a sense of community is all about. This town is the greatest mix of people and philosophies I've ever come across, but somehow we all feel we form a real community.'

Holly raised a clenched fist in the air and called, 'Where dogs matter. Hear, hear!' They both burst out laughing. 'Okay, I'll march,' she said.

'My son tells me I shouldn't carry my soapbox around with me,' he conceded.

'You've been here since the hippy years?'

'No, unfortunately. I've only been here five years. I woke up one morning and felt like I was lost in a maze with no way out, which I decided meant I must be looking for some purpose in my life.'

'I know what you mean. For me it's been a growing sense of restlessness,' said Holly slowly, articulating aloud what she'd only recently identified.

'So came the great re-evaluation of life, career, friendships and I was compelled to make a change,' he continued. 'Which meant dragging my wife and son in my wake.'

'What did you do?' asked Holly. 'Did your family feel the same?'

'I confess I was an advertising executive in

Sydney.' He pretended to hang his head in shame. 'The full-on yuppie with all the trappings. I guess we were all ready for a change, but I'd never go back,' he added. 'What about you?'

'Oh, it's too early for me to say one way or the other. I've only been here a few weeks – also from Sydney. Been mothering and doing the executive wife bit. I think it's beautiful here, but then Mosman is rather nice. Lovely home, harbour view, smart friends, busy social life –'

'And bored to tears and feeling empty. You don't have to say any more. I won't pry. You might like it here, just give each day a chance,' he said softly.

'I like that,' she said.

'Like what?'

'Give each day a chance,' she repeated.

They both sat quietly looking at the sea and the dogs. Eventually he broke the silence. 'I think I can see where you're coming from and I can tell you from experience that one day you'll want to run, run away in near panic. You'll feel you're sinking into the quicksand of indecision – stay, run, stay, run . . . stay . . . run . . . '

'Sounds depressing.'

'It can be. But stay calm and in all probability you'll be rescued.'

'By a knight in shining armour?'

'Who knows? You might be that lucky. Just remember there's quicksand in Mosman too.'

Holly turned to him and grinned. 'Don't tell me you also fled from Mosman. That would be too much.'

'No, but I'm interested in whales and the history of whaling in Australia. Mosman, or Great Sirius Cove as it was known, was once a stinking whaling shore station and the social scene there was dominated by prostitutes and carousing whalers.'

'We don't talk about such things in Mosman, my dear,' Holly said in an exaggerated socialite voice, 'and I would be much obliged if you didn't raise the subject again.'

Their laughter brought the dogs and they both stood up.

'Nice talking to you. Enjoy the walk,' said Holly.

'A pleasure for me as well. But now I have to run to catch up on my schedule. See you around.' He patted his dog then started jogging. 'Come on, hound.'

Holly hoped she would indeed see him around. She suspected she would, as everyone kept telling her it was a small place. Funny, he didn't tell me his name, she thought. Then she realised she hadn't told him hers, yet they'd ended up talking like old friends.

Billy glanced out of The Teepee salon as Matty and Erica ran giggling down the arcade from the Beach Hut. Matty gave a wave then Erica turned back and stuck her head in the doorway. 'Can you dye my hair blue, Billy? Bright blue?'

'I could, but I won't. Your mother would shoot me. Not to mention the school.'

'Boring. Mum'd love it. I'll do it myself. Bye.' She skipped away.

Billy continued trimming the local publican's hair. 'That girl . . . out of control.'

'Like her mother. Christ, Bonnie is a worry these days.'

'Been losing it in the bar again?'

'Yeah, and other places. One of the cops found her in a wild house full of young people, drugs, sex and rock 'n' roll. She was old enough to be the mother of half of them, he reckoned, including her boyfriend. She seems to be living there.'

'Maybe someone better take her in hand. Get her into a retreat place or something.' Billy unhooked the plastic cape and shook it. 'It's young Erica I feel sorry for. Wouldn't like my daughter to be running around like that. Though Matty is a good kid.'

'If Matty was mine I wouldn't want her hanging out with Bonnie's wild child. Does Matty's mother know what they get up to in town?'

'I've told Kim. Maybe I'll suggest she try to help Bonnie,' said Billy, then switched the subject. 'Any hot tips for Moonee Valley on Friday?'

'Funny you ask . . .' The two men began talking horses and didn't notice Bonnie drifting down the arcade leaving her shop unattended.

Matty and Erica hiked up to the lighthouse. Erica seemed distracted, her hands thrust in her jeans pockets, her shoulders hunched. She didn't make any chitchat, and only nodded when Matty pointed at the wheeling hawk. She watched Matty give Ramses a piece of bread and half an apple and for once didn't tease the old ram.

They sat down in their favourite spot, tucked away from the wind, the tower sheltering them. It was their special patch reserved for those times when they needed to retreat from people and be at ease, to talk and laugh, and to learn from each other. Together they were trying to find ways of coming to terms with the seemingly endless hassles of family life and being almost fifteen. Their friendship had consolidated swiftly; Matty, a popular girl, had befriended Erica, the bright loner. Gradually Erica had opened up to the idea of a close friend. She showed how much she loved music, playing her own songs on her guitar for Matty. Their shared moments at the lighthouse were times of intense conversation, music or simply two girls giggling at secrets and jokes.

Puzzled by Erica's mood, Matty decided to broach a touchy subject. 'How's your mum?'

'Okay, I guess. She's so wired all the time. And I hate that junkie house we live in.'

'Why don't you and her get your own place? She can afford it, can't she?' Matty had heard tales of Bonnie's former life in Melbourne, keeping pace with the high-flying social set.

'I don't know. The business is a bit of a mess and she spends heaps on drink and cigarettes, of all kinds. She says she came here for a new life. I don't think this is what she had in mind. She keeps saying she wants new friends, but she just keeps bringing home slobs.'

Matty put her arm around Erica's shoulders. 'Do you two spend much time together?'

Erica pulled up a blade of grass. 'She doesn't just want to be with me. But she needs me. Much more than I need her.'

'Wow. That's a tough thing to say,' exclaimed Matty, and she too plucked a stiff stalk of grass.

'It's true. I'm stronger than she is,' said Erica calmly. 'She's hanging on to pills, grog, drugs, young guys. She's too scared to be on her own. I've got used to being on my own. It's okay.'

Matty wasn't sure how much of this statement was bravado. Sometimes Erica told elaborate stories, strange anecdotes that seemed fabrications or fantasies. It was often hard with her to tell where reality, truth and dreams overlapped. She gave her friend a shrewd look. 'You drop stuff too, you said.'

'It's an escape. It makes the world look and feel good when you want. But I don't need them. You used?'

Matty was uncomfortable. She wanted to appear cool and hip, but drugs scared her. She remembered the time about a year back when both of them had come to this same spot to light up their first cigarettes. Erica did it with a great show of confidence and expressions of total enjoyment. Matty had hated the experience, but pretended to like it for a couple of sessions, then announced she wasn't smoking any more. 'Been there, done that, doesn't grab me.'

'Okay. Your choice,' Erica had said.

Now there was so much pressure from their peer group to try drugs, but Matty was frightened because of the many stories of accidental deaths. 'I'm scared that if I use it once I'd be gone, hooked.'

'Doesn't always work like that. Anyway, best if you leave it alone, Matty.'

Here it was again. Matty never knew which Erica was going to emerge. The wild child or the bored bright kid. The silly, funny girlfriend. The world-weary, almost adult. Matty actually loved Erica's unpredictable and complicated character.

'What about your mum? Still hovering over the kitchen sink and ironing board?' asked Erica.

'Yeah. Still wondering when Dad will come back. In a way it's nice having her all to myself all the time. Nice to come home from school and find the place . . .' She searched for the right word.

'Alive,' suggested Erica.

'Yeah. That's it, alive.'

'No chance of my father coming back,' said Erica, almost with relief.

'Dad will come back to stay one day. I'm sure of it.' Matty knew her father adored her, had promised her so often that he would always come back to her no matter how often life forced them apart. She knew her mother had the same faith, but sometimes it seemed to be fading, and that worried her.

'Hang on to the dream, Matty.'

'What's your dream?'

'Sail. Get a little boat and sail away. Just me. Away, away . . . over there . . .' She gestured to the horizon.

'Like Kay Cottee and that boy, Jesse . . .? Where are you going to get a boat? Do you know how to sail?'

The world-weary Erica appeared. 'Matty, you're so . . . deadly. Deadly sensible.' But she smiled and brushed the grass from her lap. 'Better get back to the shop. See what drama my mother is creating now.'

Billy was closing the salon as Matty hurried inside.

'Billy, someone's robbed the Beach Hut! The money's gone, and I think a bunch of stuff. Erica's mum isn't there, what will we do?'

Billy dashed down to the little shop. 'Don't touch anything, Erica, we'd better get the police. Where's your mother? Were you supposed to be minding the place?'

'Don't blame me! She was here when I left with Matty.' Erica's face was tight. 'I don't think we should call the police. I'll just wait, she'll come back.'

'What do you think is missing? Where were you girls, anyway?'

'We just hung around the surf club. Then we went down to the chemist to get hair dye and had a smoothie and went for a walk.'

'Do you think your mum might be up at the pub with her friends?' Billy said gently. When

Erica shrugged, he asked, 'Do you want me to check?'

'I suppose so. But I don't think she'll be there. She had a row with her boyfriend the other night.'

Billy glanced around the shop again, nothing seemed out of place. 'Was the cash drawer open? What's missing?'

Erica said nothing but idly picked a pair of sunglasses off the stand and tried them on, peering into the small mirror.

Matty spoke up. 'No, it was shut. Erica went to get some change for a drink and it was empty.'

'I see. Listen, why don't we just shut up the shop, leave her a note on the counter – she has her key, I assume – and I'll drive you both to Matty's place. You can use my mobile and see if your mum is there, Matty.'

'She'll be there, she's expecting me. I have to be home by six.'

'Fine, let's go.' Billy had a feeling Bonnie wouldn't be returning to the shop. Kim could give them both dinner then run Erica home to the nearby village of Brigalow where she and Bonnie were living. With God knows who else.

Kimberley followed Billy out to his car as the girls settled in front of the television. 'Thanks for this. You okay to take Erica home later?' he asked.

'Sure. Is this unusual? I mean, should we alert anyone?'

'I don't think it's that unusual. Bonnie often

119

doesn't come home but generally she tells Erica, from what I gather,' sighed Billy.

'It seems so . . . irresponsible. What is that woman thinking of? Not her daughter, that's for sure,' said Kimberley.

'She used to be utterly reliable. Bonnie's mother, Erica's grandmother, is a leading social figure in Melbourne. Bonnie is a bit lost and feeling sorry for herself. Trying to recapture something she never had I suspect – freedom.'

'Maybe we should try to contact Erica's grandmother.'

'Bonnie would hate that. It's not that drastic, and what's she going to do? We can't interfere.'

'This isn't interfering?' said Kimberley.

'This is being a good friend, what towns like this are all about. Looking out for each other.'

'You're right. I'd better go and turn the TV off and see if there's any homework. Take care, Billy.'

'I never do homework.' Erica was curled up in the corner of the sofa, her arms folded across her chest. 'It's so boring.'

'What about your marks? What does your teacher say?' asked Kimberley, wondering how on earth teachers dealt with such stubborn defiance.

'Leave it, Mum. Erica's okay. She's so smart. She can do stuff easily without studying, if she wants to,' said Matty.

'Lucky Erica. Well, you'd better finish your

work after dinner. I've made pasta, a salad and a banana cake. All right?'

'You mean you made it, not takeaway?' asked Erica. 'I'm so sick of Thai and Indian food from up the road.'

Kimberley left the girls to talk and thumb through magazines while she finished preparing dinner.

'Mum, can I do a modelling course?' called Matty.

'Maybe. Is that what you want to do too, Erica?'

'Nah, I'm not into hairdos and make-up and stuff,' said Erica. 'I'm a sailor. I want to sail the seven seas.'

'You will too I bet,' said Matty loyally.

'Now come and have your dinner.'

'Aren't we eating in front of the TV?' Erica stopped in the middle of the room.

'No, Erica. That's a treat on rare occasions in this house.' Kimberley's patience with Erica was wearing thin. If she says 'boring' one more time, I'll throw the dinner at her, she thought. But Erica surprised her.

'Oh, cool. We used to eat in the dining room at home before Mum and Dad split. My grandmother makes a big deal about it too. I sort of miss it. I mean not all the time, but . . .' her voice trailed off.

As they ate Kimberley wondered what life was like for Erica in a rundown house with a drifting population. She was sure Erica's grandmother would not approve of the environment her girls were living in.

Erica was silent as Kimberley drove her home. Matty stayed behind to do her homework.

'What will you do if your mother isn't home yet? Do you want me to call you later to check?' asked Kimberley.

'Nah. She's probably drinking her way through the cash from the shop. She'll turn up.'

Kimberley didn't say anything at Erica's assumption about the apparent 'theft'.

'You must come and have dinner again. I haven't seen you around with Matty's friends much,' said Kimberley as they pulled up in the quiet main street of the little town. Dim red and blue lights shone from behind the blinds and loud music reverberated from Bonnie's house.

'I only hang out with Matty. She doesn't hassle me,' said Erica, not making a move to get out of the car.

Kimberley didn't want to get into a deep discussion. She peered out the windscreen. 'Well, someone's certainly home.'

'Yeah, there's always people here. Thanks for dinner . . .' For a moment Erica seemed about to say something else then changed her mind. 'See ya.'

Kimberley couldn't shake Erica from her mind. While Matty vacillated between brimming cockiness and childlike sweetness, Erica was tough one minute, needy the next. She certainly had problems. Kimberley wished Matty hadn't befriended her, then felt guilty for thinking that. Matty, while highly impressionable, wasn't silly. Why couldn't they just have harmless teenage fun together? She recalled now that Matty had told her that many of the girls at school were 'depressed'. Kimberley had figured that simply meant they were upset because they'd been grounded, had privileges removed, a tiff with a friend. But with Erica it was something deeper and she had good reason to have major worries. Bonnie was so wrapped up in whatever misery she was going through that she didn't see the effect it was having on her fourteen-year-old daughter. Billy was right, if Matty was in deep trouble Kimberley would appreciate someone being concerned enough to ring her.

When she got home she went into her bedroom and rang Matty's teacher, glad they were on a friendly footing and Kimberley wasn't worried about her calling this late.

'Sylvia, sorry to bother you . . . no, no not a problem with Matty . . . unless *you* think so . . .' Kimberley listened to the cheerful report on Matty from her teacher before cutting in, 'Actually, I'm ringing about Erica Bitternden. I know you can't discuss another student, but it does involve Matty –'

'Oh dear, are they in trouble? Erica hasn't been at school for two days, is she all right?' Sylvia replied.

'She's fine, she was here for dinner tonight . . . it's her mother, she wasn't around and I'm a bit concerned about Erica's influence on Matty. She seems a rather disturbed child.' Kimberley was trying to tread carefully.

'She is, I'm afraid. And with good reason. Several reasons,' sighed the young teacher. 'Her mother . . . heavens, when I first met her she was so proper. She's been in such a spiral. Erica has always been difficult I suspect. And different.'

'Oh, in what way?'

'She is extremely bright, way above average. Bordering on gifted.'

'She seemed so . . . disinterested, bored with school. I hope that doesn't rub off on Matty.'

'She's typical of what we now call "star" or "new" kids. We are just realising that the boredom, their arrogance and aggression are because they are bright, not because they've a deficiency –'

'You mean like attention deficit disorders?'

'Yes, where the tendency has been to put them on medication, which in Erica's case could be highly dangerous. Do you think she is exposed to drugs at home?'

'Sylvia, Matty tells me drugs are available around the school. I assumed it was pot, surely not hard stuff.' Kimberley was finding this a painful conversation.

'Drugs are everywhere. We all have to watch for the signs. It would be helpful if you could keep an eye on Erica when you can. For Matty's sake as well.'

As Kimberley put the phone down all the accumulated tensions associated with being a single mother with a vulnerable teenage daughter seemed to break out of the corner of her mind where they'd been painstakingly confined. She felt fear clutch at her heart. She knew that she and Bonnie had similar problems, both were struggling to cope. Seeing Bonnie wallowing so desperately undermined her own shaky confidence. Thank God for friends like Mac and Billy. As Kimberley poured herself a coffee she thought of all the other good friends she had in The Bay and felt comforted.

When Matty went to bed, Kimberley gave her a long hug.

'What's that for, Mum? Are you upset?'

'I'm just glad you're you. You will come to me if ever you have a problem, won't you, Matt? No matter how bad you think it is. I'm here for you, not to judge you, to help and love you. You know that, don't you?'

Matty leaned over and hugged Kimberley. 'I know, Mum. And I'm here for you, too.' She kissed Kimberley's cheek and snuggled down in bed.

Kimberley pulled Matty's door closed, her eyes blurred with tears.

Erica was trying to sleep, and she refused to cry. She squeezed her eyes shut as they burned with unshed tears. She was stuck on the sofa again, some couple had crashed in her bed. She didn't know where her mother was. What had happened to her life? In Melbourne her mother was at least at home every night. Watching TV. Sure, with a drink. But she was there, nicely dressed, in a nice house. Everything was always neat. Sometimes Erica despised The Bay. Maybe she should run away. She could go back to Grandma's. No, she'd hate that. She tossed under the cover. Besides, she couldn't leave her mother. Bonnie was racing downhill out of control. Erica had to be there to pick up the pieces. And there were still times when they could laugh together. At least in the beginning The Bay had made her mum lighten up. But dark clouds were on the horizon and Erica was scared. For her mother. And for herself.

Amber loved her early morning jog and swim. On weekends she went to Mighty Beach, during the week she stuck to Ten Mile. At eight o'clock she had to go up to the farm to see to her mother.

This morning was misty, threatening rain. Mount Hazard was obscured by cloud. The water was blissfully warm. As soon as she dived through the curling waves she felt relaxed and peaceful, yet energised. There was something about being in the sea, and this part of the ocean more than anywhere else, that gave her a sense of connection. What with she wasn't sure. She loved the feeling of being wrapped and nurtured by the soft water, and gazing at the beautiful beach with some old holiday houses screened behind the dunes and the mysterious mountain range with the distinctive peak of Chinamans Hat. But greater than any of the pleasurable sensations there was an overwhelming pull that dragged her into the water. A feeling of purpose, or some need. She couldn't put her finger on it, so she simply surrendered to her instinct and stayed in the water longer than she should.

Most week mornings this part of the beach was empty. Sometimes a long way up there would be someone doing yoga, or skinny-dipping. But this morning, when Amber finally left the ocean, she saw a woman further along the sand wandering towards the water, staggering rather than walking. She hadn't noticed her before, she must have been stretched out or sitting on the sand. There was something odd about her gait that made Amber pause as she towelled her hair. It was too early to be drunk.

The woman was wearing a kind of sarong, more like a sari, wrapped around her body with one end trailing over a shoulder. She stopped, doubled over for a moment, appeared to sway, straightened, then walked into the water. She didn't pause, didn't turn. As if hypnotised she steadily waded deeper. Amber dropped her towel and took a few steps, mesmerised by the scene unfolding. The woman fell into the rip and, without attempting a stroke, was dragged out.

Amber broke into a run, certain now that she knew what the woman was doing. By the time she had run up the beach and started into the surf, the woman was floating, seemingly unconscious, and was being tossed around by the breaking waves. Amber put her head down and swam hard, but when she next looked from a wave the woman was nowhere to be seen.

Trying not to panic she trod water for a moment until she saw a length of red fabric drifting near a dark brown shadow.

She reached the cloth, reeling it in until she felt the weight of the woman and saw her bunched up against something solid in the water. As Amber reached her she saw that the woman had, by design or accident, butted against one of the piles of the old jetty. At very low tide its few broken teeth jutted out of the water.

Amber grasped the unconscious body and began striking out for shore. But within a minute the woman began gagging and started to struggle, trying to push Amber's arm from across her chest.

'It's all right, just relax. Relax,' Amber shouted, trying not to sound as desperate as she felt. The weight and strength of the fighting woman and her wet sari could drag both of them under. But then Amber felt her feet touch the sand and soon she was able to pull the woman onto the beach. She collapsed beside her, panting with exertion for a few seconds.

She rolled the woman's head to one side and immediately she coughed, vomiting water, then began spluttering.

'You're okay. You're safe,' Amber shouted, making sure she understood. 'Don't worry about the vomiting. Get it up, get it out, okay.' She glanced quickly up and down the beach but there was no one in sight to give a hand. The spluttering gave way to crying, and the woman's eyes opened to stare at Amber in disbelief.

Amber hugged her and smoothed her hair back. 'It's okay now. You'll be all right.'

The woman had another burst of coughing, then took several slow, deep breaths and regained her composure, managed to sit up and leaned her head on her knees.

Amber put her arm around her shoulders. 'How do you feel now?'

The woman took a breath and lifted her head to reveal a tortured face. 'I wish you hadn't done that.'

'I could say the same to you,' said Amber. 'Do you want to talk about it? Did it just come over you . . . or have you been planning this?' She studied the woman who must have been in her mid forties and looked vaguely familiar. She'd seen her around The Bay but Amber couldn't place her.

The woman wiped her face with a corner of the sari. 'I just felt drawn to the water. It seemed an easy way to . . . fix things.'

Amber sat back on her heels and looked at the distressed woman as she slowly and awkwardly tried to unwind the tangle of material wrapped around her body. That's one helluva way to fix things, she thought. 'Here, let me help. That's a nice bit of material,' she added, trying to introduce something normal into the abnormal situation. 'My name's Amber, by the way.'

The woman responded vaguely. 'From India. Silk, you know. I wore it because these girls . . .'

Then her voice faded away and the explanation was left up in the air. As an afterthought she added, 'Bonnie. I'm Bonnie.'

Amber had heard the name. She didn't comment but decided that they should move to the shelter of some large rocks against a sand dune. 'Come on, Bonnie. Let's get up the beach a bit.'

There was no resistance to the idea and they walked slowly, hand in hand, to find a sandy alcove between two large boulders. Amber then made a quick dash over the beach to get her clothes and towel. She handed the towel to Bonnie who ran it wearily over her hair and face.

'Thanks.'

'You haven't been here that long, have you? Any family with you?' Amber asked, trying to sound casual.

There was a long pause, then a deep breath, almost a decision-making signal, before she replied, 'About a year. I have a daughter. Teenager.'

It was as if the word teenager was a trigger to her emotions. Bonnie burst into tears, but struggled to remain in control. 'For God's sake, don't tell her about this. Promise. Please. Not a word to anyone. You know what this place is like for gossip. She couldn't handle it.'

'Okay. I promise. Everything strictly confidential, just between us,' said Amber with sincerity. 'Do you want to keep talking, or just rest?'

Bonnie leaned back against a rock and closed her eyes. 'Fixing things,' she eventually whispered.

'I've been trying to do that for years. Ever since I split with my husband, family and friends in Melbourne, and ran. And this is where I ended up.' She took a handful of sand and let it run through her fingers.

Confessional time, thought Amber. Her mind raced back to her teenage years when she and her girlfriends often sheltered in places along the beach and told each other of their inner agonies.

Bonnie talked as if to herself. 'Never had time for me. But it hasn't worked out, has it? I'm getting old and I don't want to be old. Haven't lived enough.'

Sounds a bit off the planet, Amber decided. 'You been on stuff?'

'You name it, I've tried it.'

'Maybe it's time to get back to reality.'

Another silence, another handful of sand dribbled through her fingers into a small peak. 'Reality. I'm not sure what that is any more.'

'Listen, Bonnie,' said Amber firmly, 'you've got to make at least one more effort, right? There're people who can help you. You're not the first person around here who has run hard from the past and fallen flat on their face. You need to spend some time at the Dolphin Centre for starters.'

'What about my girl, she's only fourteen?' And that brought another bout of tears.

It was time for action, Amber decided, and she reached for her T-shirt. 'Here, put this on until you get home. Come on, up you get.' She pulled Bonnie to her feet and the sobs disappeared as they struggled to get the wet sari off and the T-shirt on. 'I'll run you home and get in touch with some friends I've got at the Dolphin Centre. They'll work things out for you. Some therapy, something you haven't tried. How about that?'

She walked Bonnie to the car. When they were buckled in, Bonnie surprised her by throwing the bundled-up sari over her shoulder onto the back seat. 'I never want to see that again.'

The remark didn't make much sense, but Amber let it pass. The last of the early morning mist had gone and the brightening day gave sparkle to the white hem of breaking waves that crashed against the rocks of the Cape.

'Look, Bonnie, it's going to be a lovely day out there,' said Amber with forced cheerfulness.

Bonnie scanned the beach and looked at the rip where she had almost thrown away her life. A pair of dolphins appeared, and with impeccable timing they leapt out of the peaking wave together and made a graceful curving dive. It was as if they'd been given a cue to endorse the joy of being alive. 'I suppose I should say thanks, Amber,' she said hesitantly. 'And thanks for listening to me.'

'No worries, Bonnie. We all have times when we need someone to listen.'

Chapter Five

On board the Lady Richmond, March 18th, 1896

We have not long departed from the Kermadec
Islands. We stopped at Sunday Island for provi-
sions – goat's meat, milk and Tahitian limes and
oranges. Several whalers were passing through
who had been at sea for a year or more on the
Southern Ocean without replenishing supplies.
Several crew were suffering from the scurvy so the
fruit planted many years ago by American settlers
– the Bell family, I believe – was most welcome. I
was intrigued to learn that this island has its own
postal service. Each ship sends a boat to the tip of
the island, and when the tide is low there is a cave
which one can enter. Here the crews leave letters
in a large wine carafe to protect them from the
moisture, and collect the ones left previously.

The islands of the South Pacific are tranquil and beautiful to behold, yet such treacherous waters surround the reefs leading into the lagoon.

The crew was eager to go ashore and barter with the natives, though my husband fears more reason for their haste was to fraternise with the maidens. Such happy creatures, unashamed at their nakedness, immodest by our standards. My husband did quite stumble over his explanation to me that to these native women, the coupling of men and women out of wedlock with little pre-amble is not considered lewd or against God's will, but a sign of welcome and hospitality. Quite a departure from our standards of decorum. But as my dear husband also noted, these wild lusty islands are very far – in all ways – from what we know. Different as my homeland of Australia is from his childhood in Norseland, though at least we share a Christian heritage.

My husband has talked much lately of Nor-way, the land of his birth, describing vividly the deep still waters of the fjords where, between the icy cliffs, the sounds of a faraway farm echo for miles up the valley. He talked of the village and the fishing fleet, but yet cannot bring him-self to share completely with me that terrible break between himself and his parents. What could have happened to cause a boy of nineteen to run away to sea, n'er to return?

I do believe his home is on the sea. My dearest has lived such a short time ashore.

How I thank the day I ventured with my father to visit his agent friend at the Mosman ship yards, where we first became acquainted.

I have no regrets choosing a whaling master as my beloved and travelling with him. Lars is a good and true man, all the crew from the officers to the cabin boy respect his firm hand and knowledge of the sea. Like other captains' wives who choose to be with their husbands at sea, the choice of being far from him for two years or more a trip is too hard to bear. So despite the privations, I appreciate the wonders and excitement, the fears and travails, of life on a whaling barque. I miss the company of other women – ships carrying other wives meet so infrequently and if the weather be poor it is not always possible to transport us to the other ship. The frustration of being so close to female companionship and not have the occasion to exchange womanly talk – a gam – is hard to bear. Sometimes we have waved our kerchiefs from the deck at each other and that has been the only contact for many months. Oh how I do long for one day living ashore in a home of our own!

Hannah Nilsen blotted the entry in her leather-covered journal, closed the book and stowed it on the shelf above the small triangular table fitted into a corner of the captain's stateroom. It was a cramped but rare private space in an overcrowded whaling vessel.

Their living quarters consisted of two tiny rooms. The stateroom had an ingenious swinging bed, which was suspended from stone-weighted gimbals and moved with the motion of the ship. This meant Hannah never suffered the sensation of swaying independently of the *Lady Richmond*'s pitch. She also blessed the privacy of the small 'head' or water closet which had a basin and washstand. The second cabin, where she had hung a drapery to divide them, was the aft-cabin with a fold-down table that was the captain's desk, a trunk used both as a table and as storage for clothes, and a large horsehair sofa and two small chairs.

Hannah had longed to fill the cabins with personal 'fripperies' to make them more homelike, but the weather and motion of the boat made it impossible. Near a porthole, secured to the bulkhead, was the polished wood and chrome barometer presented to Captain Nilsen by the ship's owners – an American company, Richmond Whaling. On the captain's desk sat the ship's log and several beautiful scrimshaw ornaments – a delicately engraved whalebone formed into a yarn basket and her sewing bodkin made from baleen, the firm but pliable substance taken from the mouth of a humpback whale. From the beam above the shelf swung a cage that held a parrot whose cheerful squawk kept her company while she sewed and knitted or wrote in her journal. Each day, unless foul weather prevented it, Hannah took the birdcage to a sheltered spot on the deck and hung it securely from the rigging.

It was here one morning that she glanced out to sea and saw, far distant, the spout of a whale and raised the call before the lookout.

The South Pacific, at sea, March 22nd, 1896

I received good wishes for my whale spotting from the crew, for they secured two whales, one delivering forty barrels of oil.

Such a frenzy of activity erupts at the sighting of a whale. After so many days and weeks of tranquillity – indeed, boredom for most of the crew – it seems chaos and disorder take over. Men race about hauling gear as the boats are lowered and the chase is on. I see on the faces of the men such excitement and determination, while for me I can only wait and pray that they all return safely from this gruesome task. I fear especially for my beloved who refuses to stay on board but leads his men after the monsters in such a teacup of a boat. These creatures of the deep are often the size of three or four of the boats lashed together bow to stern.

Once our fine harpoonist, the American black man Tully, has the whale fast, the most fearsome part of this great game begins as the beast tries to escape by sounding or charging across the sea. And while the men talk of this 'Nantucket sleigh ride' as they are pulled across the ocean, I can only wait. And it seems an eternal wait. I recall the terrible tales of the monsters crunching and smashing the boats to splinters, men's limbs being ripped from their body caught in rope coils, or being pulled under the sea.

I did not see the kill as it was too far even with the glasses. But I was mightily relieved when those great carcasses were lashed alongside and all hands and dear Lars back on board. Then came the dreadfully odorous and frantic cutting in and trying out of the blubber where the valuable fat was peeled off and boiled to oil. A dead whale in this heat becomes very sour and the stench almost unbearable.

The first time I was witness to this event my husband had me take a seat in one of the boats slung on the starboard side. But such a grandstand seat I passed up after that. They cut the head of the sperm whale which is divided into sections. One holds the spermaceti, a fibrous fat used for candles and creams. In the other, a fine clear oil was bailed out, for it is highly valuable.

Once the best of the blubber is cut from the carcass, it is scarfed with a sharp blade in a spiral fashion around the body and a man is lowered onto it where he buries a hook into the spiral cut at the head. All this while horrible sharks circle, attacking, and I am fearful should a man fall he would be devoured in an instant. Once the hook is pulled the blanket strip of blubber peels away like the skin from a fruit. This cutting process is arduous and very messy. The decks are awash in oil, fat, slime and blood.

Birds hover over the greasy sea and sharks patrol to snatch and bite at any chance.

As the blubber lands on the deck it is hacked into chunks, minced and sliced down to the skin in order that it more readily release its oil. This is then dispatched to the dryout tubs on deck, fires burning beneath, to boil down the oil. The fires are started with wood, then fuelled with the scraps of body tissue that float to the top of the cauldrons. These burn and give off a black smoke and blacken all on deck. On many occasions passing ships offered rescue, fearing we were on fire.

The clean up following this procedure is hard work. Washing the decks thoroughly is but one part. The men, their clothes and equipment require much ingenuity from boiling garments in lye and dunking them in tubs in the sea, to drying them on the rigging and repairing them as needed before it all begins again. But this is why we are here, and with no oil there is no pay for the men. Nor, indeed, recompense for the captain.

It is a tough and lonely life and once again I long for some quiet harbour where I can gam with other ladies. And even more, how I long for a home ashore close to peaceful waters.

So ends this day.

Stolle helped Holly drag an old pine table out of the shed and set it up with assorted chairs in the front garden, then looked down at Tiny Bay Beach through the trees. 'Bloody beautiful spot. You got a buy and a half, Holly. No wonder developers were salivating . . . even a low-rise apartment complex here would be a stunner if every room had a view like this.'

'Don't even think about it,' said Lynn, who was setting out teacups. 'Holly should be congratulated for saving this bit of Bay heritage.'

'Your kids can sell it off to developers for squillions,' Stolle said with a grin, quickly ducking before the women had time to throw anything at him.

'That's a terrible thing to stay, Stolle,' Lynn admonished. 'And what are you going to do with all your worldly goods and chattels? They wouldn't raise fifty bucks at the market.' She went on, 'Just because you don't own anything doesn't mean that everyone who gets something together goes after the big bucks.'

'It's okay, Lynn,' said Holly quickly. 'That's how all our friends back in Sydney think. Enjoy every cent and live the lifestyle you want – even if you can't afford it – and let the kids make their own stash. Property is something you keep trading up, a commodity for a more glamorous life, a status symbol of what you've achieved. Andrew has always regarded houses as investments. I never felt we gave the children a sense of roots, of belonging to a place. We moved from the Northern Beaches to the Eastern Suburbs and then to Mosman. Andrew never kept up with old neighbours, just the property prices. That's why this place means so much to me. It's got a family history, I feel I belong here. Silly, I know, when I just moved in but I want to make something of it.'

'You want to show your old man you can be as astute as him,' said Stolle. 'You just picked a difficult way to do it. But this could be a real showplace if you can stick it out.'

'Oh, I'm going to do that,' said Holly with a sharp edge to her voice. 'If only to show you blokes that I can rescue this place and make a financial go of it.'

'Bugger them, Holly. You do it for yourself,' said Lynn. 'You only have to prove things to yourself, no one else. Anyway, Mitchell said he'd probably get up here tomorrow to see you about taking over the building renovations, if you want.'

'Well, I hope he's reliable. Time doesn't seem to mean much up here. "Probably tomorrow" could be a week or more.'

'Don't stress. Things all happen when they're meant to,' said Stolle.

'See you soon,' Lynn called as they left.

Holly was grateful for their help. Thinking back to their first meeting, she wondered what Andrew would make of them now being her best friends. He would regard them as hired help, not social equals, that was for sure.

Holly changed then hesitated as she caught sight of herself in the mirror. Tailored grey pants and a pale aqua silk-knit sleeveless top, tasteful heavy gold bracelet and chain with a small antique medallion. Understated, elegant, expensive looking. Suddenly she felt all wrong. There was a certain 'look' here that she couldn't put her finger on. Perhaps it was just the fact that anything went. She pulled down the smooth French roll and let her hair flick onto her shoulders, framing her face, hoping she looked less dressy.

Then she hurried outside as she heard a car – someone arriving far earlier than expected. But that would be right, she figured. Lynn had told her that guests in The Bay turned up early, or very late, often with a bunch of friends in tow you weren't expecting. Or not at all, as in – 'Things came up. You know how it is.' She opened the French doors onto the verandah and was surprised to see Eddie get out of the car.

'Hello, Holly. Remember we met at the Goddess Night ding? I was wondering if I could gatecrash your tea party?' He strode across the lawn with a disarming smile.

'It's my first tea party and you have the honour of being my first gatecrasher. Welcome aboard.' They exchanged exaggerated handshakes, which conveniently masked Holly's slight shock. She had tried to accept that values, attitudes and behaviour here were very different from those she had lived by in the city. The Moon Goddess Night had confirmed that beyond any doubt. But it was still very difficult to adjust, especially when these differences came marching through the front gate . . . like Eddie. She noticed that he gave her outfit a quick once-over, a look that confirmed her earlier concern about her choice from the wardrobe. Too bad, on with the show. 'So what is the big attraction here for you? I'm quite mystified.'

'Pictures,' he announced. 'I'd like to get some shots of the tea party.'

'Whatever for?' exclaimed Holly with a smile. 'This is not the stuff of even regional news.'

'I told you the other night about making a doco based on The Bay, didn't I? Well I think I'm onto an angle that will sell, or at least get up some interest among the right people with the money bags.'

'Don't tell me,' said Holly, 'I have star potential. Hollywood is waiting.'

Eddie chuckled. 'No promise of stardom, Holly. No, it's as much the house as you. It's one of the few originals around and a good link between the past and the present, and perhaps a clue to the future of the area.'

Holly could see how a short sequence of a tea party in the garden of the unrestored historic house could work for the storyline. 'I'm sure it will be okay with the guests,' she said. 'But I'll have to tell them what's happening.'

'That's fine. I don't want to bother anyone. Just shoot it wild, as we say in the business. Fortunately I took a couple of shots when the house was up for sale with the big signs outside. And now the rebirth, so to speak.'

'Initial labour pains only,' said Holly.

While Eddie went back to his car for his gear, Holly poured them both freshly squeezed orange juice and pondered on the big arguments for and against development she had heard so far. Some claimed that tourism, like the current backpacker boom, guaranteed the town's economic future. Others argued that the place would become overrun with tourists and accommodation development, destroying the laid-back appeal of the place. She was glad she wasn't the mayor straddling both arguments. Her plans for Richmond House would be approved by all sides, she hoped.

Eddie accepted the orange juice with a clinking of glasses. 'Good luck, Holly. And I hope Richmond House helps you find what you came here for.'

'We'll see,' said Holly with a slight note of doubt. 'And what did you come here to find?'

'Still working that out, believe it or not. It's a kind of elimination process. Knowing what I don't want before I find out what I really want. Now back to business, I'd like to get some shots of the guests arriving.'

'You're excused. Go and hide in the bushes.'

To her surprise he almost did exactly that, and set up in an overgrown area of the shrubbery that provided a slightly elevated angle on the table. He was such a charming man, mused Holly. Thirtyish, obviously creative, comfortable with technology and a determined battler. She wondered about his personal life. Yes, at the full moon evening he had made a reference to an ex-wife, and a child.

She'd never been curious about knowing the personal details of people's lives before. You met and chatted about where you lived, what your husband did, what school your children went to, what new restaurant had opened. Even over long lunches with women friends nothing too personal was ever exchanged. It would be considered prying and very poor taste. Gossip about third parties was different. Yet up here, it seemed personal sharing was de rigueur.

'I can see it. Oh yes.' Nola Florens stood in a the-atrical pose in the centre of the sitting room. The women had wandered around Richmond House exclaiming at its possibilities, the views, the lovely old wood, the ambience. Holly wasn't sure if Nola was going to break into an operatic solo or a recitation. But after clutching her turbaned head she pointed at the small window alcove.

'Make it bigger, frame that view. Make the windows floor to ceiling, it's the focal point of the room. And I know just the fabric to frame it.' She spun around. 'That little fireplace opposite should be huge and above it – an enormous mirror that reflects the view from the bay window. Let the light in, to hell with fading the cushions.'

She placed a plum-coloured fingernail against her matching lips. 'Mmm. I think pale lemon and duck-egg blue. Sun, sky, water. Flowers of course. But subtle, a bit olde worldy. Bit of the William Morris meets Nola Florens, eh?'

'Sounds lovely,' Holly said, smiling. 'But I'm not sure that my budget will run to it.'

'I know exactly what will fit in here because I have yards, rather metres, of it, my dear. Mouldering away in my warehouse in Sydney. What say we get it up, with a couple of things that might suit the bedrooms? The wallpaper too, of course. Just as a trim here and there. This humidity plays hell with the stuff. How are you going to cool this place?'

'I'm relying on the ocean breeze and fans. They're romantic and with the house opened up more it should be comfortable.'

'Windows were meant to be open. I hated living in a sealed house in the city. Curtains have to move and dance, not be rigid, pleated in place. You know, you don't even need curtains up here . . . it's so private. Just token drapes to frame each beautiful picture through every window.' She patted Holly's shoulder. 'A lot of love went into this place, make sure you have a builder who will give it the attention it deserves.'

Once they were all settled in the garden, Amber passed plates of sushi to the other guests and Lynn handed around cool drinks while Holly poured tea.

Mac was in deep discussion with Kimberley. 'So what is going on with Bonnie if you've got Erica staying with you and Matty?' she asked.

'Erica is such a clam. All she is saying is that her mother has gone to a health farm for a couple of weeks. Her mother disappeared for a short time, maybe that was the catalyst. Anyway, Erica is staying with us on weekends. How she stands that madhouse during the week when she has homework to do I don't know. I've told her to bring her washing with her on Friday night and I send her back with food to snack on during the week. She's starting to unwind and relax a bit more. She and Matty enjoy each other's company. I get the feeling Erica hasn't spent a lot of time just being a carefree teenager.'

'What health farm? Do you think someone talked her into drying out? Poor Bonnie, let's hope she's getting her act together. I'll ask Billy, he'll know what's going on, I'm sure.'

'Now, Mac, I never thought you'd be running to the hairdresser for gossip,' said Amber, who was walking by with a platter of finger food.

'There's gossip and there's caring concern. You know how it is in a small community. Newcomers or not, we have to look after each other.'

'Indeed we do.' Amber smiled politely, not wishing to argue with the older woman, but Mac gave her a shrewd look.

'There's something you're not telling. But I won't try to find out.'

Amber turned away, avoiding Mac's gaze, wondering just how psychic she really was. Reading tarot cards and handwriting was one thing, but sometimes Mac had 'flashes' that were prophetic.

So far there hadn't been any chat around town about Bonnie's incident at the beach. Amber had simply backed up her story to her daughter – a foolish morning plunge to help wash away a big hangover, and a misreading of the surf. Amber had fortunately been nearby to help her escape from the rip. The three of them had agreed to keep it to themselves. There was no need to explain her retreat to the Dolphin Centre for 'treatment'. Bonnie's reputation for wild living over recent months could be the cause of anything. Erica had no idea her mother had attempted suicide and was able to give her emotional support without the burden of that knowledge. Amber was touched by just how much Bonnie responded to Erica's help, and how sensitive the young girl was to her mother's need.

Thanks to Amber's contacts, admission to the Dolphin Centre was arranged with a couple of phone calls. The following day they all drove to the therapy centre high on a hinterland hill with remnant rainforest and filtered views of the distant ocean. A scatter of cabins ringed the main house, where they found the admission office and were shown around the counselling rooms and gym.

It wasn't until they were walking away from the car towards the front steps that Bonnie showed signs of breaking down. Tears flowed and she mumbled in a confused state. 'Oh, no. Oh, God. What's going to happen? I'm frightened.'

Erica threw both arms round her mother and hugged her tightly. 'It'll be all right, Mum. You'll be safe here. Nothing to worry about, Amber has told you that. Really. C'mon, Mum, show 'em a bit of your old self. This is a chance for things to change for us.'

'She's right you know,' said Amber. 'Let's go. No turning back.'

Bonnie recovered, wiped the tears away and smiled in gratitude at them both. 'That's what I said when I first arrived at The Bay, full of hope, full of problems. No turning back. Not as easy as it sounded then. It's all become such a mess.'

'We'll make it, Mum. You've just got to get a bit stronger.'

Bonnie looked at her daughter with pride and love, then turned to Amber who linked arms with her and steered her towards the front door. 'She's a strong girl, Amber. Maybe these past few months have helped make her that way, so it's not all bad, huh?'

'Same goes for you, Mum,' added Erica gently.

It had been a hectic twenty-four hours for Amber and Erica. Arranging the Dolphin Centre had been the easy part. More complex was getting a three-minute course on running Bonnie's faltering shop, which Amber had agreed to manage for the time being. 'All care but no responsibility, Bonnie.'

That had been the simple foundation of the deal. Along with an invitation from Bonnie. 'Put some of your products in there too. Might help a bit.'

'Done deal,' said Amber as they had hugged.

Now came the hard part, kisses and tears. A gentle, smiling man with a name badge that said 'Cheyne' took Bonnie to her room, and Amber and Erica walked back to the car holding hands.

'They're not going to do anything . . . awful to her, are they?' asked Erica.

'Of course not. But it's going to be hard for your mum to get her willpower functioning again. They're very caring and careful. They look after people with all kinds of problems, from grief to addiction, to just losing the plot a bit.'

'How come you know them?' Erica asked, catching Amber off guard for a moment.

She hesitated, then replied. 'My mother spent some time here, too.' She didn't say any more but seeing Erica's questioning look, she added, 'Yes, they helped her. A real lot.'

While the other guests were still enjoying tea in the garden, Mac wandered into the kitchen and found Holly on her own. 'Can I help?'

'Thanks, Mac, I'm just boiling more water. More juice needed out there?'

'Wouldn't go astray. A lot of chatting going on, makes us dry.' She glanced around the old kitchen. 'This will have to go. Can you imagine cooking on that wood stove?'

Holly sighed. 'I get a bit overwhelmed sometimes with what I've taken on. I'm hoping the new builder Lynn and Stolle are sending will work out. I need someone who can see what I can. I'm afraid Andrew's designs are very clinical. When you walk around the house, you start to make small changes in your mind as you see things. Nola gave me some great ideas.'

'And where is your husband? Down at the beach? Avoiding the ladies' tea party?'

Holly gave her a curious look. 'No, he's in Sydney and heading off to Bangkok soon.'

Mac frowned. 'Oh, I thought I saw him in town yesterday. I could have sworn it was him . . .' She shrugged and gave a bright smile. 'Oldtimers setting in. I'll pop back outside. That devastatingly handsome Eddie wants to talk to me for his film.'

Eddie had framed Amber in his viewfinder several times during the tea party shoot. She was just so damned beautiful and full of youthful energy that his creative instinct told him to get the shots. Creative instinct, bullshit, he thought when changing angles. Sex urge more likely. Sort that out later, get it in focus.

'Get it all in focus,' Amber said in opening the conversation when he put down the camera and joined the women. The line was so close to what had just gone through his mind that the shock almost made him drop the scone he had bitten into.

'Ah yes. In focus. Are you a blow-in like me?'

'Sort of. I've been back from Sydney a couple of months, the old folks had a farm that went bust. I'm a fully qualified beach bunny, done the horse riding bit in the hills.'

'Well I have similar qualifications,' responded Eddie. 'I'm going bust on a farm too. Probably because I let the fruit and avocado trees do their own thing. I just hope the camera yields a better meal ticket.'

Amber smiled and picked up a platter. 'Have some cheese.'

'I like the way you smile when you say cheese.'

She blushed, was unable to think of a smart response, so settled for a real smile.

'Where's your farm?' Eddie asked.

'Up where the developers will never find it, I hope,' she said with some bitterness. 'It makes me angry that so many farming families that worked hard for several generations had to leave before they could get the benefit of the boom in real estate. My folks were among them. Sold their land too cheaply. Still, Mum has the old house and her garden.'

Eddie had heard the story so often in the past two years. It was the story of The Bay, but it applied to a lot of other places along the coast as well.

'Gotta circulate with the cheese,' said Amber. 'See you.'

Tina Cook finished the paperwork in her office at the lighthouse reserve and set out on another scheduled patrol. 'Showing the flag' she called it. A few tourists were around as usual, hanging over the railing or looking through the mounted telescope. An overweight woman draped with a big shoulder bag, camera and binoculars hailed her in a broad American drawl. 'Say, ranger, where are the dolphins? We were told they're always here. We've been on all the beaches round about and haven't seen one.' She sounded irritable, and her remark seemed to suggest that Tina, as ranger, could make them appear.

Tina gave a shrug and smiled nicely. 'The dolphins choose when to appear, ma'am. They're not on the payroll. You're really lucky, because you have the chance to make yourself comfortable at one of the lookouts and do the relaxation and meditation bit while you're waiting for them. A chance to get in tune with nature, you know what I mean. People pay big money for that sort of opportunity. Enjoy your day.' She turned and went down the walkway before the American could reply.

A dilapidated car rolled up to her and Eddie leaned out the window. 'Hi, we spoke on the phone. Eddie Harley. Can you spare me a few minutes?'

Tina swallowed the flippant remark that came to mind. Who wouldn't spare time for this attractive man? 'Of course. You're after some archival stuff for your film, right?'

Eddie got out of the car and shook her hand, thinking few women would look that good in baggy khaki shorts and a drab shirt.

'How can National Parks help?' Tina asked.

'I was hoping to plunder the archives.'

'They're not official. Some stuff belongs to the Maritime Services Board, some to local families, the so-called historical society. It's all kept up here on National Parks property because it's secure, I suppose.'

'So let's make it unofficial. Can you help me?'

'Come over to what passes as my office and tell me what you're trying to do.'

Eddie sipped the bad instant coffee she'd made him as he stumbled through his vague theme for the documentary. 'It's a bit fuzzy, but talking it out seems to help clarify things a bit. Maybe I can draw parallels with past events that impact on today.'

'Where do you think The Bay should go, Eddie?'

He paused, sensing this was an important question to her. 'Well, I've only been here a couple of years. I know what I came for, but things are never quite what one expects.'

'You're disappointed?' she asked.

'Not in The Bay, I mean other aspects of my life didn't quite work out as planned.' He turned his coffee mug, avoiding her eyes. 'But I feel protective about the place. Sort of like I slipped in under the gate and I don't want the hordes to follow. Is that being selfish?'

'That's a question the whole town has to answer.' She leaned forward. 'Have you heard about some big development planned down along Mighty Beach?'

'There always seem to be rumours that some celeb has bought a chunk of prime land, the white-shoe brigade are heading this way followed by the fast food and resort people. None have arrived as far as I can tell.'

Tina still looked serious. 'They're a subversive

lot. They keep hammering away. You hit them on the head and they go away, wait a while, then slither back and try again. Like cane toads. We have to be on our guard and mobilise people power. It's a funny thing about this place. You wouldn't find a more diverse group of people – who disagree on everything. Yet when it comes to keeping out the big boys, they speak as one.'

'I was asked to shoot some footage for a green group showing how beautiful and pristine parts of The Bay are, and then they took me to other areas that have been stuffed up. I was shocked at the bad sewerage system, it's a huge issue. Soil erosion, the pollution in the creeks and rivers, the loss of some of the wetlands, some truly ugly suburban housing estates . . . The rest of the country looks on this as paradise, but there's a serpent or three waving bucks and slithering into the garden.' He drained his coffee, suddenly embarrassed.

She applauded him. 'Seems to me like you're getting a story together. There are several people out in the hills working on answers to some of those things. Maybe you'd like to meet them.'

'Old hippies or young guns?' asked Eddie. He didn't want to waste money on unusable footage wandering after a bunch of radicals or spaced-out weirdos.

Tina heard the sceptical note in his voice and changed tack. 'Both. But you wanted the historical stuff. Let's work forward from that. Follow me.' She took a bunch of keys off her cluttered little desk and headed outside.

'Hey, this is great. We get to climb all the steps?' He tilted his head back and looked up at the top of the lighthouse as Tina unlocked the old wooden door.

'I do it every day.'

No wonder she looked so fit. He walked into the darkness then Tina flipped a switch showing the round stone walls and a steel spiral staircase in the centre.

'Nice and cool in here,' he remarked.

'The walls are thick. Like a good wine cellar.' Her footsteps clanged on the narrow iron treds. 'Follow me.'

Daylight shone in from the tiny latched windows, and Eddie was glad to see they were near the top. Had Tina deliberately skipped so quickly up the stairs to test him, or was it just that she was familiar with every step? 'How many times a day do you do this?'

'At least once, it keeps me healthy. Want to take a look from the top?' They stepped through a small doorway onto the windy parapet that surrounded the tower and were hit by the brilliant sunlight.

'Oh, wow.' Eddie was struck by the panorama spread before them. 'How stunning. Got to bring the camera up here.'

'It is fabulous . . . sunrise and sunset are best.'

Eddie felt like a boy getting a ride on a fire engine. 'This is fantastic!' he called to Tina as he gazed out to sea. 'I'm going to walk around again.' He set off, hanging onto the railing as he circled the top, taking in the three hundred and sixty degree view of the coast, the sheltered bay, the ocean to the horizon, across the town and away to the hills.

'There's more. Not for public display though,' said Tina when he came back inside.

He followed her down the spiralling stairs to the lower level, past the 'engine room' where the light mechanism took up most of the space. 'It's really a magnificent structure.' He gazed at the French glass prisms.

'Over seven hundred of them – all original,' she said. 'The whole thing floats in a mercury bath, quite ingenious. It was powered like a grand-father clock in the old days, cast-iron weights on chains are in the central pillar of the stairwell.'

'So now it's powered by electricity.' Eddie peered beneath the light at a 12-volt car battery. 'Is that the back-up for a power failure?'

'Yep,' laughed Tina. 'The light never stops turning. A photo-sensitive mechanism turns it on and off at dusk and dawn.'

'Why does it keep turning?' asked Eddie, watching the slow revolution of the huge light.

'Concentrated UV rays could damage the glass or focus a beam of light strong enough to start a bushfire or damage someone's eyesight.'

At the bottom of the stairs Tina unlocked a door to one side of the tiled entrance and beck-oned him inside. The room was once used by the lighthouse keepers on their watch. There was an old comfortable swivel chair, a bench that served as a desk, and a chest of drawers with a Primus stove and old kettle on it. A tin mug hung on a hook with an old chart of the coastline beside it.

Tina pulled open the chest of drawers, revealing piles of folders filled with papers and pictures. 'This is recent stuff from various places like the library, the old people's home, the local newspaper when they became computerised.' She bent down and tugged at a large trunk. 'This is the old stuff.'

Eddie helped her pull it out and manoeuvre the old lock. When the lid was open the smell of camphor was overpowering.

'I didn't know what to do so I tossed in the mothballs. Seems to be working. It's cool in here so the humidity hasn't got to anything. I check them every couple of months. Have a delve,' she offered, sitting back on a chair watching him.

Eddie caught his breath and with some reverence began to pull out old books, an ornate photo album, a slightly watermarked family Bible with a family tree itemised in the front, old ships' logs, several framed pictures of vessels, and then a leather-bound book caught his eye. He drew out the heavy volume and lightly smoothed the cover before opening it.

Inside the fly leaf was written in a neat, flowing hand, '*The journal of the* Lady Richmond, *as kept by Hannah Nilson, begun at sea in the year of Our Lord, eighteen hundred and ninety-five.*'

Eddie looked at Tina. 'I'd like to read this.'

'I can't let you take it off the Cape. But bring a packed lunch any day and camp in my office.'

'I'll be back as soon as I can.' He watched her repack the trunk. 'Have you read all this material?'

'I've skimmed through it. I don't have a lot of spare time up here, you know. One day I'll tell you what my job involves.'

'I'd like that.'

'I was just kidding. It's pretty boring most of the time.' She locked the door behind them and they stepped out into the sunlight. 'I don't know what use this old stuff might be, but you said you wanted to start at the beginning.' She was rather looking forward to the idea of Eddie hanging around and delving into 'the archives'.

'I'd like to start right now but I have to collect my daughter from her surf lesson.'

'Oh, right. Well maybe I'll see you soon then.'

'You will,' Eddie promised. 'You certainly will.'

Chapter Six

The Log of the Lady Richmond,
September 14th, 1897

We are in Southern Pacific waters. Temperature 81 degrees F. Seas calm. Wind N-NE.

We are blessed this day by fair weather and a goodly breeze. It has brought much relief after high humidity. Mrs Nilson gave birth to a healthy boy with the Captain's assistance at 2.15 this morn. The Captain informed the crew and toasts to anoint the wee one's head were raised. They have named him Sven Richmond Nilson I am informed, after his paternal grandfather and the Richmond owners of our vessel.

The Captain hopes to reach the shores of New South Wales in three weeks hence as Mrs

Nilson desires that the child be christened in the company of her family.

George J. Bain, First Mate

Hannah fell back on her pillow, glad the baby was feeding well. She was tired and had suffered as other wives had told her she would. But if this is wifely duty then so be it. The prize of a fine strong son was worth it, as had been the joy in her dear husband's eyes. This great intimacy, she thought, had given their marriage added strength. But how she wished to share her child with her own mother. Lars had told her the *Lady Richmond* would be heaving down at the new dock at Mosman so she could spend time at Sydney with her parents. After the christening they were to sail south to Twofold Bay for half a year as they had been told the whaling outlook was promising.

'My dearest Hannah. How I hated to see you suffer so.' Lars Nilson sat at the edge of their bed and tenderly took his wife's hand. 'You are still pale.'

'But I feel very well, Lars, and see how rosy and happy our son is.' She drew the baby from her breast. Lars laid a finger against the soft cheek and the boy's eyes sprang open, showing pale blue that matched those of his father. But swiftly the pursed lips sought once more the comforting milk-filled breast.

Lars chuckled. 'He is a fine one. When you feel able, some time on deck in the fresh air will do you good. The crew have rigged a shaded spot with sail canvas where you will be cool and comfortable.' He paused for a moment. 'Should we have another child, I hope you will be cared for in more hospitable surroundings. I knew what had to be done, but I confess, I was fearful. I felt I'd rather face a maddened whale. It is a large responsibility to see mother and child delivered safely from the ordeal.'

Hannah smiled at his confession. Fear was not an emotion she ever associated with her husband, and it was strange to hear it on his lips. 'Dear Lars, I think you and Sven will always share a special bond because of this. And I have never regretted coming to sea with you. Not once.'

October 7th, 1897, at sea

I gather my strength every day and little Sven grows so sturdy. I give thanks for all these blessings.

My heart aches at the knowledge that Mrs Daniels of the Franklin *lost her babe after just three days. Though it seems should they have been ashore with the very best of doctors, little could have been done to save the poor tiny infant born before its time. Not all news I have recently learned is so sad. There are many whales this season and Lars believes he knows the direction they are headed. Of course the rest of the fleet are so inclined as well. I have learned this after a wonderful gam was enjoyed by us all when we sighted the* Addison. *As we were to leeward we held back while Captain Bartholomew ran us down to windward and came alongside. Mrs Bartholomew was lowered into the whaleboat in the gaming chair – a barrel cut down with a seat and hung on a rope so we ladies may preserve our decorum in moving from one ship to another.*

Young Sven was highly admired and passed around without a whimper. I was pleased the Steward managed to make sweet cakes for the occasion as I have been too indisposed to venture to the galley, which pleases Cook and Steward who rule their domain like jealous kings. Mrs Bartholomew kindly brought preserves and currant wine, and relieved us of one of the baby piglets. She agreed with me that it is distressing to carry animals on board as one does get attached to them. When Cook descends with his cleaver I cannot bring myself to enjoy the feast. Mrs Bartholomew regaled me with tales of their most recent catch – a sperm whale so large her husband persuaded her to walk between its jaws. She declared six men could stand in it in comfort. And more astonishing, inside one of its three stomachs was a giant squid as long as one of the whaleboats!

Tina read this entry aloud to Eddie. 'Can you imagine what it must have been like for those women?' she said as she lowered the journal. 'Having babies at sea, and all that time alone! How they must have loved their men.'

'Probably better than being alone in a faraway country, not knowing for months on end how they were. What would you do?'

'I'd be the captain of the ship,' declared Tina. Then she said quietly, 'What a wonderful woman Hannah must have been, and yet no one, not even her husband, considered what she did as out of the ordinary. Today's liberated women might learn a lot from these early women.'

October 12th, 1897,
close to the eastern coast of Australia

We came upon a large pod of whales travelling south and were witness to a rare event, which I believe even these hardened whalers found a touching sight.

The herd formed a circle around a large female, all moaning and speaking to each other – or so it seemed – as she gave birth. I could but sympathise as she twisted her body before the calf emerged tail first and began breathing and suckling. I'm told the whale mother's milk is highly rich in fat. After this event the boats moved in and tried to draw the mother away as she was a fine specimen.

*I could not stand the sounds which came
from that giant creature as they prised the baby
from her. She lunged and took the newborn in
her jaws to protect it as the other boats went for
the outside herd. The mother's fight was in vain,
the baby lived but such a short time.*

*I had to go below as I found the scene too
distressing. Lars put it down to my own recent
experience of birth. It is the first time I felt there
was something special we shared with these
creatures. I now believe that they too feel loss,
pain and anger at their fate. Not a cheerful state
of mind for the wife of a whaling captain.*

'Even then,' Tina said, 'the guilt was starting to
creep in. She was feeling like this despite everything she knew and all she had been exposed to.
And she didn't have the knowledge we have now
about how unique whales are.'

'We still feel guilty about this today,' said
Eddie. 'Even though we weren't there and weren't
responsible. It's hard to imagine throwing a harpoon into the head of such a wonderful creature.
Whaling was such a horrible, messy business.'

'It still is a horrible business even with new
technology,' agreed Tina. 'They just kill more, and
more quickly.'

'And in the name of need and so-called
research. It's just greed,' Eddie said. He glanced
out the office window at the tourists strolling
around the headland. 'Ironic, isn't it, that this

town was once a whaling station and now attracts people who want to watch the whales.'

'At least we acknowledge the past and celebrate the present with some awareness of what happened and how necessary it is to make amends,' said Tina. 'It's so rewarding when I talk to schoolkids about cetaceans, looking after the ocean and beaches. They're really switched on to it all.'

'I wonder what Hannah would think if she came back today,' mused Eddie.

'I hope she'd approve,' smiled Tina. 'We try our best.'

The Forester nosed down a dirt track to the gates of a farm, turning away from the distant house to the long sheds. Curly hung her head out of the window sniffing the pungent breeze, her ears back, assaulted by the sounds of hundreds of chickens. Holly parked outside a small galvanised-iron building and rapped on the door. A smiling young Indian girl opened it and led her to the cool-room filled with roses. The young girl joined two other women who were trimming the flowers and tying them into bunches.

'Hello, Mrs Singh, how are you this week?' asked Holly.

'Very good, very good. You like the same?' The plump woman was wearing a cotton sari with an incongruous woolly cardigan over it and thick gloves, not so much for the cold but as protection against the thorns. She spoke in Hindi to her daughter who hurried away and returned with a bucket filled with pale peach-tinged cream roses. Holly held out her own bucket and the girl transferred four large bunches of Honor roses into it.

'Eggs? Many double yolks today,' said Mrs Singh.

'Oh yes please, a dozen will be more than enough.' Holly paid, thanked Mrs Singh, smiled at the other woman and followed the young girl out into the hot sun. As she put the flowers into the back of the car, the girl brought her the eggs.

'I'll bring some cartons back next week,' said Holly, waving goodbye. The Singhs were such a friendly family, hardworking and resourceful. They ran a big stall every Sunday at the market and supplied produce and flowers to shops in town.

Two more stops at farms along the winding dirt road completed her shopping. Old boxes that years ago held the milk cans left at the gate for collection by butter factory trucks were now used as mini stalls, displaying kilo bags of fruit and vegetables and an honesty box. For a few dollars Holly had bought a pile of delicious, fresh, organically grown produce. While she still enjoyed the Sunday markets, she found this peaceful drive a delightful way to buy her supplies, not only for the bargains but the sheer joy of driving through the exquisite rolling countryside. Fat Friesian cows grazed in lush green paddocks fenced by old drystone walls made by the first settlers. It looked quintessentially English, until you lifted your eyes to the volcanic mountain range to the west and the slash of brilliant blue ocean to the east.

A sense of calm always came over Holly as she drove along this road. A feeling of wellbeing, that everything was going to work out, that she could manage whatever obstacles might be ahead. She couldn't put her finger on what it was. As well as the picture perfect setting perhaps it was also a nostalgia for another era when life was ordered by the seasons. Sometimes she imagined she was back in the pioneering days, at other times the 1950s – until she rolled into the outskirts of The Bay to find a hitchhiker dressed in strange garb, with a backpack, drum or guitar, and maybe a dog, thumbing a ride and holding a sign that said 'North'.

She was putting the produce away when Curly barked. It was a welcome bark, not her 'Who are you?' warning. Holly peered out the window at the unfamiliar truck, then saw the dog hanging out the passenger window. It was the man from the beach with the elegant vizsla.

'Hello, Romany. This is a nice surprise. Are you here to remind us of the dog rally tomorrow?' Holly asked as dog and owner came towards her.

'Well that's one reason. I'm Mitchell.' He held out his hand. 'Sorry, I haven't been able to get here before this. I had to finish a job.'

Holly was a bit taken aback. 'Oh, that's all right. I hadn't realised when we met at the beach.'

'Me either. But when Lynn described you and

from our conversation I figured it must have been you.'

'Please come in. The dogs can play. Curly is thrilled to have a visitor.'

'Always wanted to see in here,' Mitchell said as they walked inside. 'Hmm, wonderful, isn't it?'

'Please look around. I'll make tea. Or coffee?'

'Either. Provided it isn't dandelion or some sort of herb. I need the caffeine,' he said lightly. 'So you want this to be a guesthouse? A B & B, Stolle said,' he called out from the next room. 'Are you going to live in here too or away from the house?'

'There's an old shed I thought I could extend as separate quarters for me, or whoever ends up running the place.'

He stuck his head back into the kitchen. 'You're not planning on staying?'

'I do have a home and family in Sydney,' said Holly.

'Ah yes, I remember. Beautiful downtown Mosman.'

'It is beautiful. Nowadays. Depends on what you want, doesn't it?' said Holly a little defensively.

'You might have to choose,' he said calmly. And before she could answer, went on, 'This is going to take a big chunk of your life and you'll get attached. Are you fixing it up to sell as a going concern or as a potential business?'

'Sell! Heavens no. Well, I don't think so. I hadn't thought that far down the track. I just want to get on with it. Maybe by the time it's finished I'll want to get rid of it.'

He gave her a quizzical look. 'Do you really think you could part with this place? You're attached now, whether you know it or not, and you haven't started to make it the way you want it to be.'

'You're right.' She turned away, his intense expression was making her uncomfortable. 'Milk?'

After a slow inspection they sat with their mugs of tea and Holly showed Mitchell the plans Andrew had drawn up. He looked at them carefully then asked, 'And what changes do you want made?'

She tried not to smile. 'What makes you think I want changes?'

'Because you're living here and you are getting to know the moods of the house, where the light is needed, where you like to sit and read. What view you want to look at most, those sorts of things.'

'You're right. I have to confess there are some things I want changed. I'm at a loss about others. And there are things I want kept intact.'

'I understand what you mean. Would you like to look at a couple of places I've worked on? A lot of old homes in one street were being ripped down for shops and units, but once some of the owners saw how an old place came up with renovation, they changed their mind. So we saved the last few.'

'You must have done a good job. Best form of advertising, so I'm told,' said Holly.

'Thank you. It's very challenging to take what looks like a pile of junk and renovate without destroying the soul of a place. Not always that easy, but when it works the client is happy and I get job satisfaction. Win–win, as the jargon goes.'

'I'm pleased to hear it. The last builders here seemed intent on ripping the place apart rather than renovating.'

'Holly, don't worry. I only do one job at a time and Richmond House will have my full attention. And my assistants know what's expected of them.'

Holly relaxed. 'Great. Then let's walk through the place again.'

Their last stop was the widow's walk.

'This should be kept, of course. It balances the structural design and it's a nostalgic part of the house, I'd say,' mused Mitchell. 'It gets the wind, facing out to sea like this, but it could be made into a small private roof garden, or perhaps a sundeck.'

Holly didn't answer, her attention was focused on the distant horizon. In her mind's eye she could see the faint outline of a ship.

'Holly?'

'Oh, sorry. I was daydreaming. I can't help thinking about the woman who lived in this house and the times she must have stood up here.'

'The original owner was most likely a sea captain. His wife probably spent a lot of lonely, anxious hours here,' said Mitchell.

Holly turned to him. 'I think so too. I just know so . . .' She looked away. 'It sounds silly but

171

I can feel the presence of someone in the house. It doesn't bother me, it's not a haunted house, but I feel she is here watching me, or hanging around for some reason.' Holly gave an embarrassed little laugh. 'My imagination runs away a bit in a place like this.'

'Oh, I find it a lot,' said Mitchell calmly. 'Houses absorb feelings, moods, from those who live in them for a long time. I sometimes think spirits or souls hang around when there's unfinished business. What do they call them . . . earthbound spirits?'

Holly was surprised to hear the builder talking about spirits in such an accepting way. 'Do you think unfinished business, as you put it, is ever resolved? What happens when the place is pulled down, or changed?'

'I don't know, I'm only guessing.' He hesitated. 'Maybe you'll understand this . . . I just figure that sometimes fate steps in and alters people's lives before they're ready. Oh, I don't know, I guess it sounds silly, but I would say I believe in ghosts. Not ones you are supposed to see. No, the ones we sense.'

She didn't answer. It all sounded odd, and she started a little when he touched her arm. 'Don't be alarmed. This place has the feeling that a lot of love was shared here.'

'I'd like to think so.'

As they returned indoors Holly wondered what Andrew would have made of this conversation. She knew he'd tell her The Bay was turning her into an airhead. And she knew she wouldn't tell him.

She also didn't send him the local paper the following week with a large front-page photo of the protest rally to allow dogs on Tinderbox Beach. In the centre of the picture, marching with a little army of colourful characters and their dogs and banners, was Holly leading Curly. Curly wore a bow and trotted beside Romany and Mitchell. Holly thought she'd send the paper to her children. After all, it was her first protest rally.

That night, feeling so proud of her public stand, she told Andrew about taking part in the protest march. She bubbled over the phone, 'There were all manner of people, and our dogs. There were some great speeches. I was so impressed, it wasn't just about allowing dogs on a beach. It was about a lot of fundamental principles, about freedom, lifestyle, over-regulation, bureaucratic arrogance.' Then she stopped, sensing disapproval in Andrew's silence.

Eventually he spoke, slowly, very deliberately. 'Holly, how could you? That's utter stupidity. How could you get involved with that rabble? You will ruin your name in the town as a serious businesswoman – if that's what you want to be. God almighty –'

'I want to be a member of the community. I care about things that affect the town.'

'And if the ferals and local dropouts decide to march naked down the main street to protest about not being able to fornicate in the park, you'd march too?'

'Andrew, you don't have to be so silly. It's just that people can unite and speak with one voice about things that genuinely concern them –' Holly began, but he cut her off.

'I find it hard to believe you would lower yourself to take part in a protest, Holly. For dogs! It'd be funny if it wasn't so ludicrous.' He changed the subject to practical matters and Holly bit her tongue.

Eddie's car had broken down again. Resigned to his situation he shouldered his camera gear and started walking the last kilometre to the farm.

He was surprised to see Laura's car parked in the driveway as well as another he didn't recognise and the front door wide open. He glanced at his watch. School wasn't out yet so she hadn't brought Alice up to visit. Nor had she rung to say she was coming. It annoyed him that she still regarded the farm as her property.

He could hear her voice as he stepped up onto the verandah. 'It needs heaps of work, of course, but you can see why we liked it. If someone worked the farm it would be a good investment.'

'Depends. There's more value in the land to develop as an MO – multiple occupancy – or eco-village.'

Eddie didn't recognise the man's voice.

'Would a development application be approved, do you think?' Laura asked with great interest.

Eddie had heard enough. 'Can I help you guys? I'm sorry, Laura, have I missed an appointment? I don't recall us arranging a meeting here.'

She stepped forward with a thin smile. 'Now, now, Eddie. This is Dick Armstrong from Armstrong Real Estate. I thought he should give us an appraisal of the farm, perhaps a few ideas of . . . other places.'

'What for? I'm not moving. Or selling.' Eddie put the camera on the table and turned to the agent. 'Sorry to waste your time, Mr Armstrong.'

'Eddie, be practical. There's no way you can manage this place. We need the money.'

'Er, if there seems to be some misunderstanding I can come back.' The agent turned to Laura. 'Maybe this is a little premature, perhaps you two should talk things over and get back to me.'

'That won't be necessary, Mr Armstrong. My wife, my ex-wife, doesn't seem to grasp the fact that we've done a property settlement. The farm is mine. She got practically everything I own and a cash settlement. Look around. I'm down to bare essentials.'

'Why don't I leave you for the moment?' The agent began backing out the door. 'I'll be in touch, Mrs Harley.'

'Don't bother,' snapped Eddie.

Laura spun on her heel. 'How dare you talk like that. You're totally out of line and wrong as usual. When are you going to wake up –'

'You're the one who's out of line, Laura.' Eddie went to the sink to get a glass of water.

'Sorry I can't offer you a drink. No fancy glasses and you cleared out the wine cellar, if you recall.' His anger evaporated. He was tired and felt defeated as he always did in the face of Laura's bulldozing.

'Don't be so pathetic,' Laura said. 'Do you want to have this out here and now, once and for all?' She folded her arms and glared.

'Laura, we've done this. I've given you and Alice everything I possibly can, at least allow me a leaking roof over my head.'

'Buying this property was my idea, remember! We need the money. The Bay is no place for us any more, we're not on holidays. I want Alice to have a bit of sophistication, go to a good school. So we'll have to get rid of all this land. It's only fair.'

'Fair!' he exploded. 'Give me a break. You have everything. There's still a mortgage on this place. It's zoned rural for the next five years, maybe longer. No fancy development is going to happen way out here. And I like living here.'

'We'll see about that. You'll have to find money for school fees, and speaking of money there's a stack of unpaid bills over there.' She pointed at the small table.

Eddie stared at Laura like she was a total stranger. 'You just don't get it, do you? Alice is very happy in The Bay. She loves the local school. She's ten years old, we're not talking university and finishing school yet. And what damned bills?' He strode to where she had left a pile of envelopes. 'What are these? You're responsible for your own bills. I give you an allowance for that, I'm paying your rent, I paid for your car. What more do you want? Oh don't answer that.' Eddie rifled through the bills. 'What's this – David Jones and Myers! If you're ordering stuff from them you pay for it.' He turned the bill over and read aloud, 'Clothes, cosmetics, accessories. And what's this? An account for hairdressing – on the Gold Coast! What's wrong with The Teepee in The Bay where everyone else goes?' He threw the bills back on the table.

Laura snatched them. 'I don't intend to be just like everyone else in The Bay, as you put it. Look around you, Eddie, they're flakes and freaks. I don't want Alice exposed to all this weird stuff.'

'Since when? It was your idea to move here. I had a good job and was quite happy in Sydney.' Eddie could feel his temper rising. 'There's no point in going over this again. I'm going out to feed the chooks.'

'That's right, walk away, typical,' snapped Laura. 'Well, Alice and I are moving to the Gold Coast. Going to make something of ourselves, not wander around some pseudo beach town with a bunch of lost souls.'

Eddie wasn't going to ask what brought this on. He didn't want to know. Laura was always irrational, but she used to be more of a delightful ditz who could make him laugh. Later he discovered she really wasn't very bright and the ditzy manner covered a devious streak of self-preservation and self-indulgence.

She headed out the door, firing a parting shot. 'You can be an absolute shit, Eddie, without even trying.'

Holly sat on cushions on the floor under the yellow pool of lamplight, with sketches and plans and a notepad spread around her. The faint regular wash of the waves, the rustle of palm fronds, Curly's gentle snore, the occasional pattering of a possum on the roof were now comforting and familiar evening sounds. The phone rang and the long-distance bips suddenly made her heart race. Was there a problem with her children? She fell into her old habit of fretting immediately, expecting the worst.

'Holly, it's me,' said Andrew.

'Is everything all right? I haven't heard from the children –'

'Give it a rest. Let me at least say hello. How're things?'

'Fine. The new builder is great. How are the kids?'

'I don't know, no one ever calls me unless they want money. They're busy, I guess. Now listen, I'm off to Bangkok tomorrow, be gone ten days at least. I need you to sign some papers, asap.'

'Oh, all right, send them up. What's going on? Why so long in Bangkok?'

'All a bit hush-hush, hopefully we'll be doing a big resort complex.'

'I thought Thailand was already full of resorts.'

'There's a lot of money up there, this company invests in properties all around the world. It's an international consortium. Now about these papers. They're at a solicitor's office in The Bay, Pearce and James in Dive Street.'

'Why there? Why didn't you send them to me here?'

'They need a JP to witness the signature, you know the usual rigmarole. Just do it tomorrow, would you?'

'When are you coming back up here? I'd love you to see my ideas and it gets a bit lonely. I miss you –'

'Now, Holly, you knew this was how it was going to be. And ideas for what?'

'The house, oh lots of things.'

'What do you mean the house? I'd drawn everything up specifically. Don't you let some hick builder start changing those plans. We agreed –'

'That I would run things,' Holly cut in. 'Don't worry, Andrew. I'm sure you have a lot more important things to worry about.'

'Well, yes frankly, I do. Look, I might come up for a weekend when I get back. How's that?'

'Lovely. Whenever you can fit it in,' said Holly slightly facetiously.

Andrew didn't notice or chose to ignore it. 'I'll call when I can. But you know how it is . . . and the time difference –'

'Yes. I know how it is. I hope everything goes well with the deal.'

'Me too. Don't forget those papers. They'll be expecting you in the morning. Take care. Bye.'

'Bye, Andrew.' Too bad if she had other things arranged for the morning. Andrew had become used to her not having any life outside his. As it so happened Holly did have some free time, but her days were getting busier. Mitch was there every day. She'd gone with him to look at materials and been into the council as they were making a change to the plans. Nola had been terrifically generous and Mitch had patiently listened to her advice about the colour scheme. Initially Holly had trailed behind Mitch and his two assistants – Rob with the shaved head and Larry with the ponytail – when the heavy work of removing the walls and windows started. But the more she watched them the more at ease she became. Mitch was careful, had an eye for the small details and respect for the original builder's work. She knew Richmond House was in caring hands.

The following morning, Holly found the solicitor's office above the second-hand bookshop. When she introduced herself the receptionist in slacks, sandals and tie-dyed loose top greeted her cheerfully. 'Hi, Mrs Jamieson, we've got some papers for you to sign. Want a tea, water, anything?'

'No, thank you. Er, is Mr Pearce or Mr James here?'

'Oh no. Peter is out surfing and Gordon is down in Sydney. Letitia is here, she's a solicitor and a JP, and knows all about it. I'll get her.'

A very glamorous young woman in a navy pants suit with slick dark hair and dark lipstick strode into the reception area. 'Hello, I'm Letitia

Sweetman. Thanks for coming in. We just need you to sign these papers as you and your husband are co-directors of your family company. Here on page three . . .' She flipped through the papers.

'The family company? I thought this was a business thing.'

'His business company requires him to move finances, give guarantees, which he does through his personal directorship. As you also own assets you have to sign off on these transactions. Just a formality. Sign here where the X is and I'll witness it.' Holly took the pen, wondering if she should sit down and read through what appeared incomprehensible legalese. But Ms Sweetman had the second set of papers ready for her signature. She smiled at Holly. 'Sorry, I'm in a bit of a rush, have to get over to the courthouse.'

'There you are,' said Holly, signing quickly. 'You'll get this straight back to my husband? He seemed anxious to have it done quickly.'

'We have it all in hand, I'm couriering them to Andrew in Bangkok. Thanks so much for stopping by.'

As she stepped outside into the sunny street it occurred to Holly that Ms Sweetman seemed to be on very familiar terms with her husband. Her firm must have had other dealings with him, perhaps through the purchase of Richmond House. Holly glanced at her watch, which she was wearing from habit, though she'd been teased about it. She was due to meet Nola Florens to look at the fabrics she'd had sent from Sydney. Holly was thrilled she was offering to give them to her for Richmond House: 'Consider it my heritage donation, dear girl. Otherwise they'd rot away.' And she was just as interested in seeing Nola's penthouse apartment overlooking Main Beach.

Billy stopped at the doorway of the Beach Hut on his way back from the TAB. 'Hi, Amber, how's it going in here? Selling any of Bonnie's rubbish?'

'Don't be like that. Though it is a bit tacky; can't compete with the better shops around. Surprising for someone from such a classy background. I'm selling a lot of my products, though. I feel guilty.'

'You needn't be. Once customers get used to popping in they'll keep coming back. You should get Bonnie to upgrade this holiday gear. How's she doing by the way? I haven't seen Erica around either, s'pose she's with Matty.'

'Bonnie is struggling a bit. Has good days and bad days, she might need to stay at the retreat a bit longer. But keep that quiet. These women in town love to gossip,' Amber explained.

Billy gave her a warm smile. 'It's terrific the way you're looking after Bonnie, but lighten up and let rip occasionally. Act your age! No charge for the advice,' he quipped.

'Ah, don't worry, I can be a wild woman when I want to. I just prefer to rage far from The Bay.'

'Yeah sure,' Billy said as he headed back to his salon. He didn't believe her. Amber seemed to carry a lot of baggage she didn't share. Always willing to help others and she was developing a great little business with her beauty products, but there was a shadow behind her eyes. Billy decided when the opportunity presented itself he'd draw her out.

Eddie and Alice were on boogie boards riding long breakers from the Point onto the sand. 'This is so cool,' shouted Alice.

Eddie was the first to tire and settled under the shade of a pandanus palm at the edge of the sand. He had really enjoyed the mid-morning surf with Alice. It was probably one of their last opportunities for a relaxed time together before she moved to the Gold Coast to live with her mother. He wouldn't miss Laura one bit, but seeing less of Alice would be hard.

She came running up the beach, still full of energy, dropped her board, shook her hair wildly then accepted the proffered beach towel. 'Ta. Fantastic, wasn't it?'

'Didn't tire you out, I see.'

'No way. I just felt sorry for you sitting here all alone.' She adopted a mock sexy pose, which looked slightly absurd given her skinny body.

He flicked his towel at her, which started a wild towel fight, punctuated by squeals and laughter. 'I surrender,' said Eddie at last.

Alice flopped on the sand beside him. 'I suppose an ice-cream from the Whippy van is out of the question?'

'We can lash out, even though I'm pretty broke,' he added unnecessarily. She was well aware that financially, times were tough for him.

'Still haven't got a job?'

'No. But I'm working on it. One day the big break will come.'

'You gotta hang in there, Dad.' She started humming a tune he didn't recognise.

Eventually he cut in. 'How do you feel about the idea of going to Surfers?'

Alice screwed up her nose. 'Not thrilled. But then I didn't think it was such a great idea moving into town from the farm. I loved the horses and the space, and all that, but now I like being in town, near the beach, near my friends.' She doodled in the sand with a stick for a few moments. 'I was thinking, maybe I could stay here,' she said suddenly.

'Sweetie, you'll make new friends and you're only a bit over an hour away. Your mum seems to think the Gold Coast has a lot more to offer.'

'Whenever I say the Gold Coast to people here they say it's horrible.' Alice looked worried.

'You know how it is, honey. People like where they live. And not everyone wants high-rise apartments and the glitz of the Gold Coast. The Bay is . . . different. Special. But it's not a place for people to find good jobs, be in the mainstream. Your mum wants you to have the advantages of a city.'

'Why don't you move then?'

'It's not that easy, Alice. Money is one thing. And for the moment I want to try to have a bash at doing what I've always wanted to do. There's a big creative arts community here, different from Sydney, a lot of talented people. It's where I want to be. But, now, it doesn't suit your mother.'

'I don't like her friends and I don't want to live in a high-rise box.'

'You'll still be close to the surf,' said Eddie.

'Yeah. That's good, but I still want to go up to the farm and ride Sampson.'

'You know you can stay at the farm any time you want,' Eddie said gently, concerned at the change in Alice. Without Laura hovering, she was painting quite a different picture.

'I like everyone here. And even though you're not my real dad, I think of you as my dad.' Alice drew a deep breath; Eddie found he was holding his. They'd never made a big deal about the fact that when he married Laura he had willingly taken on the responsibility of Alice as his own. This was the first time she had raised the matter in an adult context. 'So I was wondering, if it's all right with you . . . could I stay here with you? Let Mum go to the Gold Coast? I wouldn't be any trouble.'

Eddie struggled to stay composed. He was so touched by the sense of family responsibility she evoked that he had to fight back a choking feeling that could have led to a tear or two. Humour was the safety valve to prevent personal injury. 'Well, I gotta admit you've learned to cook a mean omelette.'

'I'm no trouble, you know that,' she said, hoping it would help.

'No trouble, apart from some mad girly tantrums,' Eddie said lightheartedly.

Her face broke into a big smile. 'So it's all right then? I'll stay with you and Mum can go up there, and she can come back on weekends and stuff.'

'Hey, wait a minute. We'd better talk this over with her. There are a lot of things we'd have to think about . . .' Then seeing her crestfallen face, he quickly added, 'I would really love to have you stay with me. I'm just sad things haven't worked out with me and your mum. But we both want you to be happy and want what's best for you. You will always be my girl.'

'Then I'll tell her I want to stay with you.' She stood. 'I'm going back in one more time.' As far as the ten-year-old was concerned, her future was settled. Eddie watched her go, mentally cursing Laura.

Alice was confused, lost and insecure. Who wouldn't be feeling lost living with Laura? But there was no way Laura would allow Alice to stay with him. And was he ready or capable of taking on the care of a stepdaughter approaching puberty? Alice had been tricky at times, but he had believed it was because of Laura's influence and he felt reluctant to put his foot down. There was always the fact that she wasn't his child, and Laura was forever pointing that out. Alice's father lived in Europe. He had no interest in her and didn't give them any financial support. Eddie had never delved too deeply into the relationship; he'd embraced Laura and Alice was part of the package.

In Sydney he wouldn't have contemplated taking on the care of a young girl. But here he would have the support of all the women in the area. So many of the men Eddie had met here – with their earrings, ponytails, and gentle drifting nature and vague goals – were not aggressively masculine. Maybe this was the time to . . . how had someone described it? Explore his feminine side. He couldn't help laughing at himself. What he really wanted, eventually, was to be in love. To share his life with someone who loved him, desired him, thought he was smart and funny and made him laugh. Someone to have fun with. Life seemed a little short on fun these days. And, he had now learned, he needed someone with a creative, intellectual streak who understood and supported his work, work that demanded creativity and some serious thinking. But no matter what, the issue of Alice's future would have to be addressed.

Andrew put on his designer sunglasses as the plane came to a halt at the Brisbane international terminal. From his first-class window he could see the sun bouncing off the tarmac.

At the baggage carousel, he barely had to wait a minute before his expensive leather bag with its priority tag appeared, and he was through customs and immigration in no time. He hoped she'd be there and he didn't have to wait. The past week in Bangkok had been hectic.

He saw Letitia waving from outside the

arrivals, her car illegally parked at the entrance. 'Good one. I was hoping I wouldn't have to walk through the boiling carpark.' He slid into the passenger seat. 'So where are we going?'

'There's a meeting at the Marriott in Surfers then we're taking two of them back down to The Bay,' she replied. 'You got all the documents I sent up? Your wife didn't even read them. No problems there.'

'Holly trusts me.'

She glanced at him, arching her eyebrows and smiling faintly. 'More fool her. I wouldn't.'

'I bet you will later in bed,' he retorted with a smirk.

'Probably. God knows why.'

'Simple, darling. We're made for each other,' Andrew said, grinning. 'We know exactly what the world is all about these days – grabbing life by both hands and having a ball, consolidating our future as winners in the new economic era.'

They kissed briefly then Letitia pouted. 'At least I'm right across your version of grabbing life by the balls.' And as Andrew laughed she fell silent, concentrating on manoeuvring her way out of the parking lot.

She liked sex, particularly with Andrew. However, her legal training and personal struggle after her alcoholic father died had made it difficult to readily accept the obvious gap between the new generation of rich go-getters and the fast-growing army of poor – the losers, to her mind. There were issues of morality that bothered her in her more serious moments. She often wondered just how her father, about whom she knew so little, would have handled such challenges in his legal practice. Nevertheless, some glittering prizes certainly looked as if they were up for grabs in The Bay, and the temptation – and risks – were irresistible.

Chapter Seven

Twofold Bay, June 11th, 1899

I am most relieved to record my news after many weeks absence from this task. We are all well rested and enjoying time ashore as the Lady Richmond *is repaired and refitted after so long at sea. She is a faithful and sturdy ship but I am reluctant to spend such a long time at sea in future. Especially since the recent birth of our second son, Erik. How different to give birth to my child ashore! And with family to care for us and admire our second blue-eyed boy. Lars is exceedingly pleased with our lad, and Sven is quite intrigued with his baby brother.*

I have been much preoccupied with the arrival of our owner, Captain Richmond. Like many of the Yankee whalemen, he is a dashing fellow, most gregarious and humorous. He has big plans to extend our fleet and set up new stations. He talks after supper most expansively of branching into other ventures on the northern coast. Privately Lars is fretful his master could turn out to be another Mr Ben Boyd!

But Lars has given his undertaking to manage the new whaling station. So we are moving from the south-east of New South Wales to the north-eastern tip; to a place called Beacon Bay, which is far less developed than here. At last it will be a long arrangement and for me the most encouraging news is that we are to build a large and comfortable company house to be our own for some years to come. To have rooms to spare and a kitchen of one's own, and the opportunity to sew curtains is a dream come true at last. Though how we are going to furnish a large and comfortable abode after so long at sea remains a small mystery to me. Lars and Captain Richmond promise me it will be a splendidly warm and peaceful setting in which to raise my sons.

I thank and trust in the Lord.

Hannah Nilsen

It was like being at sea – disorientating and isolated. Bonnie felt cast adrift from all that was familiar, and yet, as she settled into life at the Dolphin Centre, she came to like the routine, the minutiae of each day. There had been times of great darkness when she felt that the waves of depression, insecurity and shaky ill health were going to swamp her. But as her body adjusted and the toxins were flushed from her system – despite the humiliating experience of colonic irrigation – her spirits lifted. The days of doubt and queasiness had left and she felt safe, the seas were calm and she was steaming towards a distant port that would hopefully be her final destination.

For too long Bonnie had been stuck in one place and then shipwrecked on a wild isle with frantic companions. What had seemed a fun, mad ride had spiralled into a crazy netherworld. She was living out an adolescence she'd never had. She had gone from nicely brought-up schoolgirl, to proper young woman, to mature and sensible twenty-something bride. There had never been time to cut loose, laugh too much, experiment, or play hard with happy girlfriends. She was the responsible wife and mother, straight from the pages of a 1960s women's magazine. That was until her husband ran off with his secretary.

Then, over forty, she discovered drugs, booze, imprudent sex, and silly escapades with foolish people half her age who didn't seem to care what happened to her. Greg, her young boyfriend, had not been to visit. It was hurtful, but it made it easier for her to think about starting afresh. She had learned at the Dolphin Centre that she'd been dealing with childhood baggage, living out repressed rage at parental negligence, at emotional abandonment. Money had been the answer to any crisis or ruffle in their daily existence – an unsatisfactory substitute for the affection she craved.

Her cool, elegant mother had held her daughter at arm's length, not wanting Bonnie to move into her personal space and raise an emotion, or crumple her immaculate dress. Her remote, demanding father had been hard to please. Bonnie felt she never measured up in her parents' eyes, despite over-achieving in all she did. She had made the right marriage, had her own beautiful daughter and saw her life beginning to mirror that of her parents. Except for the divorce she hadn't seen coming.

It had been painful dealing with all this. But now she saw that her perceived shortcomings were only in her own eyes. She could approve of herself and now start looking after her real needs. And as she'd dealt with the emotional side of her life, so too had her body responded to the healthy food, nutritional supplements, early morning walks and yoga. Between one-on-one therapy sessions there had been group sharings that made her problems seem minuscule. At first she thought she'd never be able to bare her soul in front of others, pummel a cushion and cry, reach out and wrap her arms around a stranger. In the visualisation at the end of each stretching and yoga class, Cheyne asked them to imagine they were dolphins. The most joyous, carefree, playful yet strong and intelligent creatures in the ocean. They were in an environment that took them back to the womb, suspended in safe warm water, close to mother's heartbeat.

When Bonnie swam in the pool at the centre she felt gloriously free and fit. Now she wanted to feel the same in the sea. The episode at the beach when Amber had rescued her seemed part of another life. A new life was beginning and she hoped she was strong enough to hang on to what she'd found here. This was merely the first step in a long journey. By being here she had acknowledged her problem and felt pride in dealing with it. She chose to forget it had not been her choice to come to the centre.

She had talked frankly with her therapist and agreed that she and Erica should develop a more stable environment. She would be more involved in Erica's life and give her shop more attention. As it was the Beach Hut wasn't worthy of her taste and resources, Bonnie decided. She'd upgrade. Ideas were beginning to swirl in her head. This was all positive. She couldn't imagine that she could go backwards, not now, despite the constant gentle advice that it would be so much harder 'outside'. She was being 'armed for re-entry', as Cheyne put it. Several people at the centre were returnees who'd slipped and been lured back to their old destructive lifestyles. Bonnie was determined the change she felt in herself was going to be permanent. God, how glad she was she'd ended up in The Bay, and that there were people like Amber around. She hoped Erica was spending time with her.

Amber, however, had little time to spare for playing mothering roles. Since taking over the

Beach Hut as caretaker-manager she had greatly increased her turnover of beauty products. Word of mouth recommendation helped, and the passing trade of shoppers attracted to the Beach Hut made extra demands. The Hut was busier than it had ever been, but Amber soon learned that Bonnie had not been smart in her choice of stock. Some was a waste of space and cash. A monster sale would have to be held as soon as Bonnie was capable of taking over again. The teenage set related well to Amber, and that proved good for business. Matty and her friends often called by on their strolls through town after school.

Of all the shops, Matty enjoyed spending time at The Teepee with Billy. She was fascinated by hair-styling and make-up techniques. Billy had grown used to her dropping by and politely asking if she could watch him cut and colour for a while. One day Matty was surprised when he asked how she was coping with homework, of all things.

'Okay, no worries. Some assignments are easy, some are hard. That's life.'

'True enough. And this is relaxation time, a break from the grind, eh? How about making it pay as well?'

Matty was puzzled. 'What do you mean? Do something . . . for you?'

'Yeah, like grabbing a broom, sorting out the magazines the customers thumb through, they can get grotty after a while. Maybe tidy up what passes as my office.' He pointed over his shoulder to a screened-off corner of the shop.

'You mean real work and pay, like money?'

'Like money. But not much.' He grinned at her, then at his client in the mirror. 'Said too much now, haven't I?'

'Stop it, Billy,' retaliated Matty with good humour. 'That'd be great. Saturday morning only though.'

'Done,' he said. 'We'll sort out the details next Saturday. By the way, where's your pal?' He had noticed that Erica seemed to have stopped hanging out around town with Matty since her mother had gone to the Dolphin Centre.

Matty looked uneasy and glanced at the woman wrapped in the plastic cape whose head was covered in silver foil strips. She was reading a magazine and paying no attention. 'I don't know where she is. She hasn't been at school and she's not at the house.' Once or twice Matty had seen Erica playing her guitar alone at the beach or in the park, but she did not intrude.

Billy stopped what he was doing. 'That's a worry. Has Amber heard anything? Doesn't the school ask where she is?'

'I thought she might be visiting her mum. She's coming home soon.'

'Well that's good. Mmm, would you excuse me for a tick?' he said to the woman in the chair. 'Matty, why don't you mind the phone, take any appointments if someone calls. I'll only be two minutes.'

He hurried down the arcade to the Beach Hut. 'Amber, Erica seems to have gone missing. Do you think we should do something about it?'

'Matty mumbled something but she seemed a bit vague when I asked,' she replied. 'I think they've had a parting of the ways. Erica's been hanging out with those space cadets from the house.'

'I hear Bonnie is due to come out of the retreat joint soon. What's the score? A bit soon, isn't it?'

'I rang the Dolphin Centre this morning and they said someone could pick her up on Saturday. They were keen that she had some friends around to support her. The drop-off rate is pretty high if you go back into the same situation.' Amber shrugged. 'I offered to take Erica with me when I go to get her, so she knows that much. Maybe I should talk to Greg, Bonnie's boyfriend, see what he knows.'

'Better you than me. More your age group,' said Billy.

'Ha! I don't have anything in common with him,' Amber said quickly. 'But I'll check him out tonight on the way home.'

The house was a mess. Takeaway food containers littered the main room and music thudded down the hallway. The hippy, Indian-inspired decor of silk cushions, mirrored Rajasthan throws, saris draped at the windows, and a brass vase with wilted flowers looked seedy and neglected. The place had not been cleaned in weeks, and the stale odour of pot and alcohol hung heavily. Amber waited as a vague young girl went to find Greg.

He emerged from a bedroom looking sleepy and dishevelled. 'Hey, what's up?'

'I'm a friend of Bonnie's. We're a bit concerned, we can't find Erica.'

'What's it to you?'

'Like I said, I'm a friend. I would have thought you'd show some concern for Erica.' She looked pointedly around the room.

'Man, don't hassle. Erica is cool. She'll be back when Bonnie rolls in.'

'Back? Where is she?'

'She's turned into quite the music lover.'

Amber didn't like the smirk on Greg's face. 'Meaning?'

'Hey, come along. There's a doof happening, a big one. The Vibe Tribe, Goa Trance. Starts tonight. People coming from everywhere. You up for it?' He was awake enough now to take in Amber's beauty.

She tried to sound nonchalant. Dance parties and especially these drug and techno music raves in secret locations were definitely not her scene. There'd been occasional stoushes with the police and council and she knew how serious the rave scene was in cities. Several teenagers had died at these all-night parties from drug overdoses and accidents. This would be a bad scene for someone as impressionable as Erica. 'Yeah, I've been to a few. So where's it happening?'

'At the Rocks. Few miles in, real wild west with a gorge into it so lookouts can delay any unwanted company. There's a big natural amphitheatre in there, sound'll be amazing. People have been holed up in some of the caves for days. Everyone else is packed into the bowl. You gotta hike in. Wanna come with us?'

'I'll get there. Thanks for the tip.'

'Any time, babe.' He gave her a parting leer that was an invitation.

Amber couldn't understand how Bonnie had existed in this dreadful house with these slimy people. She drove quickly to check out the scene with Kimberley.

'God, what a nightmare,' Kimberley exclaimed after hearing the rundown. 'What are we going to do? How do we get Erica out? I've never been to the Rocks, too spooky for me. Always makes me think of Hanging Rock. Do you think the police will close it down?'

'I suppose so, eventually. But there are no neighbours to complain about the noise out there, and it seems like they have things well organised. The only thing we can do is go there and look for her.'

'What! There'll be thousands of drunk, doped fluoro ferals.'

'I know, but have you got a better idea?' Amber was a little shocked that Kimberley wasn't more supportive. Her own daughter could be swept up in this scene.

Kimberley pulled a packet of cigarettes out of the kitchen drawer. 'Bring your coffee outside. This calls for a smoke.'

They sat in green plastic garden chairs, Kimberley dragging on her cigarette and Amber sipping the last of her coffee. 'I'd go with you, but frankly, I don't think I could stand it. Mac reckons that whole Rocks area is haunted. I mean, those weird-shaped bald rocks are so prehistoric. But you can't go on your own. Maybe she'll be okay. I mean, I did some pretty wild things when I was fifteen.'

'The drugs then weren't like what's around today. E-ing on Ecstasy is only part of it. There's all kinds of speed, MDA, ketamine; I mean stuff that can blow your mind out of your body.'

'How do you know all this?'

Amber gave a small shrug. 'A doctor friend I knew. He was treating my mother for a while.'

'How is your mum?' Kimberley trod carefully knowing Amber rarely talked about her family life.

'Hanging in there. So, are you going to tell me Erica isn't going to drop something? Do you think we should talk to Matty?' Amber asked. 'She might know something.'

Matty's eyes widened in shock as Kimberley and Amber told her about Erica. 'A doof party? At the Rocks? That's freaky. Who's she with?'

'Good question. We think those flaky ferals from the house. I knew I should have insisted she stay with us the whole time. I feel so responsible,' Kimberley said.

'Don't, Mum,' said Matty quickly. 'Erica is different from my other friends. She needs her freedom. That's why I hang out with her. Someone has to keep an eye on her.'

Kimberley looked at her daughter with some pride. 'Erica is a troubled soul. I'm glad you're being such a good friend.'

'So, Matty, what do you think? Is Erica going to get into the drugs at this doof, or is she there for the thrill of it and the music?' Amber asked.

'She'll try anything that's offered. She has tried stuff before, not with me,' she hastily added to reassure her mother. 'But up there at a rave with those joes . . . well, you know it would be hard to resist, I reckon.'

'Okay then. I'd better see if I can find her,' said Amber with more assurance than she felt.

'Can I come? Maybe I might be able to find her,' said Matty eagerly.

'No way. I hate the thought of that creepy place and I certainly don't want you there. And Amber, I don't think you should go alone either,' said Kimberley.

'So what are we going to do?' said Amber. 'For Bonnie's sake we have to do something.'

'Eddie. He's strong, trustworthy, and I think he'll be interested. He's met Erica at the markets and he knows Bonnie.' Kimberley headed inside to phone him.

'Are we ready for our little adventure?' Eddie said, grinning as Amber opened the car door.

'I've been having one of those girlie panics of what to wear. I feel like such an interloper.'

Eddie looked at her tight black jeans, loose

black sweatshirt and her auburn curls tied back in a dark green ribbon. She looked very young, barely out of her teens. 'Got comfy shoes on? Could be a very long night, these things don't get going till after midnight.'

'Oh, you've been to many?'

'No, I jumped on the net and did some research. I plan to shoot what I can, but I'll have to rely on the natural light. Don't want to draw attention to us with a camera light.'

'So who goes to these doofs?' Amber asked as they drove out to the highway. 'Seeing as you've done some research.'

'Doofs are a bit different here from the teenage raves overseas. They seem to attract a more politically aware, activist, anti-materialism crowd. They're not a totally druggy thing. Lots come for the dancing and the music, but it's pretty powerful music, almost a drug in itself.'

'I'm amazed they can get these things together in the middle of nowhere and keep it so quiet.'

'I think quiet it ain't,' said Eddie. 'But we're going to find out.'

The road began to rise, rainforest giving way to small farms, then scrubland bordered by steep cliffs. On the peaks of the cliffs were massive granite balls balanced atop each other, so precarious it seemed a breath would dislodge them. Gradually the road narrowed and great rock formations closed in on either side. Amber found herself holding her breath as she gazed up at the weird sentinels silhouetted against the starry sky.

They had been driving in silence for a while when Eddie pointed ahead to the glow of lights. They were passing through a rough narrow gorge, surrounded by sheer rocky cliffs; it was as if they were driving through a tunnel. Amber slipped down in her seat to peer up at the tops of the rocks. 'There are people up there.'

'Sentries. This old bomb of a car won't seem suspicious.'

Around a bend they were suddenly confronted by a makeshift roadblock. Half a dozen people were milling around with torches and gas lights shone at the barrier. They were collecting money and issuing instructions. Ahead of them a stream of cars was slowly moving into a huge field. Amber could hear and feel the muffled throb of music.

Eddie hit the brakes and reversed. The road was too narrow to easily do a U-turn but he swung the car around, and for a moment Amber thought he was heading straight into the rocks. But he'd spotted a space between large boulders, just wide enough to park in.

'This way we can get out easily if we have to. It's going to be mayhem in there with all the cars and vans.'

They got their backpacks, his camera bag and two blankets and walked up to the barricade where a man in a long, well-worn trenchcoat was taking the entry money. In the distance they could see hundreds of cars parked in a field and a line of others snaking into it.

'Follow the ropes to the ampitheatre, to the right,' the man said, then he turned his attention to a van jammed with people that pulled in behind them. Amber and Eddie set off to where white ropes ran from the field through the split in the rocks, and joined scores of people tramping from the parking area.

'Why were some of those people at the road-block wearing goggles?' whispered Amber.

'Night vision glasses. They probably have tele-scopic ones on the ridge tops . . . easy to check out people arriving.'

Temporary power lines were looped above their heads with the occasional weak lamp hang-ing from them. It was darker once they reached the ropes and Eddie went ahead, glancing back at Amber. 'There's a bit of a climb, watch your feet in case there are small loose rocks. Do you want the torch?'

'No. It's okay, I'll follow you.' She was shout-ing but her words were ripped away by the torrent of noise that came from behind the cliff. On a rough patch of ground Eddie reached back to offer his hand which Amber grasped like a nervous child. He was ten years her senior and she felt safe with him.

When they reached the top, Eddie and Amber both gasped in amazement. They were at the edge of a huge bowl topped with massive rocks like giant marbles. Spotlights waved eerily across the swaying, bouncing crowd in front of a stage where banks of sound equipment flashed and screamed, the sound rocketing off the ancient rock walls. Amber shuddered as she felt the sound waves hit her. The energy from the dancing crowd was equally forceful and she grabbed Eddie's arm. 'This is *unreal*.'

'Worshippers before the altar of sound,' Eddie shouted back and grinned. Putting his mouth close to her ear, he said, 'I'm going to take a shot from up here. Whatever happens, don't move too far from me, I'd never find you in all that.'

'There's no way we're going to find Erica. It's impossible!' she shouted.

'We can try.' He pulled out the video camera and stood to one side as a laughing group pushed past in their personal cloud of dope.

He concentrated on getting some wide shots, then grabbed Amber's hand. 'Let's head towards the stage. I want to see what kind of power they have. It's either massive generators or they've illegally plugged into the power grid.'

'If we get separated, let's meet at the right-hand side of the stage, if we can get there,' Amber suggested. She could see the crowd moshing right up to the stage.

They flung themselves into the thick of it and Amber found she was being swept along in the frenetic, excited, happy crowd. She glanced at a couple who were chanting, 'Doof, doof, dance, dance.' The girl swung around and bumped into her. 'Dance your heart out.'

'Great, eh?' said Amber, and felt her body responding to the beat.

The girl threw back her head. 'I'm tripping, it's *grrreat!*'

The bass speakers thumped out the hard-core rhythm as the techno tribes gathered in the amphitheatre screamed, 'Faster . . . faster . . .'

Eddie focused his camera on the glazed, ecstatic faces lit by the roving spotlights. Amber, who'd been moving to the half beat suddenly felt breathless, as if she might spin away out of control and take off like a top.

'Slow down,' he said. 'Don't go with it, that's getting over 160 beats a minute. The repetition is like a trance!'

Amber shook herself, imagining what it must be like if you were stoned or drunk or tripping out. The sound was overwhelming, blanketing, dictating. The euphoria dissipated and she felt fearful. How easy it would be to lose control here. If Erica was in this . . . She didn't want to think about it. But the thought brought her back to the reason they were there.

Eddie lowered his camera. 'Let's get through this mob.'

They were swept along among the seething, swaying, bouncing, jumping, head shaking, shouting mass of bodies. Amber clung to her bag and the blankets, scanning faces looking for Erica. It was too crowded for Eddie to lift the camera to his eye. People shoved between them, heads and arms swinging. In seconds Amber was pushed into the tide in the opposite direction. Eddie tried to elbow his way towards her but another group was blocking his path.

Amber was scared. This was not fun. God, why was she doing this? Bonnie better get herself together and start looking out for her daughter. But Amber feared that a vulnerable, lonely girl like Erica could easily gravitate to a world where drugs made you feel good, appeared to solve problems and made you part of a group. It was a world where all that mattered was the next trip, the next hit.

Erica curled her body tightly into a ball. She was a cat. A bear. A baby. She'd been flying. She'd immersed her whole body in the music. She'd been so happy. What was happening? Her skin felt like it was burning, thin and dry as paper. She was shivering. All the colours had gone, and now she was alone. Where was Greg? He'd taken her stash, everything. She did remember that. How was she going to get away from here? Her body was bruised, abused. She didn't remember much about the sex. Greg had given her pills and torn her clothes. But as the waves of euphoria and then a strange drowsiness overcame her, she didn't care about her body, the pain, the intrusion. Everything was in slow motion like it was happening to someone else and she was looking down from far above, watching the rape of a young girl in a smoky cave. Even the music below seemed far away. Maybe they'll come back and bring more Es. Anything. She didn't want to be here. She wanted to feel as wildly happy and wonderful as she had . . . When? How long ago? But she was feeling sick, she was going to throw up. She was so thirsty. So dry.

At the back of the stage Amber found a small chill-out tent. Inside several people were lying on sleeping bags and camp beds, with a woman watching them, although she didn't look like anyone medical. She ducked back out and to her relief saw Eddie, filming a young unconscious man being carried into the tent.

'No sign of her?' he asked.

'Nothing. It's impossible. I think I want to get out of here.'

'We've given it our best shot. My head is banging. Keep close, I reckon we can get out over the back.' He headed to where a wall of hessian was pinned to frames, wiggled underneath the gap at the base and helped Amber through.

The mysterious hills rose around them, a few fires and lights dotted at the base. 'People must be camped up in the caves,' Eddie said.

As they walked around the edge of the arena, a chanting group staggered from the caves, heading back into the endlessly dancing crowd. 'There's Greg, Bonnie's boyfriend,' Amber said. 'He told me about tonight; said Erica was coming.'

'He'll know something about her then.' Eddie grabbed Greg by the arm.

'Hey man, what the hell –' Greg spun around, and Eddie immediately saw that he was drunk, stoned or both.

'Greg, hey, we're looking for Erica. Did she come with you?'

Greg swayed, clicking his fingers and looked blankly at Eddie. Amber moved closer.

'Hi, Greg, it's Amber, Bonnie's friend.'

Whether it was recognition of Amber or just the fact she was a pretty young woman, he lurched at her. 'Gorgeous baby, let's dance.'

Eddie pulled Amber from Greg's arms. 'Erica, man, where is she?'

Greg turned away. 'Let's go –'

'Please, Greg, where is Erica?' Amber shouted.

One of the other men with Greg looked at Amber and laughed. 'She's fucked, man. Really fucked.' The group turned the corner of the hessian wall and disappeared.

Eddie took Amber's arm. 'Let's go.'

They didn't speak much until they were driving away. It was 3 am.

'Do you want to go to Bonnie's house and wait for Erica? Or grab a few hours sleep?' Eddie asked.

'I'll go home.'

He glanced at Amber's worried face in the glow from the dashboard lights. 'Why did you do this, Amber? What is Bonnie to you? You really put yourself on the line for Erica.'

'I had no idea what we were getting into. Thanks for coming along, Eddie.' Amber paused. 'I suppose I owe you an answer. I can't help thinking if someone had been around to help my mother she might not be the mess she is –'

'You don't have to tell me,' interjected Eddie.

'Maybe I should. I never tell people anything really personal. I suppose that's why I've never had intimate friends. I don't like people getting too close to me.'

'Bit hard in The Bay where everyone thinks they know everyone else's business,' he said quietly. 'But you could have a lot of support and good friends if you wanted it.'

Amber spoke in a low voice. 'I grew up here but Mum left for Sydney after my dad died. I went to uni and she tried to make a new life for herself. But it didn't work out, she got really depressed and I only saw her for quick visits, it was too difficult. So I didn't know until she was hospitalised that she'd become addicted to painkillers and a stack of prescribed medicines. She was a chemist junkie . . . had accounts and doctors all over the city. I brought her back here to our old farm to try and get her better. She kept trying to suicide and she's recovering from breast cancer. She is always so depressed. It makes me feel the same to be with her. And that makes me feel guilty.'

'Jesus, Amber, that's tragic.' It explained a lot to Eddie. How sometimes she had seemed far older than her years, her drive to succeed in her business, her insistence on natural healthy products without chemicals, her caring attitude towards others. 'No other family?'

'Mum's sister is interstate. Dad didn't have much family. They were in the timber business here and moved away when forestry started losing money. They all blamed the greenies. They moved down the south coast.'

'And where do you stand on the logging issue? You were scarcely born when the fight to save the Big Scrub started.'

She almost smiled. 'It wasn't easy being the timbercutter's daughter. I stayed in Sydney till I couldn't stand it any more and figured it'd be better for Mum up here, and that I could get my business going here rather than in the city.'

'Yeah, there's a lot more awareness and sympathy to eco-health and holistic beauty up here. Amber, you're pretty special. I think you'll win out and be a big success,' said Eddie kindly.

'Oh, I intend to be.' Amber spoke resolutely, without hesitation.

Mitchell took off his hat, ran his fingers through his hair and went to wash his hands as Holly poured them cold drinks. They had settled into a routine of lunching together on the verandah, and while it was a simple meal Holly found herself putting a lot of thought into it. Mitch sometimes brought fresh crabs or fish a mate had caught or unusual fruit and vegetables from another friend's bush food garden. Holly had become very keen on finger limes and planted one in the garden.

The renovations were still at what she called the messy stage, but she could see that Mitch and the boys had things under control. Over lunch they caught up on everything from world events to

Bay gossip and eventual dreams. They didn't talk about their private lives – not that they avoided it, but their respective families didn't seem part of this small world of the old house, the garden and the view from Tiny Bay out to sea.

Holly passed the bread and cheese as Mitchell turned his head. 'That sounded like a car. The others went for a surf, are you expecting anyone?'

'No. Could be Lynn or Stolle. Nola was sending someone up with paint colours – specially blended.' Holly rose and went into the house as a figure came through the open front door.

'Andrew! What a surprise. Oh darling, how lovely!' Her reaction was instantly tempered by faint annoyance. 'Why didn't you tell me you were coming? I could have picked you up.' She lifted her cheek for his perfunctory kiss. 'You're just in time for lunch. Come and meet Mitchell.'

'Let me change and get comfortable.' Andrew headed for the annexe glancing out at the verandah. 'My, that looks cosy. Keeping the hired help happy?'

'Andrew, he's the builder and . . .' She hesitated to say 'designer' to her esteemed architect husband. 'And he and his workers are doing a fantastic job. I'll show you around and you can see for yourself. Here, I'll set you a place.'

'Don't worry, I've eaten. I had a meeting on the Gold Coast and drove down. Any wine?'

'No. But I can chill some.'

'Don't bother. I'll have coffee.'

Andrew and Mitchell shook hands and Holly

fled to make the coffee. When she returned Andrew was sitting forward listening intently to Mitchell. They were discussing some land. Andrew leaned back in his chair and glanced at Holly, seeming to change the subject. 'Anyway, I have my hands full with my Asia project. I'll let Holly be the first in the family to experiment with property development in The Bay.'

'Richmond House is scarcely development. It's restoration. Development is the last thing we want. Seems quite enough going on from what I hear.' Holly spoke lightly.

'Really. You're keeping up with local issues?' asked Andrew.

'I am. I've become really involved in the local community. I've made some lovely friends. And I told you about Nola Florens. She's being so kind.'

'God, she must be a hundred years old. You're not using any of the old leftovers she offered, are you?'

Mitchell shifted uncomfortably. 'Some of the stuff I saw is pretty classic; suits this place.'

'Well, Holly always had a penchant for the olde worlde. My taste tends to minimalist. Contemporary. I suppose old fashioned suits the B & B ethos,' Andrew said. 'I believe the appeal of The Bay will be for modern, up-market design. Folksy has had its day here, I'd say.'

Mitchell spoke quietly but his voice was tense. 'You mean massive resort complexes like you're building in Asia? Five star, Gold Coast style?'

'I'm relaxed about all of that,' said Andrew

easily. 'The Gold Coast criticism is passé. When you look at what has been built in Bali, Gulf of Thailand, Mauritius, the Caribbean, The Bay will be begging for the same.'

Mitchell glanced at Holly who kept her eyes down, refilling coffee cups, not wanting to take sides. He decided to plunge ahead. 'As individual structures, stylistically, those resorts are spectacular, in stunning locations. Unfortunately, our infrastructure won't support such large developments here. And we fought very hard to overturn a council hell-bent on high rise. Three storeys is our limit. The Bay can't swallow too many people. Water, sewerage, power; not up to it. This is a small country town –'

Andrew cut in. 'Yeah, well I've heard that before. Ask the people of Pattaya, Chiang-Mai, Ubud, what they think of all the new jobs, new money where there were once so few opportunities –'

'Goodness me, how did we get onto this?' broke in Holly with a tight smile. 'The Bay isn't going to allow a huge resort complex, I hope.' She gathered up the plates, signalling the end of lunch.

Andrew pushed his cup away. 'Nothing stays the way it was, dear heart. Isn't that right, Mitchell? As a builder you should know – things get torn down and replaced. There is always a thirst for the new. Only the old appreciate the old; the money goes where the new, the clean, the flash, the plush, the fun is. And the big demand is from the baby boomers.' Andrew rose. 'Nice to meet you. I'm going for a swim. Then I have to meet a couple of business people downtown. Make a reservation somewhere for dinner, Holly.'

'Am I invited?' She was smiling but her eyes were icy.

'Certainly. Ask one of your new girlfriends along if you like. I'll be talking business.' He nodded at Mitchell and went indoors.

'Sounds like a fun night. I'd better get back to work.' Mitchell left more hurriedly than normal. Their companionship of clearing the dishes was abandoned. He decided to go and collect some window fittings rather than stay at the house. He thought Andrew was arrogant, superficial, and money oriented.

Andrew walked down to the beach, deciding Mitchell was homespun, unsophisticated, idealistic and impractical.

Holly was irritated at Andrew and also confused about Mitchell's low-key hostility. What different men they were. They were both operating in a similar world – that of construction, deconstruction, design and creating personal space. Yet both were looking at that world from totally different viewpoints.

Although the telephone conversations with Andrew had become shorter and shorter as their daily interests diverged, Holly was now surprised and confused at the complexity of her feelings towards him. It was as if the unexpected visit and the awkward lunch had been a catalyst, bringing to the sharp edge of her consciousness feelings that had been buried for a long time. She had always agreed with her husband on practically everything of any consequence. He made the decisions, she endorsed them. He expressed the opinions, she adopted them. It was comfortable, until recently.

They had both realised that buying into The Bay was the beginning of a new chapter in their relationship. Holly was certainly surprised at how it was turning out. After lunch, she sat down, looked out to sea and quietly analysed the confusion of her emotions. She was now comfortable disagreeing with what Andrew said, and if necessary, saying so in front of him. It was a new feeling of freedom and power; a very heady feeling.

After his swim Andrew drove into town for his meeting. Holly thought it might be nice to drive in together but Andrew had left before she could suggest it. She made a reservation at Vincent's, an expensive restaurant overlooking Mighty Beach. Then she tried to think who she could invite. Lynn and Stolle wouldn't work, Mitchell and his wife were out after the experience at lunch. Billy was charming, though she hadn't met his wife; might be hard for them to get a babysitter at short notice. Nola rarely went out in the evenings and, despite Andrew's disparaging remarks, she was entertaining. A dose of the Grand Dame could be fun. And maybe someone else. Handsome and charming Eddie; he'd fit in anywhere. Holly decided to ask Nola and Eddie.

'Sounds fine. I have invited two local businessmen and they're bringing two friends along. Did you book somewhere?' Andrew poured himself a scotch and soda.

'Yes, Vincent's at eight.'

Andrew sipped his drink as he wandered around the house eyeing Mitchell's work. He made no comment but went through every room and ended up on the widow's walk to watch the sunset.

Holly took a leisurely shower, and spent time putting on her make-up and fixing her hair. It was getting late and she wondered where Andrew was as he hadn't dressed. She turned off the radio in the bedroom and went through to the sitting room expecting to find him in front of the TV watching the early news. She turned on some lights and stepped outside.

'Holly, is that you? Get the hell up here!'

Curly began barking and Holly went into the garden and looked up. Andrew was on the widow's walk. 'What's the problem?'

'I'm locked out, I can't get down. Come and open the infernal door.'

Holly rushed inside and up to the attic. She paused in the little bedroom. There was that feeling again. She glanced around. An old lace curtain fluttered at the small dormer window. Funny, she thought it was closed. Andrew must have opened it. The narrow bed was rumpled, cushions that had been stacked on an old box were scattered on the floor. She took all this in quickly, at the same time noticing that a photo in an old-fashioned walnut frame hanging on the wall was tilted.

Without thinking she reached out and straightened it. The stern-faced man and his bride in her large bonnet stared back at her.

'Come on, Holly, where are you?' The doorknob rattled.

She went to the door and looked at the brass key in the lock. She turned it and Andrew hurried angrily into the room. 'Get the builder to change that lock first thing tomorrow!' He strode from the room without a backward glance.

Holly stared at the lock then gave a puzzled look around the room. 'Why did you do that?' she asked softly.

Andrew and Holly were the first to arrive at the restaurant. Ray, the owner, came immediately to their table. Holly was surprised he seemed to know Andrew but then he turned to her. 'I'm told Nola Florens is coming tonight, that's great.'

'Oh, how do you know?' she asked. She hadn't mentioned names when she made the reservation.

'She rang to find out what we were serving tonight, if we had her favourite wine and a comfortable chair.' He pointed at the chair with arms and a cushion at one end of the table.

Holly laughed, Andrew looked annoyed and then everyone arrived at once.

Holly was grateful at the fuss Nola created as she was escorted through the restaurant, where it seemed most of the other guests smiled and nodded at her. She made her stately way across the room as Andrew's two business friends came to the table and were introduced to Holly, who was stunned to see they were accompanied by Letitia, the solicitor, and Laura.

Nola swiftly summed up the situation and announced to all, 'Darling Eddie is parking the Daimler. Laura, how lovely that you and your former husband can be sociable. So very civilised, don't you think?' She beamed around the table as Ray settled her in her chair.

Holly threw Laura an apologetic look but she gave a small airy wave of her fingertips and glanced at the man beside her with a slight lift of the eyebrow. Holly relaxed but then excused herself and rushed to the entrance to warn Eddie.

He bounded up the steps and she gave him a quick kiss, explaining that Laura was in their party.

'Oh, God. Never mind, at least there are a few of us. I'll tell them all about my experiences last night at the doof. Is she with the Gold Coast zillionaire?'

'He looks it, though I thought Andrew said he was a local.' She linked her arm through his as they walked through the restaurant, causing Laura and Andrew to give them a hard look which pleased Holly.

Nola Florens was in fine form – name dropping, witty, shamelessly flirting, causing much hilarity with her outrageous anecdotes. Holly could see Andrew was entranced with her. For her part, Holly had been politely attentive to the two men Andrew had introduced as 'management consultants' but quickly lost interest. Next to her Laura was pouring out her confusion over her daughter Alice.

'I just don't know whether to uproot her and take her with me to Surfers Paradise, or leave her with Eddie. I mean, even though he's not her biological father, he is wonderful with her. And Alice is saying she wants to stay up at the farm. She couldn't wait to move to the beach when I suggested it, however.'

Before Holly could answer, Scotty, the maitre d', came and whispered in Eddie's ear and he leapt to his feet, his face ashen. Laura half rose out of her chair. 'Eddie, what is it? Is it Alice?'

He shook his head, waving her back to her seat. 'No. It's something else. I was half expecting this.' He went to Holly and took her hand. 'I have to leave, there's been a fire out in Brigalow, at Bonnie's house. Erica is missing. Amber rang me, I'll see what I can do.'

'Oh, God, how awful –'

'Take the Daimler, darling. I'll get a cab,' said Nola quickly.

'Call me and let me know, no matter how late,' Holly said as Eddie ran from the restaurant.

Andrew called for more wine, attempting to salvage the dinner. Laura was telling the others all she knew of Bonnie and her wild teenage daughter.

Holly was deep in thought. She was back at the Goddess Night, recalling how Mac had looked at Erica so strangely and muttered something about a fire . . .

Chapter Eight

BY THE TIME EDDIE ARRIVED IN BRIGALOW THE
street was filled with fire and rescue vehicles,
ambulances and police cars. Red, blue and yellow
flashing lights gave the now inappropriately
named Pacific Street a frightening atmosphere that
attracted a large crowd of onlookers.

The old weatherboard and fibro holiday house
had rapidly become an inferno. Nearly all that
was left was a collapsed and blackened framework
and sheets of twisted corrugated-iron from the
roof. Fire hoses sprayed the still burning rem-
nants, creating a hissing and steaming finale to the
tragedy.

Eddie pushed forward to speak to a young
ambulance officer who was closing the back of the

vehicle. 'Was anyone hurt? I'm a friend of one of the residents.'

'We're looking for relatives. Two people have been taken to Lismore Base Hospital, another was flown to Brisbane,' she said. 'Can't tell you much, I'm afraid. There seemed to be quite a few people in the house.'

One of the last sections of standing framework collapsed, adding a huge shower of sparks to the spectacle. He turned back to the ambulance officer. 'Listen, was a girl brought out? About fifteen, brown hair?'

'You'll have to ask the police, I'm not allowed to give out information.' She was trying to sound official, but Eddie caught the look that flashed into her eyes.

'Her name's Erica Bitternden, her mother is in . . . hospital. If you're local you must know the Beach Hut, that's her mum's place.'

'Oh, yes. I know it.' She dropped her official approach. 'Listen, it's pretty bad. Two guys got out and raised the alarm. The rescue boys pulled two unconscious blokes from the front room – smoke inhalation.'

'And the girl?'

She glanced at Eddie's stricken face and lowered her voice. 'The young girl was flown to Royal Brisbane intensive burns unit. She's bad.'

'Any word on what caused it?'

'Candles or smoking are top of the list.'

Eddie turned away, rubbing the smoke from his eyes. God, what was he going to do now? He felt overwhelmed at the horror of the disaster and he hoped the woman was wrong. He went over to the senior of two police officers standing by their car. 'I'm a family friend of one of the people who lived here. Can I get some information?'

He waited for the formal refusal but the sergeant gave him a sympathetic look. 'I've seen you around, you're that film and television man. Who did you know in there?'

'Bonnie Bitternden's daughter, Erica. Bonnie is in the Dolphin Centre. Is there any word about Erica?'

'Sorry to have to tell you this, but yes, she's been flown to Brisbane. Don't like her chances. Do you know anyone else close to the mother? We'll have to break the news.' The veteran cop growled, 'What kind of a mother would leave her daughter in a house full of druggies, I ask you?'

Eddie was cautious about saying too much but felt the police should be given some information. 'From what I hear, Erica got swayed by some of the people in the house. They took her to that doof last night.'

'Those bloody events are a public menace. Do you want us to tell the mother? Or do you know her well enough to break the news to her?'

'Thanks. It would be better coming from friends. I'll let her know and we'll get back in touch with you later tonight.' Eddie knew it would be a dreadful task for Kimberley and Amber, but he would offer to drive them to Brisbane after seeing

Bonnie. He thanked the sergeant and headed back to his car.

'Eddie!'

Tina came running up to him, looking concerned. She was wearing overalls and boots and carried a hard hat. 'What are you doing here?'

'I could ask you the same thing,' he managed wanly.

'I'm on duty, volunteer rescue service. God, you didn't know anyone who was in that mess, did you?'

'A young girl, school friend of friends.'

'Oh, no. That's the kid they've flown to Brisbane. Can I help in some way? I'm about to leave.'

'Someone has to tell Bonnie, her mother. She's at the Dolphin Centre. I was thinking of asking Kimberley Dorne. Erica was staying with them on weekends.'

Tina walked beside him. 'Too bad it wasn't all the time. What shape is the mother in?'

'Bonnie has been doing well, apparently. Amber said she's due to come out.'

'I hope she can handle this one. It's a biggie.' Eddie looked confused so Tina went on, 'Do you want me to come with you? Sometimes an outsider can help in these situations.'

'Would you? I mean, I think it would be a big help. I'd really like to have you along.' Tina radiated strength and sympathy. She looked so capable. 'I feel a bit lost. I keep thinking about that poor kid, she's going to be scarred for life.

Emotionally as well as physically. She was a bit insecure, a loner, from what Kimberley said.'

'Listen, Eddie,' Tina took charge, 'we'll have to get Bonnie and drive her to Brisbane. I'll phone the Dolphin Centre and tell them what's going on so they can prepare her.'

'I was having dinner with friends. I'd better let them know.'

'I have my mobile. We'll call on the way. Leave your car and take mine. It might be more reliable. I've seen yours.' She steered him to where her four-wheel drive was parked.

'Actually, I have Nola's car. I'll call the restaurant and ask Holly to drive her home.'

The call to Kimberley was far harder.

'Oh my God, how am I going to tell Matty? I can't stop blaming myself. Though short of locking Erica in, I don't know how I could have kept her here all the time.'

'Exactly. Kim, you mustn't blame yourself. But we have to break the news to Bonnie. Do you think you can do it?'

'No! I couldn't. Oh, Eddie, please don't ask me to do that. I couldn't face her. And I've got Matty. No, I couldn't.'

Eddie was surprised at her response. 'Okay, take it easy, that's fine. I understand. Tina is with me, we're on our way to her now.'

'Tina, the ranger from the Cape?'

'Yes, she's a volunteer rescue worker, she was at the house.'

'Then she'll know how to handle it. I'm not

good at this sort of thing. Oh, poor Erica. Eddie, I have to go to Matty. Call me and let me know how she is.'

When Tina pulled into the main entrance at the centre Cheyne came out to meet them.

'How is she?' Eddie asked, immediately feeling embarrassed. How would a mother be in these circumstances? What a dumb question.

'She's in shock. Just wants to get to her daughter as quickly as possible.'

'We'll drive her,' said Tina.

Cheyne led them inside. 'I've made arrangements for her to fly up in our helicopter. But if you could go to the hospital it would be good. She'll need support whatever the circumstances. This is very tragic, coming just when she was so looking forward to her new life with Erica. Spirit can hand out some hard lessons.'

'Can one of us go with her?' asked Eddie.

'Sorry, no room. Regulations.'

'How come you have a helicopter?' cut in Tina. 'Is there a helipad here?' This was the first she'd heard of it.

'We need a helicopter for the community, and the local police often use it. They do a routine check of the hills for dope plantations. And it's useful for emergencies like this. Come and see Bonnie, she's packing a few things.'

Bonnie was pale and distracted. Eddie gave her a brief embrace and introduced Tina, who recognised her as one of the solitary women who often went to the lighthouse to watch the sunrise. 'We're coming up to Brisbane, we'll be there in two hours or so. Anything you want us to bring?'

Her voice was wavering. 'You don't have to. But thank you. I've called her father. Maybe you could bring Erica's favourite CDs. She had some at Kimberley's . . .' Her voice trailed off as she stared at the bag and scattered clothes on her bed. Tina stepped forward and began folding and packing them.

'Kimberley sends her love,' said Eddie. 'She can't leave Matty, but she'll come as soon as she can.'

'No, that's all right. I understand.' Bonnie's good manners came from habit but she just stood in the middle of the room, hands gripped together.

Tina closed the bag. 'Right. You're ready.' She looked at Cheyne in the doorway signalling him with her eyes to move things along.

The helicopter clacked above them as they drove onto the gravel road. 'They must have got special clearance to fly this late,' Eddie said.

'These communities have a way of getting things done when they want to,' said Tina dryly. 'Now, are we getting those CDs or anything else?'

'Let's just drive. If we're going to support Bonnie, we need to be there while she's dealing with whatever she has to deal with. I doubt Erica is up to listening to CDs anyway.' He glanced at Tina and said warmly, 'This is good of you.'

'If I were in Bonnie's shoes, I'd want someone there. I just hope we can help.' She paused and added slowly, groping to articulate something she hadn't put into words before, 'You know, Eddie, I sit up there on the Cape overlooking that beautiful peaceful bay and see the tourists come and go. But at other times I watch the women walk up the track then sit and gaze out to sea, looking for something.'

'Women like Bonnie?' he said quietly.

'Yeah. Some pretend they do it for the exercise, but there are a lot of lonely women in The Bay.'

'Do you think they ever find what they're looking for?' he asked, then wondered why was it only women who had to come to a place like this to 'find' themselves. Surely he wasn't the only man who felt he was at a crossroads, confused about his future, unsure what he really wanted or what his options were.

Tina sighed. 'I wish I knew. I talk to some of them, but mostly they like the solitude. And the sea is so calming. I think that's more helpful than anything I could say.'

'Do they end up staying here? Or are they restless? Like Laura, never content with her lot.'

'Some stay and grow and change, some go. Some stay in their same old bitter comfort zone, or so I gather.' Tina laughed lightly. 'Hey, I'm no therapist. But . . . '

Eddie looked at her. There was something in her voice.

'But what?'

'This might sound strange, but there's something about the Cape, the lighthouse. It's special, like in magical, or that over-used word, spiritual.'

'I'll add that to my list of research questions. I know,' he held up his hands as Tina was about to interrupt, 'I've been so slack about coming back to go through the old journals.'

'You seemed so enthused. But they're still there waiting for you. How's your project going?'

'I've been a bit sidetracked,' said Eddie ruefully. 'A few domestic things. But I really want to get on with my Bay film. I'm getting some amazing stuff. Like at the doof.' He stopped for a moment. 'Jesus, if only I'd found Erica then –'

'That's another thing about this place, isn't it?' said Tina gently. 'How people help each other. Sometimes it gets a bit incestuous, a bit claustrophobic, everyone in each other's pockets.'

'Seems to me you get five Bay people in a room they won't agree. But when it comes to big things they unite.'

'Why do you say "they" and not "we"?'

'Well, there you go. I guess I'm not sure if I'm staying or going either,' said Eddie lightly. But her remark hit home and he fell silent.

In the next two hours in the darkness of the car Tina and Eddie shared potted life stories. The events of the night, and knowing the painful experience they were facing, gave them a heightened sense of what was important in life. They talked, as strangers often do in the intimacy of a journey, but in this case it was the cementing of a friendship.

'How well do you know Bonnie and her daughter?' Tina asked.

'As well as I know a whole bunch of people in The Bay, the women's club I call it. I met them through Mac and Kimberley more than through my ex-wife. Though she was at dinner tonight.'

'That's nice,' said Tina in a non-committal tone.

'No it wasn't,' said Eddie with a slight grin. 'She was with her current boyfriend. Old, rich, boring. Newly retired to the Gold Coast.'

'Ugh. Not my taste,' said Tina, wondering how any woman would trade in Eddie. Maybe it was the money. 'How come you're an ex? Are you a wife beater?'

'Yeah, sure,' he joked. But then added thoughtfully, 'Maybe I should have been tougher. Verbally. I let her shout me down. Funny how you kind of shut your eyes when you don't want to see what's happening around you. She changed. Or maybe I never saw who she was. I thought life would be different, better, when we came to The Bay.'

'You mentioned your daughter, how old is she?'

'Ten. She's not mine, biologically. Alice was three when I met Laura. Though she thinks of me as her dad.'

'And is Mr Old and Rich going to be her new daddy on the Gold Coast?' Tina was shocked at how much she needed to know about Eddie's private life. So unlike her, but she couldn't help herself.

'Laura is probably hoping so . . . rustic and un-rich isn't her style. Not that I was a total disaster when we came here,' he quickly added. He didn't want Tina to think he was a loser. 'I still have big plans. But I'm concerned about Alice. She doesn't want to move away, so she might end up staying with me at the farm. Part of the time anyway.'

'That's a big responsibility for you. What about your work?'

'I'm working for myself at present. If it wasn't for Alice I might rush overseas, but if you're going to be a single parent, The Bay is a good place to live.'

'Yes. There's a lot of generous people there. Generous with time and care, I mean. Let's hope everyone can rally around Bonnie. She'll need it. Here we are.'

As they headed into Brisbane Eddie suddenly said, 'Oh my God, I haven't rung Amber back. I wonder if Kimberley has. Amber is close to Bonnie. They have some bond, something between them.'

'It's late. Call her when we have some more news,' said Tina. 'We'll be at the hospital in ten minutes or so.'

Eddie looked at her profile in the city lights and thought again what a practical person she was. And he thanked his lucky stars she had been there, for many reasons. But all he said was, 'I'm glad you're driving. I don't know my way around Brisbane.'

A security guard checked at the reception desk and then directed them to the intensive care unit.

Hospitals are particularly depressing late at night, Tina thought. Silent hallways, occasional echoing footsteps, a phone ringing. Darkened doorways where patients tried to sleep through their pain. Tired nurses doing paperwork and lonely rounds. The atmosphere in the intensive care unit was different. A sense of urgency, tension and switched-on professionalism dominated.

An older nurse came out of the ward and asked who they were. She spoke in a voice wearied by too many hours on duty, too much suffering, too little hope. 'Mrs Bitternden is with her daughter. Is there no other family coming?'

'The father is in Melbourne. I believe he's on his way,' said Eddie. 'We're friends and felt we could help comfort Bonnie.'

'She hasn't been doing very well. Seeing a patient with third degree burns to most of the body is a shock, of course.'

'What's the prognosis, Sister?' asked Tina.

The ward sister studied Tina, recognising the rescue service uniform and decided this was a capable, no-nonsense young woman. 'The doctor will be able to tell Mrs Bitternden more when he comes back.' Then she added in a kinder tone, 'It's not very good. But she isn't in pain. When the burns are as bad as this all the nerve endings are burned so she's not feeling anything. In fact, she's quite lucid. But I'd suggest you get anyone close to the family to come in as soon as they can.' She hurried back into the special unit.

'Oh, Christ. What does that mean?' asked Eddie shakily. 'I mean, is she saying Erica could die?'

Bonnie came out of the ward and Eddie was shocked at the change in her in a few hours. Her skin had a ghostly pallor, her hair seemed sweaty and stringy but the anguish in her eyes stabbed at him. She was agitated, her voice high pitched. She rushed to Eddie and clung to him. 'Tell them it's not her. That's not my daughter, it can't be. Dear God, Eddie, it's hideous. That's not beautiful Erica. What have they done with my daughter? What's happening?' She buried her face in her hands, her shoulders shaking.

A nurse took Bonnie by the elbow. Tina was quickly on the other side making soothing noises. They led her away leaving Eddie feeling helpless. He found himself gazing at a man dozing in the corner of the waiting room, and wondered how long he had been waiting, and why.

Tina came back a few minutes later. 'Bonnie's been sedated slightly. She's pulling herself together. We can have a few quick words with Erica.'

'I don't know that I'm up to that.'

Tina laid a hand on Eddie's arm. 'I think, as we're here, we should. She knows you.' She hesitated then told him what she'd learned from the sister. 'There might not be another opportunity. She's not going to make it, Eddie. Her body will collapse internally – the fluids, electrolytes – they're so out of balance.'

'God, how long?'

'Maybe only hours,' said Tina steadily.

'Does she know? Does Bonnie know?'

'I don't think so.'

But as Eddie stood by the bed trying to compose himself, he knew that Erica knew. She was barely recognisable. Most of her body was completely black, and she was covered in light dressings, with gauze wrapped around her head. Her eyes were strangely bright and in their depths there glowed something he couldn't quite understand. Her voice was soft and clear. 'Was it you who came to the doof? Looking for me?'

He nodded. 'With Amber. It was her idea. She was worried about you.' His voice sounded strange to his ears.

'Ask Amber to look out for my mum. And Mac and all the others.'

Eddie nodded, his eyes filling with tears.

'And give all my stuff to Matty.'

Again he nodded, feeling Tina move closer to him. Erica caught the slight movement. 'You're the ranger at the lighthouse, aren't you?'

'That's me. Tina. You go up there a lot, don't you? I remember you.' Tina now knew who the young girl was that she'd seen so often hanging over the railing watching the ocean, or sitting hugging her knees and gazing beyond the horizon, or strumming her guitar. Now the Little Lost Girl, as Tina dubbed her, was dying. At first she'd always been alone and Tina wondered why she had never come with her mother. Did they know they each went to the headland with its beacon to seek solace or perhaps answers? Then Erica had started coming with another girl. Tina smiled softly. 'It's a pretty special place, huh?'

'Yes.' Erica's eyes blinked for a moment, like an old turtle, Eddie thought.

'Look out for me. From the lighthouse. I'm going to sail past there.' Her voice was weaker and Eddie thought she must be starting to lose touch with reality.

But Tina leaned closer. 'We'll always have the light on for you, Erica. You won't get lost.'

'I know that. It's all right now.'

'That's long enough. Her mother wants to be with her.' The sister steered them away from the bed before it struck Eddie that they hadn't said goodbye. But then he couldn't bring himself to say the words.

'Let's get a cup of tea.' Tina took his arm.

'I could do with something stronger. Christ, this is terrible. What can we do?'

'Very little. We'd better ring Kimberley and Amber. And who else?'

'I don't know who else Bonnie knows in The Bay. The same group . . . Holly, Mac, Stolle and Lynn, Nola. Oh, and Billy. Their shops are both in the arcade, they seem to be friends.'

'Mac is probably the best person to get to break the news around town. And we'd better call Cheyne. He's experienced in these situations,' added Tina.

'So what exactly happened? How did it start? The fire?' Eddie asked. He hadn't wanted to get into the details on the drive up. But now there was no escaping the reality of what had happened.

'To be confirmed, but it seems pretty sure it was candles,' Tina explained, 'in Erica's room. Curtains went up. That's where the fire started. Not sure yet if it was accidental or not.'

Eddie had to get away from the hospital. 'Let's go for a walk. It'll be dawn in a couple of hours.'

Mac tapped on Kimberley's window a short time after sunrise. 'It's me, I didn't want to wake Matty.'

'Come round the back. I'll make us coffee.' Kimberley was red-eyed. 'Did Eddie ring you?'

'No. But I know. I know,' said Mac sadly. 'Have you told Matty?'

'No. I'll let her sleep as long as possible. She'll find this so hard to deal with. Thanks for coming round. It would be good if you're here when I tell her.' While she might look a trifle eccentric, Mac's loving heart and comforting arms would help Matty. And me, thought Kimberley. As well as being a friend Mac had slipped into the role of surrogate mother and grandmother for Kimberley and Matty. 'God, how is Bonnie going to survive this? I couldn't. If anything happened to Matty I'd die.'

'No you wouldn't,' said Mac firmly. 'You have to go on living. And that's what we have to help

Bonnie do. But there's something more immediate. Erica's father might want to take over. We have to help Bonnie bring Erica back here. The funeral must be here, not Melbourne.'

Kimberley stared at her, wondering how she knew these things. She didn't question for a moment that Mac knew what Erica wanted.

Andrew paced along the edge of the sand dune where it began to level out and meet straggling marshland plants and pandanus trees. A small stream ran tea-stained brown from the tea-tree lake hidden further back in the wetlands. A large abandoned tin shed and bits of rusting equipment lay about a cracked cement slab near the remains of an overgrown railway track. He was counting to himself, measuring the distance with footsteps. He turned around and went to where Letitia was sitting on the sand studying a large set of plans.

'It's looking good. Though this area is a mess, used to be the old abattoirs.' He gazed out to sea. 'What a location. Bloody madness putting a meat-works next to one of the world's great beaches.'

'I think it had something to do with shipping the cattle and meat down to Sydney and Melbourne.' She looked up from the plans and pointed further along Mighty Beach. 'At low tide you can see the pylons of the old jetty.'

'They'll have to go. Too dangerous for water sports.' He looked thoughtful. 'You know, if they had a long wharf here in the old days, what's to say we couldn't put in a marina or some kind of aquatic centre?'

'Are you joking? You haven't seen the Easter tides, and they still get cyclones along here. Come back in a couple of weeks.'

He dropped on the sand beside her and pulled her to him. 'I might just do that. You don't get down to Sydney enough.'

'I've had my hands full up here, or hadn't you noticed?'

'You're doing brilliantly.'

'Thanks. The next round might not be so easy.'

'Leave the council to me,' said Andrew confidently.

'Andy, when are you going to tell me the full story about this? If you're thinking of buying off the council, there are too many greenies in there. They'll go bananas.'

'They're not the majority. Pressure can come from a lot of directions. Don't you worry your pretty little head, I have a plan.'

'That's so sexist! I'm not your wife. Boy, I'm going to have to retrain you,' Letitia said with a patient grin.

Andrew fell back on the sand. 'Oh, I like the sound of that. Do you use whips?'

Laughing, Letitia fell across him and he clutched her body to his. She pushed the plans to one side as their mouths locked. Neither noticed the beautiful brown dog prance past, closely followed by Mitchell.

He turned away, hurriedly going down the

dune closer to the water. Why wasn't he surprised? He hadn't warmed to Andrew but he felt concerned for Holly. Did she know her husband was having it off with a young woman? He tried to tell himself it was none of his business. But there was more that bothered him. Andrew was a well-known architect; known for super luxurious five-star resorts in up-market parts of Asia. Letitia Sweetman was a solicitor specialising in commercial and real estate deals. The strip of land on which they were cavorting had attracted developers before, but none with the clout or the kind of backers Andrew Jamieson seemed to have. Holly had intimated that Andrew was more than a designer and consultant in the overseas developments, that he was often part of the consortium that built them. She had been vague, she obviously didn't follow Andrew's business dealings too closely.

Mitchell began to wonder about their presence in The Bay. He had made it clear to Holly that he was against monster developments, which was why he was so supportive of her plans for restoring Richmond House. So what was going on?

As the day passed into evening, Bonnie wished the moments could be decades. She sat beside the hospital bed holding the bandaged hand of her dying daughter. A blackened shadow of the baby she'd birthed and raised and believed would grow up to be so special. Why had God decided to take her back? Had she been such a bad mother? How was she to go on alone? She thought of the sea, the ocean her child loved so deeply. Erica had always wanted to sail single-handed over the horizon, and in her mind she was now going to embark on that voyage. But all Bonnie could feel was the increasing pain of loss, and she was drowning in that pain.

Sensing her mother's thoughts, Erica whispered, 'It will be all right, Mum. Really. You must be strong for me.'

'I can't bear this. I can't live without you, darling girl.' Bonnie could barely speak, her throat was so constricted. Never, even in her worst moments, had she ever imagined her child would die before her.

'Mum, I'll be free and happy when I go. It's too hard for me here.'

Bonnie fumbled and fled outside, gasping, trying to breathe. She wanted to cry out that she'd always be her mother, and a good one, so please live. But all the plans she'd made at the Dolphin Centre were now cruelly shattered.

The arrival of Erica's father wasn't the traumatic and emotionally disturbing experience she'd expected. They'd clung to each other, linked by the love and bond of their child, and the reunion gave her strength. For a wild moment Bonnie imagined he might take her home to Melbourne, they would share this grief and have the closeness they'd never known when Erica was alive. But reality hit when she heard him on his mobile phone to his wife, seeking comfort, needing her, not Bonnie. Once again Bonnie felt abandoned. Only strangers had come to support her, and they would be the only ones there when it was all over.

Bonnie looked up as Tina put a cup of tea in her hands. 'Drink this and go back to her. Her father says she's asking for you.'

On the Cape, above the sweep of The Bay, the lighthouse beam was dark for an instant, as if missing a beat.

Kimberley was tired. The shock of Erica's death had galvanised The Bay and the township of Brigalow. *The Beacon Bugle* screamed from its front page: 'Why Are We Losing Our Children?'

Members of Bonnie's family were starting to arrive, Kimberley had found them a house to rent and stocked the kitchen with food. Amber spent as much time as she could with Bonnie in between keeping the Beach Hut open and fobbing off curious and nosy people who wanted to know all the gruesome details.

Matty trudged home from school. There'd been a special assembly about Erica. Everyone was asking what had happened. There were whispers she had intentionally started the fire. Matty noticed her mother's car wasn't there. She was glad her mum was keeping busy and helping Erica's mum. And she was also pleased to have some time alone. Everyone had been smothering her so much, afraid to leave her on her own, when what she really wanted was time and space to think through this huge, sudden loss in her life.

The garbage can was still out the front, several days newspapers littered the driveway and mail spewed from the mailbox. Matty threw the papers in the bin and wheeled it to the mailbox to toss in the junk mail. There were some letters in it as well as the coloured advertising pamphlets – one addressed to Kimberley, a postcard from her father in India, the telephone bill. And a letter to Matty. She recognised the writing instantly and her hand shook.

It was from Erica.

Chapter Nine

THE DAY OF ERICA'S FUNERAL DAWNED STORMY GREY and windy. Bonnie had been surprised and touched by the stream of visitors, heartfelt expressions of grief, compassion and support that had swept her along in a wave of love. Many people she'd had little contact with and some she had never even spoken to before were now embracing her, somehow wanting to share her grief as if old friends, but she struggled to put names to many. Those closest to her and Erica were grappling with their own pain and anguish, made worse, if that were possible, by the knowledge that Erica had taken her own life. For it had been determined that the fire was the deliberate result of drugs, candles and curtains. Fortunately no one else had died, but the question – why? – hovered in many minds.

Bonnie's family from Melbourne – her parents, her former husband, Stephan, and a cousin – had stayed as if on an island, clinging together, marooned in the tide of Bonnie's new life. Stephan, shattered at Erica's death, thought this world of The Bay was all a bit odd. He had found it hard to come to terms with the fact that his former, proper corporate wife was looking so very different. He couldn't imagine how she had been living, and he didn't want to think about it in case he became overwhelmed with anger that her lifestyle could have contributed to Erica's death. He tried to tell himself that Erica had gone, and the nightmare of her going would soon pass. He knew he had to be seen to be doing 'the right thing', but behind the veneer of sympathy whatever happened to Bonnie now was of little interest to him. He respected her parents, though, and didn't want to add to their grief by losing it with Bonnie. Her parents were also finding this community very strange compared to their more conservative friends in Melbourne.

While Stephan thought that Bonnie's acquaintances here were an odd bunch, he was relieved they had taken on some of the burden of comforting and caring for her. Bonnie had no close friends during their marriage. She'd been one of those 'ladies who lunch' so often reported in the social pages, and was in a circle of wives obliged to entertain each other and visiting high-flyers. The rest of the time, it seemed to him, she spent tending the roses and watching television. Now here was Bonnie, on the morning of their daughter's funeral, being swept off by a strangely garbed woman called Lynn who was giving her a massage!

He was feeling dreadfully lost and wished he'd brought his new young wife to comfort him. He went outside to call her on the mobile in private.

Lynn's strong bony fingers seemed to find every twisted knot of tension in Bonnie's body. Firmly she kneaded and stroked, steadily easing what felt like great lumps of metal in Bonnie's shoulders and neck, along her spine and the backs of her legs. The smell of the musky oil, the gentle ambient music from the CD, a peaceful combination of sounds of the sea orchestrated with flute and harp, sent Bonnie drifting into a purplish hazy dream.

At one point Lynn's hands seemed to burn and Bonnie could feel heat reaching into her vital organs. She had been feeling numb, as if each nerve end in her body had been blocked. Now she experienced a white flash behind her closed eyelids and then her body went limp as though everything had been washed out of her. But, painful as it was, she felt she was alive again, even though her skin felt raw and exposed.

Then, slowly, as Lynn continued her smooth, powerful ministrations, Bonnie felt a tingling warmth flow through her; it was as if she was coming back to life again. Tears poured down her face but it was a cleansing cry, soundless and almost unemotional.

When an hour or more had passed Lynn rested her hands on Bonnie's feet, her fingertips finally trailing off her toes, as if pulling the pain and sadness from her body, then she quietly left the room. 'Come out when you're ready.'

Bonnie lay there for another ten minutes, thinking the last few days were a dream. That she'd get up and Erica would be there and they'd go to the beach, have a coffee, hang out, go shopping.

Gradually, consciousness took over and she opened her eyes, looking at the unfamiliar wall with the picture of a bearded Indian man wearing a garland of flowers and a poster of a whale throwing itself backwards into the ocean. Suddenly the awful reality of where she was, why she was there, and what had happened flooded over her and she curled on her side and began to sob.

Hearing the deep, racking cries, Lynn waited a few moments, then went in and leaned over Bonnie, holding her in a protective embrace. Bonnie stopped sobbing and began to shake, then slowly sat up, wiping her face with the edge of the massage towel. 'I thought this was all a dream. I can't stand this pain. Why, Lynn? Why did she do it? What did I do? Am I so bad? Why didn't I die instead?' She covered her face with her hands, and Lynn was stunned at her next words, 'Damn you, Amber. Damn you.'

Lynn decided it was not appropriate to ask Bonnie about this remark, though she might ask Amber. She smoothed Bonnie's hair and handed her a glass of water, which Bonnie gulped. 'I don't have those answers, Bonnie. Don't torture yourself by asking. It was Erica's choice, she never stopped loving you. She doesn't blame you.' She wanted to tell Bonnie to be strong. But then thought better of it. 'Cry all you want. If you want to yell and scream, do it. You're safe here.'

They sat quietly together until Bonnie shook her head and took Lynn's hand. 'Thank you,' she said simply. 'I really think I'm going to cope much better with the day now. I have to be brave and not let her down by going to pieces, right?' She stretched her lips in what she thought was a smile, which tore into Lynn.

By the time she was dressed and had tidied her hair, Bonnie stepped out of the small room looking almost composed. 'Lynn, what was that music, those sounds?'

Lynn picked up the cover of the CD. 'It's "An Odyssey of the Sea", whale songs. Mitchell lent it to me. Those whale songs that seem to echo around the underwater world are actually a language. Some people now believe whales have their own literature; their own *Iliad*, their own songs and stories. They change their songs every few years.'

'How do we know that?' asked Bonnie. 'It sounds too wonderful.'

'We're learning. Slowly, we're learning.'

'I wonder if Erica ever heard a whale sing? She would have liked that,' said Bonnie softly.

By sunset the weather had cleared and the group had gathered on Tiny Bay Beach. The closed coffin on the sand was shaped like a small white boat. Planted beside it was a long bamboo pole with a canvas sail. Friends and family had painted the sail with messages and pictures for Erica. Mourners were dressed in colourful, 'happy' beach attire as Bonnie had requested.

Matty had put together a large board covered in photographs and memorabilia she knew were meaningful to Erica. From Bonnie's mother came the teddy bear that had passed from Bonnie to Erica and had been in the grandmother's care. It sat on the coffin with flowers and a pile of letters held down by a stone.

Bonnie asked Amber to stay close to her as people came up to her to offer sympathy.

Frances, the warm and attentive funeral company representative, had smoothed everything. She'd discussed arrangements with Bonnie, who confirmed the stories everyone had heard now about Erica's dream of one day sailing around the world. She'd also talked to Matty and other girls in the class about Erica, her life and the funeral.

'We're comfortable doing things differently here,' she'd gently advised Bonnie and her family. 'You tell us what you want. It's a time to reflect on who Erica was, what she gave to everyone, a time to honour her. No need to rush these things. Have everyone involved as much as possible, take as much time as you need.'

Frances had listened and then guided them towards the ceremony on the beach. 'It seems to me that is how Erica would have written the script,' she had said to the family when they were planning the details. 'It is symbolic of her dream, and her character, isn't it? A celebration of her life really, a spirit setting sail.'

Bonnie had reached out to Erica's father in a moment alone together. 'Stephan, I want you to understand that I don't know why she did this. Please don't blame me. We were happy here. As much as Erica was ever happy,' she said sadly.

He put his arm around her shoulder. 'She always was such a serious little girl. I never felt I understood her. I'd hoped, as she got older, we'd come closer . . . ' He choked up and couldn't go on for a moment. Then, drawing a deep breath, he added, 'I don't blame you, Bonnie. I don't blame myself, not personally. I blame what's happened to all of us. Nothing seems the way it used to be.'

'There isn't anything I wouldn't have done to change things; to stop this happening,' said Bonnie, adding in a sudden flash of insight, 'There is no blame. Erica did this. Not us. It's up to us to deal with it as best we can.'

Being so close to Bonnie brought back too many memories that were now painful: Erica's birth, their dreams for the future. Stephan never imagined their marriage falling apart. He never imagined losing his daughter. He never thought they would be one of a mounting statistic. This agony and shame happened to other people, not us. He gave Bonnie an awkward pat and fled. He couldn't bring himself to show the emotion he felt. It frightened him. This was the most intense feeling he'd ever experienced and he wanted to push it far down inside himself. He knew it was okay for men to cry, show their feelings, be sensitive and New Age. Like the men up here in this community, he supposed. But where he came from, how he was brought up, no one gave in to their feelings. It made other people feel uncomfortable, embarrassed. So you covered up and put on a brave face. His gut and head ached and he wanted to cry like a baby or punch something long and hard. These feelings confused and frightened him. Bonnie might be the one person he could let down his guard to, but he was too scared to do so. His new wife hoped he was 'being strong for everyone'. But, by Christ, it was hard.

So here they were gathered on the empty stretch of beach, wrapped in a sunset that had broken through the clouds. Eddie unobtrusively videoed the proceedings as Bonnie had wanted.

The youthful minister, known for his folk songs, led the traditional proceedings, then asked the school choir to sing. Next he asked those who wanted to express their feelings to stand up and say what was in their heart.

Mac spoke first, briefly, but it was a warm and tender recognition of Erica's short life. 'So young, so much lost. All the potential that we can only imagine. Yet something of her will live on in all of us because, in ways perhaps difficult to define today, the dream she had is symbolic of the dream we all have – to sail towards new horizons with a sense of adventure and an open mind. I think, despite her youthful years, she would approve of the following lines from Psalm 90:10–12:

> 'The days of our years are threescore and ten,
> Or even by reason of strength fourscore
> Yet is their pride but travail and vanity;
> For it's speedily gone and we fly away . . .
> So teach us to number our days,
> That we may get us a heart of wisdom.'

Kimberley then gave Matty's hand a supportive squeeze and stepped forward. She looked around the faces watching her. She'd never spoken in public before, but her voice was firm and steady.

'Erica has given us a difficult and challenging gift. Even as a mother, and one who shared mothering time with Erica, it is very difficult to imagine the depth of anguish Bonnie and her family must be suffering. But Erica was not a child in the normal meaning of the word. Erica, frustratingly at times, knew where she was going and what she wanted from this life. She was born an old soul, and she seemed to know her time here would be brief. She came among us to teach us hard but necessary lessons.

'It is too easy not to hear the cries, to mutter platitudes, to wait for someone else to do something. It is only when something tragic, drastic, despairingly sad happens that we pause and look around us. Our children are crying out for help. We aren't living our lives as we wish. Greed, selfishness, laziness can be levelled at us all. Somewhere we have lost touch with what the family is about. The family of the home, of the community, the nation, the family of all humanity. Erica sometimes sang of this in her own songs, words that spoke of her own searching. How much worse do things have to become before we hear and understand the cries of our children? Perhaps her memorial will be in our hearts and our heads, giving us a greater awareness of the need to look after the world we're building for the children of today, and tomorrow.'

She paused, aware her words had struck a chord with everyone. Then she continued, 'Is it to be a world just about the bottom line, about dollars and time? Or should it be about caring? Sometimes it takes an act of great courage, a wild, painful, brave sacrifice, to make us take notice. Erica wants us to care. And I'm going to start caring more. I've never done much with my life. Erica has shown me I can. Thank you, Erica.'

Matty took a step towards her mother as she moved back from beside the coffin, and they fell into each other's arms, and hugged and wept quietly.

The minister read the mood perfectly. It was no time for more words but rather music, and he picked up his guitar and strummed a peaceful, gentle melody that most of those on the beach had never heard before. It was one of Erica's recent compositions, inspired so her notes said by her dream of sailing over the horizon. Her music teacher had passed the notes and music on to him.

When he had finished he briefly told the story of the music then asked everyone to join him in prayer for the safe journey of Erica across the sea as she had always dreamed.

Bonnie and Matty were the last to add their letters to the pile of tributes that would travel with Erica. Frances had encouraged them to write as a way of settling their own hearts and resolving unfinished issues in order to let go.

My best and dearest friend,

I was so mad at you for leaving us. You always did things differently, went your own way and talked your own talk. Sang your own songs. I will miss you. I learned a lot from you. I'm only just learning how much. I hope that I can learn to be as strong as you. This is hard. I'll keep you in my heart and you'll know everything that's happening to me. And when it gets too hard I'll go to our favourite place on the Cape and talk to you. I know you'll listen. Thank you for explaining how you felt in your letter.

We'll all take care of your mum. You will always be my best friend, dearer than a sister.

With all my love

Matty

My beautiful girl,

I wish with all my heart you were with me still. How many memories I treasure from the moment I first held you in my arms, you were everything to me. And always will be.

I wonder still at the wisdom that came to you at the end and how it gives me strength. It pains me I will never see you mature and blossom, hold your babies and share your life. I struggle to understand you saying it was never meant to be, and while I know I will have dark days, I'll look to the light and know you are there with me. I will do my best to uphold the promise I made to you and make each day a little better than the last. But without you in my life it will be hard. Sail safely, precious girl, you are always part of me.

Your loving Mother

Each mourner was handed a flower to bless and drop into the twilight sea.

Amber stood beside Bonnie as they dropped their flowers into the wash of waves running back from the beach.

'I have been so angry at you,' said Bonnie calmly.

'For saving you?'

'Was I? Saved?'

'You tell me.'

'I wish you'd saved Erica. Not me.'

'Erica chose, Bonnie. I don't believe she would have wanted to be here without her mother.'

'I just want my girl with me.' Bonnie's voice dropped and the tears ran down her cheeks.

'She is with you. She'll always be with you.'

'How can you say that?' Bonnie sobbed.

Amber simply hugged her.

Bonnie took her hand and they stood staring out to sea. 'It will get easier, won't it? We'll know why we're going through all this.'

'I hope so, Bonnie. I hope so.'

They stood in silence looking at the last rays of the sun fading behind the peak of Mount Hazard. Amber sighed. 'Kimberley is right. We've messed up. We have to fix things.'

Frances arranged for the coffin and the sail and all the tokens and flowers to be taken away. Later, when Bonnie chose, she would take Erica's ashes out to sea and scatter them on the ocean she loved.

It was cruisy weather; Bay perfect. Warm, fresh, sparkling with promise. A morning for a late lazy breakfast overlooking the beach, a swim, the newspapers and coffee at a favourite cafe. A day to dawdle past the garage sales of faded Indian bedspreads, recycled vintage hippy clothes, brass pots, incense holders, posters and books spread out on the grass along the streets leading into town.

Even more than usual, people lingered to talk in the street, or smile and nod at other locals. Visitors tried to blend in and pretend this was their life for the rest of the year too. For here the interaction, the inherent sociability of a community going about its business and its pleasure gave the town a vitality and cohesiveness that was lost to those from city suburbs overwhelmingly reliant on a car to make connections with others, or living in tower blocks of apartments that limited interaction to lifts and lobbies.

It was difficult to feel alone surrounded by the buzz of a close-knit community where wanderers were welcomed, everyone intent on enjoying what they regarded as a pocket of paradise. The locals acknowledged their good fortune, and even those with tenuous economic circumstances felt enriched just by being part of it. Visitors usually felt the same, if only for a few days. No one took for granted the beauty, the lifestyle, the company around them. Although when overzealous rangers and officialdom struck they were roundly attacked in council and the pages of *The Beacon Bugle*. But no one really believed they'd merely stumbled into The Bay. Being here seemed part of a master plan. Well, that was how most wanted to see it, while never admitting to affecting rose-coloured glasses.

Aviator glasses were more visible, such as those worn by the handsome man in the yellow convertible who parked in the main street and joined the meandering Saturday morning crowd. Slim, gym fit and tanned, hair that had been cut and styled very short, casual white silk-knit top, navy board shorts and sandals all added up to money and time spent to achieve a nonchalant image. He looked in his thirties, though Wesley had seen his fortieth birthday come and go. He stood out as a visitor to The Bay: too pressed, too perfect, too rich looking.

As he walked he studied the people in the street – the Rasta dreadlocks and knitted beanies; the shaved heads and robes of drummers squatting in the small park; the bands of multi-coloured people: green, orange and purple hair, glitter and elaborate tattoos and the traditional mendi patterns of henna-stained skin. Clothes ranged from beach gear to backpackers in souvenir T-shirts and bumbags, to locals in outfits reminiscent of the fifties to fancy dress. Overwhelmingly, swimwear, shorts or sarongs declared comfort and coolness as being the code. And that went for the weather and attitude, too. Cool, as in hip, had many layers of protocol, read by those who were in the same scene. The kids on skateboards and scooters, the surfies and the backpackers all had their own recognisable tribal dress, talk and tastes. A middle-aged man riding a unicycle whizzed past, ringing a bell, juggling a bar festooned with balloons, a squawking mechanical parrot atop his pith helmet. Outside the mini-mart a girl 'statue' painted silver from her hair to her toenails and dressed as an angel stood utterly motionless. Passers-by dropped coins in the small bowl at the base of the pedestal on which she posed.

Wesley Harden observed all this as he took in the cafes, pavement tables, beer garden and shops, and the post office where knots of locals met and chatted. He doubled back through an arcade, past The Teepee where he'd just had his hair done, to the beachfront where the smart holiday units and boutique B & Bs overlooked the beach. With some pleasure he assessed the surf and the mid-morning scatter of bikinis, and checked his watch. It was still early, by midday there'd be more of a social hum fusing with the surf sounds. He decided that he'd eat somewhere expensive that night. He'd heard Vincent's was the best place in town. Now, though, he'd go for a swim. The Point was a favourite spot. Tiny Bay Beach was more exclusive, but too far out of the main action, he decided. He wasn't in a rush. He had enough cash to last for a week.

Billy stubbed out his cigarette, cursing his weakness in being unable to break the habit, and stuck his head into the Beach Hut where Kimberley was talking to Amber. 'How you gals doing? Want a coffee?'

'Aren't you busy?'

'I have Matty minding the shop. She'll get me if a customer wanders in.'

Kimberley gave him a big smile, she was so grateful to him for giving Matty a paying job each Saturday morning. 'I'd love a coffee. Amber is too busy packing up her goodies for all the tourists. Word is spreading.'

'I assume the word you refer to is "Chaste",' said Billy. 'I can't understand anyone taking skin products called Chaste seriously.'

'As in pure. Don't lose any sleep over it, darling. Whatever you think, they work and that's all that matters, right? Women's business language.' Kimberley dismissed his opinion with a wave of the hand, then added, 'But don't let that stop you getting the coffee.'

Billy put the two coffees on the table in the sunny entrance to the arcade. 'So how are things going? Has Matty said much about Erica? I haven't raised it; thought it best to wait a bit.'

'Mac came round and they went for a walk and had a long talk. It seemed to help. She doesn't say much. The funeral helped her and the other girls at school. It's been a shock to them all. And there's a feeling of guilt, as well.'

'How come?'

'Erica was shunned a bit. She was always considered different by the other girls. And at their age there's so much pressure to conform, copy each other, do and like the same things.'

'I know some of the women about town thought Erica was a bit of a feral one,' said Billy. 'I confess I was down on her in the beginning. There seemed to be a lot of resentment towards Bonnie, guess it kind of rubbed off on Erica.'

'Yeah, it's not exactly common among the mums to be wealthy, good looking and living a wild, free, outrageous life.'

'It's on their wish list, I'll bet.'

Kimberley ignored the remark. 'It always struck me how protective Erica was of her mother. Almost like their roles were reversed, despite them both playing fast and loose.'

'And how is Bonnie?'

'She still has some of her family up with her. Apparently Erica's father has been understanding about her wishes. The grandparents wanted Erica buried in Melbourne.'

'I saw her early this morning. It really upset me.'

Kimberley reacted in surprise. 'You did? What did she say?'

'She didn't see me. I went up to Brigalow to drop Paula off at friends – they're going to the Gold Coast for the day – and Bonnie was sitting in all the mess at the house.'

'The old house? Where the fire was?'

Billy nodded. 'She was sitting in the rubble on a box, just pouring ashes through her fingers. Crying.'

'God, what did you do?'

'I couldn't talk to her, Kim. I couldn't go there, it upset me so much. I had the feeling she'd been scavenging for something, anything, that belonged to Erica.' He rubbed his eyes. 'When I think of my little girl, how would I cope? It was sheer grief. I guess it's starting to hit her. I had to turn away.'

They were both quiet for a moment or two, sipping their coffees in silence until Kimberley said softly, 'I would have done the same. I can't cope with raw emotion like that. That's why I feel so glad Eddie and Tina went to Brisbane that awful night.'

'Now that the funeral is over what will happen to Bonnie when her family go back? That will be hard.'

'We'll have to help her. I'm not sure how.' Kimberley sighed. 'One good thing is I managed to get hold of Matty's father in Delhi. Ashok said he'd come back as soon as he could. That will help Matty.'

'And help you?'

'We'll see. He's never around long enough to sort out my feelings. I try not to intrude on the time and space he and Matty need.'

Billy paused to think that through, then seemed to make up his mind. 'Listen, Kim, what are you doing with your life? You're bright, Matty is well adjusted and has a lot of interests, you have Mac around to help out –'

'You saying I should get a full-time job?'

'Why not? There must be any number of things you could do. And I know you need the money.'

'The single mum's pension doesn't go far, that's for sure. I've been cut back to two days a week at the glass factory, and Ashok never has money to send us.' Kimberley's face suddenly crumpled, shocking Billy. 'The fact is there's bugger all I can do. Checkout chick, waitress, shop assistant . . . not much of a résumé.'

Billy realised he'd opened an old wound. 'It's not like you to show self-pity, Kim. Look, let's talk realistically about the here and now.'

'And?'

'I think you should get your head into something other than Matty's school, your pals and life in The Bay.'

'That's most people's lives here, Billy. And don't tell me about how time slips away.'

'Life is what happens when you're making other plans, eh?'

'What does your wife do with her time apart from looking after your little girl?' Kimberley shot back.

'Hope is at kindy and Paula is doing a part-time uni course. Why don't you do a course in something?' he suggested.

'Improve my mind? I never got past HSC.' She tried to smile. 'I read a lot. Amazing what you can learn from books. Wish we had a better library here. I did think of trying to learn to use a computer but there's always such a queue for the two in the library.'

'Learning computer skills would be good. At least you'd be able to keep up with your daughter.'

Kimberley gave a shrug, sipped her coffee, and changed the subject. 'What's new in your life, what gossip has passed through the salon this week?'

'Not much, everyone wanted to talk about the fire. Though I had a strange fellow in this morning, playboy type. Wanted to know who was the richest woman in Beacon Bay. And meant it.'

'That's a bit of a worry. You didn't tell him about Nola?'

'No, I said all the women up here were either broke or paying alimony to their ex-husbands! But even if he hears about Nola, he's scarcely going to knock on her door. And she doesn't go out much anyway. I mean, she is over seventy. He looked about thirty but the dyed hair is a bit of a giveaway, I'd add another ten years.' Billy saw Matty waving that he had a customer and he stood up. 'Must dash, darling. And think about going digital.'

Kimberley dismissed him with an exaggerated flourish. 'Get out. None of that sex talk to me, thank you very much.' They both laughed. Kim felt better. It was good to talk with a male friend.

Stolle gave a whistle as he sauntered through the garden to Richmond House.

'Yo, Stolle. What's up?' Mitchell called from the top of a ladder where he was working on a window frame.

'Hi, Mitch. Found a few treasures I thought Holly might like to look at.'

Mitchell climbed down. 'She's down at the shops. What've you found?' He was immediately interested, knowing Stolle's knack for finding 'treasures'.

'Etched stained glass pictures, 1920s, I'd say.'

He followed Stolle to his Kombi where several blanket-wrapped frames were stacked. Stolle pulled one out and gently unwrapped it.

'Oh, man, that is lovely,' said Mitchell. It was a delicate coloured image on clear glass of a Grecian nymph bearing a bouquet of flowers. Etched into the bottom of the ornate picture was the word 'Spring'.

'The four seasons, each one is intact. Do you think Holly can use them?'

'Set against the light around the house, they would be stunning. I'd cut special enclaves for them, they're not right to set into windows. Where'd you find them?'

'You know me, beauty falls at my feet. In an old farmhouse, actually. They were packed in a crate with straw and not damaged. Could be copies or a very good artist. Not signed but they seemed right for Richmond House, and the price was okay. The old farmer was happy to get rid of them.'

'I'm sure Holly'll love them. It's up to her, of course. Want a coffee?'

'Yeah.' They headed into the kitchen and Stolle noticed how at home Mitchell was in the kitchen.

'Place is coming on well. Holly must be pleased. Question is, what does her picky husband think?'

'This is Holly's project,' said Mitchell staunchly. And as he poured the coffee he asked casually, 'What do you make of him?'

'Andrew? Haven't had a lot to do with him. Well he's never here. Doesn't seem too interested in this place, too busy banging up zillion dollar resorts.'

'Have you heard anything about a possible development along a strip of beachfront? Near where the meatworks were?'

'God, no. I thought the ratshit idea of ruining the beach got terminally knocked on the head ten years ago. Why're you asking?' He sensed there was more to Mitchell's question.

'Look, in confidence, I saw Andrew out there with a set of plans, and a certain lady solicitor who deals in commercial development.'

'Oh, Christ, not the dreaded Sweets. What did Holly have to say about it?'

'I haven't told her. Didn't want to pry.' Mitchell looked uncomfortable.

'Is Andrew still here?'

'Holly says he went back to Sydney.'

Stolle gave him a shrewd look. 'When did you see him down at the beach?'

'When he was here at the weekend. I can't help wondering and I don't want to ask Holly about it.'

'Do you think she knows anything?'

Mitch shook his head. 'Andrew appears to play his cards close to his chest. If he is involved in some deal, I don't think she's aware of it.'

'Let me think out aloud for a bit. If Andrew is involved in something and she doesn't know, that's awkward. If she does know and is hiding it, that's even more . . . uncomfortable.'

Mitch didn't want to mention the passionate embrace he'd witnessed. 'I don't think Holly is the devious type. But I'm not so sure about Andrew. That strip of beach and the wetlands are like a sacred site with locals now.'

'Perhaps it's time to do some digging then.'

'So how are you going to do that? You can't just front up to Letitia Sweetman.'

'There are ways and means. I know a mole in council and our intrepid local rag keeps an eagle eye out for these sorts of rumours. In fact I've got a gig with them; doing the "Buzz" column. They discovered I did journalism at uni before coming here. Amazing what quality gossip one picks up at the markets. Ear to the ground, voice of the people, that sort of thing. *The Beacon Bugle* was started for just that reason.'

'Keeping the bastards honest?'

'And clean, and green. And independent. It started as one man's vision, a lone voice in the media wilderness, now it's owned by the community.'

'Yeah, it's a good little paper. But sometimes it's a bit over the top in its criticisms of progress,' Mitchell said.

'Depends on how you define "progress", mate. When a small local newspaper is run by a bunch of ferals, activists and intellectuals, it makes for stimulating reading.' Stolle grinned. 'I'll put some feelers out. If a deal has been done over that land, there'll be hell to pay.'

'A resort there would be a disaster. Residential subdivision probably worse,' Mitchell said.

'Services like the sewerage system can't cope with the people here already.'

Stolle looked angry. 'Might be time to get out the green paint.'

Mitchell chuckled. 'I heard that story soon after I bought here. When the council put in the first set of traffic lights and then a big clock in the main street, they kept being smothered in green paint.'

'Council gave in then. No one seems to miss the lights or a clock,' said Stolle. 'I'll have a word with the boys and girls at the *Bugle*. You mention it to Holly and see what pops out of those pretty lips of hers.'

Holly was thrilled with the glass etchings and began to plan where to put them. As they looked at possible settings for the exquisite panels, Mitchell casually remarked that Stolle had heard there were plans around for a big beachfront resort in town. 'Rumours only, but where there's smoke –'

'You're joking. One of those international resorts? Here? Where exactly?'

'Rumour again, but the word is Mighty Beach. Be a bit of competition for the B & Bs and guest-houses, wouldn't it?'

'I don't care about competition, Richmond House is unique. But a resort, even a sympathetic one, just doesn't seem right here. Maybe Andrew can find out who's involved. He has masses of contacts in the city. He can plug into almost anything for the cost of a lunch. Sometimes only for the cost of a phone call.'

Mitchell threw up his hands. 'Hey, easy. It's just a rumour. Let's wait and see. But I'm impressed that you've already become a green-thinking guardian of The Bay.'

'I know it's only been a few months, but you're right. I really care about this place,' she said softly. 'I've asked my kids to come and visit, I want them to see what I'm doing. And, well, I miss them.' They both knew the spectre of Erica hovered for a moment.

'I'm surprised they haven't been up before this, the place is a mecca for the sun–surf worshippers. My Tom finds any chance to get up here. He's around the same age as your kids. And they must be curious to see what you're up to,' said Mitchell, convinced now that Holly knew nothing about any plans to develop the land at Mighty Beach.

In Sydney Letitia and Andrew sat at a candlelit dinner.

'So when are you going to tell her?' asked Letitia, giving the red wine in her goblet a slightly agitated swirl.

'Letty, I have to do this in my own way. She doesn't have a clue there's anything going on. She's so wrapped up in her little project at The Bay.'

'Well, I'm not going on like this, flying down here every couple of weeks. You sneaking up there to see me. You're both too well-known in the area now. Sure we have a business arrangement, but that's a secret too. When can we have something out in the open?'

'We did. Up in the dunes under the full moon a couple of weekends ago.'

She kicked him in the shins under the table.

'Steady, kid!'

'Get serious. When?'

He reached for her hand. 'Letty, please be patient, just a while longer. This has been pretty dramatic for me. For both of us. When I met you in Bangkok six months ago I thought you were bright, beautiful and sexy, and then we discovered we were both up there exploring the market for venture capital. We think alike, Letty. We both want to get our share of the big bickies, and we are going to do very nicely out of this one, believe me.' He raised his glass in a toast, and gave her a big smile. 'To our share, Letty, our share.' She returned his smile and they both sipped their wine.

'It seemed like fate when Holly decided to move to your home town. I mean, what are the odds on that?' Andrew said as he topped up their drinks.

'In Bay-speak they'd tell you we were meant to be,' said Letitia with a hint of a smile.

'Yeah. But we can't let even a whisper of this get out. It could jeopardise the development. I don't want Holly rocking the boat.'

'You said she'd have no claim on it!'

'Financially, no. That's well covered, but she

could cause problems with objections. Last thing I need is some forensic accountant prying into my affairs. They can untangle the most complicated offshore network.'

'What's this "offshore" bit? Is it going to make that sort of money for you?'

'It'll make a reasonable killing.'

'It's risky. Why not try an enviro-friendly, low-key luxury resort?' Letitia asked.

'It'll be enviro-friendly enough, and it's right up there with what the market wants. This concept is aimed at the next generation of grey power. That includes half the council for a start. We're hitting the world's biggest market, rich, retiring baby boomers.'

'There's something I can't explain that's bugging me about this project,' said Letitia. 'I can't put my finger on it, but the feeling is always there. Probably sounds stupid to you, but every time this scheme comes up on my daily agenda I feel odd, like . . .' her voice trailed off and she looked down in embarrassment.

'Like what?' Andrew asked gently.

She took a deep breath. 'Like someone is looking over my shoulder.' They both fell silent; Andrew was totally lost for words. 'Well, say something,' she said finally, struggling to keep her voice down.

'Okay. Once the signatures are on the contracts you'll feel on top of the world, believe me. Just think of dollar signs and the world will be instantly brighter. I've been down this path before.' He then expediently changed the subject. 'By the way, I'll be back up there in a week or so. Holly has our kids visiting. I'd like to see the draft contracts while I'm there, how are they coming along? Our Thai friend is due out here soon.'

They began talking about some of the contractual details and Andrew immediately felt more relaxed. Whenever Letitia made even the slightest comment about their future together he tensed. Separating from Holly was in the too-hard basket and would stay there for quite a while. The young woman sitting opposite him was a nice little romance on the side, but letting a dalliance rip apart a marriage of over twenty years was an outcome he didn't want to think about.

'Eddie? It's Cheyne here from the Dolphin Centre.'

'Hi. What can I do for you?'

'After watching you video Erica's funeral, it occurred to me you might be just the person we need to do a little filming for us.'

'For the Dolphin Centre? Sure, I'd be interested. What did you have in mind?'

'Actually, it's for the community. The Dolphin Centre is just part of the Creative Community Collective up here. We have a couple of projects under way, but before we launch them we'd like the wider public to know more about us as a group.'

Eddie had trouble making the connection. 'I thought the Dolphin Centre was part of the Shahvanas?'

'It was, then the Dolphin Centre broke away, becoming a commune of over a hundred hectares.' He went on to explain that while it had grown out of a quasi-religious group of followers of some late guru, the commune now used modern technology and entrepreneurial business ventures to enhance its diverse services and alternative lifestyle philosophy.

'There are a lot of cults and groups in this area,' Eddie said.

'The Bay's tolerance is part of the attraction. There's everything from Osho to the Raelians, to inspired individuals who believe they have the holy grail for peace, love and happiness. Wish it were so easy,' Cheyne chuckled.

'So what's this collective?'

'In a few words, thinking, caring people who share common values and a world view of how we want the future to be. There are people all over the world who think this way but feel invisible until they find like-minded people. Perhaps we don't necessarily agree on how to bring this about or put principles into practice, but by working and thinking together about how we lead our lives, we hope we might help bring about a wiser, saner life.'

Eddie grinned. 'Sounds interesting. I guess I need to come and talk to you about it. Can you give me a hint about this project now?'

'We'll show you the concept when you come up, get across what we want to say, and to whom. Then you can work out a filming budget for us, okay?'

'Sure. How about next Wednesday morning?'
'Good one. Ten am.'
'Ten it is.'

Scotty, the maitre d' at Vincent's had reserved his best table on the terrace for Nola Florens. The French champagne she'd ordered was chilling, her special menu prepared. Scotty was curious about Nola's companion. She rarely dined out unless it was with a group. But he was quite surprised when she arrived in her queenly style accompanied by a handsome younger man wearing Armani and a little too much expensive cologne. A family member? No, he was being too attentive in an almost flirtatious manner.

Scotty unfolded the damask napkins. 'An aperitif?'

'Just bring what I've ordered, Scotty dear, thank you.' Nola turned her attention to the man opposite. 'So, Wesley, tell me more.'

Chapter Ten

A LIGHT NOR'-EASTER OFF THE SEA MADE THE
temperature on the beach perfect for sunbathers.
The waves rolling in at the Point were not big but
beautifully shaped for excellent breaks as they
reached the surfers sitting astride boards and surf
skis, or paddling boogie boards. It was a rising
tide and the surf was going to get even better over
the next couple of hours. Days like this were common enough at The Bay for the locals to take it all
for granted, but for visitors out there positioning
themselves for the next good break it was a time,
a place, and a surf that kept them smiling. And
what's more, being a Monday, it wasn't overcrowded; no crush of schoolies, no weekend mob.

Holly was sitting on the sand watching

Melanie and Marcus, who were waiting side by side on their boards for the next big wave.

'The view almost beats Bondi,' said Marcus, deadpan.

'Yep,' Melanie replied. 'A spread of apartment towers just above high tide would make it perfect.' They exchanged grins. 'Mum's got it made. I mean that house is just so well situated and she can come down here any time, any day. God, what a life.'

'Except we're not here, or Dad,' said Marcus. 'I wonder how much she misses us.'

'I thought she'd never manage this on her own. In Sydney Mum seemed to like the idea we were in the same city, even though we didn't see her much. Now it's like she's making a new life for herself.' Melanie sounded faintly aggrieved.

'So you keep saying,' said Marcus, signalling an end to the conversation by throwing himself flat on his board, shouting, 'Out the back. Out the back.' He began paddling towards a wave that was building up for a break, and Melanie took off after him.

Holly was so happy to see her children enjoying themselves. They each led such separate lives these days. Richmond House was absorbing all her time and she was feeling fulfilled, but she realised it hadn't always been that way. She thought back to when the children were young. They had made her feel fulfilled, too, but in those days it seemed it was her time that was occupied, not her head, her spirit or her soul. Of course she loved, adored, her two children. But now she wished she'd also taken time out for herself. She might have been a more interesting and happier mother.

The children, and their father, had accepted her role without question. She devoted all her attention to the home, their entertainment, ferrying them and their friends to school, sport and social functions. And then one day they were out the door with scarcely a backward glance, on to university, living with friends, driving themselves, hardly any time to come home and visit. This was good, she kept telling herself. This was expected. So why had she felt resentful? Slowly it had dawned on her as she talked with her new friends in The Bay: she felt that she was a shell, she had never explored her inner-self. What did she want from life? She'd never dared dream great dreams, the women's movement had never touched her. There also came the sneaking thought that to dive into the dark waters of her soul would require more courage than she felt she had.

'What are you daydreaming about, Mum?' Melanie carefully put down her surfboard, dropped to the sand and began drying her hair.

'I was thinking how my life has changed since I came to The Bay.'

'Yeah, it's a fantastic place, like being on holiday all the time.'

'It's more than that. Much, much more.'

'Like?'

'Heavy stuff, Mel,' she warned with a smile.

'Test me. See if I faint.'

'It's about feeling I belong to a community, and knowing that a sense of community really matters and helps makes individual lives more meaningful. How's that for starters?' She passed the sunblock, then went on. 'I'm still coming to grips with what it all means, but there you are.'

Melanie said with a smile, 'Go on. I'm coping.'

'Okay. It's also about a new range of relationships between women, of trust and support, and exploration of oneself.'

'Consciousness raising. Wow, Mum, better late than never. Is that what this deal with the old house is all about?'

Holly chuckled. 'Well maybe your father would think so. I suspect he thinks it's all a bit self-indulgent. He can't see a fast enough profit.'

'You could sell it after next New Year,' Melanie responded seriously. 'Keep it through the holidays so we can bring our friends up, then sell. You'll make money on it, if you don't spend a fortune on the renovations. Bit of paint, plant lots of geraniums. Your builder seems very fastidious. That's expensive.'

'Is that all you think I'm doing? Just trying to make a fast buck? And then what?'

'Hey, don't get your back up. Do something else. Fix up another place somewhere. I mean The Bay is a nice place, for a holiday. But you wouldn't want to live here.'

'Why not? You don't know what's here. There's a lot more than the beach. This is a cutting-edge community.'

'Hello, Mum! Your home is in Mosman! With Dad. I can't see him fitting in with the greenie guru dopeheads up here. Can you? And you can't spend your days running a guesthouse. God, make some money and enjoy it.'

'I am enjoying myself,' said Holly stubbornly. 'Listen, I'm going up to the house to get lunch. You and Marcus come when you're ready.' She softened her voice. 'Or do what you want. I just want you to enjoy yourselves. If you'd prefer to hang out here or eat downtown, do it.'

'Lunch at the house will be great. I'll have a sunbathe first though.' Melanie was making amends too. So often there were these little sparks between them; if not stamped on they could burst into small fires.

When the kids had first arrived Holly had felt clingy, she had missed them and thinking about Erica made her appreciate how lucky she was. But soon enough the daily bickering had surfaced. It seemed they could never please each other. Holly desperately wanted them both to feel the way she did about Richmond House. But they didn't see it through her eyes, with all its romance and history. They saw an old place being renovated with perhaps too much adherence to its heritage; that it was in a stunning location where they could bring their friends to surf and party.

It occurred to Holly as she hiked up the hill to the house that perhaps she shouldn't snuff out the sparks, but let a healthy cleansing bushfire rush over them. Like in nature, when it took a fire to renew the country. She'd never had an adult confrontation with her children. There had been petty fights over childhood issues like keeping rooms tidy, coming in late, appropriate friends, but they'd never communicated on a serious level as adults. She didn't think they would have listened if she'd disagreed anyhow. She suspected her children didn't regard her as someone with whom to have any deep intellectual debate. But with her new feelings of self-confidence and independence, she would welcome it. Now she didn't feel she had everything to lose. She wanted to be her own person. And, she suspected, while there might be some conflict, they could only respect her for it.

Holly felt in her bones and heart that she was coming to terms with who she was, her potential, her aspirations, her value, her contribution to those involved with her on a regular basis, the community and, hell, the planet. Her children, and her husband, would have to understand and accept her on these new terms. She was undergoing a gentle transformation, which would affect them all.

She was surprised to find Mitchell at the house. He had said he would keep away while she had her children there so as not to disrupt the family, and he apologised. 'I need the handles and brass hinges to try to match them. Stolle found a guy who can make anything from Asian antiques to copies of pressed-metal ceiling panels.'

'Great. Want a cup of tea?'

'Thanks, but no. I have to see a client.' He gave

her a second glance. 'Are you all right? You look tense.'

'It's the old syndrome of being chief cook and bottle washer. And punching bag,' she said with a small smile. 'I'd got used to just looking after me.'

'Everything okay?' He knew she'd been anxious that her children love Richmond House as much as she did.

'Kids. When the house has been fixed up they want to bring their friends here, then sell it and move on. I might as well be running a caravan park.'

Mitchell was tempted to remind her that he thought that seemed to have been her plan when he'd first met her. 'It's the nature of children to be selfish. Which is why we should look after our own needs as well as theirs. You do what feels right and good to you. Unless there's a financial constraint –'

'It's not that. Though I have sunk my own savings into this, and Marcus is pressing me to help him fund his own business.'

'That's ambitious. He hasn't left uni yet, has he?' exclaimed Mitchell. 'What kind of business?'

'He's been designing websites and doing graphic work. Andrew thinks he's pretty good.'

'There's probably money in it. But he's a bit young to be talking about his own business, isn't he?'

'I don't really know. My world, our world, seems to have been left behind by this new generation. Do you think that, or is it only me? I can't help feeling the ground is constantly shifting under my feet since I came here, forcing me to review practically every aspect of my life, all my values.'

Mitchell had heard her talking this way before, and it hurt him to see her like this. With the memory of Andrew and Letitia Sweetman still vivid in his mind he was torn between whether to say something or hope Andrew would come to his senses and see the treasure he had in Holly. 'Listen, Holly, we all go through periods of change in our lives. And this place tends to accelerate change, to bring about an awakening,' he said.

'I didn't come here to change my life. I just wanted to add something,' she said, sounding very unsure.

Mitchell hesitated, then said quietly, 'Would you like to experience something special? It's probably a once in a lifetime thing that I think you might enjoy, but it might also help you think about things – you, your life, your future – in a different way.'

'Gosh, like climb Mount Hazard to see the sun rise, or spend three hours in a float tank?' she joked. Then said seriously, 'Seeing as you put it that way, how can I say no? I'm game for anything these days.'

'It's nothing scary or dangerous. But you need a week away. Come on the whale-watch expedition with me. I'm involved with the Oceania project so I go every year . . . it's really special. A week on a new catamaran sailing off Hervey Bay watching the whales. There's a group of us that go for research, collecting skin samples the whales shed for DNA testing, all kinds of things. But paying guests come along because it's, well, phenomenal.'

'Do you see whales? For sure? I'd hate to wallow around without seeing a whale. Like, close up?'

Mitchell laughed. 'Oh, yes. They know us, we have the same ones come to us each year. We know them all. There's even a rare white female that puts in an appearance if we're lucky. They come right up to the side of the boat. It's something that's hard to describe. You have to be there, as they say.'

'It sounds fabulous. I think I've earned a break. I was planning to go back down to Sydney but now I have the children here, I don't feel the need . . . ' Her voice trailed off.

'Listen, think about it and we'll talk more. I'll introduce you to Trish and Wally who run it.'

'Great. Oh, Mitch, Mac asked me if a group of ladies from the aged home could come up for a tour of the house and I'd show them what I'm doing. I'm not ready, nor is the garden, but they seem to love any outing so I agreed. But I thought maybe we could get rid of the old timber and some of the building stuff from the garden.'

'Sure thing. No problem. See you in a couple of days. Cheers.'

After videoing yet another wedding of a Japanese couple on the lighthouse reserve Eddie wandered over to Tina's office to take up her invitation for 'a cuppa'.

'Another session of creative shooting?' Tina asked as he entered.

'Don't knock it,' Eddie said. 'Bread and butter stuff, and it helps kick along the town's tourism business. At least it's better than doing a wedding on top of Mount Hazard at dawn. Did that once, and don't want to repeat the experience.'

'Milk and one if I remember.'

'Ta. Have you brought over any of the old things from the lighthouse yet?'

'Knew you'd ask. Over there.' She pointed to two large cardboard boxes of papers, books and folders. 'I've already given in to temptation and spent a few hours browsing, and it's fascinating. I'm starting to make an archival index on the computer.'

Eddie sipped his tea and glanced at Tina, then walked over to the boxes. 'Some pretty dry stuff amongst all this. You prepared to wade through it all?'

'History was my favourite subject at school and uni,' she said. 'For a while I contemplated becoming a history teacher.'

'Can't imagine you confined to a classroom,' said Eddie. 'You show me what to put down and I'll add to the archive as I go through the boxes. How about that?'

She quickly brought up the file on her computer and they sat together as she explained the system. Then she pointed to a desk in the corner of the room. 'That can be your research centre,' she declared. 'No one is using it. And when you've finished, you can buy me a drink.'

Eddie was soon totally absorbed in the old diaries, journals, ships' logs and notes kept by the lighthouse keepers. He found anecdotes and records of events that were straight out of the pages of a boys' own adventure book or a swashbuckling movie. They were so interesting he kept reading extracts to Tina until she interrupted.

'Rule number one. Reading aloud only permitted for major discoveries, or sexy bits. I've got work to do, you know.'

'Okay. But what an amazing lively town Beacon Bay must have been in the old days. Full of a lot of hard-drinking working men, from the sound of it.'

'Some of the older women of the town have told me The Bay was not the place for refined young ladies. It was considered a bit down at heel and working class. It was a place for slumming, before it became a place for sunning.'

'Very nicely put.'

'Flattery will get you anything,' she said, and returned to her paperwork.

Eddie picked up a new file, forcing himself to concentrate. The variety of information was at once enlightening and confusing; so many diverse impressions, so many interesting stories. Everything he read gave him fresh ideas for his developing documentary. He became so engrossed that he didn't notice Tina leave to make her final patrol of the day. When she came back he still had his head down, carefully scanning old black and white photographs.

'These are great photos, if you like slaughter-houses. Nineteen-fifties. Where'd they come from?' he asked.

'Sid Wainwright donated them. He was the last meat inspector at the abattoir, near the whaling station. Sid only had a box brownie with one speed and one aperture opening.'

'Well he had a good eye for framing a subject, even if there is a lot of blood in these shots,' Eddie said. He flicked through some yellowing news-paper clippings. 'Sid had funny ideas about what made news, judging by what he kept. Some bloke hanged himself under the jetty one New Year's Day. "Gruesome start to the year" the local rag called it. And here's another tragedy, "Bomb Blast Kills Boy", an unexploded World War Two bomb a kid found in the sand.'

'Yeah, it was from a whale chaser the Ameri-cans commandeered for an ammunition boat in the war. The crew got on the turps and crashed it into the old jetty. That was hushed up. The wreck is a favourite spot for local divers,' said Tina. 'Sid has the story, among many. He's one of the town's great ear benders. He only needs an audience of one and he's away.'

'You mean he's still around? How lucid is he?'

'Sid? He's in his eighties and seems in good shape. But he's deaf as a post without his hearing aid and you can't get away from him for hours at a stretch.'

'I've got to talk to him. How fantastic to get *that* on camera: the old boy reminiscing around the town. How it was, what happened, what he thinks of it all now. Where can I find him?'

'No worries there, I've got his number,' Tina said and tossed a set of keys into the air and caught them. 'It's lock-up time and you owe me a drink. Remember?'

They sat under palms in the patio of the Big Pub and took in the state of the surf just across the road. The usual locals having an early sundowner were talking about the recent local rugby league team victory but lack of crowd support was a worry, and the run of brilliant weather that was giving the tourists a fabulous season. There were also the backpackers, many of them from overseas, reading mail from home, writing postcards and entries in diaries, and comparing travel experiences.

At one table Holly was having drinks with her children, who were both a little sunburned, and laughing at the photos they'd just collected from the chemist around the corner. Billy and his family were eating hamburgers, Stolle was talking to a man and scribbling notes. The back of his T-shirt was emblazoned with the motto 'Globalisation Sucks'. The hard sunlight that dominated the day had softened, the nor'-easter was dying down, and the ocean glare had been replaced by a subdued blue. It was as if The Bay was taking a breath before an evening of frenzied enjoyment.

On rocks by the beach a handful of drummers and a couple of didge players were warming up with impromptu bursts of music, in preparation for their evening ritual of sending the sun down in a crescendo of sound. Several people danced on the sand, each wrapped in their interpretation and enjoyment of the rhythm.

'Are you going to bring Sid here for a comment on the changing scene?' said Tina. 'There was a funny old pub on this spot in the twenties.' Not waiting for a reply she went on, 'Have you settled on a theme for this doco yet?'

Eddie took time to answer. 'Probably end up being several themes, but one thing is obvious. Paradise found, paradise for sale, paradise lost.'

'I know what you mean. We must have passed a dozen signs just on the way here, all saying "For Sale. Development Opportunity".'

'Everyone keeps saying this place is so special, but just how far will they go to keep it like that in the face of development pressures? The Bay is a hot site on the web, on the itinerary of half the world's backpackers, on the agenda of every Aussie teenager, and in the eyes of every greedy developer who passes by.'

'A good question to ask. Best of luck in finding an answer,' Tina said, raising her glass. 'You're up against the Greed is Good tidal flow. We'll even lose our beaches if we don't put in offshore reefs because of our building interference. Making headway against that is like paddling . . . well, you know.'

Eddie nodded, and they both tuned in to the drummers who were lifting the tempo as the sun dipped towards the distant ranges.

Sid's old brick and weatherboard house tucked on a small block right across from Tiny Bay Beach was a gem.

'I knew every inch of The Bay so when the missus and I decided to build I bought the best bit of land. I still don't get tired of looking at that,' he said, pointing to the sweep of ocean stretching to the horizon. 'The Cape is to the left so the lighthouse beam peers into our kitchen every night.'

Beyond the headland, across the bay, were the distant ranges and the length of Mighty Beach disappearing into the northern haze.

Sid was steady if cautious on his feet, white hair stood in tufts that refused to lie flat, there was a gap or two in his cheerful smile and behind his thick lenses his eyes were a washed-out blue. He wore a hand-knitted vest over a shirt with the sleeves rolled up above the elbow. Touches of 'the late missus' were everywhere. Photos and mementos crowding table and shelves, crochet on almost every surface, the handiwork of Mrs Wainwright, whose basket of thread and crochet hooks rested beside her leather chair in the glassed-in sunroom. Here Sid sat, occasionally glancing at the empty chair beside his own.

'The missus and I sat here to watch the sunset most nights for over fifty years,' he said. 'They never seem as bright as they used to when she was here.' He gave a bit of a smile. 'Might have to clean the windows, eh?' He ran a finger across one of the glass louvres. 'Now, young man, what do you want to know?'

He relished the company, and sipping his sherry told Eddie how he'd come to The Bay as a young man to work in the abattoir that was next to the whaling station. 'Both were messy jobs, so the set-up close to the beach was convenient. And in those days it was away from the town centre. Town has spread a bit. Just a few fishing shacks along the beach in the sixties.'

'Yeah, now look at the development,' said Eddie. 'This will soon be a place only for rich people. I can't afford to live near the beach.'

'Greed. Gets everyone in the end. I have 'em banging on my door a couple of times a week. My kids will probably knock this place down and put up units.' He sighed. 'But we've had good times here. Watched them grow up on the beach down there.'

'Tell me about the whaling,' Eddie asked, to change the subject.

'You've never smelled anything like it,' he said. 'By God, it was a stench. A lot of the men who worked at the whaling station never really got rid of the stink. Didn't help marital relations,' he said grinning. 'You always knew when one of the local girls for hire had been with a bloke from the whaling station.' Eddie smiled and Sid gave a bit of a wink.

'So you were the local meat inspector?'

'That's right. I was also hired to be the whaling inspector. Whaling had stopped before the war and was just getting going again in 1946.'

'What did you do?'

'I had to measure the whale, check it wasn't undersize, or milk filled or pregnant. I had to write a lot of reports along with the gunner's report about the actual kill.'

'What were the whales used for? I thought once petroleum and electricity came along, that wiped out the need for the oil.'

'The oil – it smelled like cod liver oil – was in demand for food products in Europe after the war so it was sent by road tanker to Brisbane and shipped to England. It was also used in all sorts of things like processed stock feed. The meat was used in pet food. Some was sold to fishermen on the coast here as bait for traps. I even had an American come out wanting to buy the whale meat to feed minks on big mink farms.'

'Uh, oh,' exclaimed Eddie. 'Killing whales to feed minks for fur coats! The animal libbers wouldn't like that.'

'People weren't so fussy back then.'

'Was there a lot of interest around the town when whales were caught?'

'When a whale was pulled up on the jetty onto the railway flat top and a small engine – we called it the green frog – hauled it to the station, it was like centre court at Wimbledon,' declared Sid. 'In those days no one thought about saving the whales. Not until the damage was done.'

'I guess they had no idea what they were doing. Killed off their one industry, eh,' Eddie remarked.

Sid picked up an album from the small table beside him and pulled out a newspaper clipping. 'This only came to light a few years go. The International Whaling Commission had very strict regulations and yet listen to this *Herald* article I kept.' He adjusted his glasses and read, 'Files kept secret for many years have revealed that the Soviet Union systematically slaughtered a large part of the world's protected whale population, selling some valuable meat to Japan.' He lifted a finger for added emphasis, 'Long buried documents show that the Soviet Ministry of Fisheries, in a military-style operation lasting forty years, deceived the commission about the number of whales it slaughtered.'

'God, by how many?' asked Eddie.

'By thousands.' Sid continued to read, 'As a result of the plunder, the humpback whale herd around New Zealand and Australia was exterminated by 1966. Six years later, the sei whale herds in the Indian Ocean were destroyed, and by 1975 the sperm whales north of Hawaii had all but vanished.'

He put down the clipping. 'Bloody criminal. As bad as the Japanese today,' said Sid, unselfconscious at his change in attitude towards his one-time profession.

Eddie was hooked by Sid's strong, clear voice. He looked good too, probably be even better on the screen. He briefly explained to Sid what he was trying to do with the documentary and was comfortable about asking him to play a role, convinced that inside the old man was a performer just waiting for the right stage. 'Why don't you take me and my camera on a tour of The Bay and talk about how it used to be?'

'Ah, no one is interested in the ramblings of an old geezer like me,' he said modestly. But Eddie could see he was flattered.

'Let's go back to the old whaling station and you can describe what it was like. We can use the photographs that are around, including yours.'

'I'll think about it, young fella. Let me think about it. Might be orright.' He smiled, and Eddie knew he had the old man on board. 'But there's nothin' up the beach now, you know that. Mighty Beach is nothin' but a beach now.'

'All the dunes and the bush belong to the council, don't they?' said Eddie.

'Little bit where the parking lot is, but the rest is privately owned. Used to be the whaling station property. Americans owned it, until it went bust. Dunno who has it nowadays. Worth a bloody fortune, I'd say.'

Kimberley arrived at The Teepee in a linen dress, carefully applied make-up and yellow sandals with small kitten heels. Billy reacted by covering his eyes as if hit by a blinding light. 'Who is this vision of loveliness?'

'Come off it. I need my hair trimmed and could you blow it for me so it looks, you know, together.'

He flourished the plastic cape like a bullfighter as she settled in the chair, then swept it around her. 'Big date? Meeting with the school principal?'

She looked smug. 'None of the above. Try job interview. Final call back. Been through two interviews already.'

'Kim! Brilliant! Doing what? Hell, it doesn't matter. Hey, was it because of what I said the other week?'

'Yes. You sort of tipped me over the edge. I was feeling so low and useless, then after Erica I felt I had to pull myself together.'

'I meant to say, what you said at the funeral – really powerful, Kim. Made me think, I can tell you.'

Kimberley flushed but looked pleased. 'I didn't think I could say two words in public, and especially feeling so upset.'

'So what's the job?'

'I haven't actually got it yet. You know it's strange when you put something out into the universe what happens. The minute I decided I wanted to get a proper job, do something – bingo! Things fell in my path.'

'Like?' persisted Billy.

'Working in the council. Some fancy title like Community Liaison Assistant, but really, it's just a jumped-up dogsbody. I'm helping all the councillors who are out and about, answering the phone, taking messages, listening to people's complaints. I have to do a weekly report on community concerns for the councillors to pass on for action. Also write a newspaper column based on what's getting people talking to each other and to the councillors. The column will run in the council's weekly advertisement. I'm no threat to Stolle,' she laughed. 'He fancies breaking the country's biggest scoop in his column one day.'

Billy nodded his head approvingly and rested his hands on her shoulders. 'I'm knocked out. It's fan-bloody-tastic. And so quick. You're really an action girl when you put your mind to it.'

'We'll see how it works out,' she said hesitatingly. 'I've started a crash course on computer skills.'

'Bravo. But how are you going to cope with such opposites as Jimmy Bright and Tricia Rich? She's a greenie and he's pro-development. He voted for the new arcade and road bridge of shops and is behind the eco-hamlet down by the lily ponds.'

'Eco-hamlet my foot,' said Kimberley. 'Read housing estate!'

'You're going to have to hone your diplomatic skills. How can you work for two people who loathe each other that much? And there are a lot of tensions among the other councillors, and the staff. A regular hothouse of intrigue.'

'Maybe that's why I'm there. To help build bridges. They can talk through me instead of yelling at each other. It's going to be interesting – if I get it,' she added.

'You'll get it. You look professional, personable, you're a local, you're committed to the town. It's a cinch. What's Matty think?'

'She's thrilled. She was a bit impressed I'd got my act together, as she put it. It's only a few hours a day, but enough to get off welfare.'

He finished blow-drying her hair, flicked the cape and helped her out of the chair. 'Go get 'em, gal.'

It was late afternoon. Shadows stretched and the waters of the bay were calm, reflecting small clusters of clouds in the softening sunlight. Holly, Marcus and Curly walked slowly along Mighty Beach enjoying being by themselves for the first time since she moved north. They walked in silence for a while, taking in the tranquillity of the long beach and the music of the surf.

'Are you and Mel enjoying it up here?' Holly asked, breaking into their thoughts.

'Ten out of ten. A totally cool place,' he laughed. 'Never thought we'd have a place up here.'

Holly smiled. 'I like it too, but Melanie thinks I should sell up as soon as Richmond House is renovated.' She glanced at her tall son beside her, waiting for his opinion.

'Mmm, it makes sense. But you have to have a successful business going to get your money back. The idea is to establish a trendy B & B, you're not just doing renovations, right?'

'That's the plot. It means a longer investment of money and time.'

'And you don't mind that?' He picked up a stick and tossed it for Curly.

'Like you said, this is one of the top spots in the country. I think my place will do very well.'

'So just how long do you see yourself staying here?' he asked. 'What does Dad think? It's the first time you've been separated for so long. Are things . . . okay between you?' he asked gingerly. He'd never talked so intimately with his mother before.

Holly squeezed his arm. 'Everything is fine. Funnily, better than it's ever been. I think I needed this time alone. All the years I spent being a wife and mum, when I look back now it was a bit like being a mother hen and suddenly I was facing the prospect of becoming an old chook. I mean, I don't regret a minute of it and I hope you guys think I did a good job.'

'What do you mean, an old chook? You're no boiler, Mum. You're looking the best I've seen you in years, and I notice you're causing a few heads to turn at the beach.'

'Thanks. Mums need that sort of compliment. It's hard to explain, but it was like all my feathers were being pulled out.'

'You had bald patches in your protective pelt?'

'Exactly. I needed time to repair myself, find the missing bits. Find out who I was.'

'So you're finding yourself up here in The Bay?' Marcus was struggling to keep the cynicism out of his voice. This didn't sound like his Mosman mother.

'Now don't give me a hard time like Mel did. I'm not abandoning you. Or your father. He's involved in a huge new project; that's his feathering, his fulfilment –'

'Do you know much about it?'

'Not much. Frankly, I've been so busy with my own project I haven't been following his life too closely,' she said with some satisfaction. For once she wasn't playing second fiddle to Andrew and she hoped her kids were impressed with what she was doing. 'I was hoping you guys would be happy I'm leading my own life.'

'Oh, yeah. It's great. It's just not how we've always seen you.'

'You know the essential things never change,' said Holly with a rush of affection. 'The fact I love you, I'm here for you, no matter what.'

Curly trotted back with the stick and dropped it at Marcus's feet as if it was something he'd forgotten on the sand. She made no bouncing effort to indicate she'd love him to throw it again, feigning nonchalance as she walked at heel. 'She's dying for you to throw it again,' said Holly. 'The attitude is part of the game.'

Marcus laughed with her and tossed the stick to the edge of the wet sand. 'Mum, seeing as we're talking about, well, dreams, aspirations, new lives –'

'My God, don't tell me you want to get married or something!'

'No, calm down. It's the same old passion. The internet business idea. It's a dead-set winner but I need money. I have all the details, business and financial proposals, backers who'll come in with advertisers.'

'How much money?' asked Holly cautiously.

'Quite a lot. It's setting up the office support that is expensive. Keeping that running until the cash flow reaches a certain level is what I'm trying to secure. Maybe you'd like to look at the whole business plan. I brought it up with me, just in case.'

Holly was surprised and flattered. 'You mean I'm being treated as a businesswoman and not just Mum who's a soft touch?'

'I never thought that. I wouldn't ask you for several thousand dollars without some sort of security.'

'That much? Mmm, that could be tricky,' said Holly.

'Look, forget it. Don't worry about it. I'd ask Dad but you know how he is. He just wants me to finish uni, then get into the real game. Something hot, like waste management.'

'That's not unreasonable. And it's only a year away.'

'I know, but opportunities like this are only there for a short time.'

'Yes,' said Holly. 'A lot of people who launched dotcom companies over the last couple of years also only lasted a short time.'

'It was an inevitable shake out, Mum. We've

learned a lot and can see the way to go forward more clearly now. We know this idea will work. I have pretty influential people interested in getting involved.'

'So why don't they put up the seed money?'

'They will, I'm sure, but I have to bring something to the table, show them I'm serious.'

'Let me see your business plan,' said Holly, wondering how on earth she'd find the money when she'd put everything of her own into Richmond House.

That evening over a bottle of wine Marcus went through his proposal for a graphic art service on the internet using a smart new software program he had developed. He ran through the people involved, the short and long term turnover projections.

'I have to say it all looks impressive. But any business is a risk, as your father says.' Marcus waited and Holly gave him a small smile. 'As an investor do I get shares?'

He grabbed her hand. 'Then you'll do it? That's great, Mum. We'll put you on the board!'

Holly was elated to see the light in her son's eyes. While she understood the basics of his web business concept, she had no idea whether or not it would succeed. But she wanted to give him the opportunity to have a go at his dream. Like she was doing.

Chapter Eleven

Beacon Bay, May 10th, 1901

How I enjoy living here. Such a grand day yesterday. We took the two boys into town in the sulky for the Federation festivities, which culminated in the switching on of the light of our brand new lighthouse. It is an elegant structure, freshly painted white, gleaming brass and polished wood. A new gold coin was buried in the sandstone base for good luck. The rough old stone beacon – soon to be pulled down – looks most insignificant beside it. However the beacon has served its purpose for many years as a signal to sailors and whalers.

The Aboriginal people, many full bloods whom we rarely see in the district, along with the mixed races here performed a beautiful ceremony.

But to begin the day's proceedings.

Along the promenade – as we call Beach Street, the sandy road along the beachfront – there were flags and banners and many people strolling in whatever finery one possesses in this place. Quite a few had travelled by steamer up the coast and rivers, others had come by the train.

At Arabella Street, where the Jetty Hostelry and Wright's General Store sit on opposite corners, a huge archway stretched over the road. It was made from young saplings and wire and decorated with flowers, native greenery and displays of locally grown produce including the new crop of sugarcane. Many archways through the town were decorated with our coat of arms and appropriate expressions of our new status as one country. The bandstand was similarly bedecked with flags and the musicians played well. But when it came time for the official party to arrive, Mr Blanchard, the town clerk, appeared on the platform to announce that they had been delayed at the Honeysuckle Creek crossing due to minor flooding and the absence of the punt. However, he declared that proceedings would commence as planned, seeing the ladies of the town had prepared delicacies too good to let spoil. At this there was a hearty cheer and the band struck up a jolly tune. Later in the day an ox was roasted and kegs of ale tapped for the men.

The boys had a ride along the beach on a

camel led by one of the Hindoo workers from the market gardens, followed by a ride in the little train that carries goods from the sheds lining the jetty to the vessels. So many ships of all description were crowded into the bay, many of them gaily decorated to make the whole scene most festive. The weather could not have been kinder. Sunny, a slight breeze to cool us and the great blue sky as clear and bright as you could wish. The sea sparkled like a crown jewel, the waves long and gentle, and when several dolphins appeared, cavorting through the breakers, there was much excitement as it was considered an excellent omen.

There was a great picnic on the racecourse – a rather poor excuse for such a title but it serves its purpose – and children with their fathers competed in sporting events for prizes. These were modest but by the fierceness of the competition one would have thought they were competing for nuggets of gold!

Speaking of which, there has been much talk of the possibility of goldfields being opened up in the ranges of Mount Hazard. A French geologist has been exploring the ridges and taken away samples. And there have been gentlemen of quality visiting the town staying at the Jetty Hotel who say they are investigating new opportunities in 'the paradise of the Richmond'.

This has not been received well among the populace, the common feeling being that if there are riches to be found in the district, the local people will do the finding and reap the rewards. Lars explained to me, as best he understood it, that Mount Hazard and the ridges around it are the remains of an ancient volcano and the valleys formed by the flow of lava from its peak.

Goodness knows what minerals or makings of our planet have been thrown out by the eruptions. It is not easy to know what truth there is in all this talk and what it might mean for the future of our town. There, I have written it: our town. I do so truly feel I belong here. I dread the day Lars might want to return to his frosty homeland, but sad as it is I take some comfort in the knowledge that he still has not shown any desire to reunite with his far-off family. He was much moved, as were we all, by the visit of Captain Richmond and his praise of the contribution Lars has made to the efficiency of the station and the success of the whale catch. The bonus presented to Lars in the form of shares in the company is greatly appreciated.

Eddie stopped reading and pondered on the diary entry: goldfields, shares in the company, how exciting it must have been then. There seemed to be so much opportunity, so much to look forward to. He picked up the diary and walked outside the lighthouse keeper's cottage to find Tina remonstrating with some tourists who had climbed over the safety fence to pose for photographs at the very edge of the headland.

She strode back to him, shaking her head. 'Galahs, think they're so smart. That's a long drop.'

'That's why they do it. Human nature. The thrill of the possibility, remote as it may be. Didn't they teach you at ranger college about the absurdity of human behaviour?'

Tina shrugged. 'Reality is different from the classroom. I'm still coming to terms with that. Anyway, what has your latest session with the past revealed?' She nodded at the journal in his hands. It had become something of a joke that Hannah was 'the mystery woman' in Eddie's life.

'Gold. She talks about goldfields around here. Did that ever come to anything?'

'I don't imagine so. Though on the early parish maps there are outlying areas marked "gold-fields".'

Eddie stared across the bay to the misty peak of Mount Hazard. 'I bet there's something to it.'

'There's gold in them thar hills, eh Eddie,' she said with an exaggerated drawl. 'The real wealth in those days and now, for that matter, is in the soil, in the red volcanic soil that will grow almost anything in this climate.'

Eddie followed her back inside. 'Hannah talks about the Hindu market gardeners. Where did they come from?'

'Probably brought in to work in the sugarcane farms up north like the Kanakas.'

'Shanghaied, blackbirded, kidnapped, you mean. Not exactly willing indentured labourers,' said Eddie.

'When you look at old pictures of the locals you can see different races in many of the faces,' Tina said. 'Aboriginal, Indian, Chinese, Caucasian. They all seemed to mix in and intermarry.'

'Like Broome,' said Eddie. He closed Hannah's diary. 'I'll get back to that. I have to go and meet Alice and her mother. The big move.' He gave a half smile. He'd quickly realised Tina was sensitive to the situation between himself and Laura, and the sharing of young Alice. In one way her discomfort pleased him. It hinted that she had more than just a friendly interest in him. On the other hand, he hoped it wouldn't frighten her off from deepening their relationship. He enjoyed Tina's company – they'd been for drinks and an occasional meal together – and they were both engrossed in exploring the contents of Hannah's journal and the other archival material.

'So Alice moves in with you as of today?'

'Yep. We're starting to cart all her gear out of the unit and back to the farm. God, she's got so much stuff. I can see where my money goes. Not to mention Laura's shopping habits. I hope Alice doesn't expect the same rate of acquisition from me.'

'Maybe she needs other stuff, non-material things,' said Tina cautiously. 'Like your time and attention.'

Before Eddie could reply, she tossed her car keys to him. 'Take my truck, it'll save you a couple of trips. More room. I'll take your bomb home if that's okay. See you back here tomorrow then?'

'Tina, you're a champ.' He blew her a kiss and

glancing at his watch knew he'd be a few minutes late. Laura hated it when he wasn't on time, yet she had no compunction keeping him waiting an hour or more.

As he drove along Beach Road he wondered what Hannah would make of the rows of holiday units and small hotels facing the grassy tree-lined strip across from the sand. He thought of her spending a day with her two boys enjoying a ride along the beach, games and a picnic: simple pleasures. The weight of caring for a young girl facing puberty pressed in on him. Laura had tried to turn Alice into a young sophisticate, doing the kind of things she liked to do: shopping, eating out, movies, parties with too many adults. Perhaps the biggest impact he could have on Alice would be to allow her to enjoy what was left of her childhood. He hoped that somehow together they would find the right influences in The Bay to help her make the transition to womanhood without too many hassles. Not that Laura was abrogating her responsibilities, but she liked to be mum only when it suited her.

Eddie bounded up the two flights of stairs to the unit to find Alice sitting on the top step surrounded by bags. 'How's it going?' He bent down and kissed her.

'A nightmare,' replied Alice with an air of boredom. 'She can't find a ring, a sweater and a pair of shoes.'

'Yours?'

'No. That wouldn't matter. Hers. I know she left them up at Jack's on the Gold Coast. She wore them up there weeks ago.'

'And came back shoeless, topless and ringless?'

Alice grinned. 'She has so much gear up there. She shops out Pacific Fair every trip.'

Eddie sat down beside her. 'You're not going to miss that kind of thing, are you? Shopping and stuff?'

'No, I have enough clothes. And I don't even like a lot of the things Mum buys. I know you aren't rich,' she added.

'There's rich and rich,' said Eddie cheerfully. 'I'm richer than you think. We'll manage. And Alice,' he squeezed her shoulders, 'don't ever feel you can't ask me for something you need or want.'

She leaned against him without answering and he felt she was close to tears. He gave her a quick hug, smiling as he said, 'But just 'cause you ask, doesn't mean you get. Everything's negotiable, okay?'

'Okay.'

Laura came out and stood looking at them for a moment. 'It might be nice if someone came and gave me a hand with all this stuff.'

'That's what we're here for,' said Eddie. 'I brought a friend's small truck. You'll need something bigger, no doubt,' he said wryly.

'No way,' said Laura in the dismissive tone that irritated him so much. 'I am not taking this crappy furniture. Jack's place has been done by Berlotti.'

'Bully for Berlotti.' Eddie wasn't going to ask what or who was Berlotti. 'Now which is Alice's pile?'

Alice was silent as they drove through the hinterland above The Bay.

Her mother's farewell had been brief, a quick hug, a few last words of advice about her hair and not to forget Cindy's birthday party. She'd call her every night and see her the following weekend, 'As soon as I'm organised, sweetheart.'

The mother–daughter heart to heart sessions about the new parenting arrangements had been uncomfortable to the point of tears for Alice. Laura did all the talking and Alice just nodded. In Laura's mind it was all settled. It was far preferable for Alice to stay with Eddie and her school friends in The Bay than in Jack's pristine apartment on the Gold Coast surrounded by oldies. Laura hinted it was sort of temporary, and that with luck one day they would be back together in a lovely big house.

Alice looked at the lush countryside flashing past, and as Eddie began whistling happily they exchanged smiles. She had learned long ago that her step-dad was a dreamer, but his dreams never made sense to her mother, or so she said. He was always seeing life in terms of stories, long stories, short stories, stories that could be told with pictures. It was something that Alice struggled to understand. It seemed so much harder to grasp than the simple idea of a lovely big house they could all share. Yet the very mystery of Eddie's dreams attracted her to him. She was suddenly startled out of her reverie.

'What are you thinking about?' he asked.

'Nothing much, Dad. Just looking at the bush, the mountain. Pretty, isn't it?'

'Yeah. Much better than looking from one flash apartment on the Gold Coast to another flash apartment next door.' Eddie pointed towards Mount Hazard. 'Besides, did you know there's gold around here? Some of the land was goldfields in the old days.'

'Is it still there?'

'Could be. I was going to have a chat to old Sid, he knows everything. Maybe we could go and pan in one of the creeks running down from the hills.'

'Pan in a creek? What's that mean?'

'Gold panning? Haven't you done the goldrush days at school?'

'A bit. History isn't my favourite subject. I don't see the point in hashing over stuff that happened ages ago. Our teacher keeps banging on about what trouble we're all in now. You know, pollution and conservation and stuff.'

'Fair enough. But if we look at what happened in the old days we can see where they went wrong, or what was better back then. The past can be a sort of a map for the future. Help us find our way around better today.'

'Umm.' Alice didn't sound convinced. 'Maybe the gold stuff might be good for a project I have to do. We're supposed to look at something that was special to our area in the last hundred years. I was thinking about the lighthouse. Would Tina help me?'

'You bet,' Eddie replied. 'We both will.'

The new togetherness began as soon as they reached the farm, making trip after trip between truck and bedroom to unload the bags of clothes, CDs and stuffed animals, a stereo, books and posters. Eddie had given the room a fresh coat of paint and built a desk along one wall in front of the big windows that looked into the fields. The curtains and bedspread were pale lilac dotted with tiny lemon daisies, and on the desk there was a jug of yellow daisies, picked that morning.

'Pretty basic, but I figured by the time you put your gear around you'd make it how you want. I'll move my old computer in from the front room if you like.'

'Dad, it's great. I love it. I really do.' Alice hugged him tightly, and Eddie held her to him with unstinting affection.

'Welcome home,' he whispered in her ear. 'Welcome home.'

While Eddie prepared dinner Alice rambled over the top paddock greeting her horse. 'You look fat and lazy. Have to get you back in shape. The boss is back!' She rubbed the horse as he nuzzled her, looking for the apple she always had. 'You remember, don't you, Sampson? Bring you up a treat later. Just checking things out,' she told him. But she felt bad about neglecting the horse she'd pestered Laura and Eddie to buy. 'We're gonna have fun,' she told the old horse. As she headed towards the house Alice spotted a new lamb from the small family Eddie had bought to help with the lawn mowing. She sighed with a feeling of contentment. Chooks, a lamb and her old horse; she was glad to be back. Eddie had promised they'd still have time for surfing on weekends. She hoped her mother would be happy with Jack up on the Gold Coast, because she knew she was going to be very happy here. Secretly she was glad to be out of the daily turmoil of life with her mother.

The decision for Alice to move back up to the farm with Eddie had not been an easy one for the three of them. Laura suffered pangs of guilt but consoled herself that she had a right to a life and it was best for Alice.

For Eddie the sense of responsibility had been overpowering at times. But he wanted to do this – for Alice, but also for himself. He'd thought long and hard about how best to support her on the journey through her teens and had come to the conclusion it had to make spiritual, emotional and physical sense to her. Somehow he had to impart a means whereby she could look into her own dark places and construct a way forward, and decide what to let go of and what to keep. She had to learn to find the balance in her life and trust outsiders.

He looked back on his own childhood. It seemed to him technology had eaten into kids' lives too much, they'd lost a sense of beauty, of naturalness, of what connected the world to them, to their life. Perhaps he could instil in Alice a respect and enjoyment of the natural world, to feel part of a community as well as a family, so she realised that it was there to support her no matter how fractured it appeared.

'Do you want some help, Mitch?' asked Holly. There was a touch of urgency in her voice as she saw just how much building rubbish had to be moved out of the garden before her guests arrived from the old people's home. 'Thanks so much for doing this. Andrew would've helped but he's out playing golf. An important game, he claimed.'

'To fanatical golfers every game is important,' Mitch said. 'No, I don't need you trying to play builder's labourer. This is no job for someone in bare feet. Where are the kids?'

'Marcus is surfing, again, and Mel is at The Teepee seeing what wonders Billy can do with her hair.' Holly sat on a stump that was used as a chopping block and watched him haul the rubbish into his trailer.

'You don't play golf?'

'Hate it. Do you?'

'Spoils a good walk, I reckon. Curly and I prefer the beach.'

'There, that's starting to look better. Can't

have the ladies tripping over old floorboards. Just a couple more near you and I'll be on my way.' He moved towards her then froze and hissed urgently, 'Don't move, Holly. Don't say anything. Just don't move.'

She immediately sensed danger and like Mitch she froze and struggled not to panic. Her eyes locked on to his and asked the question.

'Snake. Brown.' His head inclined slightly to the left. She tried to follow his gaze without moving, but couldn't see anything. She was about to look back at Mitch when the snake slowly came into her range of vision, right beside the stump. It stopped and lifted its head, seemingly concentrating on Mitch.

'When I move, you go,' he said quietly.

In an acrobatic movement Mitch suddenly sprang towards the snake and instantly bounced back, neatly out of reach of the striking reptile. Holly had moved as instructed, with almost as much speed as the snake. After a dozen steps she turned to see Mitch throwing pieces of firewood at the heap by the stump.

'Where is it?' shouted Holly, still shaking in fright. 'For God's sake be careful, Mitch.'

'It's in the heap. Probably been its home for some time.'

He walked over to her and put his arm around her shoulders. 'Hey, calm down. You're safe.'

Holly felt weak at the knees and for a moment leaned her head against his shoulder. She felt his arm tighten just a little, and it was a comforting feeling. Neither of them spoke for a while, then Mitch pulled away slowly. 'Better call Frankie the Snakeman. He's on the emergency list I put on your fridge door. Use the mobile number. He might come before the ladies arrive if you're lucky. I'll keep a lookout while you call.'

She took a deep breath. 'Oh yes, the ladies! You're right.' She turned and ran to the house and with a wave over her head signalled she had heard his instruction to lock up the dogs.

Frankie was straight to the point. 'I'm close by. Be there in five minutes, don't take your eyes off it.'

She found Romany and Curly lying in the sun on the back verandah and coaxed them indoors and locked them in. Then she stuck her bare feet into her gumboots and walked as quietly as she could across the lawn to stand near Mitch. 'Where is it?'

'Still in the woodpile. Go stand around the other side, not close in case it makes a run out that way. Be careful, these things can kill you.'

'Why don't we just kill it if it sticks its head out?' said Holly, picking up a hardwood garden stake.

Mitchell grinned. 'Where's the budding conservationist we've been nurturing?'

Before she could answer there was the sound of a vehicle in the driveway. 'Ooh, I hope it's not the ladies.'

Holly raced to the front of the house and saw a small van with a vivid serpent painted on its side.

Frankie was pulling several long poles with metal pincers on the end from the back of the van.

'Hi, thanks for coming so quickly.'

'Where is it? Is someone watching it?'

'Yes. It's a big brown. Under some wood.'

'Woodpiles. The Hilton Hotel for snakes.' He spoke with a faint accent, and Holly glanced at him, taking in his army fatigues tucked into thick boots, the braided ponytail, the protective wrapping around his wrists, a cloth sling hung loosely around his neck. 'You look well prepared.'

'I never take chances.' He spotted Mitchell and went towards him just as Holly heard more cars crunch on the driveway and she hurried to the front door.

Mac looked at the dishevelled, gumbooted hostess with a grin as she helped several elderly ladies from the cars. 'Dressed up for the occasion, I see,' she quipped. 'You're making the rest of us look rather overdressed, my dear.'

Holly swept a nervous hand through her tousled hair. 'A slight hiccup, Mac. Tell you about it later. Sudden change of plans, morning tea inside first. Okay?'

The guests were clustered in the front garden, organising walking sticks and handbags.

'Hi, Holly. Where do you want to start?' asked Lynn, glancing at her gumboots, shorts and T-shirt. It was unlike Holly not to be perfectly groomed for visitors. 'We got the right day, didn't we?'

'Yes. Right day. But as I said to Mac, morning

tea first so that everyone has the energy for the walk.' Holly bustled them towards the front door.

Mac spotted the van with its colourful serpent, looked at Holly and raised an eyebrow mouthing the word, 'Frankie?'

She nodded and Mac whispered to Lynn and soon they had the group of ladies settled in the sunroom for tea and biscuits.

Mitchell appeared a few minutes later and nodding at the guests said, 'My mate and I are just going to take a spin around the garden.' He gave Holly a broad grin and surreptitious thumbs up.

Later as they toured the house one of the ladies peered out the window. 'Goodness, what are those men doing to your garden? They're whacking sticks around like a pair of African beaters.'

'Oh, I'll go see, please excuse me.' Holly dashed outside.

'Frankie, thanks so much. Are there any more, do you think?'

'Most likely. We tried to flush them out. They're shy, they'll keep out of your way. Unless you surprise them.'

Mitchell touched her arm. 'Frankie will come back and give you a snake-proofing session.' He gave her a worried look. 'Are you okay?'

'Yes, is it safe to let the old dears loose?'

'Any snake will hear them coming a mile away and hide. Don't be afraid, young lady,' Frankie said, smiling.

'I hate snakes,' shuddered Holly. 'They give me the creeps.'

'There is no place that's without a demon or two, even the garden of Eden,' said Frankie. 'You carry your fears with you wherever you go.' He gave her a steady look and suddenly it seemed he was telling her something. 'Sometimes one has to confront one's demons, yes?'

They stared at each other for a moment or two. Impulsively Mitchell took Holly's hand. She was grateful for the touch. What a good friend he was, she could never have managed so many things without him. She realised with a shock how much she relied on him. When there was a problem she automatically thought of Mitchell, not her husband. Holly dropped Mitchell's hand, suddenly suffused with guilt. Frankie's dark brown eyes were still riveted on her face. She straightened her shoulders. 'Thank you for this. I'll get my bag and pay you.'

Frankie touched her arm. 'I will come back, fix me up then. Don't be concerned.'

'You should have seen him grab that snake, whip it into the bag and into his van in a flash,' said Mitchell. 'Let me know when he's coming over and I'll snake-proof any doors or holes he points out.'

Later, as the ladies finished pottering around the grounds, admiring the view and Holly's plans for the old garden, Mac drew her aside. 'Has Frankie taken away your intruder?'

'Yes. I hated the idea of something so evil in my grounds. I was on tenterhooks every time one of the dears stuck their walking stick into a bush or touched a plant,' laughed Holly.

Mac didn't join in her laughter as she usually did. 'Be careful how you walk. Be alert, danger has a habit of popping up where it's least expected. Even in the heart of the home.'

'Oh Mac, enough of your superstitions. Frankie and Mitch are going to snake-proof the house and check out the garden.'

'A snake can shed its skin but it's still the same snake,' said Mac enigmatically.

Holly was saved from replying as the ladies from the rest home came to thank her and say goodbye.

Alone in the house, she took meat out of the freezer for a barbecue and wandered through the rooms the ladies had so admired. Frankie and Mac had unnerved her and for a moment Holly wished she could talk to the woman who'd first lived in the house. Did she have to deal with snakes and other nasties on her own? Protect small children perhaps? The house then was isolated from the township, with no snake catcher at the end of a phone. It struck Holly that she'd always had help on hand when she needed it. Would she manage on her own with no handymen or helpful friends?

Andrew was there to open the wine, the cleaner, Judith, took care of the house in Mosman, Andrew called in repair men, the shops delivered, his secretary arranged trips and service for the company cars, the beauty parlour rang to remind her it was time for her monthly hair and nails treatment, a neighbour's son walked Curly in the park. Andrew regularly reminded her how privileged she was, as were the children, and it was all due to how hard he worked.

Holly came to rest in the attic bedroom that led to the roof. She sat in the rocking chair looking out to sea where clouds were beginning to build up. She had always accepted that she was lucky: she had position, privilege, healthy successful kids, an ambitious and achieving husband who provided them with an up-market lifestyle. Why had she always felt she should be grateful and accommodate all the family's wishes? She might not have been out there in the corporate world, but she certainly made life comfortable and pleasant for them. She had given up the idea of doing many things that appealed such as art classes, when Andrew objected, arguing that she had to be available to entertain clients at a moment's notice. When she'd been invited to accompany a newly widowed girlfriend to Italy, Andrew had simply looked at her in astonishment, telling her it was out of the question that she traipse around Europe on her own. They'd go skiing to Aspen instead, it would be useful for business contacts. Never mind that Holly hated the cold.

Like a snowball rolling downhill, getting bigger as it went, so many small incidents began to assume large proportions in Holly's thoughts. She felt angry. Damn it, she had a right to a life of her own, some pleasures of her own; she wanted, she needed, to prove to herself that she was an independent capable person.

Is this what Frankie had meant about confronting her fears, her sense of inadequacy? She'd never properly analysed her motives for buying Richmond House, but now she could see there was a lot more to it. She had a lot of emotions swirling about in her head. The snake incident had triggered something in her. She had good friends in The Bay who liked her and admired what she was doing. Andrew simply didn't understand. Nor did her children. But that was okay, they were busy with their own lives. Maybe I'm just tired, she thought. Perhaps she would take Mitchell up on his offer to go to Hervey Bay and spend a few days on a boat, whale watching. It was the lure of time out at sea that was most attractive. And Mitchell's company. It occurred to Holly that she and Andrew never sat down and just talked like she did with Mitchell. Well maybe tonight they could re-establish the family bonds.

She pulled the window shut in case it rained and smiled at the empty room. She felt comforted, as if she'd shared her thoughts with an old friend. Another woman who'd had her own struggles, in a very different time.

Andrew looked on appreciatively as Letitia wiggled her hips and got just the right posture and balance for another drive down the lush fairway of the Brigalow golf course. She swung the driver with confidence and determination and the ball soared straight towards the green.

'Good shot,' he called.

'Stand aside and let the men in,' was the reaction of Sam Mann as he strode to the tee, squaring his shoulders and tensing his stomach muscles in a futile effort to get a bulging beer gut into a semi-respectable state. He stifled a little groan as he bent down to position the tee and ball.

Letitia flashed Andrew a quick grin and he gave her a wink as Sam swung with huge energy but indifferent style at the ball, sending it off in a disastrous hook.

'Ah balls,' he sighed and followed his golf partner, General Chidchai, to their buggy. 'Off bloody form today, right off,' he grumbled, tossing the wood into his golf bag.

The former Thai general turned financier was politely sympathetic. 'We all have our off days, Sam. If they were all confined to the golf course it would be a great blessing. It is not as easy to cope when some serious business is involved, don't you think?'

Sam was quick to agree, having decided long before the General had arrived and Andrew had introduced them that the safest approach was to say little and agree with him as much as possible. Tolerating Asians, let alone trying to understand them, had never featured on Sam's agenda. Good for bloody cooking, was his narrow assessment of their role in the world. But now some really big money was at stake and he was working hard to make a good impression. 'Hope our course comes up to the standard you're used to, General.'

'So like Thailand in many respects,' he replied, looking around the lush forested hills and the sprawl of palms around the Brigalow course, well inland from The Bay. The General refrained from commenting on the luxuriousness of the courses he was used to at home. 'Not as many people,' he added with a smile.

'Yeah, tourists are thin on the ground here, all down at The Bay. That's the place everyone wants to be,' said Sam, pleased at the way he had turned the conversation into a sales pitch. 'The course in the town would be crowded at the moment with visitors. Crowded most days, for that matter. Everyone wants a slice of the action up here.'

'I am more used to investing in city projects, Sam, so this is something new for me. Are you sure you can get the right workers at the right price for this project if it gets the nod from the council? And, will it get the nod, as you put it?'

Sam tried hard to match the General's cultured and flawless English. 'I appreciate your concern, but relax. I've got a certain amount of backroom influence at council. And I've never had a problem with workers getting out of line.'

'And your unions? They can cause headaches to a big operation. Is that taken care of also?'

'You bet. Once we get the go-ahead, we're ready to spring into action.'

'I must say I was impressed with the site when you took me out there yesterday. It is everything Andrew promised, and it is even better than the video images you sent me,' the General remarked as they pulled up for the next stroke.

'It's one hell of a site. You're right there. And it can take the biggest proposal that's been done on this part of the coast. Or possibly the whole coast.'

The General gave a slight smile which Sam didn't notice.

In the other buggy Letitia polished her expensive sunglasses. 'So when are we making the big announcement?' she asked Andrew.

'When the General says he's in.'

'Meaning once we have the money guaranteed, it's full steam ahead?'

'Now that I've signed the deal with Sam I can't wait to get started on drawing up the subdivision plans. The project management work will be great when the development takes off.'

'So what are you showing the General?'

'I have a pile of concept drawings of how the site could be developed, to show him we mean business.'

'He seems pretty impressed with the area and the town.'

'Wait till he sees the drawings, the whole idea is brilliant.' Andrew reached around for his club.

'Sam is getting tetchy,' said Letitia. 'I think he's being pushed by the Sydney owners of the land. Their solicitor wants everything kept low profile for the moment.'

'Sam's a typical developer, can't wait to scorch the earth.' Andrew gave a chuckle. 'Just do as his company solicitor instructs you. But the proverbial is going to hit the fan when the plan is put up for public comment.'

'A lot of people are going to hate the whole concept,' warned Letitia.

'I think our lobbying of certain councillors is paying off,' said Andrew calmly.

'Ahh, the softening-up process. It was smart to invite them to Sydney for that informal dinner,' said Letitia. 'But there are two rabid greenies in council. They could hold things up.'

'Hopefully they'll be swung around when a straw poll shows them to be out of step. You've arranged for *National Colour Magazine* to do a spread on the future of The Bay as we discussed?'

'It's all happening. The local rag isn't going to be impressed, but they're a bit radical anyway. Most of the locals don't take them too seriously,' said Letitia.

'What's black and white, and read all over?' joked Andrew. 'Black and white in thinking, a bit too red in their politics if you ask me. To the local media there's only one way to go, no compromise ever considered.'

'By compromise, you mean doing it your way,' said Letitia with a smile, resting her hand on Andrew's leg.

'Don't put me off my game,' he grinned, squeezing her hand. 'I wish I could see you tonight but Holly has arranged a bloody family barbecue.'

'How cosy.' Letitia withdrew her hand. 'Why doesn't she suspect anything? You're not sleeping with her, are you?' she demanded.

'I told you. She does nothing for me any more and she doesn't seem to care. Not like you, sexpot.'

Letitia didn't answer but stepped from the cart, pulling out a four iron as she watched Sam swipe his ball into the grass fifty metres down the fairway. He cursed and Andrew slapped him on the back. 'Good thing you only play for fun, eh Sam.'

'Very funny. Go ahead and take your shot, General.'

They watched the slim, short Thai man carefully take aim with deep concentration and execute a deft swing that sent his ball down the fairway to a position just short of the green.

Andrew glanced up at the sky. 'We'd better hurry. It's going to rain.'

'Always rains here at Easter,' commented Sam. 'Ever since I was a boy.'

'I'd forgotten you grew up here. What did your folks do in The Bay?' asked Andrew.

'Dad was a dairy farmer, one of the ones who didn't sell his land for a fortune,' said Sam. 'Tried bananas and went bust. Mum grew flowers for a bit. They sold up when no one wanted an old farm out in the hinterland. Moved down the coast to Port Macquarie.'

'But you stayed on in The Bay,' said Letitia.

'Started as a builder. Even did a stint on the council. Thought it might help me get some projects pushed through.' He grinned. 'Believe me, I know how councils work.'

'So what happened to your family farm?' Andrew asked.

'Our old farm is now part of Richmond University. They've set up some research project worth ten million bucks.'

'What sort of research?' asked Letitia.

'Alternative bloody medicine crap or something.'

Sam stomped to the buggy and Andrew whispered to Letitia, 'Might explain his desire to do something big and prove he's worth something to the old Bayites.'

'I reckon he just wants money to cushion his old age,' she answered.

'Don't we all.'

'I plan on having a bit of fun first,' she retorted as she addressed her ball, hitting a long smooth shot onto the fourteenth green, which irritated all the men.

Andrew and the General sat on the balcony of the luxurious serviced apartment Sam had arranged for the General's visit. Sam had excused himself, 'To attend to a few pressing matters.'

Andrew waved his glass towards the view of Mighty Beach. 'I hope you have been comfortable here?'

'Indeed. Sam has thought of everything. The service has scored ten out of ten.' He gave an appreciative lift of his eyebrow and Andrew grinned to himself. Good old Sam had connections with the best escort service on the Gold Coast and used it to give added value to the meaning of 'serviced' apartment.

'Here's to our mutual interests.' Andrew raised his gin and tonic in a small toast.

'Indeed, and thank you for making the introduction. Having spent time going over your concepts I can assure you that there will be adequate,' he gave a slight smile, 'more than adequate, funding available once rezoning of the land goes through the council.'

'Sam has matters well in hand there,' said Andrew.

'He seems very confident,' said the General. 'I won't ask for unnecessary details.' He delicately sipped his drink. 'Who presently owns the land, by the way?'

'No one seems to know. The owner has a Sydney solicitor acting for him and all communication is through that solicitor. Sam is the source of all knowledge about the solicitor and the land. He tends to prefer to keep a low profile on things until we need to go public with a big PR and promotional push.'

'Very wise,' agreed the General. 'It's a sensible battle plan to keep one's head down until the field ahead is clear.'

'Something like that,' said Andrew, suddenly thinking Sam and the General were not unalike in their strategic game plan.

The General smoothed the knife crease in his slacks. 'I will return to Bangkok and await news of approval of the rezoning and design plans.' He paused and fixed Andrew with a steady gaze. 'I trust, as in the past, that you will look after my interests?'

'Of course.'

'When you first described it to me in Bangkok last year, you called it – and I noted your words, Andrew – you called it an interesting little project. A slight understatement if I may say so, now that I am across the whole concept.'

'Well, I didn't know that much about it then. My connection with Sam's associate was, er, rather informal.'

The General gave a nod of understanding. 'I enjoyed meeting her again. She has a nice style with a golf club. Turned in a better card than you, if I recall correctly.'

'She scores well in many sports, General,' said Andrew with a straight face, then they both burst into laughter.

Bonnie sat on a big boulder, still warm from the sun, as she watched the fading colours of the sunset. Further along the beach a group was drumming together. They looked like a flock of colourful birds: wild haired, faces painted, bodies pierced and tattooed. They let their fingers create the music, one setting the rhythm, the others following, before another broke away to play solo for them to follow. They swayed, hunched over their hand-made drums, nodding in a wordless communication that was exhilarating, subtle but total.

'Thought I might find you here.' Amber's soft voice broke Bonnie's reverie.

'I like this spot at this time of day. Being near the sea makes me feel closer to Erica.'

They sat in contemplative silence for a few minutes, both thinking of Erica. It was Bonnie who spoke first. 'So, what news?'

'The new shop fixtures arrived. Billy says he and Stolle will fit them. Nola Florens dropped in and gave me a couple of great ideas. The display area for Chaste is going to look great. All silver, mirrors and glass shelves. Clean looking.'

'Very appropriate. What else came?'

'New clothes racks, the white shuttered doors to the change rooms, oh and the light fittings. We'll need an electrician to do those. The Beach Hut is starting to look more beach chic . . . for beach chicks, eh?' laughed Amber, pleased with her pun.

'I'm very happy you're managing the place so well. But no, we're not changing the name to Chaste Chicks,' said Bonnie with a brief smile. 'We should make it official, don't you think?'

'I'm just grateful to you for letting me sell my products and learn about retail. I don't need anything official. I'm happy to stay in there as long as you want.'

'Well you stay in there and run it or I sell it,' said Bonnie. 'I have different interests these days. The time I'm spending working at the Dolphin Centre is very helpful to me and I hope to some of the others there.'

'Healing too?'

'As much as one can heal from a deep wound

to the heart,' she sighed. 'We are seeing a lot of disturbed people. Deeply depressed and confused.'

'Young people?'

'One or two, mainly middle-class, middle-aged women, along with two men. One is trying to recover from his wife's apparent suicide.'

'Why apparent? And why are affluent, intelligent, middle-class people so depressed?' asked Amber.

'He thinks his wife was brainwashed into leaving this world. And what is more alarming, they've all been involved with the Shahvanas.'

'Oh, that's frightening. Sounds like a familiar pattern around the world. Who runs them?'

'Some leader from Midwest America has found the way into the everlasting light where all is warm, beautiful, peaceful. It's called On High. They try to reach the High where everything is blissful. I wish,' sighed Bonnie.

'It's a bit scary. How come these people are at the Dolphin Centre?'

'They're so depressed we're worried about them taking their own lives. With their families we are trying to pull them through, but the effects of this On High program are deeply ingrained. Heaven knows what's happening to those who are still in the group.'

'God, how can this mob be allowed to function?' Amber said angrily.

'Hey, this is The Bay, home of spiritual tolerance,' said Bonnie with some bitterness. 'They're registered as a church, a quasi religion.'

'Do the members have to hand over their money and stuff?'

'You've got it. It seems this master leader of the group has a money radar that can figure out to the dollar what to get out of people. The church is acquiring land, houses, shares and cash.'

'I don't suppose there's any point in going public with this?' said Amber. 'They're just one of many groups that say they have the key to eternal happiness.'

'When I first came here I couldn't believe some of the stuff that was available,' Bonnie said. 'I thought I was escaping from the wild city to a sleepy seaside town that embraced holistic health. Instead I found a hell of a scene. Well, that's all old news.' There was a touch of bitterness, regret, in her tone.

'Everyone is looking for answers,' said Amber quietly.

'If only people would drop the garbage, expecting demigods to give them answers when it's all in front of their noses.'

Amber glanced at her. 'Meaning?'

'I couldn't be in more pain, yet the most effective healing is what's around us.' Bonnie pointed to the sweep of the bay, shining in the sunset, the curve of sand where the wetlands bled into the lushness of remnant rainforest. Above that were the hinterland and hills, lush, tropical, fecund. 'Nature. It's what people have instinctively known all along; it's a balm for the soul. Poets and musicians tell us. It's why we lunge lemming-like to the sea and the bush to escape, even briefly.'

'I wish my mum understood that. It might help.'

'How's she doing?'

'Good days and bad days. I feel so helpless. She's so . . . closed up. She shuts me out. She's just waiting to die. In pain, filled with anger and bitterness. She feels her life has been for nothing.'

Bonnie took Amber's hand and squeezed it. 'I'm sorry, Amber. Don't take it on board as your trip. We parents are a hopeless lot. We inflict hurts and stupid actions that damage our kids without realising it half the time. I'd give anything to have my time over with Erica. But I can't.'

'Yet she understood, she forgave you, she loved you,' said Amber insistently.

'Oh, I know that now,' Bonnie said calmly. 'Like Kimberley said, Erica taught us all something. Which is why I'm trying to help others. I'd like to help you and your mother.'

'Bit late for that, but thanks anyway. I wish I could take away some of the agony she feels. I don't just mean the pain from the cancer, but her whole attitude about what a bad deal life has dealt her. That she deserves it somehow. Life has never treated her gently. She always railed against the world, thinking everyone was always against her.'

'I know what's hurting you,' said Bonnie quietly. And when Amber didn't or couldn't answer, she said, 'You're afraid you'll be like your mother.'

'Please God, no,' cried Amber. 'That's what frightens me the most. I'm too scared to get involved with anyone; scared that I'll ruin it. Like she did. She gave me this idea I'd never be happy. Life doesn't treat you fairly, so don't expect to be happy.' Tears rolled down her cheeks.

'That's her problem. Not yours. Listen, Amber, take me to meet your mother.'

'Oh, she'd hate it. She doesn't like pity, she hates how she looks, the way she is. Yet when someone does walk in, she is charming and sweet and it kills me.'

'She's probably faked her true feelings all her life. You know, if nothing else my time here in The Bay, turbulent as it's been,' she paused, almost allowing herself to smile, 'has allowed me to let go of all my old stuffy inhibitions. For a short time I was a wild, free woman. Not wise, but hell, I lived for a few months like I'd never lived before.'

Amber gave a wry grin. 'So that can't be all bad. I haven't felt free to do that yet, Mother wouldn't approve. It's like she knows everything I think or do. And it holds me back. I hate to say this, but I think she's hanging on refusing to die because she doesn't want me to be free of her.' Amber dropped her head in her arms. 'Oh what an awful thing to say. It's like she's spinning some web around me so when she does die, I'll be caught; I'll never be free to be me. I'll always be trying to be what she wants me to be.'

'And what's that, Amber?' asked Bonnie gently, rubbing her shaking shoulders.

'I don't know. To be like her, I guess. And you know what,' she lifted a tear-stained face, 'I don't want to be like her! I don't like my mother!' She started to cry again. 'Oh God, I shouldn't have said that. I'm going to be cursed for saying that.'

Bonnie shook Amber, forcing her to look into her face. 'It's all right to say that, Amber. Listen, you and your mother need to come to some understanding, some resolution or she is going to die and you're going to suffer for the rest of your life. Your mother is an emotional mess. Whatever happened in her life before she got sick has nothing to do with you. Believe it or not, deep down she wants you to be happy more than anything else in the world.'

'No she doesn't, she goes to great trouble to make me miserable,' retorted Amber.

'She doesn't know anything else.' Suddenly it was so clear to Bonnie. 'Let me visit. Trust me, Amber. Hell, what have you got to lose? Your relationship couldn't be much worse.'

Amber wiped her face with her sleeve. 'The thing is, we don't acknowledge there's any problem. We do this weird dance of me being the caring, dutiful daughter, her being the frail, grateful mother. Behind that facade there's an incredible battle for dominance and power going on.' She gave a bit of a grin. 'If it wasn't so sad it'd be funny. I swear I won't be sucked into her game, but she gets me. Every time. And I come away furious with myself for fighting and losing yet again.'

'So like I said, you've got nothing to lose. She'll be perfectly lovely to me and you'll think I'll think you're mad and been grossly unfair on your mother.'

They rose and began to walk along the beach. Bonnie linked her arm in the young woman's beside her. 'But Amber, I'll know how it really is. Without you saying anything. So don't fight it.'

As they walked towards the town they both felt calmer, accepting, and grateful for each other. A skittish twilight breeze cooled their faces and the tangy smell of the sea began to lift their spirits. The Bay was working its magic once again.

Chapter Twelve

HOLLY GLANCED OUT THE FRENCH DOORS ONTO THE patio where Andrew was fanning a barbecue soaked by a passing shower less than an hour ago. She knew by the set of his mouth that he was cursing under his breath.

'Marcus, go and see if you can help your father with the fire.'

'You need a proper gas barbecue instead of that old iron plate. Or just use the griller. You know Dad is not the happy camper type.'

'That old thing out there *is* a proper barbecue. If you guys don't watch out, I'll produce a camp oven to cook in for the rest of the weekend,' Holly retorted.

'You've been roughing it here too long, Mum.

I bet you could swing an axe with the best of them,' teased Marcus. 'I'll take some of the dry wood from the firebox.'

Holly gazed up at the twilight sky where the last of the rain was heading out to sea. Between the grey clouds was a deep bruised expanse of greeny blue and arching across the bay was a pale rainbow. How lovely it looked. Mitchell had told her with winter they'd be going into the rainbow season. He promised her double rainbows. She was about to call to Marcus and Andrew to look at it, but saw they were in a heavy discussion over the state of the fire. She returned to the kitchen.

'Salad, new potatoes, garlic focaccia and corn on the cob. Sound okay?' Holly asked. 'With rib eye fillets I bought in Casino. It's close by and the best beef in the country!'

'Um, yes. Whatever.' Melanie had her head in the current issue of *The Beacon Bugle*. 'God, just listen to some of the things in the Classifieds: massage therapists, Buddhist teachers, and every kind of yoga. What's dolphin brain re-patterning? And listen to this, "Come to satsang and enter the space of silence. Be part of the psychic circle, ecopsychology workshops, prophetic and aurasoma readings". How about Tibetan pulsing healing, or craniosacral balancing? What a load of rubbish. How do you cope with these weirdos up here, Mum?' Melanie said, laughing. 'Though I suppose your circle isn't into any of this stuff.'

'My circle of friends might surprise you, Mel.

Perhaps you'd like to make the salad.' There was a touch of tartness in Holly's voice.

'No rush is there? Where are we eating?'

'In the garden, unless you guys think it's too cold. I have some flame torches we could light.'

'The garden? It's been raining!'

'I thought it might be romantic. The moon will be out, the lighthouse is shining, the rain has gone.'

'And the mosquitoes and cane toads will be out in squillions.'

'You guys,' Holly sighed, trying to be good natured. 'No soul, no feeling for romance.'

'Talking of romance, take a look outside at the sky,' Marcus said as he walked into the kitchen.

Melanie gasped. 'You mean there's something out there better than a website pic?'

'Ha, ha, very funny. Yes, take a look at the real world out there. Great show under way,' he replied.

'Yes, that's the clincher,' Holly declared, 'we're eating outside. Setting the table or making the salad, take your pick.'

'I'll do the salad,' offered Marcus.

Melanie flounced outside with the tablecloth, plates and cutlery.

Marcus began ripping up the lettuce from the crisper. 'Mum, I hope you don't think I've gone overboard with this computer scene, lost touch with the real world.'

'So you're telling me, again, how great your web, e-commerce dotcom company idea is?' she said with a wry smile.

'No, I wasn't at all. It's just . . . You seem so tetchy, defensive. Different from how you used to be. You challenge us all the time. Like we're trying to put you down or something. You've changed since you've been here.'

'For better or worse?' she asked, trying to speak lightly. But her heart was twisting.

Marcus didn't come back with a flippant response as she expected. 'Now that's not easy to answer. Sometimes you seem really cool, really with it. And then you seem so strange, well, different. You talk about things, do things, you never did before. You even look different.'

Holly took a step back and looked down at herself.

'I think it's good,' he said. 'Great. Really natural, relaxed, casual. You don't look like you did at home – just from the hairdressers in clothes that would have paid my rent for a month.'

'Oh, Marcus, that's nonsense.' She laughed but felt strangely pleased. 'Anyway, as I said, I've decided to help you out with your dream. So don't mention anything to your father, or sister. Let's keep it between us for now. Okay?'

'Whatever you say, boss. Now what else goes in this?'

There were flowers on the table, the food was spread out, Holly had lit citronella candles and placed them around the lawn, and the wind had dropped. Everything was perfect at last, she thought.

'All those candles could start a bushfire,' Andrew said, pulling the cork from the shiraz.

'They're pretty and practical. I've been eating out here a lot,' Holly explained. 'I'd love to have the garden subtly lit. Imagine lights shining into those old palms. Be gorgeous for dinner parties.'

'Yours or for the paying customers? If I were you I'd be serving meals indoors. Keep it simple or you'll be a slave to a bunch of people you'll never please,' said Andrew.

'Remember, Mum, how you always complained about our dinner guests,' Melanie reminded her. 'They wanted to smoke, half the women were on a diet and wouldn't eat the food, there was always someone with an allergy. You used to make Dad's secretary keep a file on every dinner guest.'

'And what they ate,' added Marcus.

'That's so I didn't serve the same people the same dishes,' Holly protested. 'We did do an awful lot of entertaining, didn't we, Andrew?' She winced as she thought of the work she'd put into those dinner parties. Then she'd sit down to a bunch of faces around her dining-room table whom she didn't know well, if at all, and couldn't have cared less if she never saw again.

Andrew poured the wine. 'You knew it was part of the job. It probably would have saved a lot of friction if we'd just taken clients to restaurants.'

Marcus jumped in, deciding it was time to change the subject. 'So, Mum, what's the big news in the district at the moment?'

Holly was lost for words. She couldn't imagine anything that would count as big news by city standards. 'Well, a few problems with drugs and young people, but that's hardly news. It's been a long time since there was anything happening around here that made the headlines. People keep writing to the local paper complaining that the council needs to have tougher regulations governing development in the future. That's about it.'

Andrew reacted instantly. 'The radical fringe, probably. The lotus land dwellers.'

'Have you put me in that category, Andrew?'

'No, darling,' he said, without showing that he had felt the edge in her voice. 'You're not one of those types, despite the doggy demo.'

Marcus and Melanie exchanged a quick glance.

'Enjoy the golf this morning?' asked Holly in a quick change of subject.

'Ah, not bad till it started to rain. Cruddy little course; pitch and putt. Anyone else for more corn?'

'Butter?' Marcus asked.

'Not for me. Fattening,' Andrew said, reaching for the salad.

'Since when? You've always loved butter on your corn.'

'Don't knock him for watching his health, Mum,' said Melanie.

Holly bit her lip. The dinner was a disaster – bickering, jibes and no conversation of any consequence. She thought back to their family meals, had it ever been any different? Andrew was usually late, rushing off to his study, or not there at all. Sometimes he would ask the children about their school work, but it was like reporting to the chairman of the board, scarcely a two-way conversation where he showed genuine interest in what they had done.

She recalled how he always came home, kissed her cheek and asked how her day was and then tuned out. She often joked that she could have told him she'd shot her grandmother, lost the kids and sold the house, and he'd say, as usual, 'That's nice, dear,' as he disappeared into his study with the newspaper and the TV guide.

'I had a bit of excitement today while you guys were out,' Holly said, making one last stab to rescue the conversation.

'Oh, what was that?' said Marcus dutifully.

'A snake. A big brown, deadly thing.'

'My God, where?' Melanie glanced around the darkened garden.

'Just there, near the barbecue.'

'What! Why didn't you tell me?' Andrew exclaimed. 'I wouldn't have been cooking if I'd known.'

'Oh, it's all right, it's gone. Mitchell was moving the old woodpile when it came out. He was so calm, held the fort and told me to call Frankie the Snakeman. We got rid of it, no problem,' said Holly airily.

'Good ol' Mitch,' grinned Marcus.

'Oh, sure. Had to be the hero of course,' said Andrew.

'Well what would you have done, dear?' asked Holly mischievously.

'Called the gardener. Like you did,' he shot back. 'If you move a pile of old wood you'd expect to find a snake up here.'

'Mitchell is not the gardener. He moved the rubbish as a favour. And snakes don't usually come out at night,' said Holly.

'Better watch Curly, Mum,' said Marcus.

By the time they'd finished the second bottle of wine and the rich local ice-cream, the tension had eased but it still didn't feel like an intimate family dinner. Holly was not relaxed, she felt as if strangers were visiting. What had happened to her family? When she'd first come to The Bay she'd been uncomfortable with the close warmth people exuded; how everyone hugged each other, linked arms and was so open about sharing feelings. Now she appreciated such demonstrative affection and wished she could get her children to open up more to her. She'd love them to talk to her about how they really felt, or ask her what she really felt. But as she cleared the plates, she looked back at the three of them at the moonlit table and she knew it would never be. She didn't love them any less, but she promised herself that when grand-children came along she'd make sure they learned to show and share love.

As they prepared for bed Andrew must have sensed her melancholy and he made a gesture of reconciliation. 'Are you really happy up here, Holly? If this whole idea is too much, we can sell Richmond House and you can come back to Mosman.'

She stopped brushing her hair and swung around to stare at Andrew propped up in bed. 'Why do you say that? I wouldn't give up this project. I like it here, I'm happy.'

'You seem uptight. Is there something bothering you?' He made the remark lightly but he was tense.

Holly put down her brush and went and sat on the edge of the bed. Andrew suddenly thought how attractive she looked. She was slimmer, tanned, healthier; her hair was shining and she had the skin of a thirty-year-old. She looked sexy. He hadn't thought of Holly as sexy in a long time. He pushed aside the memory of the whippet-thin body of Letitia. He held his breath as Holly tugged at her nightgown.

'It's us, Andrew, all of us. We don't seem much of a family. We don't really communicate about things that matter.'

'Like what? The kids are fine. You look great.' He gave a smile but she didn't seem to register his compliment.

'By things that matter I mean little things as well as big ones. Feelings, enjoying a rainbow, having the kids tell us what's really going on in their lives . . .'

'They're not about to do that!' said Andrew. 'Listen, money, success, learning about hard work, they're pretty important and our kids know these things. Oohing over a sunset isn't going to help them get ahead in this world.' He took her hand. 'Come to bed, stop fretting over nothing.'

She looked down at their linked fingers and

said almost to herself, 'You don't get it, do you? You really don't understand.'

Andrew made love to her for the first time in a long while, but she felt strangely detached. When he fell quickly to sleep Holly lay on her side staring out at the tops of the palm trees in the bright moonlight and felt overwhelmingly lonely.

Kimberley parked in Rous Street after cruising round the block twice looking for a parking spot. That would be noted in her next report. Parking was becoming a year-round problem, not just in the holiday season like it used to be. She left the council-issue clipboard on the back seat of the car; she hated being seen as officious and she gleaned more information over a cup of coffee or leaning on a counter than ticking off questions on some survey sheet.

She'd been to see Ian in the library, Cathy in the bank, Ron in the newsagent and Linley in the bookshop. They all had some anecdote, observation or a comment passed on by a local or a visitor. They understood Kimberley's role now and trusted her. They saw her as a conduit to air their grievances about the council or life in The Bay in general. Kimberley was circumspect in her judgement of what she considered petty whingeing and what had a basis for legitimate complaint. This interaction with the public was the most pleasant task on her long list of official duties.

She walked in the sunshine among the strolling

shoppers and tourists. People were sitting at sidewalk tables relaxing after the lunch rush. Eating was a cultural experience in The Bay, and you could find almost everything – international cuisine, health foods, vegan to organic.

Kimberley went through the arcade and waved to Amber who was busy serving customers in the Beach Hut. She noticed that the clientele looked a lot more up-market than when Bonnie had first opened it.

Billy was standing outside The Teepee smoking. 'How's it going?'

'Great. Doing the rounds. Want me to treat you to a coffee?'

'Love to but I have a tint about to come off. Have you talked to Amber?'

'She was busy. I'll catch up with her soon.'

Billy stubbed out his cigarette. 'You should, she was telling me about Bonnie. She had some news you should investigate.'

'What's that?' Kimberley asked, feeling guilty she hadn't been around to visit Bonnie lately.

'She is really into volunteer work at the Dolphin Centre. She says there are people there trying to claw their way back after being involved with the Shahvanas. You heard about the deaths of two women who'd been at the centre?'

'I knew there'd been two deaths, I didn't know they were connected to that group. You sure they're linked?' she asked. 'Not much you can do if people choose to follow some nutter.'

'They gave all their worldly goods to the

group, which hasn't pleased the families,' said Billy. 'Be a shame if the weird doings of a couple of spiritual wankers give all the other retreats and healers a bad name.'

'Doesn't come under council regulations,' said Kimberley. 'We can't be thought police.'

She was walking back to her car when a cheery voice called her name and she looked around to see Eddie and Alice. 'Hey you guys, what are you up to?'

'Been shopping for groceries,' Alice said. 'Not too exciting.'

'She doesn't understand yet that it's an essential survival skill,' said Eddie, ruffling his daughter's hair.

'*Daaad*,' she groaned and ran her fingers through her hair to restore order. She turned to Kimberley. 'How's Matty?'

'She's good. Are you settled into the farm?'

'Yeah, it's great. I've got a new lamb and another horse.'

'Why don't you bring Matty up to visit,' Eddie suggested and Alice jumped in eagerly.

'Oh, yeah, let her come. We could go riding and stuff.'

Kimberley looked at her bright face and realised how much young girls looked up to older teens. 'Matty isn't a very good rider. Maybe you could give her a few tips.'

'When can she come?' asked Alice, and both adults laughed.

'I'll get her to ring you. In fact, I was thinking

of taking a bit of a tour round the hills,' Kimberley said to Eddie. 'Doing research into some of the communities and odd bods who live up there.'

'That's interesting. I'm off to meet with the Creative Community people for my film soon. Do you want to come along?'

'You bet. Maybe I could drop Matty off at your place to spend time with Alice.'

'Cool. Tomorrow? After school?' Alice did a little dance of delight.

'Why not? Let's check in tonight. Talk to you then.'

'Mum, I'm not very good, what if it bolts or bucks or something?' Matty was reluctant to go horse riding with Alice. 'She's only a kid.'

'Think back to when you were ten, Matts. How you loved hanging around older girls. Alice needs a bit of company that's not grown-ups,' said Kimberley gently. 'She spent so much time with her mother's crowd. Help her enjoy being a girl with a pony and a pet lamb. And I bet you'll love it too.'

Matty knew what her mother meant. She had often seen Alice being dragged around restaurants and shops with Laura, and felt sorry that she had to hang out in town while cool Eddie lived up in the hills.

That night after Eddie rang to confirm the interview with the 'Creatives', Alice came on the line and to Matty's surprise she enjoyed talking to her.

'Wear loose clothes and I have a hat and boots

that will fit you. Don't be nervous if you haven't ridden a lot,' Alice said. 'Sampson is so calm. He's a great old thing. And we can go along a really pretty trail.'

'Sounds good, so long as he's not going to take off.'

'Na, you just have to show him who's boss, otherwise he'll eat all the time,' said Alice with authority.

'Can I see your other animals?' Matty asked.

'Oh yes. I'll show you the lambs and the hens and their little chickens and the ducks nesting on the dam.'

'Sounds fun. I haven't been away from town for ages,' said Matty.

'I suppose you miss Erica,' Alice said bluntly, a question many adults had wanted to ask but hadn't for fear of upsetting her.

'I do. A lot. Have you got a best friend, Alice?'

'Not really. There's a gang of us at school, we all hang out together. Sometimes I like one of them better than the others. But, then sometimes we fight a bit . . .'

Matty laughed. 'I know how it is. Well we can be best friends tomorrow. See you then.'

She hung up and gave her mother a shrug and a bit of a grin. 'She's not a bad kid,' she said, and disappeared into her room.

Kimberley and Eddie rattled over the dirt road as they wound their way up into the hills. The paddocks looked peaceful and productive, and Kimberley could see the attraction of having a farm there.

'Must have been stunning up here in the old days before the timber men hacked into the Big Scrub,' she said.

'According to old Sid the dairy men were just as bad as the cedar cutters. The Bay had the biggest butter factory on the coast,' said Eddie. 'It also had a huge piggery.'

'There are still a few pig and chicken farms around; the oldtimers are waiting to sell up for a fortune,' Kimberley said.

'Can you imagine these hills covered in houses?'

'Not for a long time, it's still a bit primitive out here,' she replied. 'No town water or services, and this road would be cut in the wet season. Bit too rugged for me.'

'I suppose these people see some value in living like this.'

'No nosy neighbours, that's for sure,' said Kimberley.

'I wouldn't be so sure. If you're part of a community in these hills, you have to be part of a group,' said Eddie seriously. 'That can mean there's very little privacy. And some very odd crops tend to do well up here in the hills, and all sorts of people are nosing around. Now, we have to look out for a red milk can on a fence post.'

They spotted the milk can serving as a mailbox and turned onto a dirt track that took them to gates and a cattle grid, and suddenly the road improved. It was graded with fresh gravel and lined with palms. In neatly fenced paddocks fat cattle and a few horses grazed. Sheds were freshly painted and they passed a large area planted with vegetables. In the distance they saw an orchard and a substantial water tank.

When they reached the main house Kimberley and Eddie exchanged a surprised look. 'Pretty impressive. A mini utopia.'

'Sure it's not a movie set?' grinned Kimberley.

Nearby was a large hall with a children's play-ground, two smaller cabins and a cottage, surrounded by gardens and shrubbery.

A tall man in jeans and a T-shirt strolled over to greet them. 'Welcome. I'm Tola. Come in and meet some of the families living here. They'll talk to you about their lifestyle, then we'll give you a look around.'

'It's lovely, so peaceful,' said Kimberley.

'Keeping connected to the earth is important. Living sustainably is the only way to go these days. Come on in.' They followed his lead and slipped off their shoes, then went into a family room off a large kitchen.

Eddie was immediately hit by a sense of yearn-ing; yearning for something he wished he had in his own life. Kimberley was similarly struck, but a cynical vein in her nature asked, was this for real? There were smiling faces around a big wooden table, the smell of freshly brewed coffee and bak-ing bread. Fresh apples in a bowl, a baby cooing in a cradle at a woman's feet – a scene of total domestic tranquillity.

With introductions over, coffee poured, and home-made biscuits passed around, Eddie began by asking who they were and what was the aim of their collective.

'We are like-minded people who've come together to live with less stress, to be healthy, do with fewer material things but have a rich diversity of life physically, intellectually and spiritually,' one woman explained.

'A big ask these days,' said Kimberley. 'Are you devising your own New Age culture?'

'We're not into tags like New Age and baby boomers,' said another. 'We're practical people from the mainstream who believe it's absolutely necessary to change how we've been living on the planet.'

'You're a bit out of the mainstream up here, how can you make any kind of difference?' Kimberley asked.

There was a reaction around the table, not hostile, not condescending, more calm patience, Eddie decided as he waited for a response to Kim's remark.

'By taking steps to show we can live in a community that's socially supportive, ecological and spiritually motivated that integrates our lifestyle, our dreams, our businesses.'

A young mother holding a baby added quietly, 'We're part of a grass roots movement around the world trying to solve global, social and environmental issues. People can make a change. We have knowledge and tools to change the world. It's about changing values and lifestyle. The big first step is for people to know they're not alone.'

Eddie leaned across the table. 'I like what I hear, but how do you make it work?'

'It's a gentle movement, where we have quality of lifestyle without taking more from the earth than we give back. An eco-village like this seems to be one answer.'

Kimberley flinched and glanced at Eddie.

'You've gone one step further than the sea change attitude,' he said. 'Maybe I've been unfocused and I could look at my life in a new way.'

Kimberley turned to stare at him in surprise.

'That's a very common response, where people recognise that a fundamental shift in their attitude is needed,' said Tola. 'And it doesn't mean doing anything too radical. As a filmmaker you can help spread the awareness through people's stories. Hearing other people's experiences is very powerful.'

A middle-aged man spoke up. 'The challenge for all of us is to preserve life on this planet and find a way through the emptiness of modern life. We need to help each other with solutions that enrich, that heal and sustain us. A community is supportive. Cities and towns can be very isolating.'

Amen, dear brothers and sisters, amen, thought Kimberley, as if she had been listening to a spiritual revivalist sermon.

The group leader then took them on a tour of the property, which included a bewildering mixture of experimental permaculture, traditional small-scale agriculture, and high-tech alternative methods of generating power and farming the land.

Eddie made notes on good visuals he might be able to use, and left them with a promise to talk again further down the production track. The visit was a successful recce, he told them.

The horses settled into a comfortable walk after cantering up a track to the top of a hill. Alice and Matty stopped to admire the view then slid down to the grass and let the horses nibble as they sat in the sun.

'You're lucky to live here,' sighed Matty. 'Our house is so cramped, so close to town. I love all this space. It's as if we're the last two people on the earth.'

'But you're close to the beach.'

'Mmm . . . And school, and Mum's work and all that other stuff. But this is really special, you know?' She scuffed her toe in the dirt, dislodging a stone and watched it topple down the hill. 'Doesn't your mum miss this farm?'

Alice thought for a minute. 'Mum was crazy about it when we moved here, but she gets bored real easy. With places and people.'

'Did she get bored with Eddie?' Matty couldn't imagine Eddie ever being boring.

'Sort of. But it wasn't Eddie's fault or anything. That's just how Mum is,' she said philosophically.

'So what's your real dad like?' asked Matty.

Alice shrugged. 'Dunno. He left when I was a baby.'

'Where'd he go?'

'Belgium.'

She had said it matter-of-factly, but Matty could see her pained expression before she turned her face away. She wondered if she should drop the subject, but was too interested to stop now. 'Do you ever wonder about him?'

'No. Why should I?' Alice stared out across the fields, her brow creasing slightly. 'Maybe one day I'll write to him; maybe even see him. If he wants to see me, that is.'

'I'm sure he does.' Matty's words rang hollow in her ears. How would she know what Alice's father did or didn't want?

'Anyhow,' Alice continued, brightening up, 'Mum says I can write to him whenever I want; whenever I feel ready. I don't think I'll ever be ready though.'

'Why not?'

Alice grinned sheepishly, and Matty saw a slight colour rise in her cheeks. 'It's kind of embarrassing, but when I was younger I used to dream about my real dad being this famous rock star or actor or something.' She lowered her eyes, regretting telling her. But Matty reached across and squeezed her hand reassuringly. 'I just know I'm going to be disappointed, that's all,' Alice whispered.

'You'll still have Eddie,' Matty offered.

'Yeah, he's pretty cool.' She smiled. 'Anyway, what about you? You don't see much of your dad.'

'Oh, my dad's great.' She laughed as she thought about her father. 'Mum says if he was around every day I wouldn't put him on such a pedestal, but I don't know. I can't be mad at him for anything. He thinks I'm perfect too. But Mum says that's because he doesn't see me every day either.'

'I don't get it. How come your dad stayed around and mine didn't?' Alice shook her head. 'There must be something wrong with Mum and me.'

'Don't be stupid! You said yourself that you were just a baby. He'd have his reasons.' Matty tried to think of some good reasons. 'He probably feels uncomfortable round your mum, or he could just hate Australia.'

'Maybe one day I'll ask him,' said Alice slowly, then she frowned. 'What would happen if I liked him more than my mum, more than Eddie?' This conversation was making her think of possibilities that hadn't occurred to her before.

'You'd like them all in different ways. You'd like your mum because you love her, you'd like Eddie because he's great fun and you'd like your real dad 'cause you could stay with him in Belgium!' Matty grinned at her. 'I'm so jealous, I'd love to go to Europe!'

'Not India?'

'No. It's hard to explain. India is such a special

place for Dad, I sort of feel like I'd get overlooked, like I'd be competing for his attention.'

They stared out at the rolling paddocks wrapped in their own thoughts.

'You know what I think about sometimes,' ventured Alice. 'Who I'm going to marry. It'd have to be somebody special. I mean, I don't want to end up like Mum . . .' she stopped, embarrassed that she was being so disloyal. 'I don't know why my parents split up. I always thought that Dad would be the best guy to marry. He was always the prince in the fairy tales, being a hero when all the others were just being dopey. I reckon Eddie's the same.'

Matty jumped to her feet, picking up the reins of the horses. 'Let's go tell him, it'll make him laugh!'

But as the girls trotted back towards the farm both were thinking of their absent fathers with a pang in their hearts.

For the first few minutes of the journey as Eddie and Kimberley headed back both were quiet, thinking over what they'd just seen and heard. Eventually Kimberley broke the silence. 'They're really into the spiritual search, aren't they?'

'Anything particularly wrong with that?' asked Eddie.

'I worry about these way-out movements. They're like religious fanatics and I'm uncomfortable with religion. Gave up the church-going bit years ago.'

'Lots did that, Kim, but you can't live by bread alone, as the saying goes. They've found something that gives their lives an extra dimension.'

'I suppose that's what Ashok, my husband, is doing in India, much as he says it's research. Are you looking for something?'

Eddie didn't rush into a reply. 'Well, I guess I am, and I suspect you are too.'

'Oh? And what makes you think I'm searching for something spiritual? I was certainly unaware of it.'

'Because you're bright, and you've been lost for a long time. Now you're discovering a way ahead with work, and with Matty. Like me. And sooner or later we all find we need to believe in something other than the material world, and subconsciously we start searching.'

'Funny you should say that. There are corporate consultants in the cities who are trying to give the new generation of fast livers and high achievers something to believe in, or at least respect. Other than money,' said Kimberley.

Eddie gave her a big smile. 'You know, Kim, your little talk at the funeral was a sign that you're well and truly on the journey.'

'To where?'

'Good question. I don't have the answer, but when you find it, let me know.'

'And you'll tell me what you find?'

'It's a deal.'

They met the girls in the barn brushing down the horses and chatting happily.

'How was it?' asked Kimberley.

'Fantastic. I was a bit nervous at first but Alice helped me and we cantered across the ridge and then took them down along the creek and through the forest.' Matty's face was glowing and it was obvious she'd enjoyed herself immensely.

'Sounds like it's time for a treat. Any of that orange cake you made left, Alice?'

'Yep. We'll be up when we're finished here, Dad, won't be long.' Alice stroked the horse Matty had ridden. 'Matty will have to do this again, eh?' she said to Sampson.

'I'd love to, Alice. Is that okay, Mum?'

'Fine by me.'

'Terrific. Love to see you here again, Matty. We'll work out the transport,' said Eddie, pleased for the two girls.

Holly watched Andrew and the two children packing his car for the trip back to Sydney. Despite the bouts of tension she had experienced during their visit, it had been good to be with them all again. Yet, she had to admit to herself, the prospect of being left alone wasn't upsetting her at all.

Andrew came into the kitchen and glanced around. 'That seems to be everything. I'll be back up fairly soon. I'll let you know. Got a few things on the boil all over the place.' He kissed her and gave a quick smile and shouted, 'C'mon, kids, blast-off time.'

Holly followed him out to the car. 'See you then.

By the way, Mac rang me wanting to know if you'd heard of any big project planned for up here.'

Andrew froze with his hand on the door handle. Holly always did this to him, dropped some bombshell right as he was leaving the house. 'What sort of project? Why would I know anything?'

'Because you move in those circles. I thought some of your builder–developer friends in Sydney might have mentioned it once they heard you have an interest up here.'

'What do you mean, interest?'

Holly sighed at his defensive attitude. 'Well, my interest. Richmond House of course.'

'Oh, of course. No, I haven't heard anything. Should I be looking into it? I mean Hong Kong, Shanghai and Bali do tend to keep me occupied.'

'Don't worry about it, Andrew. I just told Mac I'd ask you. I didn't think you'd know anything.'

'I'll make a few inquiries. We're late.' He got behind the wheel.

Melanie rushed up and kissed her and jumped in the car. 'See ya, Mum. Thanks for everything.'

Marcus hugged Holly. 'It's been really great, Mum. Thanks for you know what. I'll call you and we'll have a yarn, okay?'

'I'd like that, I really would.' She was close to tears. Before she could say any more Andrew was reversing the car and they were gone.

In the silence the currawongs' cry sounded mournful.

Two days later, Holly decided to act on her promise to back Marcus in his business project. She rang the family solicitor.

'I see.' Her cup rattled in its saucer as she put it down with a shaking hand. 'But, Thomas, that can't be right. Andrew and I agreed when Marcus was born that everything was in our joint names. The house, the shares, everything.'

She listened for a moment, then in a strained voice asked, 'What do you mean, I signed them over to Andrew? When?'

Her heart began to race as memories came back to her of Andrew handing her documents to sign. She didn't read them or know what they were. He was vague, she was a director of his company and had to sign a lot of papers. It never occurred to her to ask about them. She trusted Andrew.

'I had no idea what I was signing. Yes, yes, I realise I'll have to speak to Andrew. Tell me, what about Richmond House in The Bay? He handled the purchase of that property. Do I own it? Is it joint or do Andrew and the company own it?'

Suddenly this question was vitally important to her. She waited for the solicitor to rifle through contracts and documents.

'I see,' she said as she listened to his answer. 'So I've put all my personal money into Richmond House, and I'm taking all the risk. But it's all mine. Not only don't I have any assets to draw on to loan my son money, but if Richmond House falls over I haven't got a penny to my name. And everything else is in Andrew's name or the company. Well at least I'm still part of the company –'

Disbelief stopped her as the solicitor cut in. She felt like laughing, it was all too ludicrous. 'And just when did I resign as a director?' She shook her head as she listened to the reply. 'I signed papers in November.' She rubbed her forehead then added, 'I thought they were papers to do with buying Richmond House. Yes, I'm sure there's not a problem. It's a temporary arrangement for this new project Andrew's got under way. I'll sort it out with him . . . Yes, thank you for your help.'

Holly hung up the phone, climbed up the stairs and went out on the roof and looked down at Tiny Bay. Waves lapped on the smooth sand, magpies chortled in the front garden, the sun glittered on Brierly Rocks in the distance. How could this nightmare be happening when everything around her looked so peaceful? The solicitor's soothing voice sounded hollow as she replayed the conversation in her head. An awful niggling fear chewed at her. Of course she must speak to Andrew immediately, but something held her back. Normally she would have rushed to the phone, upset and confused by this shocking news, and Andrew would explain everything. She could hear him repeating the solicitor's words, that it was all temporary, his deals were more important, that she simply wouldn't understand these complicated business matters. Then it came to her, why hadn't the solicitor advised her about any of this? He acted for the family, the company had a different solicitor. A thousand questions began to whirr through her mind.

Leaning on the railing of the widow's walk, a slow anger replaced the shock. And a voice at her shoulder seemed to whisper in her ear.

She walked back to the room off the kitchen that was her temporary office and rang a number she knew by heart now.

'Mitch, it's Holly. Look, I have a bit of a problem, can you recommend a good solicitor in the area?'

She kept the conversation brief, then looked at the two names she'd written down. One was Letitia Sweetman. Instinctively Holly drew a line through her name. The other was Paul Maynard. She drew a little frill around the words, doodling as she thought about what she would say, then rang to make an appointment.

'Can I tell him what it's about?' said the secretary.

'Just tell him it's about a problem with a jointly owned property. I want to know where I stand, and what I can do about it before I confront the other party.'

A time was set. Holly hung up, took a deep breath, and turned her attention to meeting Mac and Kimberley down at the sushi bar for lunch as planned.

Eddie watched Tina put water, fruit, some barley sugars and binoculars into a small backpack. She was fulfilling her promise to show him a special secret place in the bush for his documentary. 'Looks to me like you're packing survival rations. We are only going thirty minutes out of town.'

Tina smiled. 'Keep that up and I won't share.'

'Oops. Sorry.'

'What are you taking?'

'Two Cs: camera and coldies. The two essentials.'

'We might be able to do a trade later,' said Tina, hoisting the pack over her shoulders. 'Now remember the ground rules, no blabbing all over town about the location of this place. As far as I'm concerned it's on my list of sacred sites. We've all got to have some secrets.'

'What about your own secrets?' Eddie asked. 'Any buried skeletons?'

'If I had I wouldn't tell. It wouldn't be a secret then anyway.'

'Did you share secrets with your best friend at school? Alice seems to have a new secret every week but with different girlfriends. I don't know how she keeps track of what she's told whom,' laughed Eddie. 'It must be a girl thing.'

'I once told a girlfriend something very special and swore her to secrecy and she tattled to other girls, and so I never told anyone a secret again.'

'I'd never tell. Would you trust me with a secret?' Eddie's tone was light but he was keen to know her response.

Tina gave him a steady gaze, thinking for a moment, then flashed a huge smile. 'You know, I think you would keep a secret. But I'm not telling you any.'

A short time later as they hiked through a rain-forest gorge, Eddie paused and said quietly, 'I can see now why you want to keep this place secret. Let me get some shots in here.' He set up the camera to capture the beams of sunlight that filtered through the canopy of tangled treetops and vines. Huge bird's-nest and tree ferns were spotlighted and among them tiny orchids and lichens clung to mossy trunks and fallen logs. The air was moist and warm. He wiped his brow. 'Wow, it's steamy, but so beautiful. How can people rip through country like this with saws and bulldozers?'

'Easy. For money. Always the cause of madness. Come on, there's a magical pool a bit further on.'

Eddie was speechless at the beauty around them as Tina led him along a small creek. Clambering over the mossy rocks and crossing the stream on a fallen log, they came to what appeared to be a rock wall.

'End of the trail?' asked Eddie. 'I hope you don't think I can climb up that!'

'Follow me,' she said and started to inch her way over the tumbled rocks to a split in the cliff face, just wide enough for someone to fit through sideways. 'Take your backpack off or you'll get stuck.'

Eddie edged his way between the rocks, then

stepped into an opening and looked onto a scene that took his breath away. Before them was a small basin ringed by curving rock walls; a silver shimmer of water slid down the far rock face into a deep crystal pool.

'Pretty special, huh?' said Tina, pleased at his reaction.

'How did you find this place?'

'Old records in the archives, and the help of a very good map. The local Aboriginal people showed some of the early settlers how to get here.'

Eddie gazed around at the towering stand of old trees and the lushness of the unspoiled setting. By the time he had clambered all over the area to get the shots he wanted, he was sweating. 'Looks inviting, doesn't it?'

'So? Shall we?' Tina answered for both of them by pulling off her boots. Eddie put the camera away and turned to see her taking off her heavy shirt, revealing a cotton camisole stretched over pert breasts. He suddenly felt hotter than a few moments before. Tina slithered over the rocks into the pool with a flash of a long slim back.

Eddie gasped as he followed, finding the water very cold. As he and Tina splashed, dived and swam in the clear pool he felt his whole body tingling. But he wasn't sure whether that was a reaction to the water or the tantalising glimpse of Tina's shapely body.

'Garden of Eden stuff, eh?' Tina was close to him and as she threw her head back to look at the sky, Eddie leaned over and impetuously kissed her throat.

Her head lowered, their eyes met and almost in slow motion they reached for each other, limbs entwining, their mouths hungrily finding one another, drinking each other's lips, tongues, faces. Eddie's feet slipped and he slid below the surface, clinging to Tina who continued to kiss him as if he would give her breath, even underwater.

In moments they surfaced and drew apart, laughing, spluttering, shaking their heads, water flying from them in sparkles. Instantly they steadied themselves and reached for each other once more. Eddie's hands pulled her body to him, feeling her breasts crush against his chest. There was more than eagerness and physical chemistry in their impassioned embrace. There was a hunger, a haste, a breaking of some dam, as if each had been waiting a long time for this moment. But it was Eddie who pulled back first as they gasped for air.

'The sky is spinning,' whispered Tina, her eyes closed.

Eddie nodded in agreement, trying to speak. But Tina put her fingertips over his mouth and pushed him against a rock where the water splashed lightly and continued to kiss his eyes, his ears, his nose, his cheeks.

Eddie felt like a baby being totally loved, smothered in affectionate gestures. He trustingly surrendered until he felt Tina's body press on top of his and his passion flared to an intense and overwhelming desire.

But as that point of no return approached he grasped her and lifted her off him, floundering for a moment as he found his feet in the pool.

'No, Tina, hang on.'

'I am.' She reached for him to draw him close.

'No. Wait. God, this is so hard. No, I didn't mean that! What I mean is . . . let's get out and talk.'

She raised an eyebrow.

'Tina, you are the most desirable, beautiful creature. This sounds so corny, but can we hold off for a minute. Man, I didn't expect this.' He hit the water with his hand.

Tina gave a low laugh. 'Did you think I brought you up here to seduce you?'

'I hope so,' laughed Eddie. Inside him swelled great waves of emotion he couldn't recall experiencing since he was a teenager. He smoothed Tina's hair. 'Do you mind if we leave things like this just for a short time. I'm feeling . . . I can't explain. I don't want to spoil anything. This is so special. It's not a rebuff,' he said hastily.

Tina drew away and studied him for a minute, his wet hair flopping over his forehead, tiny droplets shining on his eyelashes, the burning depths of his eyes, the earnest, almost fearful set of his mouth. She looked down at his hands gripping hers. 'This is bigger than we thought, isn't it?'

Eddie nodded, unable to speak, then shivered.

'Let's get out,' she said quietly. 'You're cold.'

He knew it was emotion rather than the temperature but he didn't argue, merely commenting, 'Too bad we didn't bring a towel.'

Tina reached into her backpack and waved a towel at him. 'We'll have to share.'

Eddie waded from the water. 'Anything,' he said trying to get himself back on firm ground – emotionally as much as physically. 'Do you always think of everything?' he asked as she rubbed herself with the towel.

'I figured we might get wet feet,' she laughed. It was almost as if the moments of passion hadn't happened. Her easygoing nature and good humour came to the fore, easing the tension. Unselfconsciously she leaned over and began rubbing his chest and shoulders with the damp towel. He took her wrists and held them still, looking into her face.

'Tina. Just now, pushing you away like that. It was the hardest thing I've ever done. Not my usual style at all.' He tried to grin, but his mouth trembled.

She tilted her head slightly and stared into his eyes, listening to him, to his very heartbeat. 'I felt I was getting into deep water and . . . ' He groped for words.

'And?' she prompted.

'And I don't want to mess this up. Not just rush at you – much as I want to. You're really important to me, Tina. I want to try to do things the right way. Whatever that is. Does it make any sense?'

She nodded and gave a small smile. 'Oh, yes. Very much.'

'That's good,' said Eddie with relief. 'Because I

don't know what the hell's going on.' He lightly and quickly kissed her nose and drew back. 'Except I think you're the most important thing that has happened to me in a long, a very long, time.'

Chapter Thirteen

Beacon Bay, 1907

HANNAH PUT HER JOURNAL TO ONE SIDE AND climbed the narrow stairs to the rooftop lookout. She had heard Sven and Erik's excited shouts when they'd seen the whale catcher returning to the jetty at Mighty Beach. The boys had rushed down the track to Tiny Beach, planning to go round the Point to the main beach and see the whale landed. Hannah could tell from the sluggish churn through the sea that the whaler was bringing in another humpback. Lars would be pleased. The station had exceeded its minimum quota already, so this season there would be a good bonus for everyone.

She ran her hands around the freshly painted white railing. She would dearly like some extra money to do more to the house, or take a trip down to Sydney to see her parents, but Lars told her he had a plan for the future. He had not elaborated and Hannah wrote of her concerns in her diary:

I fear Lars has finally decided to return to his homeland in the near future. For me, this country is my home and I cannot contemplate the idea of going so far to a place which seems so bleak. I have yet to tell Lars of my feelings; feelings that have become so much more complicated now that I know most certainly that I have begun a new babe. Unlike the two boys, this child has made me most unwell on many days. Until the situation is more comfortable I will not tell him about the baby and my concerns.

Hannah knew there would be a buzz of activity at the jetty as the townsfolk gathered to watch the whale landed. If it were a big one, young men would pose for photographs standing in the gape of its mouth with its strange hairy plates of baleen that strained its food. Sven, now aged twelve, and Erik at ten lorded it over the other boys as their father, being manager of the whaling station, gave them extra privileges.

Lars rarely went to sea these days, which pleased Hannah, although her husband confessed that he missed the excitement of the hunt. Bay whaling meant the men did most of their hunting within sight of the township and spent their nights ashore. Among the veteran whalers there was great nostalgia for the more exotic life in distant oceans. They told stories that younger men new to the industry envied, stories of wild and dangerous days.

Life had become more settled, The Bay was now an established port on the route between Brisbane, Sydney and Melbourne. There was much more opportunity since the farming co-operative had been established. And word was out about the good climate, the rich soil, the spoils of the hinterland there for the taking if a man and wife were prepared to work hard and put up with some privations.

Hannah felt well settled. She loved her house atop the hill with its magnificent views. The boys were doing well at school, Lars was respected in the community. Now that he was part owner of the whaling station he had to spend more time and energy on the planning and administration of the company. In return, he had been rewarded with shares in the company. He had installed the Kavanba cookers to more efficiently reduce the blubber to tallow used to make candles, and set up a large new storage tank. He also persuaded a Sydney businessman looking for opportunities on the north coast to lease part of the whaling station and establish a meatworks.

In another entry in her diary a little later, Hannah had written:

We have become quite prosperous, and like many have settled into the district as the wilderness around is tamed. The timber men have come here and are working for wages. Tradesmen and the merchants all own tracts of land. In fact, land ownership is a defining stamp in this country and it draws many men to our area. I am most content now that we own Richmond House. The children are well provided for, no matter what path they choose to follow after school.

I suppose it is understandable that Lars wishes to return to his homeland and show what a success he has become, and to introduce our fine boys to his family. Sven has expressed interest in his father's heritage, which may have sparked this plan of Lars'. I have now explained to my dear husband that with the arrival in seven months of a new child – how I wish for a daughter – Doctor Mark has counselled against a long voyage. Also, winter in Norway would not be good for my health, which is not as robust as it once was. Given it has been ten years with no blessed event and I had quite given up, Lars agrees it best I remain here. I will rely on the household help and Peter from the station will look in on me each day and help with any heavy chores.

Lars believes the whales are dwindling in number and he has taken up other ventures. For the next few seasons he is sending ships back to sea for he knows the whales' route from the

Antarctic and believes he can make the required barrels of oil back at sea. The boys are disappointed this voyage to Norway will not be part of a whale hunt. How they treasure their scrimshaw souvenirs Lars gave them. In my heart I hope my sons do not choose a life at sea.

Eddie gazed out to sea from the old lighthouse keeper's office where he was sorting through a fresh box of Nilsen family diaries, logbooks and letters.

Tina had the day off and Jeff, the other park ranger, knew Eddie was researching in the archives. Eddie was glad Tina was away. He'd only seen her for coffee since their swim in the rock pool. He was still very confused about how to handle the next step in their relationship, so he'd decided to bury himself in his research. The more he read, the more intrigued he became with the heart and soul of this brave woman, Hannah Nilsen. She was representative of that period – a pioneer in the area even in the 1900s. Hannah shared so much with her diary that Eddie now felt he understood her better than he did his own family. He wondered if she had shared as much with her husband.

Women, he decided, were better at expressing these things. He was recognising this as his days were so involved with women in The Bay. Other than Mitchell and Stolle, he didn't have good men friends up here. And he certainly didn't share anything very personal with either of them. The thought struck him, why not? Why didn't men share things the way women did? Stolle and Mitchell would probably open up and talk; they just had to give each other permission or opportunity to do so. Eddie felt that he needed to talk to another man about his confused feelings for Tina. This confusion increased whenever he thought about his relationship with Alice and, worse, when the formidable image of Laura came to mind.

He'd learned a lot about his relationship with his daughter from talks with Mac, Kimberley, Amber and Bonnie. They taught him about the delicate dance of father and daughter, male and female, youth and maturity. He'd often tried to talk with Laura about raising Alice but she'd refused to discuss anything other than superficial practicalities, such as school, budget, possessions and activities.

'I'm talking heart stuff, Laura. Communication, morals and values, being a good and decent citizen, loving oneself and others.'

'Come on, get real. She's a child. She's only interested in clothes, CDs, friends. Stop laying a whole Bay trip on her,' she laughed.

'I'm serious. At least I'm trying to get her to think about more than shallow materialistic things.'

'Eddie, she's not interested in anything deep – that's your trip. Let her be a kid and have fun. Like she does when she comes up to the Coast to stay with Jack and me.'

'I don't think our definition of fun matches,' he said quietly. 'And frankly, if you're going to let her watch videos, don't let her watch R-rated ones. She told me about seeing *Drive-In*. She had nightmares for a week.'

'God, Eddie, you're becoming a prude. She knows about sex and violence. And it's a good thing she does, naive young girls are easy targets. Mind you, some of the young teenage girls in The Bay are sleeping around with older men tourists for money. Some even get set up in a flat for a couple of months.'

Eddie had changed the subject. He and Laura were now so far apart in their thinking he was shocked they'd ever had anything in common. How could his judgement have been so flawed? That is what made him nervous about his burgeoning relationship with Tina. He wanted to be sure, to do the right thing and go slowly. He couldn't bear the idea of spoiling something he sensed was very special and important to him, and her.

A week after Andrew returned to Sydney from The Bay he had a farewell lunch with the General at East Circular Quay. The General was flying to Los Angeles that night, then on to Las Vegas. Both men were buoyant.

'A splendid place for a meal, Andrew,' enthused the Thai man, taking in the panorama of the Harbour Bridge and the city skyline. 'A nice way to wrap up a very successful trip.'

Andrew was pleased. This new link with the General made him feel that he was at last getting into the big league of international movers and shakers. He was now more than just a smart architect with a fine sense of what the moneyed market wanted in hotels, resorts and houses. Players like the General were right into snapping up the enormous opportunities associated with 'globalisation'.

'It's more than just a game for big corporations,' the General had told him over the entree of fresh oysters. 'It's a game in which individuals can achieve power and money that will make some of the empire builders of history look like . . .' He paused, seeking just the right word in English.

'Like players in a junior league. Amateurs,' suggested Andrew.

'Exactly. Small time.'

'There weren't many rules back then,' Andrew said. 'Bit different now, though.'

The General savoured the last oyster on his plate before picking up on the remark. 'Perhaps the rules will actually make it easier to build empires. Think about it. Referees might blow the whistle from time to time when someone oversteps the mark too much, but the game will go on. The bold and the brave will still be there reaping the rewards. And speaking of rewards, Andrew, you will be hearing from me soon.' He raised his glass.

Andrew reciprocated and there was a fine crystal tinkling which pleased them both.

That night Andrew had a much more modest meal: a pizza dinner with the children at a small cafe on Spit Road. Later, at home, he called Letitia to let her know he had sent off the money-man in appropriate style, then he turned on the TV to watch the late news before going to bed.

He was surprised when the doorbell rang.

He switched on the porch light, opened the door and saw a tall, bulky man in a dark suit without a tie, a man in his forties, smiling at him.

'Evening, Andrew. Late delivery.' He reached inside his coat and for a moment Andrew felt his knees go weak, half expecting the man to pull a gun. He seemed the type. His voice was unpleasantly nasal, a result of the flattened nose which appeared as if it had been broken many times. He looked very fit and strong. And intimidating. He handed over a bulky envelope.

'What this?' Andrew recoiled slightly.

The man pushed it into his hand with two giant fists. 'Compliments of the General. No paperwork necessary. You understand.'

'The General,' echoed Andrew, feeling very uncomfortable and not sure what to say next.

'There's a message from him inside. Goodnight.'

For a moment Andrew was stunned, then he impulsively ran after the stranger calling, 'Just a moment, please.'

The man turned and walked back until they were only a few steps apart.

'I just wanted to know your name,' said Andrew rather awkwardly.

'Why?'

'Well, we will probably meet again.'

There was no immediate response and Andrew was conscious that the man's eyes were staring into his, almost as if reading his mind.

'Tony,' he said at last. 'Tony. That's all you need to know.' Without any further comment he turned and walked to his car without looking back.

As Andrew shut and bolted the door he heard the car roar away in the quiet street. He put the envelope on the bar and poured himself a scotch before opening it. Out fell several bundles of fifty-dollar bills. He picked one up and after a quick flick estimated there must be around twenty thousand dollars on the bar in front of him. A note was tucked under the rubber band on one of the packs. 'The General thanks you for your consultancy work. He looks forward to continuing success.'

Andrew gave a low whistle, took a long draw on the glass of whisky, then slapped his thigh in delight. 'Big league, here I come,' he announced to the empty room. He carefully repacked the money and put the envelope in the small drawer of the bar with the corkscrews, wine caps and a silver champagne stopper.

Kimberley, Mac, Lynn, Holly and Nola sat at a sunny outdoor table at a cafe on the edge of Mighty Beach. Nola asked the waiter to adjust the umbrella to shade them as they studied the menu.

'The sun is great,' said Kimberley. 'I love this time of year. Crisp in the morning, cool at night, gorgeous during the day.'

'Provided there's no wind. But the sun is still bad for the skin,' Nola said.

'August is the windy month. I've given up on sun damage, I've learned to love my wrinkles,' declared Mac. 'And I'm going to have whipped cream on my strawberry basil tart.'

The others laughed, but Kimberley noticed Nola always kept out of the sun and only ordered a freshly squeezed fruit juice. Her discipline had kept her slim, fit and amazingly youthful looking. She doubted anyone would pick her as over sixty, let alone over seventy.

'Now, there's a reason I've gathered you all together this morning,' said Nola, acting as chair of the meeting. 'I hate to seem a nosy parker and, in fact, this is so unlike me! I kept to myself and never had many real women friends before –'

'Coming to The Bay!' interjected Holly. 'I can relate to that.'

'So then, if something has grabbed your curiosity it must be worth sticking our beaks into,' added Mac.

'You start, Nola,' Kimberley said, 'because we've already talked and I've done some nosying of my own.'

'It's just a whole lot of small things that I didn't worry about at first. But I did notice there were some comings and goings in an apartment up the road. Some well-to-do Asian gentleman was staying there and he had quite a few visitors, which made me think he wasn't on a holiday. Unless you count the glamourpuss who arrived in a white limousine with Queensland numberplates,' said Nola as an aside, which made the others chuckle knowingly.

'What kind of people?' asked Lynn.

'A lawyer, that young good-looking woman. I met her at your dinner at Vincent's, Holly. Sam Mann was there on several occasions. And so was Andrew.' She turned to Holly. 'Can you shed any light on this?'

Holly was surprised. 'Well yes and no. The Asian is a mystery. But Andrew did play golf over Easter with some local business acquaintances. I think he first met them when we were buying Richmond House last year. But there's nothing unusual about that. He's got an eye for networking and drumming up business wherever he goes.' She was a little defensive and still in shock at the news she'd received from the family solicitor in Sydney.

'Nothing unusual indeed,' said Nola, clearly enjoying the little drama. 'Until Mr Mann paid me a visit. He was desperate to dissociate himself from a young man who'd brought me a business proposition.'

'I thought you'd retired,' exclaimed Lynn.

'My dear girl, when a handsome young man invites you to dinner, the least one can do is listen.'

'You're an inspiration. I'll remember that,' laughed Lynn.

'What was Mr Mann's objection to him?' asked Holly.

'Oh, he was a bit of an unsavoury character and he and Sam had once had some business affiliation which Sam didn't seem too happy about. And here is the crux of all this, Sam was nervous because he is in the middle of some negotiations with a group of movers and shakers currently in town to do the biggest deal ever seen in The Bay.' Nola paused and looked around the table. 'Now what do you suppose that could be?'

'Sam is a wannabe,' Lynn said. 'Grew up here, was a shonky builder who went north. He came back a couple of years ago after working on the Gold Coast in development. He's never done anything of any size, or quality. Stolle worked for him once on a building project and said he'd never work for him again.'

'Holly might ask Andrew if he knows anything,' Mac suggested.

'Of course. He's been working on big hotel projects in Asia, and did all the paperwork when I bought up here, as I said. So he knows some local people through that. He had dealings with a Bay solicitor.' Holly tried to make it sound casual, but Mac saw through the smokescreen.

Nola missed the subtle signal and moved on. 'Now let's get back to the agenda. I came to The Bay for tranquillity in my old age. I didn't want to see lots of people, or get involved in local affairs. I can afford to sit in my ivory tower. So how I got involved with you lot . . .' she shook her head and laughed. 'But anyway here I am now, deeply concerned about what happens to this place.'

'Gets them every time,' Lynn said to Mac with a wink.

'I'd like to know just what is going on,' finished Nola. 'Kimberley, take over.'

'Nola spoke to me about all this and asked me, well, to snoop.'

'It's part of your job,' said Nola. 'Investigate community concerns.'

'What did you find out?' Lynn leaned across the table.

'Not a lot. But because there was such reluctance to talk in several quarters, I became very suspicious,' said Kimberley, pausing to sip her coffee.

'Go on,' urged Mac.

'Well, after a few lunchtime chats with paper shufflers, no names no pack drill, I found out that an application for rezoning has been lodged with council for a big slab of real estate in The Bay. Not sure where, but it's big, and worth a lot of money.'

'Rezoned from what to what?' asked Mac, who understood the way councils functioned.

'Apparently it's currently rural, totally undeveloped, and the owner wants it to be zoned for urban residential and commercial.'

'That will wake up the old town when it becomes public knowledge,' said Lynn.

'Of course. But I got the impression, just a feeling mind you, that no matter what the public reaction might be, approval was in the bag.'

'Some people on council have been bought,' declared Mac.

'Wouldn't be the first time,' Nola said.

'What about our green councillors?' asked Lynn.

'Outnumbered,' Kimberley replied. 'The question is, what do we do about it?'

'Oh these things can be so tedious,' sighed Mac.

'You don't know what the plan is or where it is,' ventured Holly. 'Maybe we should wait and see, it might be a storm in a teacup.'

'She's quite right, of course,' said Nola. 'And I will be the first to climb down from my high horse. But, ladies, it seems I have discovered a new passion in life and I'm embracing it like a lover. I've tossed out the young man's proposal and I'm devoting myself to The Bay.'

Her companions broke into laughter and a scatter of applause in appreciation of Nola's enthusiasm and personality. 'Raise the red flag,' quipped Lynn.

'Order, order,' commanded Nola. 'Let's all keep asking questions around town.'

Lynn added, 'Has anyone spoken to Billy at The Teepee recently? He hears all the gossip. In fact, maybe we should get some of the men on the case – Stolle, Eddie, Mitchell.'

Nola looked around the group with an air of satisfaction. 'Well done. Give me a call if you find out anything and I'll send out smoke signals.' She rose to pay the bill, looking statuesque and formidable.

Bonnie and Amber were comfortably quiet as Amber drove past Brigalow golf course, the seed and agriculture supply store, the old Masonic Hall and the showground with a hoarding announcing, 'Sunday Markets here next week'.

The road was dirt now, rising through small banana, macadamia and avocado plantations. Then they passed a long white fence with a large gate made from Indonesian carved wooden panels. Dangling incongruously between them was a brightly painted carousel horse and a sign: 'Carousel Studios'.

'What's that, way out here?' asked Bonnie.

'Music recording and film editing studios. Pretty high-tech stuff,' said Amber. 'A lot of well-known artists record there. Couple of studios and a fantastic house, a sort of music retreat. Whole gangs of people hang out there for weeks at a time doing their thing.'

'You mean, like making records?'

'Yep. Even international names plan gigs in Australia so they can work at Carousel, and have a holiday in The Bay at the same time.'

'Wow. I've probably passed someone famous on the beach without even noticing.'

'I saw Eartha Kitt at Tiny Bay Beach and Bob Dylan was here. There's a lot of movie people and pop stars who stay in The Bay. I guess they like it for the same reasons we do.'

'Nice that they don't get hassled,' said Bonnie. 'I love how everyone here does their own thing and appreciates others doing the same.'

'Yeah, even performers. They don't have to have a paying audience . . . buskers in the street maybe are looking for a dollar or two. But you know how you see people just sitting on the beach or in a park strumming, drumming, playing the didge, making their own music because they enjoy it. Not everyone wants to get into a million dollar recording studio.'

'I'd like to see around that studio some time,' Bonnie said. 'This place is full of surprises.'

'We can visit it. I've been meaning to bring Eddie out here.'

'For his film?'

'Yeah, when he's ready.'

Bonnie was silent and Amber guessed she was thinking about Erica.

They turned down a smaller track and drove under giant Moreton Bay figs and huge camphor laurels shading the road.

'How beautiful, like a green tunnel,' said Bonnie.

'I love those camphor laurels, the leaves have a wonderful smell. Beautiful wood for turning and furniture, but they've been declared a nuisance in most places. If they pulled them out of this district it would look like a disaster area,' said Amber as she swung the car off the track. 'This is our place.'

The fence sagged, the old timbers were dried and split from a century of weathering. The farmhouse, restored years before, was classic bush simplicity: painted weatherboard with bullnose verandah roof, swing windows with panes of coloured glass, wooden steps flanked by neglected, old-fashioned garden beds.

'Built in 1912. It has great pressed-metal ceilings, most of the original fittings. Mum modernised it twenty years ago but it could do with an update,' sighed Amber. 'She doesn't have the heart for doing that sort of thing now.'

'What happened to your father?' asked Bonnie.

'He had an accident and was confined to a wheelchair for several years before he died.'

'What sort of accident?'

'Got a bad electric shock while he was working on powerlines out in the bush.'

'Must be hard for an active man to see out his days in a wheelchair.'

'Yeah. It depends a lot on your attitude. He kind of gave up, felt it wasn't much of a life. You'd ask him how he was and he'd say, "I want to die." Mum thinks it's her fault, nothing she could do for him, she bored him to death. Sadly, he could have had a productive life with me.'

Bonnie glanced at Amber, hearing the catch in her voice. 'You were close to your father?'

'Very. I was an only child. He was the one who got me interested in healing plants, bit of an amateur botanist. He'd be thrilled at what I'm doing now with my beauty products.'

They walked up the steps to the open front door where a hallway ran right through the house to the back verandah. A voice called to them, 'Round the side, Amber. Usual spot.'

'Coming, Mum,' Amber replied, then added

softly for Bonnie's benefit before leading her around the corner of the verandah, 'That means it's morning tea time.'

Her mother sat stiffly at a small table set for tea. She glanced at her watch and gave a polite smile. 'So here you are, I had almost given up on you. I'll reheat the kettle.'

'Sorry we're a bit late, Mum. This is my friend Bonnie Bitternden, and this is my mother, Celia.'

'Lovely to meet you. What an entrancing place you have here,' said Bonnie.

'Do you think so? It's falling down around my ears, I'm afraid. I'm not able to look after things like I used to. The garden has gone, such a pity.'

'I think it looks wonderful! A little unruly perhaps, but that's half its charm,' said Bonnie. 'I miss my garden in Melbourne.'

'Mum, I've said before, we can get someone to come and work in the garden whenever you want.'

'I wouldn't dream of having you waste your money. You've little enough as it is.' She gestured to Bonnie. 'Working for herself at her age. Can you believe it? Home-made cosmetics. Who'd be silly enough to buy them? She's no Estée Lauder. Amber, please put the kettle back on.'

Amber hurried into the house and Bonnie sat in one of the wicker chairs. 'If we're late it's my fault. Since I moved to The Bay I've stopped wearing a watch. I operate on Bay time like everyone else.'

'At least you have a reason to be somewhere. I never go anywhere these days. My health isn't up to it.'

'Where would you like to go?'

Celia fiddled with her pearls, aware she was being put on the spot. 'Too hard, Amber is so busy.'

'We can take you out any time you want,' offered Bonnie. 'Amber has been very kind to me. And I have to tell you, her products are excellent. She's taken over a little shop I lease in The Bay and once women, and men, try her stuff they're back for more.'

'Is that so?' Celia looked genuinely pleased. 'Her father studied plants, you know.' She was about to say more but Amber appeared with a jug of milk. The enthusiasm in Celia's face disappeared and the faintly irritated tone returned to her voice. 'Well, I still prefer proper brands of cosmetics.'

'Mum won't believe me when I tell her that so many of them are full of chemicals and the exorbitant price is for the packaging and marketing,' Amber said to Bonnie.

'I can't afford good things any more anyway,' said Celia, handing Amber the teapot. 'And bring the biscuits please.'

'Whatever you're using, your skin looks fabulous,' Bonnie declared and Celia blushed at the compliment.

'Would you like to see the garden?'

When Amber returned with the pot of hot tea and a plate of biscuits she could hear her mother chatting about the garden, where she got cuttings from, what she'd struck herself, what had survived from the original flowerbeds. She listened to the warmth in her mother's voice. Why didn't she ever speak to her like that? There was always an underlying accusation in what she said to Amber. She took a deep breath, glad at least that Bonnie was there. Visits with her mother on her own were stressful. She leaned over the railing. 'Tea's ready.'

'In a minute, dear.' Her mother sounded cross at being interrupted.

They slowly returned to the verandah, Celia leaning on her stick, Bonnie offering a helping hand as Celia came up the steps. If Amber had offered to help her like that she knew she'd be brushed aside with a curt, 'I can manage. I'm not an invalid.'

'Your mum says I must see the old orchard and the rainforest by the creek. Really, this place is magic,' bubbled Bonnie. 'I think I'll have to come back with my secateurs and steal some plant cuttings.'

Amber was about to ask where she planned on putting them as Bonnie was living in a rented unit in town where she'd moved after the fire, but she bit her tongue. She poured the tea as Bonnie and Celia continued to talk gardening. 'I'd love to know the history of the house. Whoever planned this garden originally knew a thing or two,' said Bonnie.

'English, of course,' said Celia. 'It's a traditional garden but we planted tropical things in the orchard. The remnant of rainforest shows you what it must have been like.'

'It's full of amazing ferns and orchids and stunning trees,' said Amber. 'It was a wonderful playground when I was a kid.' She sat back in the old rocking chair in the sun as the two women talked. She hadn't heard her mother talk at such length without getting breathless or complaining of feeling faint for a long time. She had colour in her face and was obviously enjoying Bonnie's company. How good of Bonnie to come and do this, thought Amber, but then Bonnie seemed to be genuinely enjoying herself too. Perhaps for a brief time both women could forget the pain, physical and emotional, that haunted them.

Finally it was her mother who announced they really should get going. 'But do show Bonnie the back of the property, Amber. Be sure and point out the bird's-nests.'

As they wandered through the cool shadows of the lush two acres of rainforest, Bonnie linked her arm through Amber's. 'What a magic place to grow up.'

'It was, but I just find it so depressing being here now with Mum. I know I shouldn't feel like that. Anyway, thanks so much for making the effort, she's really enjoyed it. I gave up bringing my friends to see her as she was so mean and cranky, or seeming to be at death's door. She wouldn't stay in bed, of course. Had to get up and put on a nice dress and make-up for company. In the end I decided it was putting too much of a strain on her.'

'Nonsense. I know she isn't easy with you.

What you don't realise is that your mother is a great actress, all the makings of a drama queen. Missed her calling. She loves to perform. I can see it, and she won't pull with me what she does with you.'

'Of course not, you're company and one always has to make an effort for visitors.'

'I was just the same. See, she won't try it with me because she instinctively knows I won't buy it. I see through her because we're rather alike in that respect.'

Amber stared at Bonnie. 'I can't believe what you're saying.'

'I was a miserable bitch during my marriage, looking back. Mind you, I had good reason – a family that didn't communicate, a cold husband not interested in me as a person. I was wife and mother, not Bonnie a person. God, I didn't know who I was either.' She laughed. 'I'm still finding out. I miss Erica dreadfully and I wish she could see who I am now. I'm getting to quite like myself,' said Bonnie. 'No one in Melbourne would know me, or want to know me now!' And she burst out laughing.

Amber squeezed her arm. 'I think Erica knows very well how you're doing. And she'd be very proud of you.'

Bonnie and Celia continued to chat while Amber washed up the tea things. Then she kissed her mother goodbye on the cheek and asked if she needed anything from town.

'The community nurse will be out tomorrow, thank you, dear.'

'I'll give you a ring before I come up in case you want anything,' Bonnie said, embracing Celia.

Amber was too shocked to say anything then wondered if Bonnie was being polite. What surprised her even more was the warmth of her mother's response to Bonnie. As they drove away Amber asked, 'What did you mean about visiting again? I'll pick you up when I come up next.'

'Oh now I know the way, I'll drive myself. I'm going to do some gardening for her. Well, for me really. Can't wait to get into those roses.'

She turned and looked at Amber's stunned profile. 'It's good therapy. For all of us, Amber,' she said softly. 'I wouldn't do it if I didn't want to. And by the way, I used your mother's bathroom. It's full of your products, very well used. Don't you believe she doesn't like them.'

Amber didn't know whether to laugh or cry, but as Bonnie chuckled she still felt angry. 'Why can't she tell me!'

'Stop expecting her to say and do what you want, because she won't. Just to spite you. You both spar all the time. Get out of the ring, Amber. Let her be. She's stronger than you think, even if she is fighting a disease. She's actually happy being miserable. So let her do things her way. Besides, you've got a referee now. Me.'

Holly sat on a well-worn leather sofa next to the plump and fatherly solicitor Paul Maynard. Shirt buttons strained over his portly belly, and his red polka-dot bow tie seemed too tight as flesh over-flowed his collar. In his dark pants and dark shoes, a suit jacket on the back of his chair, he looked a formal and overdressed figure for The Bay. His office and desk were cluttered and messy, and she was pleased when he ushered her to the sofa and carefully arranged his files, pens, notebook and mobile phone on the coffee table. His secretary, who was also his wife – plump, friendly, a smart navy dress, grey hair that sprang free of combs – brought in two cups of coffee. They were warm and folksy people and initially Holly wondered whether her problem might be out of their league. Conveyancing and wills were probably their regu-lar business. But Paul nodded and tutted sympathetically as he made notes on a yellow legal notepad on his lap.

'You girls, too trusting, too nice. Cases like this have been common for years. Had my first back in the early eighties. Now, let me ask you some ques-tions. Is the company account with the same bank as your personal accounts?'

'I believe so. Andrew likes to deal with the same people he's known for some time.'

'You don't have a separate bank of your own?'

'Only recently. I opened an account here in The Bay for the business I'm setting up. I thought it more convenient for paying workmen and so on. It seems that account is all I have for the moment.

I put my own money into the business and I'm responsible for its debts.'

'Very wise. You are the sole recipient of the profits too, I take it?'

'That might be a bit down the track, but I hope so,' sighed Holly.

'Now, did your bank in Sydney ever contact you about these documents you were signing?'

Holly shook her head. 'Andrew deals with the bank, not me.'

'But the bank never rang or wrote to you independently to discuss the papers you were to sign?'

'Never. Why would they speak to me? About what?'

'To ask if you fully understood the implications of what you were being asked to sign. Or advising you to seek independent legal and financial advice.' He shifted his weight making the leather couch creak. 'Because, Mrs Jamieson, you could have signed a document agreeing to be guarantor of company debts, for example.'

'My God, I hope not! But Andrew's company is doing very well. I can't imagine why he's changed things.'

'Without discussing it with you.'

Holly looked uncomfortable. 'To tell you the truth, we never discussed financial matters in great detail. I never asked, and I guess Andrew figured I wasn't interested or wouldn't understand.'

'So why are you here, my dear?'

'I'm trying to run my own life, totally,' she said. 'And so before I ask Andrew why he's done all these things and why I don't have access to our money to help our son, I want to understand where I stand. It's not that I don't trust my husband, of course –'

'You are doing exactly the right thing. The fact is, we are looking at a clear case of unconscionable conduct by the bank in their failure to advise you of the impact of what you were entering into. A case of conflict of interest on the part of the bank and your family solicitor. Grounds to sue, actually.'

'Oh, I don't want to do that!' Holly exclaimed in shock.

'Very well. But be aware that you do have grounds.' He gave a wide smile. 'If I may offer some friendly advice, it might be wise to acquaint your husband with this fact when you have a discussion with him. After all, you are running your life and business, just as he is, and it shouldn't impact on your happy marital relationship.'

'No, of course not. I'm sure there's some explanation for what's happened. But I feel much better having talked it over with you. Thanks so much for the advice.'

Mr and Mrs Maynard watched Holly walk outside into the bright sunshine. 'I would say that young lady is in for a few more unpleasant surprises,' said the solicitor.

'At least she is taking appropriate steps,' his wife replied. 'I like to see women wake up and take control of their own lives.'

Paul Maynard smiled at her. 'Quite so, my

dear. Now what have you arranged for the rest of my day?'

Holly tossed throughout the night. She had strange, half-awake visions like weird dreams. She kept seeing the face of a woman – a woman she didn't recognise. She was young, in her thirties maybe, dark hair pulled back from her head in a severe style like a ballet dancer. This woman made Holly fearful. Who was she? At the same time she kept seeing Andrew, laughing, looking carefree and youthful.

Why was he so happy while she was racked with worry over her finances, her future, which was bound up in Richmond House? She had to make a success of it because she knew very well now that Andrew was not going to bail her out if it foundered. He was wrapped up in his own business and he regarded Richmond House as her little hobby, of no consequence in the big scheme of things where he operated. And what exactly were his business activities? Nola's bombshell that he had been seen at some Asian man's apartment with a local businessman of dubious reputation worried her more than she had let on. A golf game was one thing, clandestine cocktails quite another. The yawning gap in their communication with each other, even on things like who he knew in what she now regarded as her town, made her realise how far apart they'd grown.

The information the solicitor had given her,

although he'd cloaked it in fatherly tones, made her feel an utter fool. How could she have been so stupid? So trusting? But that was how she'd been brought up, even at the tail end of the baby boomers. She had no reason not to trust her clever, successful husband.

Holly had never felt so alone in her life. She leaned over and looked at the clock: 4.45 am. She got up. What was the point of tossing and turning? She made a cup of tea, and seeing the first pale streaks of dawn faintly lighten the sky, she wrapped her thick bathrobe around herself and walked upstairs, through the little bedroom out onto the widow's walk.

A balmy breath of air lifted her hair. It would be colder after sunrise, but at the moment it was calm. The stars were still out, the morning star bright. Below, the waters of Tiny Bay were placid, the lighthouse flicked its beam in its endless pirouette. Holly paced around the small deck. A fleeting thought made her look down expecting to see a worn path; some other woman had paced like this, concerned, fearful. How had she dealt with her fears?

Holly stopped, drew a breath, closed her eyes and stood very still. It was as if every nerve ending in her body was tuned, vibrating, waiting. And then suddenly she knew exactly what she had to do. She threw back her head, feeling the tension slip from her body. It wouldn't be pleasant but it had to be done. She felt strong and capable. As the dawn chorus began, she laughed at the sleepy birds. 'Good morning, birdies, it's a new day. Is it ever.'

Holly queued for a taxi at Sydney Airport. A new experience. No hire car on Andrew's account this trip. She hadn't given him warning she was arriving. Her instinct told her not to let him be prepared. She wanted to catch him off guard so there'd be no smooth answers. She wondered if Thomas, the family solicitor, had told Andrew about her call.

How hectic the city seemed. Gazing at the traffic round her she couldn't help flinching as the cab darted between lanes. Holly decided she'd never be able to drive in the city like this again. She smiled as she thought of how she whinged when she couldn't find a parking spot at the supermarket in The Bay.

As the taxi nosed through Neutral Bay towards Mosman Holly reflected that she'd never felt a part of her Sydney suburb. The taxi braked suddenly, flinging her forward and the driver cursed. Holly decided she'd be glad to go back home. Then she caught herself, she now considered The Bay as 'home'.

She felt strange as the taxi pulled up outside the large Mosman house. How formal and cold it looked. The garden was a bit neglected. Roger the handyman had cut the grass, swept the driveway and done some token weeding, but no one had dead-headed the flowers or done any pruning. She paid the driver, took the keys from her bag and wondered if Andrew was at work as it was barely 9 am. The doors of the double garage were closed. He normally left after a quick cup of coffee and a glance at the morning papers, leaving Holly to her solitary breakfast in the small sunroom. It was a ritual she'd always enjoyed.

She unlocked the front door, dropped her bag and heard the radio playing. Andrew must have left it on. The familiar smell of the house came to her, bringing with it so many memories. She walked down the carpeted hallway and then stopped, hearing Andrew's voice. Perhaps he was on the phone. She had been planning to see him at the office on less personal ground. Maybe she would suggest they could meet in town and have lunch together. She walked through the dining room towards the breakfast nook in the sunroom thinking she'd better call out so as not to alarm him, then she heard a second voice, a woman's voice. At the same instant she reached the doorway and the tableau before her burned into her mind.

Andrew and Letitia Sweetman were sitting over the remains of breakfast and scattered sections of the morning papers. Andrew was pouring coffee into Letitia's cup. Both were dressed for work, though Holly noted Letitia had no shoes on.

'Good morning. Am I interrupting?' said Holly icily.

Andrew leapt to his feet, putting the pot down with a clatter.

'Darling, what a nice surprise. We're having a bit of a breakfast meeting. You know Letitia, don't you?'

'Not really.' Holly could only stare at them, the wild thought going through her mind, how come Andrew never had a leisurely breakfast with her?

'We met when you came in to sign those papers and at dinner at The Bay,' said Letitia with a bright smile.

Andrew kissed Holly on the cheek. 'Coffee? Still some in the pot. We thought it safer to meet here, bit of a hush-hush deal going on. Didn't want people putting two and two together.'

'About what?' Holly went to the kitchen and got herself a cup.

'It's a long story. Letitia put me on to a developer and we're negotiating a deal. A bit complicated,' smiled Andrew.

Holly sat at the table and held out her cup. 'Well I'm not in a rush. See if I can follow your long story.'

'Well, maybe later, we do have to get to another meeting,' said Andrew glancing at Letitia, who rose.

'I'll get my things. My papers,' she added unnecessarily.

'Why are you here, Holly? Why didn't you tell me you were coming down? I've got a really heavy schedule –'

'Shall I make an appointment to see you then? I came down to speak to you, Andrew. About several things,' she said in a tight voice.

'How's the house going? No problems? No more snakes?' It was a feeble comment and he knew it.

Letitia reappeared with a jacket, wearing shoes, carrying a briefcase and handed Andrew a folder. 'Your briefing papers. Shall I call a cab and meet you at Beard and Walshe?'

He glanced at Holly. 'Can this wait, I have a bunch of people turning up for this presentation? What about lunch? I could cancel my dinner I suppose . . . '

Holly held her coffee cup with both hands so they wouldn't see they were shaking. 'Let's do lunch. I'll come to your office.'

'Right, round 12.30. There's a great new place close by. You'll like it. See you later.'

He escaped. She listened to the garage door open and close behind his car.

Holly waited before gathering her strength to walk slowly through her house.

Everything was in place as though the owners were away. She knew Judy had been in to clean, ornaments and pictures were lined up soldier-straight as she always left things after dusting. Distractedly, Holly repositioned a photograph and a vase on the small side table. The kitchen was clean except for a leftover croissant.

She opened the dishwasher. Inside were two wine glasses and a plate. She looked in the fridge, no leftovers, very little food. She peered in the dustbin under the sink. An empty bottle of one of the good old reds from Andrew's collection was all it held. She went into the lounge room. It was tidy save for the wine opener on the bar, which she put in the drawer with the others. There was a fat envelope in there too. Curiously she pulled it out and her mouth dropped when she saw it was filled with thousands of dollars.

But it was the note on top that puzzled her most. Why was Andrew being paid in cash? And who was the General? For a moment she was tempted to take the money and give it to Marcus, but instead she closed the drawer and continued wandering through the house in a daze. There were no flowers anywhere, Judy had emptied the vases.

Finally she reached the master bedroom. The cushions on the bed were not how she arranged them. But then Andrew wouldn't know that. No dirty clothes, nothing out of place. It was as if he hadn't been living here. But the shower was wet, the glass still fogged. There was a sweet unfamiliar smell, soap perhaps. Holly looked down and saw long dark hairs caught in the plughole. There was nothing else, no used tissue in the wastepaper basket.

A shower and breakfast and off to meetings. How cosy. Her plan to call Melanie and Marcus was pushed to one side.

Holly walked through the house again. Very slowly, remembering. Idly she picked up a small blue vase that had belonged to her mother, wrapped it in a tea towel and pushed it into her shoulder bag. She glanced at her watch – nearly 10 am. Two and a bit hours to fill in.

She rang for a taxi and waited at the front porch with her overnight bag at her feet. She watched birds dart around the garden, diving among the shrubs, trees and flowers she'd planted. Or had Roger planted them? Those were what her children called her pointing days. All she had to do was point and say, 'Put it there, please.' How different from life at Richmond House where she was using a shovel, dragging out old vines and cutting back dead branches with her new little handsaw.

She directed the taxi to the cinema complex near Andrew's office and bought a ticket to a film that finished at 12.15.

She barely remembered who was in it or what it was about. She touched up her hair and make-up in the ladies room and, still carrying her bag, made her way to the office.

His secretary buzzed her through and Holly firmly shut the door behind her.

'What's with the bag? Aren't you staying down? Holly, what is all this about?' He came around his desk and embraced her.

She stood frozen to the spot, not returning his brief hug.

He drew back and seeing her set face with tears rolling slowly down said, 'Oh for God's sake, Holly, you're not going to make a scene in here? Not in front of the staff. Sit down. Do you want a glass of water?' He led her to the sofa and sat opposite her.

'Why, Andrew? How could you?'

She looked so bewildered, so crumpled, so

pathetic, Andrew recrossed his legs and said aggressively, 'What the hell are you talking about?' He was feeling shaky, unsure how much Holly knew, about everything.

He'd made a few phone calls since arriving at the office. Thomas had told him about Holly's phone call and that he'd had no option but to tell her what the situation was with the papers she'd signed. But did she know about Letitia? He'd been so careful. He'd stayed every night at Letitia's hotel, except last night when they'd celebrated with a bottle of one of his best reds after a late dinner at a restaurant up the road. He hadn't wanted to chance driving back to the hotel so they'd stayed the night at the house. He'd been careful to tidy up after them as Judy, the cleaning lady, would notice anything out of order which could get back to Holly. The last thing he'd expected was Holly to walk in unannounced. It was so unlike her to do anything off her own bat. He and Letitia had gone through it all when he'd called her from his car on the way in, and he felt their story of the breakfast meeting was a good one.

'Andrew, I don't know where to start. When did it all begin to go wrong? What did I do? Was I that boring? Was our life so dreadful?' Holly asked tearfully. 'I'm really trying hard to understand . . . how it's come to this.'

'Come to what? I'm trying to understand what you're talking about.' He decided to take the bull by the horns. 'Now look, if it's about the company directorship, I've been shuffling shares

406

and things, it's only temporary. I didn't think you'd be interested –'

'Why wouldn't I be interested in the fact I have been pushed out of the business and our joint assets?'

'Do you need money? I'm just refinancing and restructuring. How much do you need?'

'I don't need money, I wanted to invest in Marcus's venture.'

'You're mad! He hasn't finished uni! Let him get on his feet like I did.' Andrew was angry.

'You forget your father gave you a loan to go out on your own.'

'That was different! I was married with two little kids.'

'I happen to think Marcus's idea is clever and timely,' she persisted.

Andrew bit the retort that sprang to his lips, thinking what would Holly know about e-commerce. 'How much does he want?'

'Ten thousand dollars.'

Andrew got up and went to his desk and opened a drawer.

He's going to write a cheque, thought Holly. He's giving in too easily. Guilt. She wondered whether she should say anything about the cash at the house. But instead he pulled out a folder of business cards, extracted one and gave it to Holly. 'Give this to him, this guy might be able to help. Very big in IT.'

'Why don't you give it to him, show you're being supportive? I'm flying back this afternoon.'

'Why are you here then, Holly?'

'I was hoping we could renegotiate and restructure our business affairs. I guess I'm not very bright at all this. I'll have Paul Maynard, my solicitor, deal with it.' She stood up.

'Who? We have a solicitor. Holly, that isn't necessary.'

'I believe it is. Thomas and your bank are in a serious breach of nondisclosure, failure to advise me and conflict of interest.' She picked up her bag, imagining the wheels spinning in Andrew's mind. She paused and said, 'By the way, is this deal you and Letitia are doing the one your Asian friend and Sam Mann are also involved in? I'd be careful, Andrew, Sam is not highly regarded in The Bay.'

'What the hell do you know about this, Holly? Who have you been speaking to?' Andrew was across the office in two strides, but Holly had the door open.

'I'll be at home when you want to talk further. That's at home as in The Bay.' She nodded at his secretary and pulled open the glass door with the gold lettering: *Andrew Jamieson. Architect, Design and Development.*

He caught up with her at the lift. 'Holly, we need to talk. This is important.'

'Then you come to The Bay. Oh, not for a week or so, I'm going whale watching. Goodbye, Andrew.' She stepped into the lift, relieved it was empty. Her bravado melted and she fumbled for her dark glasses but still the tears flowed down her cheeks.

Chapter Fourteen

Beacon Bay, 1908

HANNAH SAT BY THE SEA TRUNK LOOKING THROUGH the clothes and favourite belongings of her two boys. The idea of not seeing them for so many months was breaking her heart, but she tried to hide her fears and sadness in the face of their excitement. Lars had explained to them the potential boredom of life at sea on such a long voyage after the freedom they enjoyed at home. But to the boys it was looming as a grand adventure. And while they weren't on a whaler, they'd heard the old stories the whalers told of seafaring exploits. Lars had also, if reluctantly, tried to explain to Hannah the estrangement that had developed between him and the family in Norway.

It seems such a big mountain has grown from quite a small event. But I finally understand what caused Lars to sever ties with his family. It had not been a happy family, for many reasons, and Lars, when only nineteen, decided marriage to a younger relative was a way to escape and start a new life. There was a dreadful disagreement with his parents, he felt guilty because the girl too had been shamed and shunned, so before the wedding he ran away to sea. His father rejected him completely and when he finally wrote to his mother after many months, his letter was returned to the shipping company. He tells me he wrote to them on the happy occasion of our marriage, saying they would approve of his choice now he was a mature man. He heard nothing. He wrote again after Sven was born and received a reply from his mother telling him his father had died some time before. But she was pleased to know of the birth of her only grandson.

Lars says his mother is old and there are only a few members of his immediate family alive. Also, as Sven has been curious about his family so far across the world, he thinks it his duty to take the boys to Norway. Later in life they can choose where they wish to make their home.

I am relieved that due to the forthcoming baby I am not going on this journey. I do not speak their language and I secretly fear meeting such a strong old lady who rejected Lars's first choice of bride, even though he was a rash young man. I fear she might still be disapproving.

Lars has left the business in good order and I am well cared for with assistance for when our babe arrives. Another reason I like being settled here is the friendships among our small community.

I will sorely miss my beloved husband, from whom I have scarcely been parted. I should not complain about this separation when I think about those wives of captains who went a year or more without seeing their husbands. My days as a 'petticoat whaler' when I accompanied Lars to sea were often tedious and difficult, though enlivened by the whale hunts and the rare occasions to gam with other wives. I selfishly believe our time here in this beautiful bay is reward for the hardship, but looking back I would not have exchanged one day. I truly count my blessings, especially when I stand atop the roof walk to watch the sunset. Such a peaceful time. I've told Lars and the boys that I will make it a daily habit to watch the far horizon until their ship returns them safely to my arms.

'See, Hannah had the right idea. Watching the sunset and counting one's blessings. It's a Bay tradition,' said Eddie. 'How about a sunset walk and a quiet drink? Maybe dinner?'

Tina gave him a luminous smile and he felt a shiver go through his body. Did he read more in her eyes?

'Sounds lovely.' She studied him for a moment, then returned her attention to the paperwork on her desk.

Two days after her distressing trip to Sydney, Holly took Curly down to the beach very early in the morning. It was just on sunrise, but she had been awake for some time. Her mind was in a whirl of confused thoughts about the rift with her husband, and she hoped a dawn walk might clear her head. Mitchell was picking her up at eleven to set off to Hervey Bay. Mac had agreed to stay at Richmond House and look after Curly and Romany, and be there for the delivery of linen and china Holly had ordered.

Sunlight etched the outline of the clouds low on the sea with hot rose gold. In a few minutes the sun would burst above the horizon and the day would be on its way. But for the moment all was still and dreamy. Curly yawned and sniffed the sand; she might be slow but she was thorough. Holly laughed to herself as the dog stopped to sniff around a spot of grassed dune. Another dog had been this way and left its mark and Holly was convinced Curly was interpreting the smell to determine its breed, size, sex and age.

Suddenly Curly looked up, ears alert, and her tail began to wag as she scanned the beach and gave a small bark. Holly looked around and saw Romany in the distance, startling seagulls and dancing into the pink waves. Mitch was standing on the sand close to the water, going through his morning ritual of tai chi.

In slow fluid movements he went through a series of graceful, balancing poses. Arms outstretched, his deep concentration was evident all the way to his fingertips as he turned his palms upwards then drew them to him. It was extremely personal. Holly felt like she was spying on him, and her physical response to his lean and agile body surprised her. She quietly called Curly and turned and walked back through the dunes, the puzzled dog reluctantly following.

As she made her way home, Holly couldn't help comparing what she knew of Mitchell's life with her own and Andrew's. Mitch had walked away from a successful advertising career, and his wife and son apparently had accepted the dramatic turnaround. It seemed he was determined to embrace values that gave more meaning to life than those he had seen worshipped in the boardrooms, agencies and trendy restaurants around the city. Several times over coffee breaks at Richmond House he had remarked on how utterly stupid it was to worship the 'god of greed'. The remark usually followed references to the latest news story of a corporate crisis or the exposure of dubious moral standards of some, if not all, of the key executives. For Holly these remarks helped her to articulate her own searching for something new.

'I think many people are searching for those good old-fashioned values that guided our parents, and their parents,' she'd once remarked, but felt uncomfortable about trying to elaborate.

Mitch had laughed when she said it. 'Hey, welcome to the club.'

She wanted him to keep the conversation going, but he finished off his coffee and went back to work.

His wife Veronica, who had been an art director in the same ad agency in Sydney, was quiet and intense. Since moving to The Bay she had become increasingly absorbed in creating pottery and ceramic figurines. Holly had met her a few times, most recently at an exhibition of local craft work in the Community Centre. Veronica had stunned her by remarking out of the blue, 'Mitch tells me he's trying to talk you into communing with whales.'

'Yes, absurd isn't it, but I'm intrigued with the idea. He's so enthusiastic about whale watching that I'm tempted to do it.'

'It's his annual escape from the world,' Veronica added without any hint of criticism. 'We all need to escape from time to time. Something to do with having our own space, you know what I mean?'

'Yes, I think I do. That's partly why I'm here and not in Sydney.'

'Well then, are you going?'

'Going where?'

'Whale watching with him.'

Holly was taken aback with the relaxed way in which Veronica endorsed the idea of her and Mitch driving off together to spend a week whale watching. It convinced her, though, that she should go, and she felt no embarrassment whatsoever.

It was sunset when Mitch and Holly arrived at Hervey Bay, three hundred kilometres north of Brisbane. It had been a pleasant six-hour drive. They walked to the Urangan Boat Harbour where the sleek, purpose-built eighteen-metre catamaran *Oceania* was moored.

The Franklins greeted Mitchell warmly and he introduced Holly to the tall, white-bearded, gentle-eyed Wally and his petite, energetic and enthusiastic partner, Trish.

'Good to see you back, Mitch. How's your year been?' asked Trish in her soft English accent.

'So far it's been a very good year,' he said and winked at Holly.

'Some of the others on the trip are having dinner ashore. Seven o'clock at the Oriental Palace on the Esplanade,' Trish said. 'We have four high-school students from The Bay with us this year. Our youth program is becoming very popular.' She explained to Holly, 'Engaging the hearts and minds of young people around the world is one of the more rewarding aspects of this work.'

'While you're with us you can hear as much as you like about the work of the Oceania Project on cetacean research, or just enjoy the whale and dolphin experience,' said Wally.

'Sounds lovely.' Then a sudden thought struck Holly. 'I hope I don't get seasick.'

'It's one of the first things you have to get used to on board – the constant movement,' Wally said. 'But you soon tune in to the rhythm of the sea.' He and Trish exchanged a glance. 'You might find you adapt to nature in a whole new way. And we have plenty of remedies in case you do feel squeamish, but the waters are very tranquil. That's why the whales like it here.'

Trish showed her to the cabin she'd be sharing with three others and how to flush the 'head'. Holly threw her bag on a top bunk and grabbed her jacket and handbag. She looked in at the saloon, marvelling at how spacious yet compact everything was. The fascination with discovering even the fundamentals of small boat living, added to the unknown pleasures ahead, made Holly wonder why she had never taken advantage of living on Sydney Harbour and made an effort to get some experience on yachts. She'd hated the dinner and cocktail cruises Andrew had organised for clients, but this was different.

She joined Mitch up on deck and they decided to stroll through the township, which was built around the harbour where many pleasure craft were moored.

Mitchell paused at a selection of postcards on a stand outside a bookshop. 'Look at all these whale photos. Did you bring a camera?'

Holly nodded. 'Although if a whale comes as close as this I'll probably drop the camera overboard with excitement.'

Mitchell merely smiled.

They decided to eat by themselves as they'd be in close quarters with the others for the next week. Over their noodles and beer Holly asked, 'Why do you do this every year? If you have one great experience one year, the next mightn't be so good and then you're disappointed.'

'It's hard to explain. You'll find out. Many people come back again and again, from all over the world. Wally and Trish have been doing this for twelve years. They know how to make it memorable and their research for the Oceania Project is fascinating, and valuable.'

'What's involved in the project? Obviously it helps save the whales.' Holly had only recently begun to get an inkling of how important the whales and dolphins were to the culture of The Bay. Using dolphins and whales as a logo for products and businesses was one thing, but she was beginning to learn from Mac and others that they had a deep significance for people who lived along the coast.

'Essentially it's a non-profit education and research organisation dedicated to saving the whales and dolphins. It's also a way to study them, learn about them as individuals, their behaviour and what they can teach us. It works to protect their environment, too.'

'How did Trish and Wally get involved?'

'Well, it didn't come about by chance, but it's another case of people leaving one life to start another.'

'Doing what you truly want and believe in,' said Holly softly, almost to herself.

'I don't have any regrets,' said Mitchell, catching her mood. 'I could be making a mint in advertising back in Sydney or working on my mad dreams while enjoying life in the open air, using my hands . . . and meeting wonderful people like you.'

It was a light remark, but Holly felt the intensity of his blue eyes burning into her and she didn't trust herself to speak for a minute. How long had it been since she had felt so special?

Too long, she answered herself. Andrew and the children took her for granted, understandable of course, but it was nice to be appreciated as a warm and intelligent friend. And there was no harm in feeling like this, she decided. Holly raised her glass. 'Here's to happy days at sea.'

The following morning they sailed north-east towards the ancient beaches of Fraser Island, the world's biggest sand island, at the southern end of the Barrier Reef. Wally told them it marked the gateway to the reef for the whales.

Two hours later he navigated the big cat into the southern shallows of the lower reaches of Hervey Bay. 'We'll stay in this area of the bay for the next six days, anchoring at night on the sheltered western side of Fraser Island,' he explained.

It took Holly the first day to adjust to the rhythm of the sea, then she stopped noticing it. There was no television, no radio – other than the communication radio in the wheelhouse – no newspapers, no phones, no contact with the world outside their sheltered waters.

The routine that started on the first day consisted of rising at first light and sitting on the cool deck with a mug of steaming tea to watch the dawn break, eating a huge breakfast, then having a quiet conversation with the four students from Beacon Bay High. They were doing a school project in conjunction with Tina Cook from National Parks. It was part of The Bay's whale-watch program which Tina had set up at the lighthouse with Wally and Trish. Holly thought how nice it was to have the local kids with them, and they started to discuss what the kids liked about growing up in The Bay.

'Lifestyle, laid-back lifestyle. That's what my parents came for when they sold up in the city. I love them for making that decision,' said one of the boys with a big smile. 'They don't want to go back, but I guess I'll have to get a city job after uni. There won't be enough work around for all of us. Not everyone will be happy to work in tourism and stuff like that.'

Two of the girls had come to The Bay as toddlers and couldn't remember any other place. They had more faith in the future offering a greater diversity of jobs in the country, particularly in resort areas, 'So long as developers don't spoil everything.' They were fascinated by Holly's project and were delighted when she invited them to drop around when they were back home.

The fourth student, a well-tanned boy who was built like a front-row footballer, announced that The Bay was heaven, it had to get bigger and he wanted part of the action. 'I'm going to get a trade and a ute and lead the good life right there. I can go to the cities for hols, if I want.' He'd been born in The Bay, his father was a plumber.

The other passengers were Alex and Ivy, an American couple who worked for an international computer conglomerate as research physicists, but their main interest was in quartz crystals. In a private moment with Holly, Mitch said he found Ivy and Alex more New Age spiritualists than scientists. Then there was Tor, a shy, smiling young Norwegian backpacking student.

'Following the whales, eh?' Trish asked.

'If I was I would be on a never-ending journey,' he said.

Trish was delighted with his response, and the slight accent that emphasised his Scandinavian origin. 'Yep, that's right,' she said, then turned to explain to the school group. 'We know that all humpbacks follow similar migration patterns, whether in the northern or southern hemispheres. Seasonal timing means that whales in both areas travel north or south in the same months. So they never approach the Equator at the same time. And whales have been following these ancient routes for as long as they've been around.'

'Round the world every year,' said the plumber's son, 'be great if they could score frequent-flyer points.'

His school friends groaned and threatened to throw him overboard.

That evening it was clear and balmy, and Wally suggested that those who wanted to could sleep on deck in canvas hammocks. Mitchell, Holly and Tor agreed and after the others had gone to their bunks they settled into the comfortable slings and lay staring at the night sky.

'This is so unbelievable to see stars – so many, so close,' said Tor. 'Not like my home. I love the sun, hot weather. It will be hard to go home after being in Australia.'

'How old are you, Tor? Do you have a career?' asked Holly.

'I'm twenty-two. I am very interested in marine biology. I want to study the Great Barrier Reef. I've applied to James Cook University to do postgrad studies,' he said shyly.

They talked well into the night, enjoying the rising and starry vastness of the sky. They talked about islands, the reef, marine life, and eventually life at The Bay in response to questions from Tor.

'In backpacker hostels everyone talks about visiting Beacon Bay,' he said. 'It has to be one of the most famous places in Australia. I'd heard about it in hostels in Norway long before I started this trip. That started my interest, among other things. You're lucky to live there.'

They both urged him to stay with them in The

Bay when his study schedule allowed him to travel.

The silences in the conversation grew longer and soon it was obvious Tor was sleeping. Holly felt herself drifting, the swaying of the hammock was deeply comforting. But then a faint sensation vibrated in her body, or was it her head? She waited and was soon aware of a low sound that sent shivers through her. She held her breath and listened. A feeling of such peace came to her that she felt like she was enveloped within it. The sounds seemed to come from a long way away, or from deep in the sea. They were unlike anything she had ever heard.

'It's the humpbacks singing,' whispered Mitchell. 'They'll be here tomorrow. You'll see. It will be wonderful.'

She lay listening to the mysterious singing of the great ocean creatures and remembered what Mitch had told her of how the whale songs evolved and changed, adding to their legends and history since the creation of the planet. Their singing went around the globe like a telegraphic message. Mitch had explained that a sound of this intensity emitted within sound-reflecting layers which occurred at certain depths could be heard by the human ear at a distance of well over 25,000 miles – the circumference of the earth. Holly had begun to wonder if it were possible these wise old creatures knew our story too? To Holly at that moment it all seemed possible, that she was a speck in a great universal connection between nature, the whales, dolphins and the universe. She fell into a deep, dreamless sleep with a sensation of being protected in some womb-like place.

Holly had no idea how long she'd been asleep when her hammock was nudged and Tor's insistent voice broke into her consciousness. 'Look. It is so beautiful.'

She sat up and stared at where he was pointing then turned to Mitchell. 'Mitch, are you awake, look at that!'

'Yes, isn't it wonderful. It's a moonbow. Not uncommon but very special,' he answered softly.

'I have never heard of a night rainbow,' said Tor. 'The lights of the aurora borealis are beautiful but not like this.'

'It comes from the light of the moon instead of the sun,' said Mitchell.

In awe they looked at the pastel-coloured arch that stretched from horizon to horizon, until each fell asleep once again having shared a moment of great beauty.

The following morning was one Holly would never forget. The high-school kids spotted the first whale some distance away, and the crew let the *Oceania* drift. Wally got his video camera and Trish her stills camera to continue her ongoing photo ID research. 'It's a young adult judging by that strong blow,' she said.

'There's another!'

'Look to the port side,' called Wally to the students who were at the starboard rail. They joined Mitch, Holly and Tor as a shimmering shape rose to the surface. Holly clutched Mitchell's arm when only fifty metres away a huge humpback broke the surface, slowly, gently, in an arching roll.

As the whale turned, lifting its flukes, Trish called to Wally, 'It's Nala!'

Her camera shutter clicked and Mitchell explained, 'Nala's an old female that Trish and Wally first saw ten years ago. She's also been seen in the Ross Sea.'

'So they know them all by name?' Holly was entranced by the slow and graceful performance the whale seemed to be putting on especially for them.

'Oh yes, every whale has individual markings. They know some by damage to their flukes – nips by orca whales – or by the barnacles and colour variations,' said Mitchell. 'All the whale-watch organisations share information.'

The whale slowly submerged, and shortly resurfaced on the other side of the *Oceania* and put on another splendid show.

'It's so big, yet it can move with the grace of a ballet dancer,' exclaimed Holly. 'It's fantastic.'

She wished Melanie and Marcus were with her; tears were running down her face and she couldn't understand why. It wasn't just the immense size and gentleness, the obvious curiosity and delight the whale seemed to have in being there – for the whale had come to them – but the sense of some knowingness between this great intelligent creature and herself.

The students began to sing. It was a beautiful harmonising song they'd written about the sad saga of whales. The humpback lifted its head and using its long pectorals pushed itself towards the boat.

'It's listening,' declared Mitchell.

Closer and closer it came. The kids leaned out over the boat rail, their arms outstretched, singing to the whale.

'Kids from The Bay seem so different from the city kids my two went to school with,' Holly whispered to Mitchell.

'Maybe. Trish told me that this lot are all in the school choir. They started working up songs about whales early in the term.'

'Lovely touch,' said Holly in admiration. Then the whale nudged the boat, rubbing against the slightly rolling hull and everyone broke into spontaneous applause.

Next it pushed away and flipped on its back in a joyful breech, its massive tail flukes slapping the water and spraying them. Holly peered across the clear calm ocean. 'Will it come back?' She desperately wanted Nala to return.

Before Mitchell could answer, Trish on the upper deck called, 'Port side!' And there, breaking the surface came the leathery hump as it glided past with a *whoosh* of air. It turned and rolled and seemed to hover, its pectoral fins propelling it against the boat. Then it lifted its head and turned towards Holly, who instinctively leaned out towards it.

She found she was staring at the small bright eye that studied her as intensely as she watched it. They eyeballed each other and then the whale breathed out, a great gushy warm fish oily breath which hit Holly with a physical impact. She reached out and briefly touched the whale's head, amazed at its softness and how it stayed at the side of the boat.

Holly became totally absorbed by the incredible magic of the moment, unaware of the shouts of delight from those around her, unaware of anything but a growing sense of oneness with the whale. More tears rolled down her cheeks as the whale drifted away and then, as if waving farewell with its flukes, plunged from sight.

She stayed by the rail gazing into the empty ocean, feeling connected to the old female whale in some special way, until she felt Mitchell's arm around her shoulder. 'Powerful stuff, isn't it?' he said softly. 'The first encounter usually hits pretty hard. Tears are okay.'

She gave him a quick smile, grateful for the right words and the comfort of his arm. 'Thanks,' was all she said, knowing that was all he needed to hear.

It wasn't till later that she realised she wasn't supposed to touch the whale, but she'd felt so drawn to the old female. There was something about that deep release of breath that made Holly think of a baby's first gasp of air, of how we can live without food or water but not air. Now she understood those stickers she'd seen in The Bay: 'Don't Forget to Breathe'.

Mitchell snapped photographs of the whale as Holly wept with the intensity of her feelings. She could not believe more than an hour had passed since Nala had first approached the boat.

'Where's Tor?' she eventually asked Mitchell. She had been aware of him standing near her when the whale first surfaced, but at some stage during the drama he had disappeared. Holly went below and tapped at the door of the cabin he shared with Mitchell. There was a muffled response and when she opened the door she saw Tor huddled in a corner of an upper bunk, his back to the porthole. He looked distressed and sat hugging his knees.

'Tor, what is it?' she asked. 'Are you all right?'

He shook his head. Then put his face on his knees, his shoulders shaking.

'Can I get you something? Do you feel sick? I'll get Trish.'

'No! It is nothing.' He brushed at his face and slid down from the bunk, avoiding Holly's eyes.

'Wasn't the whale fantastic?' she said in an effort to boost his spirit, but got an anguished look in return.

'That is the problem, why I am upset. I do not understand. I wanted so very much to see them.'

Trish appeared in the doorway. 'Are you okay, Tor?' She was understanding and when he nodded she took his hand and glanced at Holly. 'This is not uncommon, the experience of being with whales can have a profound effect on some people.'

'I know, I didn't expect to be so overwhelmed,' agreed Holly.

Tor and Trish sat on a lower bunk.

He began to speak. 'It is to do with my country, the killing of whales . . . it still goes on. I feel deeply ashamed. I once went to the coast where a pod of many whales had beached and were dying. There were people there, watching, like it was a picnic.' He lifted his tear-stained face. 'I looked into the eyes of mother whales and their calves, and it was like they asked me to help and I could do nothing. Then I saw that these people had stubbed cigarette butts into their blowholes . . . and done other things. Why are people so cruel?'

'Oh, how horrible,' said Holly.

Trish sighed. 'We still have a long way to go to protect these amazing creatures. And still so much to learn. These encounters evoke deep feelings in people.'

'I somehow feel guilty about whaling. Our people invented the harpoon and we have always been a big whaling nation,' said Tor. 'Or whale killing nation,' he added.

'You can't do anything about the past,' said Holly sympathetically. 'Just think of the here and now, and what a joy it is for all of us to be able to celebrate the magnificence, the intelligence and connection we have with them today.'

'You can come to terms with that past,' said

Trish. 'These same whales we see out here, so free and beautiful, are the descendants of those who escaped the slaughter in the old days.'

There was a shout from the deck as more whales were sighted.

Trish and Holly stood up. 'Come on, Tor, let's enjoy this. They're bringing us a gift, I think,' said Holly, taking his hand.

The days blurred in a timeless blending of sunrise and sunsets, starry nights, clear warm water and the continuing visits of the whales. They were all known to Trish and Wally; one mother brought a new calf to show off to those on *Oceania*.

At night on deck the children sang, and they all talked about their thoughts, feelings, dreams, ideas. There seemed no age difference between them as they shared this unique and special time. They had bonded in a way they never would back on land.

Towards the end of the last day at sea Wally set a course to the edge of the continental shelf where the ocean floor dropped away to the deepest most secret depths – the heart of the sea. The colour of the water changed, it was dark and mysterious, eerie in the setting sun. And it was here that the *Oceania* hove to and Wally explained that an unusual request had been made by Ivy and Alex, the two 'quiet Americans' as they'd been nick-named – a little ceremony was going to be performed.

Wally's preamble failed to prepare the others for what Ivy and Alex had in store for them when they gathered on the afterdeck around a table. The Americans carefully opened a small package and unfolded a felt wrapping inside to reveal a beautiful chunk of chrysoprase crystalline quartz. It shone in the late light like a large rough-skinned green apple. Alex began the explanation.

'We know that crystals are energy transducers, meaning they can transmit and receive information. Just like we can send our thoughts and feelings through the nervous system of our bodies, a kind of electrical charge.' He paused as if waiting for questions, but no one said a word.

Ivy then spoke up. 'We can transmit that same energy into a crystal. We thought it would be fitting for us to hold this little ceremony to help heal the wounds inflicted on the creatures of the sea and start a reunion process between humans and cetaceans.'

'How can we do that?' asked Holly.

'By deeply focusing on the crystal it will receive our message, provided it has loving intent,' said Alex as he cupped the crystal in his hands.

Ivy asked them all to link hands and to think about their experiences, emotions and feelings of the past week; to think about the beauty of being as one with nature, and the moments when each one of them had made a connection with a whale.

To Holly's amazement, the quartz crystal seemed to vibrate and it looked soft, like jelly, in Alex's hands.

Wally spoke for all of them. 'Let the whales, who are the record-keepers, those who hold the history of our planet in their songs, know that we all wish to share a united world. One of peace, love and harmony, where life unites the human and the world of nature; where we all care for each other as we depend one upon the other.'

Then Alex stepped to the rail, stretched his arm out and let the green crystal slip from his hands into the dark waters. Wally finished by saying, 'Let the healing begin.' They all stood silently staring at where the crystal had disappeared, to fall to the bottom of the sea.

Mitchell squeezed Holly's hand and she in turn looked at Tor beside her. He felt her gaze and smiled. 'It is all gone. The pain I always felt in my heart seems to have gone.'

'How strange,' said Mitchell. 'I could have sworn that crystal vibrated or changed in some way.'

'Some mysteries and questions aren't meant to be answered,' said Trish.

The students, who'd seemed awed by the experience, announced they'd written a new song. So as the *Oceania* sailed back across the bay and the moon rose, they sang of the journey that had brought them together, that would bind them, for now their lives were changed and linked forever. They called it 'The Gift of Whales'.

The following morning the *Oceania* headed back to Urangan Boat Harbour, dolphins dancing in the bow wave. Holly hung over the side watching them, her hair swept off her face in the salty breeze. Mitchell stood beside her and dropped an arm over her shoulders. 'Glad you came?'

'Oh, yes. It's been magical, I really feel I've changed. Something deep inside me has moved. I can never, ever thank you enough.'

'I'm glad. I hoped it would free you,' he answered and leaned over and kissed her smiling mouth, and it seemed, to both of them, the most natural thing in the world.

A couple of skateboarding youths gave a loud, rib-ald imitation of a rooster crowing as they flashed past Kimberley as she was leaving the council chambers, and she couldn't help laughing. The recently built edifice was known far and wide as the 'chookhouse' because the architecture of the tin-shed office building was like a lot of the chicken farms in the area. The chookhouse was condemned by most ratepayers as a bureaucratic indulgence and was the subject of endless jokes. Local government was not a service that enjoyed much respect among the residents, thanks to a legacy of corruption allegations and decades of inadequate funding for essential works.

While the council generally stayed aloof from party politics, it was never free of faction fighting. In recent years, particularly since the last election, the generally pro-development bias of the council had been seriously challenged by a more environmentally conscious group of new, younger councillors. But they were in the minority.

'They're just out of the trees and wet behind the ears,' was how outspoken and long-serving councillor Jimmy Bright frequently described them, particularly when they claimed that development threatened the environment and lifestyle of The Bay. 'They don't live in the real world.'

The electoral uprising had been led by one of the local Greenies, Buck Hagen, whose campaign slogan 'Let's Buck the System' roused the town out of a long lethargy. The election had been a mini war that attracted national media interest, mainly because of Buck's methods – radical, in-your-face, cheeky – and his near defamatory actions. Not all the candidates loosely associated with the push to reform council endorsed his tactics or extreme policy stands, but 'Buck of the Bay' became known in local politics across the nation as an alternative lifestyle hero. Posters of Buck, an ageing hippy with wild, grey-streaked hair hanging around his shoulders, wrists shackled to the council gates in yet another protest, sprang up all over town, replacing the peeling pictures of Bob Marley, Che Guevara and the Maharishi.

Kimberley had only met him fleetingly, for despite his outspoken letters to *The Beacon Bugle*, his stunts and flamboyant publicity events, Buck was very disciplined in separating public posturing from his private life. Personally he embraced solitude, meditation and painting rainforest scenes that sold well enough to keep him off the dole.

Reluctantly he had stood for council and been elected. Even conservative voters figured he'd do more good from within the system than 'bucketing' it from outside.

The divided council, increasing developer interest in the town and pressures from a fast expanding tourist industry made Kimberley's new job more interesting than she ever hoped it would be. Today had been well above average in terms of the unexpected and she was now making her way up to the rooftop office of *The Beacon Bugle*.

Stolle put in many hours as a volunteer on the paper as well as writing his column. He could generally be found hanging out in the small office, particularly on the eve of publication. When Kimberley arrived he was on the phone. She tapped him on the shoulder and gave a 'gotta talk' sign.

Stolle wound up the conversation, put down the phone and leaned back in his chair. 'You look like a woman on a mission. Got something for us?'

'I think so. Is there another chair in this joint?'

'I'll find one, and a coffee.'

Once settled Kimberley wasted no time. 'I've just had my regular meeting with the councillors and just before that I picked up a juicy bit of information courtesy of an indiscretion by Councillor Bright.'

'Good old Not-so. I find it amazing the old geezer has managed to survive for so many years. Mr Bright is the definitive tumbleweed – blows with the prevailing wind. So what'd he have to say?'

'Not-so Bright has fingers in a lot of pies, I've discovered. He's made good use of his many years in council,' said Kimberley. 'Owns shops in town and collects rent from various sources. We all know he's pro-development and seems to be the leader of that faction. He has ways and means of getting them on side when he needs them, wink, wink, nod, nod.'

'That's something he's bright at,' quipped Stolle. 'His career in town has had a lot of help from Sam the Man over the years. Sam Mann was in council for years and very good at getting the numbers when he needed them. When he left council, Not-so replaced him. Bright is his stooge,' Stolle said, turning a page in his notebook. 'But that's old news. What's new?'

Kimberley was thoughtful. 'I hadn't known about the connection between Sam and Councillor Bright. That makes it rather intriguing.'

'So what's he pushing through?' asked Stolle, who knew where many of the town's skeletons were stashed.

'An application for rezoning rural land to residential/commercial has gone from the general meeting to the planning department for a report to council. I was lucky enough to overhear Bright hustling one of the boys in planning to move the application along and get a report in support of it to council asap. He said something about it being good for the health of the town; that it'd be suicide for the town to knock back a big money team, and if council refuses the plan it will go to the Land

and Environment Court and win – at council's expense, so let's not mess about with this. That was the gist of what he said.'

Stolle gave a low whistle and made a few notes. 'Okay. Big money boys. Interesting, but then every developer these days likes to use that line. Did you happen to find out what little bit of land they were talking about?'

'No problem. A relaxed chat over coffee with a workmate was all it took,' said Kimberley with some satisfaction. 'Fasten your seatbelt, Stolle, it's two kilometres fronting Mighty Beach, inland for half a k. Nothing on it, just dunes, wetland and the remains of the old meatworks.'

'Jesus, that land is worth a fortune. It certainly will need big money boys. It'll attract them like ants to the honey pot. I always thought it was crown land. Can you imagine what they'll build there?'

'I'd rather not attempt to visualise such a nightmare,' Kimberley said. 'How can we stop it?'

'We need more information. Who owns the land and who is putting up the big money, to start with. This is going to cause something like World War Three in The Bay.'

'Sam could be a key if Bright fronts in council for him,' mused Kimberley.

'You're going to have to do a little more digging, Kim.'

'No problem, I was planning to work tonight. I told Matty I'd be late.'

Stolle picked up the phone. 'I'll start a bit of a whisper in my "Buzz" column. And it might be a good idea if I called Buck Hagen. Give me a call if you find out anything more.'

Matty ambled home from where the school bus dropped her. It wasn't such fun coming home from school now that her mother was so involved with her job. They used to hang out and talk about her day before she went off on whatever activity she'd planned that afternoon. Then at dusk it was home to her desk and homework while Kimberley prepared dinner.

Nowadays the house was empty when she got home, and notes from her mother were stuck on the kitchen bench asking her to find something for dinner and start it, feed the cat, peg out the washing, or take it in. By the time Kimberley came in it was usually dark, she was tired, had a million messages to answer and wanted to claim their newly acquired second-hand computer to write up her reports.

So Matty dawdled, dreading the quiet house. She went straight to the kitchen for a drink and to check on the inevitable notes. As always, the answer-phone was flashing. After pouring a glass of soy milk she switched on Replay and her mother's voice came through. 'Matts, I'll definitely be late. Doing some research on a big development. Don't tell anyone who calls. Just say I'm out and you don't know where I am. This could be something really huge, believe me. Love you, toots. Bye.'

'I wouldn't have picked your mother as the

type to dramatise events like that,' said the male voice behind her in a slightly amused tone.

Matty shrieked and spun around to stare at the figure in the doorway, half in shock, half in joy. 'Dad!' She rushed and flung herself into his arms. 'Why didn't you tell us you were coming!' She kissed him eagerly.

'Thought I'd surprise you both. Turns out I get the surprise.'

'We thought you were coming in weeks ago. I'd given up, thought you'd changed your mind.' Overjoyed as she was to see him, Matty felt a little cheated. She always liked the thrill of knowing he was coming home and the build-up to the day. Once or twice she'd even been sick with the anticipation and excitement.

'Well, Matilda me darling, I do have a little surprise of my own up my sleeve, but more of that later. Mum's working full-time then?'

'She sometimes gets home round five or six, this is unusual.'

'If your mum is working late, then may I buy my beautiful daughter dinner down town? Somewhere nice, not the pizza joint?'

'Oh, yes please, Dad. Are you sick of Indian food? Can we go and have curry and pappadams and all the things you know about?'

Ashok laughed. 'Sure we can. You do your chores and your homework and then we'll hit the town. You've got to tell me what you've been doing and about your mum's job. And about Erica. You up to that?'

Matty nodded and swallowed. 'I can talk about her without crying now. In fact I talk to her a lot, just walking on the beach or when I go up to the headland. She's still here, still my friend, you know?'

'I do. We'll talk about that later. Indians look at death quite differently from Western society.'

Matty gave her father a hug, feeling pleased she had him all to herself, then drew back. 'Does Mum know you're here?' When he grinned and shook his head, Matty said firmly, 'We'd better tell her. I'll phone her later. Want a cup of tea or coffee?'

While the jug boiled Matty whipped into her room to change into jeans and a T-shirt, then bustled back to the kitchen to fuss over mugs and a plate of biscuits. 'Anzac biscuits, Dad. I'm cooking them these days, not Mum.'

'Is there no end to surprises?' he said. 'My daughter boasting about cooking!'

'Well, you can tell me about your surprise, then.'

'Okay, you can always get secrets out of me,' he laughed. 'I've been commissioned – and that's important 'cause it means I've been asked and given money – to write a book!'

'Wow! What kind of book?'

'They want me to turn a dusty musty academic subject into something lusty and riveting.'

'About India? About all the princes and mad monks and pilgrims, and sadhus and wars that you tell me about?' said Matty excitedly. She'd loved the stories her father had told her, taken from the depictions in early Buddhist cave paintings he'd been studying for so many years.

'Got it in one! What a smart cookie.'

'How long is that going to take? Can you do it here? We have a computer now, but you'll have to share it with both of us.'

'Your mum uses a computer?'

'Yes, she learned so she could get a job.'

'I am impressed. But I have a little laptop I've been using to put in all the research. So we can be a two computer family. And to answer the question I know you're busting to ask, this book is going to take at least eighteen months to two years. So I'm kind of home for a long time.'

'No more trips to India?'

'Not for a while and certainly not for any length of time. What do you say to that?'

'I think it's wonderful,' breathed Matty with tears springing to her eyes.

'And how do you think your mum is going to feel about it?'

'I don't know, Dad,' she answered candidly. 'That's something you and Mum have to work out.'

'Let's ring her and tell her we're going out. Maybe she can join us for dessert. Might be easier if we're all out somewhere together. She might be a bit mad at me for just dropping back into your life with no warning.'

'She's changing, Dad, she's different. But it's a good change, I think.'

Ashok stood up and rubbed the top of Matty's head. 'We're all changing, Matts. We all grow up, eventually.'

Kimberley had been glad she had a reason to stay on at the office and let Matty enjoy time with her father. Also, she needed time to adjust to Ashok's return home. His phone call had caught her by surprise. Normally she would be cranky at his thoughtlessness in just wandering in the front door, but now she had so much occupying her mind that it was just another issue to deal with. She wasn't sure how she felt. But when she glanced at her watch and decided they'd be on to dessert, she took pains to make herself look good before she left the council and drove to Matty's favourite Indian restaurant.

They hugged and all talked at once. To passers-by they would have looked like an ordinary happy family enjoying an evening out. Kimberley knew she was talking too much, too quickly; eager to impress Ashok with her job, her responsibilities, her new status. Matty was smiling proudly at her, glancing at her father who sat quietly, his head tilted, a half smile on his face, listening intently.

When Ashok emerged from saying goodnight to Matty, Kimberley was sitting on the sofa, her feet up on the coffee table, reading a council report.

He sat beside her. 'Work? It seems to make a lot of demands on your time.'

'Matty and I manage. Like I said at dinner, I'm in the middle of a humdinger. There's a gathering in the community hall to talk about the ramifications.' She glanced at him. 'Would you come? Or are you going to be working on your book, your head back there in India?' She needled him gently. It was an old story – she had often accused him of wandering around the house with his head in the clouds, not knowing what day it was, tripping over anything left on the floor.

'The book is definite, Kim. Money in the bank. I just have to deliver the goods. It's crystallised where I've been heading. It will be a heavy trip, but I think I can do it.'

'So what you said about being around to do it . . . does that mean really *being* here? Or going off into the hills some place to write, going back to India, to see the publishers in London –'

'I thought I'd set up base camp in the old den. Sort out all those boxes of papers and books and stuff I've dumped in there over the years. Unless you want to move, find somewhere bigger? We could use some of my advance. Just rent for the time being. Maybe if the book works we could buy a small place.'

She stared at him. 'Buy a place? Have a mortgage like real people? The great wanderer put down roots?'

He took her hand. 'Kim, there comes a time when we find our way home, know where we want to be, and who we want to be with. You know I've been restless, searching for I didn't know what. Which wasn't to say I didn't love you and Matty. But until I could love myself, be at peace with myself, I wasn't going to be any good to you both.'

'So have you found whatever you thought you were looking for, Ash?' Her voice was tired, almost resigned. They'd danced around this question time and again.

'Maybe, maybe not. What I do know is – I need, I want, to be with you and Matty. I want to be part of your lives again, to be involved in the trivial, the day to day. I want to cook dinner when you work late like tonight, I want us to run the house together, I want to be involved in Matty's school, her friends. Listen to your adventures at the council. Read you what I've written occasionally.'

'All the things you've never done,' said Kimberley.

'You know the saying, a journey begins with a single step.' He stood up and pulled her from the sofa and wrapped his arms around her. 'Walk with me, Kim. I'm ready to follow you.' He kissed the top of her head.

She could smell his familiar scent of sandalwood oil, feel the softness and strength of his lean frame. She felt her body relax and melt into his. 'Let's just walk beside each other.'

Arms around each other they walked slowly down the hall to the main bedroom.

443

Chapter Fifteen

Beacon Bay, 1910

IT HAS BEEN TWO YEARS SINCE I HAVE HAD THE *heart to lift my pen and address my dear journal. So many memories are recorded here and how it breaks my heart to recall them. I am alone, I have longed for merciful death to take me as it has taken my beloved Lars and our two young ones. Why did I always feel in my heart that the sea would claim those I love most?*

'Oh my God.' Eddie had started reading Hannah's journal aloud to Tina as they did each week when they sat with a coffee in the lighthouse office. But the dramatic opening on this page had caught them by surprise.

'What happened?' Tina leaned forward, and Eddie slowly continued to read.

It was a storm in the Bay of Biscay that took them. I know little other than the formal short letter of advice and regret from the shipping line. There were some telegraphed stories in the Sydney papers that I eventually saw, but no mention of my loved ones. The shock was so great I lost my little baby girl by miscarriage and my own health has been weak. More, it was my mind that troubled me most. The nightmares still haunt me. My dear mother came to be with me but Father is frail and she returned to Sydney. She confessed she found this house too sad, too lonely.

'Oh, that poor woman,' whispered Tina. 'She lost everything. I can't imagine how I would cope.'

Eddie reached out and squeezed her hand. 'No wonder there is two years between this and the last entry.' He picked up the diary and resumed reading.

While our township grows, I keep to myself and have, I am afraid, something of a reputation as a strange lady recluse. I spend each morning and evening on the walk atop the roof as I promised Lars I would wait and watch for their safe return. Often I believe I see the old Lady Richmond sailing towards me and hear the cries of my sons. I wait for the day I too will be taken from this house to be with them. I pray my soul will be set free of this place. I have only death to look forward to. How happy we were here, now I know not nor care what will happen to me. I am ashamed for feeling thus, other wives have faced tragedy, but my heart aches that I agreed to Lars taking the boys so far away to a family that never cared about us. How can the God I believed in so devoutly abandon me like this? I have not returned to the parish church. Perhaps I must do so to ease the anger and pain that consumes my days.

Eddie finished softly reading Hannah's heart-broken words. Silently they both stared at the page of distinctive spidery writing.

'Do you suppose she saw out her days here, alone?' asked Tina. 'I'll have to ask Sid if he can tell us anything about her. I feel I know Hannah now.'

'I can just imagine her, pacing around that widow's walk,' said Eddie finally. 'What an incredible tragedy.'

'Life can change in an instant. Makes you realise how you have to grab at happiness when you can,' Tina said as she rose and went to him, and without another word they kissed.

They'd kissed before, but this time they realised the emotion they felt had a special edge. The great love Hannah had known, her too brief a time of happiness, her pain and tears affected them deeply. Without either saying the words, they knew that this time they had to plunge ahead and take their own chance at happiness.

Tina straightened up and wiped her eyes.

Eddie closed Hannah's journal, drew a breath and looked at Tina. 'Well, are we going to give it a go as real partners? I'm willing.'

'One way to find out. Let's just take it day by day,' she replied. 'No pressure, no commitments, what will be will be, as someone once said.'

Eddie leapt to his feet and hugged her, his heart light, a sense of freedom and joy overcoming him. 'Tina, I feel wonderful. You're wonderful. Life is wonderful!' He picked up Hannah's journal and kissed it. 'Thank you, Hannah.'

'You're crazy. Gorgeous but crazy.' Tina laughed. 'Let's go for a walk around the headland. Then I have to hose the goat droppings off the steps.'

'You're so romantic,' Eddie said and followed her outside where the whole world looked sunnier and brighter than it had for a long time.

Buck Hagen and Stolle were having a beer in the Pier Hotel, the 'old' pub that had been done up in the centre of town. They sat in the back room talking quietly.

'You going to run with this story in a big way next week?' asked Buck.

'Yeah. Have to run something on page one, I imagine, even though we don't know too much. But

I'll be dropping a pebble in the pond to cause a few ripples before the tidal wave. For that we need more info, like who is really behind this whole deal.'

'This might help.' Buck slid an envelope across the table.

'Fell off the back of a truck, did it?' Stolle grinned.

'Copy of the rezoning application. Doesn't give you much that's new except the name of a solicitor in Sydney who is representing the owner of the land, one Beacon Land Holdings.'

'Thanks, mate. The solicitor is probably a front for a network of companies, even offshore interests, to mask the identity of the real owners.'

'You might start looking closely at the connections and relationships of some of the players.' Buck sipped his beer. 'Bloody nice drop,' he said appreciatively.

'Always tastes better when the adrenalin is flowing a little faster, right? Now what sort of links have you come up with?'

Buck ticked them off on the fingers of one hand. 'Seen together several times in recent months at the local golf club . . . Sam the Man, one-time councillor, developer, sometime scoundrel and small-time entrepreneur; his stooge in council, Not-so Bright; and Andrew Jamieson, well-known socialite architect and concept designer who has worked on mega resort developments in South-East Asia, mainly in Thailand.'

Stolle acknowledged this with a nod over his beer.

'At the latest golf outing, not here but in less public Brigalow, Sam and Jamieson had the company of General Chidchai for a pleasant eighteen holes. Now a little search on the internet last night revealed that the General has an interesting background. Spent a lot of time with units on the Burma-Thai border back in the dubious days before the government ordered the army to get really serious about cracking down on the drug trade from across the border.'

'Struth, you're moving the game into the big league, Buck. Surely The Bay doesn't rate that sort of attention,' Stolle exclaimed, clearly sceptical.

'We live in a fast-changing world, mate, and there's a lot of big money drifting around these days looking for something that is an earner and a cleanser.'

'Nah. That's stretching it, linking the deal to laundering drug money.'

'Perhaps. But it might be worthwhile keeping in mind. Anyway, I'll bet a quid the General is in on the deal.'

'I'll pass on the bet, thanks, Buck. Who else?'

'Every good plot has a woman, preferably lovely, available and a player. Enter the luscious Ms Letitia Sweetman . . . currently playing with none other than Andrew Jamieson. She made up the numbers for the Brigalow game. She also acts for Sam when required, on legal matters only, that is,' said Buck.

'Yeah, well, Letitia does have style and brains,' said Stolle. 'And Sam's missus wouldn't tolerate any sexual indiscretions by him in this town. She'd murder him if he did. You sure about Letitia and Andrew?'

Buck nodded and his expression left no doubt in Stolle's mind. Buck had one of the best networks in the area when it came to knowing what was going on, who was getting on, and who was about to.

'No point in trying to get info from Letitia, and I don't expect you'll get too much joy from the Sydney solicitor, but give him a ring,' said Buck, taking out his pocket diary and making a couple of brief notes. 'I'll chat up a media mate or two in Sydney and see what I can find out. Given our town's past and present profile for off-beat stories, they'll be interested to get a break on this one. When is the inevitable public meeting?'

'Nola's little group of revolutionaries, which includes my Lynn, will no doubt be setting that up. Probably the middle of next week at the Community Centre. They'll want you to speak.'

Buck made another note. 'It's good to see the community waking up again. They get complacent, newcomers get comfortable. Town needs a kick in the butt every so often. Watchdogs go to sleep in the sun. It's not like the big smoke, you know. We still have time to take evasive action.'

'Yeah, as soon as things get good, the sharks circle. They come here and see dollars and development opportunities when the rest of us see lifestyle, a slower pace, fulfilment,' sighed Stolle, thinking back on the many words he'd written along those lines.

'We've won wars here because so many of us are misfits,' said Buck. 'We've reinvented ourselves. But you can't relax. There're always going to be the sharks, lazy and greedy councils, general apathy. We need a total upgrading of environmental concerns, the whole local government scene needs overhauling, if you ask me.'

'Steady on, Buck. You can't do it all, and you can't do it alone,' said Stolle, seeing Buck becoming morose. 'We're a community and that's what we're fighting for. And we have to do it together.'

There wasn't much time to organise the Sundowner Mob, as they now called themselves, for a meeting at Nola's on Saturday afternoon, but everyone responded to Kimberley's phone call. 'Big news,' was all she had to say to get an instant acceptance.

It was another perfect sunset, and Nola ensured that the hospitality was just as good: dainty hors d'oeuvres made and served by her 'home assistant', drinks in fine crystal.

Holly got a special welcome from the others, Nola particularly enthusing over her suntan and relaxed demeanour. 'It obviously did you the world of good, darling. Such a sparkle in the eyes.'

Holly produced a set of postcards, all with the same photo of a mother whale and her calf throwing themselves joyfully out of the sea. 'I wrote, but never got around to posting them. It's a photo Trish Franklin took of Nala and her calf.'

Mac turned the card over and read the brief message and smiled at Holly. 'Happy writing,' she said, 'very distinctive and very you.'

It was a remark that momentarily puzzled Holly, but she was soon distracted because everyone was taking a keen interest in the photographs and asking questions.

'What an experience it must have been,' said Bonnie enviously. It was her first time at a Sundowners gathering and she had been surprised to be included, but Nola had insisted. With her volunteer work at the Dolphin Centre and the Creative Community, Bonnie now felt she had a role in The Bay. Nola had telephoned to invite her and said she was impressed with what she'd heard from Amber about her generosity to Amber's mother.

'It's only time. And I like pottering around in her garden,' she said, but was grateful to Nola for subtly acknowledging her changing lifestyle.

'Giving people time is a precious gift, Bonnie. We look forward to your contribution to our group.'

Bonnie looked intently at the postcard. 'I might have to make that trip to Hervey Bay myself,' she said quietly.

'I can't put into words how it affected me,' admitted Holly. 'They say it's a profound, often life-changing experience, and I can understand why. There's so much I could talk about, but I'm sure whales aren't on the agenda at the moment.' She turned to Nola. 'What's happening?'

Nola took charge. 'Would you all please settle down so Kimberley can satisfy our burning curiosity. Kimberley.'

'Well, take a firm grip on your drinks, folks. A Sydney-based company is making a bid to develop most of the beachfront at Mighty Beach. Their rezoning application is before council staff for assessment.' She paused until the expressions of dismay subsided. 'Okay, there's more. Councillor Bright is pushing the application and Stolle thinks that could link the deal to Sam the Man. Lynn.'

Lynn took the cue. 'Yeah, it seems that after Sam quit sitting on council donkey's years ago, he stage managed Bright into the vacancy and they've been very close buddies ever since. Bright apparently owes his commercial success to deals Sam cut him in on. Now, it's likely that the deal is linked through Sam to that little gathering Nola witnessed in the apartment over yonder, and that the Asian bloke is involved. He might well be the big money backer of the deal.'

There was another outbreak of exchanges among the women but Holly didn't hear what anyone was saying. Her mind was whirling, trying to come to terms with the obvious and irrefutable knowledge that Andrew was probably in on the deal as well. And the trail wound sordidly back to his trip to Thailand last year. As she struggled to get her anger under control she became conscious that the little gathering had quietened and everyone was looking at her.

'Yes. I know what you're all thinking, and

you're probably right. Andrew could well be involved, though to what extent I'm not sure. What we've heard ties in with some remarks he made to me recently.' She paused and took a deep breath. 'On a slightly different subject I'd like to say a word or two, because it won't be long before the gossip grapevine puts it about. I'd prefer to say it straight to people I regard as my friends. Before I went away to Queensland I took a trip to Sydney to see Andrew, and to cut a long story short, we seem to have hit the wall. But where we go from here, I hadn't wanted to think about. I'm now thinking a little more clearly. I don't believe I can see a future for Andrew and me any more.'

There was a stunned silence for a moment before Nola rallied and took command. 'Holly, darling, that was probably one of the hardest little speeches for any woman to have to make and we love you all the more for telling us as friends, together like this.'

Mac leaned across and gave her a kiss on the cheek and took her hand.

Nola pressed on. 'Now, we'd better get cracking. What do we do? Organise a public protest?' She paused, 'I take it we are all in agreement we don't want this ghastly plan to go ahead?'

'No way!'

'Absolutely not.'

'Stolle has spoken to Councillor Buck Hagen and I reckon he'll be moving along those lines before the next edition of the *Bugle*. If this development goes through it will be the end of The

Bay as we know and love it,' said Lynn quietly. And it didn't seem a melodramatic statement to any of them.

'We'd better let him know he has support, right. All in favour?' asked Nola with authority. There was a round of applause in support. 'I shall make an appropriate statement to the *Bugle* then,' she added.

'As I'm on the council staff I can't make any public comment,' Kimberley explained. 'I believe Nola would be an effective community spokesperson.'

As everybody agreed, Nola smiled. 'I think grey-haired old warhorses can put the wind up councils. We have time and inclination to stir. Now, let's top up our drinks and enjoy what's left of the twilight.'

The women chuckled as the bottle of champagne was passed around. The queenly and glamorous Nola and the wonderfully eccentric Mac in her purple hippy clobber could scarcely be described as grey-haired warhorses. But stirrers – definitely.

It was then that Mac took Nola aside. 'I'd like to thank you for providing this little forum and hospitality for such a diverse group of women. Some very lovely friendships are being forged here, very lovely indeed.'

Her sincerity touched Nola deeply, and impulsively she reached out and gave Mac a hug and whispered, 'Thanks, Mac, thanks.' She pulled back and took Mac's hands in hers. 'You know what we're acknowledging here is that we're all changing, all responding to what life offers. The Bay encourages that, doesn't it?'

Mac smiled. 'You're right. You know I once read a line that went something like this, "Life whispers in your soul and speaks to your heart." '

'A lovely line.'

'Yes, but the trick is taking time to listen.'

Mitchell completed the final sequence of movements in his morning tai chi routine, stretched and stood, hands on hips, looking at the sea.

'Now run down and dive in,' instructed a steady voice behind him.

He turned in surprise then grinned at discovering Eddie had his camera focused on him. With a shrug Mitchell jogged to the water and dived through the waves, his sleek body silhouetted against the early morning light.

Eddie filmed him swimming strongly then panned to the right as several dolphins arched through the backlit waves. 'Ah, wonderful stuff.' Eddie turned off the video and sat on the sand waiting for Mitchell, tempted to strip off and dive in the water, but his training to never leave his camera was too strong.

Mitchell joined him, rubbing himself with a towel then pulling on a T-shirt. 'What's this Eddie – "Candid Camera"?'

'The sexy side of life in The Bay,' laughed Eddie. 'You had clothes on. I've just shot a long soft-focus segment of Drew's nude beach yoga class and a couple of fabulous naked Danish girls who were most co-operative. They were being chatted up by Robbo, our local well-hung stud.'

'Our favourite lawyer?' laughed Mitchell. 'Makes a change from filming weddings and rallies, eh?'

'From what I hear there's going to be a lot more rallying. Kimberley is on the warpath,' Eddie said. 'A lot happened while you were blissed out in Hervey Bay. How was it?'

Mitchell sat on the sand beside him and didn't immediately answer. Eddie waited, suddenly aware Mitchell was giving his light question some heavy thought.

'Eddie, it was special. It is every year. But this year, Holly made it really special.'

'Yeah, I've heard it can be mind blowing. I've only filmed whales from the air, not up close. So, Holly really got into it?'

'She did. But what I meant was, she made me feel special,' Mitchell said slowly. 'I suppose the whole experience is conducive to bonding. But I have to say, I've come ashore with a bit of confu-sion.'

'Ah,' said Eddie, suddenly understanding. 'Deep waters afloat and ashore.'

'Holly has become a good friend. The months I've been working up at Richmond House . . . I don't know, we never ran out of things to talk about, laugh about, share. I realised I'd never had that in quite that way before. I suppose because we're both married it took the pressure off . . . but out there at sea, it was like we were starting out again in life.' He stopped and gazed at the water and gave a shrug and half grin. 'I wish.'

'I know exactly what you're saying,' Eddie said. 'I've been through two marriages. Things start off in that hot rush of adrenalin, sex, fun, and the next thing you're looking at this strange woman across the breakfast table thinking what the hell are you doing here?'

'Oh, things haven't got to that stage with Veronica,' said Mitchell hastily. 'Nothing unpleasant. It's just that we seem to have run out of things to say to each other, do together. I blame myself for dragging her up here.'

'I thought she was into her ceramics with all the pottery people,' said Eddie. 'Laura never got into anything but spending what little money I had left.'

Mitchell chewed his lip, finding it difficult to get out his next remark. 'Veronica did drop a bombshell on me as a welcome home surprise.'

'Oops, mate. I think I know what's coming.'

'It's not that serious. I mean she doesn't want to leave me or anything. Well, I mean . . . it's just that she wants to go back to Sydney. Has a job,' said Mitchell in a rush.

Eddie stared at him. 'That's not leaving you? Or are you supposed to pack up and go back too? Do you want to go back to Sydney?'

'Hell, no. Would you?'

'No. No way,' he said quickly, then paused and

spoke slowly. 'Well, maybe. I mean I think I might if Tina said she was moving to Sydney.' His face cleared and he said with some relief, 'She's never going to leave here.'

'You and Tina – how serious is it?'

'Now, very. I've been in a bit of a mess about it all. When you make two mistakes you think you have to be a lousy judge. But she seems so different, so special . . .'

Mitchell smiled and nodded in agreement.

'I was very cautious. I didn't let on I was so smitten with her. Didn't tell anyone, even myself,' said Eddie. 'I was scared I might do the wrong thing. Didn't even try to sleep with her and for me, well, that's a bit of a record. Used to be easy Eddie . . . easy come, easy go. I treasure this girl. I've never felt like this.'

'I've found the friendship part is really important. My old mum used to say friends first, lovers later. Now I know what she meant,' said Mitchell.

'So what are you going to do?' Eddie asked sympathetically. And when Mitchell didn't answer, he added, 'I think you know very well.'

'It's not that simple.'

'These things never are. You and Holly are good friends. That counts for a lot. Mind you, Andrew seems a bit of a shit, wouldn't surprise me if he was playing around with his secretary.'

'Or solicitor,' blurted Mitchell.

Eddie gave Mitchell a hard look. 'In Sydney?'

'As well as up here. I saw Andrew and Letitia together on the beach a long time back.'

Eddie let out a low whistle. 'Now I reckon there's more to that than just having the hots for a younger bird. That woman is dangerous. Devious. Ambitious. She's one of those reptilian bitches that eat soft men like us for breakfast.'

'In that case Andrew can hold his own.' Mitchell made an attempt at a joke.

'Andrew is a businessman. He and Letitia Sweetman are well suited,' said Eddie. 'The question to my mind is, who's using whom?'

Holly had agonised over making the phone call to Andrew. So many small things now added up and she saw an ugly picture emerging. The extended trips to Bangkok, mutterings from other partners in Andrew's company and a comment or two from their wives at cocktail parties that she hadn't understood at the time. Phone calls in the evening when she'd answered and the caller had hung up, or Andrew had picked up the phone and spoken in a low voice. The dubious company he was keeping. His evasiveness. And thousands of dollars in a bundle in the drinks bar at their house. Mac's comment that she'd seen Andrew in The Bay when Holly didn't think he was there. And most devastating, the fact that he'd tricked her into signing all those papers, effectively removing her financially from their marriage. Not to mention the issue of Letitia Sweetman. Well she was glad. He was a stranger to her. And she was now determined to fight for her share of their assets and take a stand against whatever involvement he may have in this development at Mighty Beach. But being the fair person she was, Holly still wanted to give him an opportunity to convince her he was not part of this scheme which looked like igniting the town.

They briefly exchanged small talk about Marcus and Melanie, then Holly drew a breath. 'Andrew, there's something else . . . about The Bay –'

'About Richmond House? I hope you're not going to ask for money. I told you I had to consolidate everything, just temporarily of course.'

'Would that have been to invest in Beacon Land Holdings?' Holly glanced down at the points she'd written on her notepad.

There was a moment of stunned silence. 'What do you know about that? Who told you?'

She sighed, hearing the note of panic in his voice. 'Andrew, the news is out about the development of the beachfront by some group and you're said to be one of the people involved.'

He gave a sharp short laugh. 'You make it sound like I'm a criminal. Holly, this is a business deal, a big one, with very reputable people. It's going to be magnificent.'

'So why didn't you tell me about it? I'm living here, in business here, for God's sake!'

'Because you've never taken a bit of interest in what I do –'

'That's rubbish! You never tell me anything! Never speak to me. You treat me like an idiot,' she shouted, breaking her promise to herself to keep cool and calm.

'So what do you want to know? I'd appreciate your telling me just what wild rumours are being bandied around about a very legitimate enterprise that could set us up for life.'

'Set you up, Andrew. I'm not a part of your business, our company, or our marriage any longer,' she snapped. 'Just what sort of a deal is it? What do you plan to build on that pristine strip of land?'

Andrew suddenly became placatory. 'Holly, I'll come up as soon as I can. I'll bring the concept plans I've been working on and you'll see what a sensitive, necessary, visionary project this is.'

'Fine. Though how sensitive and visionary it could be with the likes of Sam Mann involved with some shady Asian investor, I fail to see.'

There was another brief silence and Andrew sighed. 'Is that what you've heard? My, the gossip-mongers must be out there beating the drums,' he said with an attempt at lightness. 'The development is for a company in Sydney, Sam is just dealing with the legal adviser to that company, which represents the owners of the land.'

'Who are?'

Her sharp question stung him, for Andrew realised he didn't actually know who was behind Beacon Land Holdings. Letitia had put the deal to him after they'd met at a party in Bangkok and started their affair. Later she'd introduced him to General Chidchai, who was looking to invest money in Australia. Andrew had his suspicions but it didn't bother him how the General and his friends had acquired the money. Letitia had introduced Andrew to Sam back in Sydney and things had started rolling along. When he'd seen the potential money to be made, Andrew wanted in as an investor and not just a hired designer and architect. That's why he'd needed to cash in all the family assets. Under normal circumstances Holly would never have known, he'd have had enough money to do his own thing. The shadow of Letitia hovered over him. It was so incredibly ironic that Holly got a bee in her bonnet about doing something with her life and picked – of all places to do it – The Bay. He shook himself as these thoughts spun through his mind.

'Holly, I'm not at liberty to give you that kind of information. Trust me, the Beacon development is something you'll be proud to know I was a part of creating. Wait till you see the whole concept. Just don't talk about this until I see you. I'll be up in a day or so, as soon as I can.'

'I don't care how wonderful your concept is. The issue is, nothing should be built on that land – for lots of reasons. It's beautiful and unspoiled and it's used by everyone in the community. You'll put up something for rich people.'

'Well it's too late. The rezoning is going through council, and when the people see what we are giving to the community, it will be a different story.'

'Andrew, I'm telling you, people are going to fight this. And I'm going to be in the frontline.'

'Oh, God, like you were at the dog rally? Get real, you're in business there too, remember. The development will advantage everybody.'

'I am in business, no thanks to you. And when I open the doors of Richmond House I can say I've done it all with integrity, with the help of good and decent people, and all with my own money.' Her anger had dissipated and she felt close to tears.

'Fine, Holly. I'm withdrawing as your guarantor – conflict of interest. You realise if this little B & B doesn't make a dime, you're left with nothing.' He sounded snide and mocking. Andrew had taken pride over the years in being a tough bastard in business and Holly could hear the pleasure in his voice.

'Nothing to you is a lot to me, Andrew, but you couldn't even begin to understand that. I guess we just call it quits then. On every level.' Her voice was drained of emotion.

'I guess so.'

'Goodbye, Andrew.' She hung up before he could say anything else. What was there left to say? Later would come the painful task of telling their children and families, of sorting through possessions. She started to shake and headed to the kitchen.

Andrew immediately lifted the phone.

'Letitia, what the hell is going on? Holly has

464

just rung to ask me what I know about Beacon Land Holdings. The shit is going to hit the fan, she says. Who talked? We wanted to stage manage the release of this for public comment. We have our own media and PR people to do it. What happened?'

'Calm down, it's a small town. Once the DA went in, there'd be some talk. We can handle it. Certain people jump up and down but there's nothing much they can do. Sam has things under control.'

'I'm coming up tomorrow. By the way, who is the owner of that land? Who is Beacon Land Holdings that Sam's acting for?'

'That doesn't matter, Andy. Everything is being done legally. Sure there could be front companies, but that's par for the course these days. The minute after council votes through the rezoning application, we get paid. The locals shouldn't be a problem. This is too big to stop.'

'My wife has informed me she'll be in the frontline against it. Or should I say my soon to be ex-wife. Holly and I have called it quits.'

'Oh. That could be a complication we don't need. She's well liked in town.' Letitia didn't sound as thrilled at his news as he'd expected.

'Dinner tomorrow night then? I'll check into the Big Pub . . .' He had no intention of staying there and he waited for Letitia's invitation to stay with her, but it didn't come.

'I'll get Sam and the PR woman down from Brisbane to come and eat with us. We'd better start thinking strategies.' Letitia sounded distracted and they said goodbye without their usual endearments.

Mitchell and Eddie pulled up to Eddie's farmhouse and Mitchell leapt out of his truck and went to the large Esky tied in the back. 'Hey, come and grab a handle, there must be over twenty kilos of fish in here.'

But Eddie was standing by the truck glaring at a small white convertible with Queensland numberplates parked by the shrubbery. 'Shit. I hate the way she just turns up like it's her house.'

'Who?' Mitchell moved towards him.

'Laura.' He scowled.

'She visits Alice, doesn't she?'

'Yeah, but I've made it clear she has to plan these things, doesn't just walk in unannounced. Typical. Let's get those fish in the freezer.'

They carried the Esky between them round to the back into the laundry where Eddie had installed a second-hand freezer.

'I'll get some freezer bags.'

Eddie went into the kitchen and was rummaging in a drawer when Laura spoke behind him.

'Hi, Eddie. What's new?'

He slammed the drawer shut. 'I might ask you the same thing. Damn it, Laura, I've asked you to call before you come up here. I hope you're not taking Alice back with you . . . this is an unscheduled visit. She has stuff to do tomorrow.'

He glared at her and Laura was struck as she had been when she'd first seen Eddie at how handsome he was. 'You're cute when you're mad.'

'Give it a rest. Where's Alice?'

'She's searching the internet for something. Been showing me her room. You've made this old dump look quite decent.'

'Alice and I are very comfortable. Of course if I had some money it'd be much better. But I give all my money to you. Nice car by the way.'

'Present from Jack.'

'Good of him. Excuse me, I have to get these out to Mitch.'

She followed him through to the laundry and greeted Mitchell. 'What a heap of fish! Have you guys been fishing?'

'No, hunting, Laura. What's it look like?' snapped Eddie and Mitchell laughed.

'We took a friend's boat off the Cape to film a sequence of deep-sea fishing and this is what we caught,' said Mitchell.

'Filming fishing? Making a sporting film now?' asked Laura.

'I'm actually shooting The Bay's lifestyle,' said Eddie calming down. 'All the nice things one can do here. Tomorrow it will be the kayaks paddling round the Cape with the dolphins.'

'Alice is going to be a star in it. She's looking forward to it,' said Mitchell, sealing the fish into freezer bags.

'Of course, it's probably a bit tame compared to the exciting life you lead on the coast,' Eddie said.

'I wouldn't say that,' she answered. 'Good to see you, Mitchell. Eddie, we have to talk,' she added ominously as she went back through the house.

Eddie and Mitchell exchanged a look. 'Another one of those talks. Guess what it's about?' said Eddie.

'Alice?'

'Wrong. Money.'

'Eddie, it's not my business, but surely you can't keep supporting her like you say you do, plus care for Alice,' said Mitchell quietly.

'Be careful, mate. You have all this to look forward to. Your wife will get half your super too, you know.'

Mitchell shrugged. 'I haven't thought about any of that. I mean the word "divorce" has never been mentioned between Veronica and me. She's down in Sydney already, doing her thing, enjoying her job. They wanted her to start straightaway, so we agreed she should go for it. She's got her ceramics, and now she says she's going to do textile design. She and our son Tom have the house, they're happy. I'm happy up here. Seems a fine arrangement to me.'

'A word of advice – get things drawn up now, legally, while you're still friends. I've had to learn the hard way,' sighed Eddie.

'Okay, thanks. It might give me an opening to ask Veronica just where she sees our future going. Certainly not together,' said Mitchell.

Eddie shut the freezer and held up two large

snapper. 'Come back for dinner. I'll sling them on the barbie.'

'Done. I'll finish distributing the fish and clean up and see you about six. I'll bring a salad and a bottle.'

Eddie retrieved his camera gear from the truck and waved to Mitchell as he went back into the house dreading his talk with Laura.

Alice walked in holding one of the fish. 'Wow, Dad, these are great. Are they for tonight?'

'Yes, Mitchell's coming over.'

'Great.'

'Have you done the chooks today? I have to talk to your mother then I'm taking a shower.'

Alice looked from one to the other. 'You could just ask to be left alone to talk, you know. But I'll do the chooks. We get big brown eggs every day,' she said to her mother.

Laura watched Alice head down through the garden. 'She seems very happy here. The next thing she'll be wanting to wear gingham skirts and broderie anglaise tops.'

'What's that mean?'

'Just she's a little bit wholesome, Miss Country meets RM Williams, you know.'

'What's wrong with that? You want to dress her up too much. She's never worn any of those clothes you bought her.'

'That's because she doesn't go anywhere smart with you.'

'I imagine she gets enough of the high life with you and Jack.'

'Can we drop this, please? I have something to say.' Laura fiddled with the pepper and salt shakers on the table.

'Fine.' Eddie folded his arms and leaned against the sink. 'Shoot.'

'It hasn't worked out with Jack. Nice guy and all that, but well, the age difference caught up with us I guess. He's boring.'

'You mean he's showing old fart tendencies? Wanting to watch telly and you want to go dancing?'

'Golf actually. He plays golf, then watches TV. And all his friends, and their wives, are old. I don't think they like me. Well, we don't have anything in common.'

Eddie felt a chill creep over him. 'So what are you saying? I hope you don't want to take Alice up there full time.'

'No. I know she likes school here and all her friends . . . It's me. I'd like to move back here. Looking back, we had good times here.' She gave a tremulous smile.

'Here? You don't mean, here, in this house?' Eddie's voice rose.

'I miss you, Eddie. We did have fun in the beginning, lots of fun.' She tried a sexy little laugh. 'Couldn't we try again? No commitments, just a family again –'

'Christ, no way, Laura! We were never "a family", it was controlled mayhem most of the time. This is the most stable Alice has been since we met. And you and I are history. I'm sorry, but I've moved on, there's no going back for me.'

'Couldn't we at least try? I mean, no sex, just be friends, under the same roof. It'd be good for Alice to have a real family situation, just for a while. Till I get my own place settled –'

'Laura, grow up. Alice has been given a sense of stability these past months, I'm not going be a hypocrite. You can't keep running to me every time you have a problem. I have a life of my own now.'

'What's that mean? Are you seeing someone?' Her eyes narrowed.

'That's none of your business. And don't ask Alice about my life, it's not fair to her. Listen, you have a unit, move in there.' The last thing he wanted was Laura back in town, but anything was better than having her move in with him.

'It's rented.'

'So rent something yourself. Go back to your parents and sort yourself out. Then make a decision. That's the best plan,' he said again. 'Definitely.'

'You want to get rid of me,' she pouted.

Alice came through the back door. 'Four eggs today.' She looked from Eddie to her mother, the tension between them still thick in the room. 'Oh, are you still talking?'

'Not really. I've said all I'm going to say.' Eddie looked at Laura. 'Have you talked this through with Alice?'

'Talked what through? What's going on?' asked Alice sounding worried and glancing from one adult to the other.

'Tell her, Laura.'

'All in good time. Alice, honey, I had to talk to Eddie first. But he's not being at all understanding and now I don't know what I'm going to do.' She started to cry and sank onto a kitchen chair.

Alice gave Eddie a bewildered look. 'What's going on?'

'Your mum and Jack have split up.'

'Oh. I'm not surprised. He wasn't her type. Just rich,' said Alice with a mature assurance that stunned them both.

'That *is* her bloody type,' snapped Eddie.

'You're mean, you're not trying to understand,' wailed Laura and released a fresh flood of tears.

'Understand! That's just what I am trying to do. Why in God's name do you want to move back in with me?'

'Mum wants to move back here? With us?' yelped Alice. 'What about Tina?'

'Tina?' Laura lifted her head, her eyes steely bright through her tears.

'Mum, you're not going to make me leave here. Please, I don't want to leave.' Alice began to cry.

'Oh, for God's sake.' Eddie took two strides and drew Alice to him. 'Stop crying, sweetie, nothing is going to change. For us. Your mother has to sort herself out. Now we'll help her. But there comes a time when everyone has to grow up and start managing their own life. On their own.'

Alice gave Eddie a grateful look then knelt by

her mother. Laura now had her head on her arms on the kitchen table. 'Mum, it'll be all right. You'll be all right. Can't you stay down at the beach and we can see each other a lot more? Just till you get, you know, settled . . .' Alice patted her mother's head.

'Well, I can tell when I'm not wanted. You didn't even ask me to dinner.' She wiped her face.

'You hate fish,' said Eddie dismissively.

'Mum, where are you staying?'

'I haven't got anywhere to stay yet,' sniffed Laura. 'I just came straight here. I thought I'd be welcome.' She glared at Eddie.

'You could have phoned.'

'You were out fishing. Enjoying yourself,' she snapped back.

'Mum! He was filming!' said Alice.

Laura got to her feet. 'All right, I'll go to a motel and phone in the morning and arrange to see my daughter.'

Mitchell called out to Holly as he carried the box of fish into the kitchen. 'Fisho – delivery as promised.'

'Only come in if they're really fresh,' she answered.

'Madame, these monsters were swimming just two hours ago. I've cleaned them. They're ready to bung in the freezer.'

'Wonderful. Thanks so much. You've given me far too many.'

'Serve them to the guests. Hey, why don't you

come up to Eddie's for dinner? He's throwing some on the barbie.'

'I can't, thanks. Too much to do.'

'Okay, but we have to sit down soon and finalise some thoughts on your advertising brochure that we've talked about. I've come up with a few ideas for you to look at. And Sagaro has put together a great website idea.'

'Give me a call on Monday. And don't forget the meeting in the community hall about the Mighty Beach development. Andrew is coming up to show me his concepts.'

'We'll all be keen to know about that,' said Mitchell.

'I hope we get a good roll-up. Stolle has stuck flyers around town. Be sure and bring Veronica.'

Mitchell busied himself with the fish and didn't look at her. 'Um, Ronnie has gone back to Sydney. Got a great job in a gallery with a studio she can use for her work.'

Holly was taken aback, but forced what she hoped was an appropriate response. 'That's great for her. She must be pleased. Will she commute? When did all this happen?'

Mitchell straightened up and gave her a slightly embarrassed, perplexed look. 'This week, and commuting is out, Holly. She's moving back into the house with Tom. She feels she's run the distance up here.'

'Oh,' said Holly quietly, the silence in the room so intense she could hear the clock ticking. 'And you?'

'I'm staying.'

'There seems to be a lot going on in people's lives at the moment,' she said simply.

'I suppose Mac would say there's some planetary upheaval in the universe at the moment,' he said and gave a small grin.

'Seems like it. Thanks for the fish, Mitch.'

He nodded, then walked back out to his truck and drove slowly down the driveway.

Chapter Sixteen

SAM PACED AROUND HIS LIVING ROOM IN A QUIET street in one of the original housing estates in The Bay. Large trees and established gardens disguised the dreariness of brick suburbia – so out of place in the tropical casualness of the rest of the town. Housing developments now had to meet more sensitive regulations pioneered by a talented woman architect and developers were obliged to follow her brief and leave a band of native trees and vegetation around the buildings.

Freda Mann had lived contentedly in the pleasant environment, rarely taking any interest in her husband's business activities. When Sam talked of selling up, leaving The Bay and retiring to a more up-market place, she took little notice. Sam had always talked big. She was happy to stay exactly where she was.

His wife was out at bowls and Sam picked up the latest edition of the local paper and scanned through the page one story again: 'ALMIGHTY ROW BREWING'. He was amused by the headline, which was typical of the *Bugle* style. However, he realised it was necessary now to organise some headlines of his own, some positive reaction, to emphasise that the project would be environmentally friendly and create lots of jobs. Of more immediate concern was the reference in the 'Buzz' column that tenuously linked the General with the project. Who the hell leaked that? Sam asked himself over and over. Oh well, keep calm, he told himself and read the 'Buzz' paragraph again.

Vultures sighted
We're used to having sea eagles hovering over Mighty Beach, but a new species has been sighted in the area – vultures. Not the feathered kind, either. They've flown in from Sydney and as far away as Bangkok, so I've been told by well-informed local birdwatchers on the civic scene. The Asian subspecies are noted for their fat wallets and are known everywhere as Development Vultures. Their activities concerning Mighty Beach will come under discussion at the public meeting on Tuesday in the Community Centre.

Sam settled into his high-backed swivel chair at his desk in the sunny room overlooking his back garden which served as his office. Having read the paper that morning he had been expecting a call from Councillor Jimmy Bright.

'Hold it, Jimmy. Hold it. All the story said was the rezoning application is being considered for a report to council. The report said, correctly, that the land is owned by a Sydney company. The rest of the story is about initial community reaction and the predictable concerns about impact on the environment. Nothing we hadn't anticipated, apart from the story getting out sooner than we wanted.'

'Yeah. That's true, but this new organisation of women that came out of nowhere to announce they're going to oppose the project sounds like a nuisance we hadn't anticipated. Nola Florens, of all people!' exclaimed the councillor with disdain and dismay. 'She's done bugger-all but drink and swan around ever since she sashayed into town. What the hell is she up to?'

Sam had a little laugh. 'Sure, she's a wild card I hadn't expected. I can't explain her change of style. Maybe she's had a religious experience.'

'A bad batch of wine, or an overdose of caviar more likely.'

'Maybe, but her network reaches well beyond this neck of the woods, so that makes her a bit of a worry. Media and the like.'

'Okay. Okay. But there are many relative new-comers making noises. Eddie, that television bloke, for one, and even Andrew's wife, Holly. Now what the hell is going on there? Have they split? And how has the Sydney connection reacted?'

'Calmly,' replied Sam quite casually. 'As for Holly's involvement, I'll talk to Andrew, but maybe she got wind of you know what with whom.'

'Play with fire and you get your fingers burned,' concluded Jimmy Bright, now feeling relaxed. 'Some people never learn. See you later at the club, Sam.'

The *Bugle* story added to Letitia's nagging but ill-defined concerns about the Mighty Beach project. She'd been uncomfortable ever since the telephone call from Andrew alerting her to Holly's outburst the previous weekend.

After pouring her second cup of coffee for the morning she rang the Sydney representative for Beacon Land Holdings, the solicitor Maxwell Hamilton. They had spoken many times since he first contacted her in connection with the rezoning application by the company he fronted. Since then he had taken her and Andrew to dinner at an exclusive club near Parliament House on two occasions when she was in Sydney 'on business'. Sam Mann had recommended her to Hamilton as a legal representative in The Bay when Sam had been chosen as the development manager. For Letitia the connection had been lucrative and had enormous potential, which fitted in very nicely with her ambitions to be a huge success – financially – as quickly as possible.

Just hearing the affable and mature voice of the silver-haired lawyer was reassuring. 'How lovely to begin the day with a call from The Bay. I imagine it's another beautiful day and you are all congratulating each other for being there and not in Sydney. What can I do for you, Letitia?'

'Oh, it's nothing earth shattering, Mr Hamilton, but I was wondering if you had heard about the public reaction here to the rezoning application? It was all over the local rag this morning.'

'Yes, my dear. Sam gave me a call at an hour he associated with bowel movements of the sparrow,' he replied. 'Filled me in completely. There's nothing untoward in what's being made public. I expected it would raise some concerns, but Andrew should be able to address those with some expertise.'

'There are some coffee-shop rumours suggesting shady deals done a long time ago to do with that land on Mighty Beach. Nothing definite, but you know ... They've had a week to gather momentum,' Letitia said, trying to give the call added justification.

'Momentum and exaggeration, no doubt,' he replied, politely dismissing the reaction. 'Be assured, Letitia, that everything about this deal is above board. After all, your father was closely associated with the company that sold the land to Beacon Land Holdings so long ago. It was gilt-edged, that was how he put it to me. Good fellow, all very tragic . . .' He sighed, leaving the sentence unfinished. He was thinking about the sad demise of a promising solicitor he'd studied with at law school. Drunk himself into an early grave leaving a wife and very young daughter.

Letitia was stunned, speechless almost. She'd known her father and Hamilton had been to law school together, but couldn't recall either of them ever mentioning a business connection. She quickly closed the conversation. 'Yes, indeed. Of course,' she fumbled. 'All right then, back to the daily grind. Bye.'

For a while she paced around her smart unit with its distant ocean view and agonised over what to do next. She had to get the whirlwind of thoughts in her mind under control. Suddenly she stopped, quickly swallowed the last of the near cold coffee and rang the office. She was relieved to hear she had no appointments, told the secretary that she would be late and to refer people to her mobile for only the most urgent matters. Then she drove to the industrial estate and parked outside a self-storage shed in the complex.

The lock had rusted up and required some lubricant from the car tool kit, and some hissed curses, before it opened. It had been a couple of years since she had needed to unlock the shed. It was filled with possessions from the family home, which she had packed up when her mother was admitted to the Brigalow Nursing Home. After rummaging around for ten minutes she found some tea chests identified by marker pen as 'Daddy's Files'. She knew from a couple of previous hunts for some of his old legal papers relevant to her own clients that the search this time was not going to be easy, unless she was lucky.

The atmosphere in the Community Centre was almost festive as friends greeted each other. There was also the occasional head shaking and exclamation as people wandered up to the large display board propped in front of the stage. On it was a map of the land in question and a series of photographs showing its pristine state, children in the small park in the reserve, birds in the wetlands and a lovely shot of the full length of the beach with a couple in the distance walking their dog. A large sign declared 'Save Mighty Beach' with a petition beside it which almost everyone signed.

Rows of chairs were set up facing the stage and a trestle table by one wall held a hot water urn, cups, milk, instant coffee and tea bags for people to help themselves. Nola glanced at her watch and looked around the rapidly filling hall. 'Better get the show on the road in a few minutes. Looks like everyone who wants to be here, is here.'

Holly nodded agreement. 'It's a good roll-up considering the short notice and little publicity. All we need is Buck Hagen and he'll turn up for sure. Best of luck, Nola.'

She was about to move off the stage when Nola called her back and in a softer than usual voice said, 'Holly, I hope you're not too upset about the way this is going, given the certainty that Andrew is involved. I mean, you're more or less committing yourself to being in the frontline of opposition.'

Holly took Nola's hands in hers and squeezed them in a gesture of appreciation. 'Thank you for thinking about my feelings at this time. I am so grateful that with all the pressure of the evening you can find the time to give a thought to me.' Holly leaned forward and kissed her cheek. 'Thanks, but I'm handling it all okay so far, and I'm determined to stay in the frontline, as you described it. Very determined,' she added.

'Wonderful, darling. Absolutely wonderful,' said Nola as Holly moved off and then went to a seat a few rows from the front.

Stolle sat with Lynn at the front and flipped open his notebook. 'The pro-development lobby has a few reps here, I see,' he said and pointed towards a group of local builders and business types in the centre of the hall.

'Going to be a good night out,' Lynn said as she checked the tape in a small recorder linked to a microphone on the stage. They were going to record the evening for community radio. 'Also the people from Coast Care are here, the Natural Heritage Preservation Society, a few other environmental groups, the wildlife carers and our local member of State Parliament. And to complete the cast, my opposition has just arrived – ABC Radio.'

Setting up another microphone on the stage

was an attractive woman with a tape recorder who introduced herself to Nola. 'I'm Fiona Wyllie, I host the breakfast show on regional ABC. I'd like to tape the proceedings and get a few words from you and some of the others here for tomorrow morning's program. Local radio news will use some of it too.'

'Delighted,' declared Nola. 'You might be lucky and score something unexpected.'

There was a stir as Buck Hagen strode in looking rumpled and distracted, clutching a folder of documents. He sat beside Sid Wainwright in the front row.

Nola tapped the microphone, which crackled and caused the crowd to start hushing each other as they looked expectantly at the dramatic figure before them. Nola had dressed for the occasion in a gold and scarlet print caftan and matching turban. She was wearing emerald jewellery and looked, declared Lynn, 'like the high priestess of The Bay'.

'Fellow citizens, welcome,' she said and the room grew quiet. 'Thank you for coming. You're here as I am, not just because we care about The Bay we love, but also because we care about what we're going to leave for future generations. A special part of The Bay is under threat. Let us begin by asking why. Why here? Why this strip of land, why this bit of beach? Why choose to build on an area of land that has been regarded as a public reserve for years, that has sensitive wetlands and dunes, that is unstable for construction and would require massive infrastructure, and also is culturally significant to our Indigenous people?'

The instant but subdued reaction in many parts of the audience caused Nola to pause. She decided not to elaborate, particularly since the local middens and sacred sites had been well documented by the Aboriginal custodians of The Bay's indigenous history.

Then she sailed on, raising an arm for dramatic effect. 'The main reason this land is sought for development is its beauty. And beauty means big bucks. But beauty is something that cannot be bought. Such natural beauty is given by God. Once we allow it to be taken away, we lose it forever.' There was a burst of applause.

'There's a lot of ugliness in this world. So a place that is unique, that is as beautiful as any place in the world is a place to be treasured. This tiny stretch of land which we can all own, all share, all appreciate, should not, must not, be taken from us and buried beneath bricks and mortar!'

'Hear, hear.' There was a roar of approval from most people in the room.

The small knot of pro-development supporters looked disgusted and shook their heads in disbelief. 'Get real, what about jobs, the future of the town?' called one of the group.

'Debate on this issue is welcome,' said Nola. 'Informed debate,' she added pointedly and glancing at her notes went on. 'A member of the community has asked to speak, one of our writers, Shelley Neller.'

There was a scattering of applause as Shelley made her way to the stage. 'See, this is an issue that is getting the thinkers to speak out in public – not something they normally do,' whispered Lynn to Stolle.

Slim and quietly spoken, Shelley was gently firm as she explained she felt compelled to speak on behalf of 'The Bay tribe'.

'Our tribe goes beyond radical green clichés,' she began. 'Our tribe is the epitome of social and cultural diversity. We have old people and young people, businessmen and businesswomen. Doctors and lawyers, students and teachers. We have musicians and builders and hairdressers and artists. We are people from the hills and people from the coast, and we are a hell of a big tribe!'

Members of the audience called out in support, and with her dark curls bouncing, Shelley continued in a stronger voice, 'We know that our unspoilt landscape and friendly small-town atmosphere are our greatest assets. We value our lifestyle and our sense of community. Big companies don't understand that we are not into greed and instant gratification – if we were, we would all be living up the road at the Gold Coast!' At this there was a roar. Shelley summed up by pointing out that mega developments were not what this tribe wanted for their community.

Stolle wrote furiously knowing this would be a front page story for the *Bugle*.

Nola thanked Shelley and said, 'Now I'd like to call on Councillor Buck Hagen.'

Buck ambled onto the stage and the attitude of the audience became more relaxed. They all knew him, and even his opponents agreed that Buck always put on a good performance. He nodded in acknowledgment of Nola, then scanned the hall as if plugging into everyone with individual eye contact. Buck didn't mince words or bother with niceties, and that made many of his performances in council meetings such a highlight. Wisps of hair not restrained in his ponytail sprang around his face, his shirt needed ironing and he had the air of a weary puppy dog who just wanted a good feed and to curl up in front of the fire. In a gentle voice that seemed at odds with his large build and perceived belligerent persona he greeted the audience, now jammed in with standing room only.

'Yeah, g'day. Glad to be here. Look, this is important. It's not just this bit of land at the Mighty Beach reserve, special and beautiful as it is. It's about what we want in our community. It's about us deciding what we want to happen to a significant area of land, believed till now to be public land. It's about outsiders coming in and wheeling and dealing over our heads to manipulate and con us. Not that I'm saying there's anything illegal about this plan,' he added, lifting a hand in a placatory gesture. 'But there is a lot of undisclosed issues in this whole procedure. Why don't the owners of the land come forward and speak to us? Why are they hiding behind their lawyers' skirts? If this development is such a bloody good idea, why don't they tell us what they're wanting to build, tell us right now?'

Again there was a muttering of agreement and Buck continued. 'Like a lot of people, I've been fighting for this community for a long time. But it can't be left to the old brigade alone to keep The Bay the kind of place that makes it unique – a little bit of paradise as it is constantly called, particularly by the increasing number of newcomers banging on the door. The problem is that for a lot of folk these days finding a little bit of paradise is like finding a potential goldmine. Unfortunately for us, ruthlessly exploiting a goldmine is considered by them as the only way to go. Generally speaking, greed is their religion and to hell with anyone who gets in the way. Their argument that if they don't do it someone else will is not acceptable!'

Another burst of applause followed by brief remarks between members of the audience and Buck sensed it was time to wrap up. 'There are many relatively new people in our community and they must be made aware of what's been won, what's under threat, and how quickly we can be undermined by the greed of money grubbers, who mostly don't live here. So if you want to live here, in a place you chose because it's clean, green and beautiful, then you bloody well have to fight for it.'

He strode from the stage to strong applause and a few exchanged smiles.

For the next hour there was heated discussion

about the threat to Mighty Beach and conflict between the vision of the conservation faction and others who saw the need for compromise if the town was to economically survive and provide more jobs in the future. Several speakers emphasised that from a strictly legal point of view, the rezoning application was in order. The full details of the project would be revealed and publicly debated at some future occasion, if rezoning was approved.

Eventually Nola called everyone to order. Then without expressions of dissent the meeting passed a motion to form the Mighty Beach Action Group to take appropriate steps. 'So I'm calling for volunteers for a small steering committee. Have we a nomination for chairperson?'

There was a moment of silence then Mac rose to her feet. 'I would like to nominate Holly Jamieson.'

'Seconded,' called Billy, lifting his arm.

Holly was shocked. 'Oh, no I couldn't. I mean –'

'Go for it, Holly,' whispered Amber.

Nola flashed a smile towards Holly. 'It's an important frontline job, Mrs Jamieson, do you accept nomination?'

Holly glanced over her shoulder to Mitch who gave a thumbs-up and a huge smile. And in that moment, Holly felt some kind of strength, a sense of purpose, along with a devil-may-care feeling of release. She stood up and addressed the audience through Nola. 'I'm flattered that as a relative newcomer I could be considered worthy of such a role.

Yes, I accept and will do my best to reflect the wishes of the community.'

Nola ran through a few more nominations for the committee, which were agreed to, and handed over the meeting to Holly to close. 'Keep it very short and sweet, my dear,' she whispered as Holly stood before the microphone.

'Ladies and gentlemen, thanks for your vote. I hope our committee will deliver the goods, with the help of the wider community, of course. As it stands the outcome may well depend on votes in council, so we have to ensure that our representatives really hear what we're saying. These days, it seems to me, that at too many levels of government, on too many issues, the people in power say they're listening, but really they aren't listening and don't want to hear what the people are telling them. There's a big difference. Thank you, goodnight and thanks for coming.'

The applause this time was punctuated by some cheering, and a brief chant from the teenagers present: 'Save Mighty Beach . . . Save Mighty Beach. Yeah.'

As Holly stepped down from the stage a young man with a shaved head, a lot of body piercing and tattoos stopped her. 'Hi, I'm Clive. I run one of the tattoo parlours. I'm with you guys one hundred per cent. Look, what do you think of this?' He pushed up his shirt sleeve to show a tattoo on his arm – 'Save Mighty Beach'.

'Oh, my, that is dedication,' said Holly, slightly startled.

'It's only temporary, it'll wash off in a couple of weeks. I thought you might like to give 'em out to people.'

'Well, thank you. It's different from bumper stickers.'

Next a tall, distinguished-looking man introduced himself to her. 'Hello, I'm Alec Shand, I'm a QC. I've seen the light and retreated from the city hurly-burly.' They shook hands and he introduced his attractive wife. 'We're living up here now and I have chambers not far away. If I can be of assistance please call me.'

Holly thanked him profusely and was interrupted by Fiona asking for an interview.

Letitia met Andrew at the airport and embraced him. It seemed to Andrew that she clung to him a fraction longer than normal. Then she pulled away and was all business, filling him in on the latest gossip and radio feedback from the public meeting. 'It's really stirring the hornet's nest. Those friends of Holly's are going off in all directions, mad as hell.'

Andrew shook his head. 'I don't know what's happened to her since she moved up here. She's a totally different person.' He was silent for a moment, thinking that despite their differences Holly had blossomed into an intriguing and interesting woman. Far more so than when they were living together in Sydney.

'The tourist people should promote The Bay as

the place you go to change your life, rather than concentrating on the scenery and the opportunities for dropping out,' Letitia said in a tone that surprised Andrew. It sounded cynical and lacked her usual energy.

He rested his hand on her thigh as she drove. 'You're going to have a big change in your life too. When this whole thing takes off, so do we!'

'Change. Yes, I want a change. No more small town for me,' she said fiercely, in a sudden switch of mood. 'It's money, Andrew. Big dollars to change my life.'

Andrew was slightly taken aback at the vehemence of her tone. But it was her ambition and thirst for money that were among the things that had attracted him to her. He decided to match her businesslike tone. 'So where and when do I give the presentation?'

'At the Bay Best Motel, there's a nice convention room. We've got the model set up, display pictures, video screen, brochures, press kits. Drinks and food, of course.'

'Who's been invited?'

'Media, councillors, key community and business leaders. A couple of the opposition people. You'll do the main presentation, Sam will be there to answer questions.'

'Sounds great. How is Sam handling the pressure?'

'He's taking it all very calmly, and he's managed to calm down his old mate Bright. He freaked out for a while.'

'I'll have to calm Holly down. I'd better see her right after I check in. Car organised?'

'Yes, just sign the papers at the desk,' she said, then added in a more subdued voice, 'You might not find calming your wife as easy as you think.'

'Don't worry about that,' he said, leaning over to kiss her cheek, totally missing her slight tensing. 'Lunch?'

'Afraid not. I have a few things . . . to deal with.'

'Dinner. Even better.' He kissed her again as she dropped him outside the serviced apartment the General had used.

Letitia glanced up at Nola's penthouse wondering if she was watching. Too bad. Andrew and Holly's marriage was over. Just the same, Letitia liked to keep her private life private. She wondered how long it would be before her name was raised in connection with this now contentious scheme, which, in Bangkok, had seemed so simple, so straightforward.

Andrew had rung Holly, so she made coffee and an apple cake which she knew he liked. When he walked up to Richmond House he was surprised at the changes. The garden was bursting with early spring blooms, it was beautifully maintained and dotted about were those touches he recognised as so Holly – a rustic love seat, urns filled with geraniums, an arbor with exotic climbers drooping fat trumpet-shaped flowers, small statues and fountain all discreetly placed among the tropical greenery.

The verandah looked inviting with chintz-covered wicker chairs, a lounge and a table set for morning tea with a vase of roses in the centre. He called out and went indoors to where Holly was putting the coffee and cake on a tray.

They greeted each other awkwardly, neither pecking the other's cheek. Instead Holly busied herself with the tray. She somehow felt this might be the last time she and Andrew would share morning coffee together. She felt calm, resigned to the change they were both facing. For once she felt more at ease than he did.

He glanced around the house marvelling at the restoration, the peaceful ambience, the combination of beachy casualness blending with classical good taste. 'You've done a great job, Holly. It all looks very comfortable. Tasteful. I'd stay here,' he tried to joke.

'I had help, so much help from so many friends,' she said.

'You've really settled in here, haven't you? More so than in Mosman. So what are your plans?'

Holly carried the tray to the verandah. 'More to the point, Andrew, what are yours?'

He didn't want to discuss this, for if the truth were known he didn't have any plans. He hated this upheaval. He had liked his ordered life in Sydney with Holly, the excitement of his affair with Letitia, the lure of fame and riches with his involvement with Beacon Land Holdings. But the sudden notoriety, disturbed business partners and a distracted Letitia were items he hadn't expected to suddenly turn up on his agenda.

'My main focus is to get this project up and running. Believe me, Holly, it's nothing tacky. I have put a huge amount of time and effort into this whole thing.'

'So it would seem.' She sipped her coffee.

'My reputation rests on this project coming off.'

'That's a shame.'

He looked at her. Her calmness unnerved him. 'I trust you're not going to go out of your way to make trouble with the development.'

'Hopefully the rezoning won't happen, but I have to tell you, Andrew, I was elected president of the action committee to save Mighty Beach.'

He was so stunned that he slopped coffee into the saucer. 'You! Head of a rebel rabble! Don't make me laugh,' he scoffed. 'Well, we'll all quake in our boots. C'mon, Holly, what are you and your pals going to do? You have no idea of the immensity of the backing, the scope of this thing.'

'Don't underestimate me like you've always done. Or the people of this town,' she said evenly. 'So just how big is big and what is the whole thing?'

Andrew felt he was on the back foot. He hadn't planned to go into details at this point. With some irritation he recognised the significance of Letitia's earlier remark about calming Holly, and cursed her for not telling him of Holly's leadership role in opposition.

Now he had to win her over, impress her, ruffle that cool exterior that was so annoying him. He wished she'd get mad, hysterical, weepy. Anything other than this almost serene arrogance.

'Okay, here are the essentials. The development is called the Beacon, after the first navigational aid in The Bay, before the lighthouse,' began Andrew. 'It's a new way of looking at community living – your own private realm where everyone is still linked to one another like spokes in a wheel. The concept is designed for those who want security, support, entertainment, health care in superior surroundings.' He was conscious that to a large extent he was reciting much of the presentation speech he had carefully rehearsed for the public briefing later in the day, but pressed on. 'It's mainly for people at a time in their lives when they want to savour the fruits of years of work.'

Holly handed him a slice of cake. 'So it's a private community that's expensive, exclusive, and for secure do I read "gated"? And given the factors of health care and entertainment at a special time in your life – what you're building is an upmarket retirement village. Am I right?'

Andrew swallowed his mouthful of cake and sighed. 'It's far, far more than that.'

'That's what I thought,' said Holly. 'I figured a resort, expensive holiday townhouses or units. Just who do you envision moving into the Beacon?'

'Baby boomers. It's big business. They're starting early retirement in droves and they are not about to settle for the kind of places they put their parents!' Andrew leaned forward, genuinely enthusiastic for the first time in the conversation. 'I tell you, Holly, this will be an international prototype for living out the last third of your life in real style. Believe me, people from all over the world are going to want to live there.'

'Andrew, the so-called "community" you're talking about is exclusive and elite. How will those people blend in with the rest of The Bay?'

'They don't have to! They will be self-contained in many respects. The best food, fresh produce, basic commodities will be sold in the Beacon Store – more up-market than anything in Sydney. Plus an internet service means that anything they want can be whizzed to their door.'

'So the bourgeoisie don't have to mingle with the plebeians. And the locals in The Bay get to do the menial jobs,' said Holly but Andrew missed her facetious tone.

'It's beyond anything you can imagine. It's a definite goer. It's going to make me.'

Holly stood and moved away from the table, then turned to face her husband. He clearly didn't know what to do or say next. She looked at him in silence, a penetrating look that disturbed him, reinforced in him that new awareness of how much she had changed, and how much about her he no longer understood.

'Andrew, if you think your slick slide show is

going to win over the people here, you are so wrong. You haven't said one word about the environment, the coastline, the wildlife, the contribution that place makes to the total mood, feel, even thinking of this community. Not one word. It's against everything The Bay stands for – one for all and all for one,' was all she could think to sum up the unique spirit of The Bay community. 'I'm afraid your concept has only strengthened my resolve to stop it.'

'You have no vision, you're just doing this to spite me.' He slammed his cup down. 'You've never supported my ideas.'

Holly bit her tongue at the injustice of his remark. Then angrily she snapped, 'Don't talk to me about vision. You should talk to Bonnie about what's happening with the Creative Collective out here, now that's a community vision. One that embraces everybody, those less fortunate, those who are comfortable, who want to share beauty and tranquillity and have a quality lifestyle. Where a sense of generosity of spirit, open hearts and open minds rule. A true community needs youthful energy, creativity, it needs to embrace a diversity of views, of culture. Not just who can afford to live here – which in your world means just rich people.'

Andrew shook his head in amazement at his wife's outburst. 'I can hardly believe what I'm hearing. You're living in a total fairyland, so far removed from what's happening in the real world. For God's sake, get with it, Holly. This dreamy stuff you're coming out with is absolute crap.' He stamped out of the garden without looking back. But he heard her final question.

'Who is behind your scheme, Andrew, who really owns it? If I were you I'd ask a few hard questions.'

He drove angrily back to the apartment. Holly's question had unnerved him. Despite Sam's, the General's and Letitia's assurances, along with those of the respectable old solicitor in Sydney, he didn't have a clue who actually owned the land on which his dream plan was to be built. To worry him even more, his mobile rang and General Chidchai was on the line from Bangkok, dispensing with any preamble and sounding tense.

'Andrew, I am deeply concerned at the news I hear from Australia. You know I don't like problems. I thought you were looking after my interests in this project.'

'Everything's under control, General. You're referring to the slight public concern in the local media . . . it was to be expected.'

'Perhaps. But I don't like my affairs being mentioned, even in the local press. I prefer to keep a low profile. This business could cause trouble if it gets picked up by the national media. I am a little disappointed that you didn't call or even email me about developments. We have an arrangement, remember.'

Andrew stiffened and silently cursed his lapse. The pressure of events in The Bay as well as the emotional complications involving the two women in his life had dulled his usually sharp attention to such detail. 'Of course, General. Your interests are indeed being watched. Later today we are making a media presentation on the rezoning application.'

'Good. You're my man on the spot . . .' Unsaid was the implication that Andrew was a paid hand to do the General's bidding. Andrew could feel himself sweating. He hadn't forgotten the late-night visit from the heavyweight mystery man 'Tony', who'd delivered the package of money. 'I can expect matters to be dealt with quickly and efficiently, yes?'

'No problems, General. Sam has it all under control.'

'I expect that you also keep on top of Sam, yes? This is not the time for friends to fall out. Business is business, Andrew.'

'I understand.'

'By the way, does the name Eureka Developments Limited ring any bells with you?'

Andrew thought for a few seconds. 'No, afraid not. Why do you ask?'

'Oh, it has just popped up.'

'Like a jack in the box,' responded Andrew in an effort to lighten the exchange.

'Yes, but perhaps not quite as amusing. Goodbye, Andrew.'

The line went dead. God, thought Andrew, that man trusts nobody. And it came to him that you wouldn't get a second chance if you put a foot wrong with the General.

The briefing for councillors and media began with Sam welcoming everyone to what he described as 'the prescription for curing the long-term economic and employment ills facing the local community'. It was a project that ultimately would involve hundreds of millions of dollars to develop fully, he explained, and at every stage only the highest environmental and design standards would be accepted by the owners of the land and the financial backers. He then invited Councillor Bright, chairman of council's Planning and Development Committee, to speak.

Bright emphasised that the rezoning of the land from rural to residential/commercial would be a long process. 'I want to point out that the concept drawings being displayed are not related at this stage to a development application. What is presented in the development application, if rezoning takes place, will be subject to another round of planning and staff reports. Furthermore, the State Government will also have an overriding say, given that the land in question is sensitive coastal property. Having said that, may I add that personally I think the project has tremendous potential and the community will benefit significantly from an appropriate development of the area.'

Andrew then made a presentation with elaborate architectural sketches and graphics that suggested the development would have a higher than required percentage of open space, significant sections would be devoted to walkways and cycle paths for public use, and there would be more points of public access to the beach, whereas there now was only one trail from an improvised parking lot.

Letitia stood at one side of the conference room concentrating on the reaction of the media. All the regional stringers for radio, television and metropolitan dailies had turned up.

Question time had no surprises until Stolle's turn came.

'Only one question, Mr Jamieson. Is General Chidchai definitely associated with the project and to what extent?'

Andrew glanced at Sam, who reluctantly gave him the nod to answer. 'Yes he is. He has seen the project concepts, walked over the site, and is enthusiastic about putting substantial finance into it. That, I can assure you, is good news for The Bay. I have worked with him on other projects, and he has very high standards and appreciates the need for achieving a balance between economic development and environmental protection.'

Sam felt good. They had anticipated that question and Andrew got the answer word perfect.

'One more question, if I may,' said Stolle, still on his feet. 'Who really owns this big slab of land? Who is behind Beacon Land Holdings?'

Sam grimaced, Andrew stayed perfectly calm. 'A Sydney development company that has been waiting a long time for the right circumstances and the right funding source to make this development a success – for investors and the community. I am sure that at the development application stage the owners will be going very public indeed.'

Over drinks afterwards Sam, Jimmy Bright, Letitia and Andrew agreed that the presentation had been a resounding success.

Holly sat in the front garden overlooking Tiny Bay Beach. She had been mulling over the advertising material Mitchell had drawn up and while she liked it, she wished she had some historic photos of Richmond House. She'd asked Sid to see what he could find, but so far he'd had no luck and no one could ever recall seeing old pictures of the house or its original family, the Nilsens.

She closed her eyes in the warm sun. It was a moment of peace in what had been a hectic and emotionally draining few days. Why had she become involved in this anti-development move- ment? What had happened to her marriage? How was she going to manage financially? Could she forget the whole thing and just go back to life with Andrew in Mosman?

Holly opened her eyes with a start. God, no. What was she thinking? When things seemed too hard her answer had typically been to run back to the familiar – no matter how miserable – or stick her head in the sand. Too late for that, she chided herself. She stood up and went back into the house. As she put the kettle on Curly began bark- ing and there was a call from the driveway. She peered through the French doors and saw a young man calling out, and as she opened the door she recognised the tall blond boy.

'Tor! You came! How lovely.' Holly embraced the shyly smiling Norwegian. 'Welcome, come on in, I was just making tea.'

'That is so Australian,' he said, grinning, as he shifted the bulky backpack from his shoulders. 'Always making tea.'

'I can make coffee,' laughed Holly. 'How are you? Where have you been since Hervey Bay? Come and tell me your news.'

Tor gazed around. 'Oh my, this is wonderful, so lovely. I thought you were rebuilding some old, what do they say here – shack.'

'It was very rundown. I'll show you photos later from when I started.'

Tor followed her to the kitchen and when he saw the front garden he stopped. 'The sea. You can see it . . .' He was at a loss for words to express his obvious surprise and joy, and went outside to take in the view until Holly called that the tea was ready.

'This is so very beautiful. You are open for customers now?'

'Not quite, but I insist that you stay here as my first guest. Mitchell would love to see you, too. Perhaps we could ask him for dinner tonight. Do you have plans? Obviously you haven't landed anywhere yet if you're still carrying that big backpack.'

'Oh, that is so kind of you. Are you sure? I don't wish to impose.'

'Of course not. Now tell me what you've been doing.'

'I went to Cairns and then back to Townsville and met with the professor at James Cook University. I can begin my studies. I will be there for eighteen months. After that I hope I can work out here.'

'Your family will miss you.'

'They understand that it's important I come here,' he said quietly. 'Maybe they will visit me in the summer here.'

'Good idea. Escape the European winter.'

They chatted more and Holly showed him the photographs Mitchell had taken on their whale-watching trip. 'Now I'll show you to your room, then I have to go into town. Have you looked around The Bay yet?'

'Not very much. I hitchhiked in and they dropped me at the bottom of this hill.'

'Great. I can show off our little township. I'm sure you'll want to go surfing and see the beaches.'

'Very much. But I'm not an experienced surfer.'

'Too bad neither my son nor Mitchell's son are here, they'd have you standing up on a board in a day. Not to worry, we'll sort something out.'

'Holly, you are very kind.' He stood shyly. 'This is so good of you. It means very much to me.'

'Oh goodness, Tor, it's nothing. The Bay has a reputation for opening its arms to strangers. We've all been strangers in a new place at some stage in our lives, so we know how nice it is to find a doormat that says welcome.'

At the supermarket in town he helped Holly by carrying her groceries to the car. She pointed out some of the sights and older buildings, the popular places to eat and drink, and then cut through the arcade to make an appointment with Billy at The Teepee.

'Hail the chief!' Billy called out. 'Our fearless leader!'

'Yeah, Holly, save Mighty Beach!' Matty was in the salon and gave a rallying cry.

Seeing Tor's quizzical expression Holly briefly filled him in on their fight. Meanwhile, Matty only just managed to control her reaction to her first sighting of Tor as he came in with Holly. She had never experienced such an emotional impact and despite the shock she loved the feeling. She listened with great interest as Holly explained they'd met on the whale-watching trip. Tor was very handsome with his blond hair, blue eyes and tall build, and Matty thought he looked like a movie star.

'How long are you here for?' Matty asked.

'I am not sure.'

'Matty, Tor wants to learn to surf, could you teach him the basics? There must be a spare board somewhere he could borrow,' Holly suggested, and Matty nearly hugged her.

'You bet. I have Erica's board. Might be a bit short for you, Tor, but it'll give you the idea. This afternoon?'

'I'll drop him off at your house, Matty. Maybe Alice would like to go too, she's pretty good,' said

Holly, but Matty quickly squashed the idea. She didn't want to share this fabulous newcomer with a kid.

Billy grinned at Holly, picking up the vibes from his fifteen-year-old assistant. 'The tide will be right, and the wind's coming from the right direction so there should be some good sets coming in. Go for it. You can even have an early mark, Matts.'

Holly returned to Richmond House and rang Mitchell to invite him to dinner, then went up to the attic bedroom and put fresh sheets on the bed for Tor.

She thought he might enjoy the little room. It was really a spare room, not one of the large guest rooms with an ensuite, but it had a wonderful view from the dormer window across Tiny Bay. She glanced at the door that opened onto the widow's walk. He'd probably like that more than the window view, she decided. She fussed around the room checking there were coathangers in the wardrobe, and arranging a towel on the end of the bed.

She was looking forward to having the young man stay, partly because she missed her own kids and their energy. She hadn't told them of her involvement in the Mighty Beach campaign, and was nervous about it as it pitted her against their father. Being objective about the children, she knew they would probably opt for supporting the development, even if it was a 'yuppie baby-boomers third age refuge', as Mitchell called it. Melanie and Marcus were very money conscious, and if Andrew made a lot of money then eventually it would benefit them.

Holly smoothed the bed cover and went downstairs to read some of the letters and petitions that were beginning to come in from the public about Mighty Beach.

By the time Tor arrived at Matty's house, Eddie had been organised to shoot a little sequence of an overseas backpacker enjoying his first experience of surfing in The Bay. He hadn't been able to resist Matty's enthusiastic request when she telephoned him after Tor had left the salon.

'Please, Eddie, he's absolutely perfect for your film, believe me. And it's going to be a fabulous sunset later.'

It was getting late when Eddie drove them to Tinderbox Beach. The surf there had a poor break because of a gutter near the shore, but it was scenic. He took shots of Matty giving Tor a lesson on the sand, showing him how to kneel and stand on the board. They were nice shots because of the background of headland and lighthouse. Afterwards they drove to the lighthouse to check out the view and how the waves were breaking on other beaches.

Tor gazed around the long length of Tinderbox on the southern side of the Cape, the curve of The

Bay that ran into Mighty Beach and in the far distance Ten Mile Beach.

'Paradise, isn't it?' said Matty, standing close beside Tor, grateful that Eddie had left them alone to visit the Parks office to check if Tina was there.

'Beautiful. And that,' he pointed to the lighthouse, 'is the guardian angel of paradise, yes?'

Matty looked at Tor with near adoration in her eyes. 'This is my special place. I always came here with my friend Erica.'

'Yes, it is special. I can feel that.' He looked out to sea for a moment before continuing. 'We all need lighthouses in our lives. They can be a warning light to alert us to dangers ahead, and also a comforting light, helping to show us the way home.'

They spent a hugely entertaining hour at Mighty Beach laughing at Tor's attempts to stand up on the board, and cheering him when he finally managed to balance for a minute on a modest wave. It was getting close to sunset when they headed for a final sequence at Tiny Bay.

'It's going to be a knockout sunset, let's just get some pretty shots of you both lying on your boards,' said Eddie. 'It's very calm, you don't have to go too far out. Anyway, you're sheltered in the lee of the Point.'

It was a flat surf so other riders had moved on, leaving the sea for Matty and Tor. Matty gave a little prayer of thanks and flashed a big smile at Tor as they paddled out.

Eddie filmed the sun sinking onto the peaked volcanic hat of Mount Hazard, then zoomed back to the two figures floating on their boards on the glassy molten-coloured water. In his viewfinder he saw Matty's arm point and both their heads lift. Panning to the sea in the direction she had indicated, Eddie felt that Lady Luck was about to deliver one of those bonus moments cameramen dream about.

There, rising slowly in the distance, was a whale, its spout a golden streak in the setting sun's rays. The last of the whales were still heading south after their sojourn in the breeding grounds of the north, but this was unexpected.

Matty sat up on her board, clapping her hands in sheer joy. The whale sank from sight and they waited until it next appeared. To their amazement it had moved inside the lee of the headland and breeched, its tail flukes cracking on the water as it rolled.

'Wow, unreal,' squealed Matty.

'Magic, magic, magic pictures,' exclaimed Eddie to himself, taking care to keep the camera steady and the action perfectly framed.

But then something happened that later no one could fully explain.

Tor rolled off his board, perhaps trying to sit upright – or was it deliberate? – and began swimming out towards the whale. Then both of them, as if responding to a signal, sank beneath the surface.

For Tor it was as if the world had stopped and he was in another, dreamlike place where time and reality blurred. Later he would recall in exquisite detail the watery sunlight before him suddenly blotted by a huge dark shape gliding to a stop within touching distance. His hands stretched out and he felt the living, pulsing smoothness of the whale's skin. Then he recognised, quite clearly, the profile of the whale's head and the eye looking at him. In the moment of contact he saw and knew and understood, and all fear left him. All that had happened was meant to be and the incident represented the closing of a great circle. In an exuberant joyous explosion he burst to the surface at the same time as the whale rose and flung itself out of the water in a massive salute to life.

Tor laughed and cried. Matty paddled to him and took his hands and added her voice to his in absolute happiness as the whale slowly circled them. Then, as suddenly as it had arrived, showing its flukes in a farewell wave, it was gone.

'What was that! What happened? Wow! Unbelievable.'

They paddled their boards to the shore in the fast fading light. Eddie turned off the camera and sat back to reflect on the wonderful sense of communion that he had been privileged to record. What he didn't know was just how much it meant to Tor.

Tor only had time for a short rest before getting dressed for dinner with Holly and Mitchell. They settled in the sitting room lit by candles and toasted each other with a Hunter Valley wine. Outside, a big moon streaked the ocean.

'So how's your first day in The Bay been?' Mitchell asked.

'Overwhelming,' said Tor, and tried to explain what had happened with the whale. 'It was so quick, yet it seemed a lifetime to me.'

'You say Eddie caught it all on film?' Mitchell said incredulously.

'I have goose bumps,' said Holly.

Tor leaned back in his chair and for a moment sat with eyes closed and both hands clasped under his chin as if praying. Then he opened his eyes and straightened up. 'My dear friends, because of this happening today I believe I must tell you my story,' he said slowly. He took a small sip of the wine and then looked directly at Holly. 'But first, you say I am the only guest here? You do not have family in this house? Some other person?'

Holly looked at him strangely. 'Just Mitchell for dinner. There is no one else living here. Only Curly.' She pointed to the old dog stretched out by the sofa. 'Why do you ask?'

'There was an old lady. I was dozing, felt some presence, and with half-opened eyes saw her sitting at the foot of my bed. Then, as if I imagined it, she was gone.'

'Dreaming,' said Mitchell gently, reaching to take Holly's hand which tightened in his.

'No. She's here. I've seen her too.'

'She is a ghost, yes?' said Tor. 'She was the same woman I glimpsed from the garden, when I looked up at the roof this morning while you were making the tea. I had the sun in my eyes, but she was there on the walkway. When I moved, she was gone.'

Holly nodded. 'I believe it's the spirit of the woman who built this house, Hannah Nilsen.'

'Ah, then that explains much. Perhaps she is at peace now. I believe she has been waiting for her family to come back.' He paused and gave a small smile. 'You see, I am Tor Nilsen. I am a direct descendant of Lars Nilsen who built this place.'

'Good Lord!' exclaimed Holly. 'You're a Nilsen. Oh, how extraordinary.'

'I'd never given a thought to what your surname was,' said Mitchell, equally astonished. 'This calls for topping up the drinks.' He reached for the bottle and filled the glasses. 'What else do you know about the family connection?'

'Not much. It was so many generations ago. Lars and their two children left here to visit Norway. Their ship was sunk in a storm. All were feared dead. But the younger son, Erik, was saved. I have something to show you.' He walked to the sideboard and picked up a large envelope he had brought downstairs. 'I have some of the family documents, some letters and photographs. My grandmother gave them to me before she died last year. She put the story together. Perhaps you might be interested?'

Holly and Mitchell looked at each other, then Holly rose with her glass. 'Another toast. To the Nilsens.' They drank and then she walked over to Tor and hugged him tightly. 'Welcome home, Tor.'

Chapter Seventeen

THE DOCUMENTS WERE NEATLY STACKED IN PILES ON the dining table – yellowing, musty smelling, incriminating.

Once again Letitia paced around the room, staring at them. They were only a small part of her father's meticulous records that she kept in storage – boxes and boxes of files containing the dry documentation of ordinary legal transactions so necessary to the conduct of business, life and death. Conveyancing contracts, property settlements, wills, divorces, business deals, neighbourhood disputes, hundreds of minor court cases, thousands of letters, the very fabric of life reduced to clinical formal legalese. Yet behind the words were untold stories of passion, heartbreak, wrongdoing, greed and desire.

The selected files on the table related to the Mighty Beach project in a way that had shattered her normal composure. They were a spectacular chronicle of what surely must have been the most appalling chain of events in her father's legal career, and in his personal life. Examining them for the first time had made her feel ill. Looking at them now was just as emotionally devastating.

Her mother had dismissed him as worthless, and Letitia never found out – if indeed her mother knew – why her father had become an alcoholic. He had certainly not been the inspiration for Letitia to study commercial law. It had seemed a smart way to get out of a small town and into the fast lane. Now it appeared that her father had been involved in what could be one of the biggest deals the region had seen.

This revelation, and more importantly who was behind it all, had stunned Letitia and completely unnerved her. The knowledge, gleaned from her father's old files when he had been the solicitor acting for the owner of Beacon Land Holdings, presented her with an ethical, moral and emotional dilemma.

By the time Andrew arrived to take her out to dinner, the files were nowhere to be seen. The table was set for two.

'We're eating in! Splendid, very romantic,' he said, settling himself as Letitia poured drinks.

'There are some things I thought we should

discuss in private,' she said, handing him his scotch.

'Excellent. Of course. What's for dinner?'

'I don't cook much. It's takeaway Thai from down the road.' She sat opposite him, swirling the ice in her vodka and orange. 'Let's run through the history of Beacon Land Holdings for a minute.'

'Oh, you want to talk business? I thought we covered everything in the media presentation.' He was disappointed.

Letitia looked serious so Andrew made no further attempt to stop her. 'When we met in Thailand, I was there checking out potential investors in a big project in The Bay. I had been commissioned to do this by Sam Mann, my client, and the Sydney owners of the land, Beacon Land Holdings. We happened to meet and you introduced me to the General. He liked what he saw, agreed to come in, then Sam and Beacon commissioned you to design the project.'

'Right,' said Andrew in a jocular tone, trying to lighten the mood. 'We both scored and got a good gig with great potential and lots of fringe benefits. We got to collaborate in more ways than one. I'll drink to that.' He smiled broadly as he downed his drink.

Letitia didn't return his smile. 'So who else was involved, do you know? Going way back? This is important, Andrew.'

He put his glass down and spread his arms. 'Hey, baby, what's the problem? Why the cross-examination? What's up?'

'I'm just trying to get the matter completely clear in my mind.'

'The only other person I know of is the Sydney solicitor fronting Beacon Land, Maxwell Hamilton. Good bloke. Old school tie type. You were with me both times we met for dinner.'

'So you don't know that my father studied law with Max Hamilton? Or that my father was involved in selling the Mighty Beach land to Beacon in the seventies?'

'Your father? Christ, I had no idea. What was he in all this?'

'He acted for the owners of the land when it was sold to Beacon.'

'So he was a local solicitor doing his job, what's wrong with that? I hope everything in the deal was legit, no sloppy paperwork,' said Andrew, suddenly worried.

'Despite my father's drink problem, every "i" was always dotted, every "t" crossed in his paperwork.'

'That's great,' Andrew said with relief. 'Who owned the land before Beacon?'

'Another company, I'm still looking into that. It's a little cloudy.'

Andrew sensed from her tone that she had no more to say. 'Well then, let's eat, drink and be merry.' He handed her his empty glass for a refill. 'I'll help serve up the takeaways,' he offered half-heartedly.

But dinner was a desultory affair, and the love-making following it was disappointing. Andrew flew back to Sydney the next morning, first making Letitia promise to keep him abreast of every event as it unfurled.

The digital video editing suite in which Eddie was putting together some sequences of his documentary was in a pleasant rural setting. It was more reminiscent of a holiday ranch than a high-tech service facility for creating sound and video productions.

One of the hip chicks who frequented the complex wandered in to tell him he had a visitor.

He didn't lift his head from the small screen and control panels in front of him. 'Hi, Ali,' he called. 'I won't be long, honeybun. This looks so good.'

'It isn't Alice.'

His heart sank at the sound of Laura's voice. How the hell did she track him down? He spun around. 'This must be important. What's up now?'

'Maybe it's a social call, Eddie,' she smirked.

'All the way out here? I'm working, Laura.'

'Working?' she repeated cynically. 'While you're working who is keeping an eye on Alice? She told me you'd be out here and I was curious. There're a lot of strange people wandering around.'

'They're musicians. And Alice is quite safe while Matty's here.'

'I want to talk to you about Alice. Us. Me –'

'Laura! This isn't the time or the place. I pay

for my time here. I have to get a rough edit done to send down to Sydney. I have a lot of interest in this. Lots of appeal to the cashed-up baby-boomer demographic.'

'Bully for you. Listen, I have a job offer.' Seeing his expression, she amended it. 'A kind of an offer. An opportunity. But if I get it I can't really keep Alice with me. We need to sort something out . . . legally. On paper. Formal custody, they said.'

Eddie felt his heart lurch. The thought of Alice being dragged away from him really hurt. It wouldn't be good for her, Alice was settled and happy now. More, he'd miss her. Incredibly so. While his relationship with Tina was a great joy, Alice was the focus of his life and Tina accepted that. She was terrific with Alice. Didn't play surrogate mother or interloping girlfriend, just an affectionate interested, good friend. Alice, and Tina, liked it that way. 'Where is this job?' he asked.

'Out of Brisbane.'

'Out of . . . meaning you're travelling, like a sales rep or something?' He couldn't see Laura in any such job.

'Publicity director for a hotel chain. It would involve a lot of travelling to the South Pacific, maybe Asia. Up-market places.'

'That's right up your alley,' Eddie said. 'So what about Alice? I think she should stay here, she's settled in school.'

'I think so too. I'll be down every month or so for a weekend, or she could come up. In school hols I could take her to one of the resorts. If I get the job.'

'I really hope you do.' He meant it. 'I agree about having the arrangement on paper. Get old Paul Maynard, he's a good man. What are you doing with all your stuff, the unit here?'

'The renters are out, and I was wondering if you knew anyone who might want to take it over and keep a bedroom free for me. So I can stay when I come to see Alice, keep a few clothes, that sort of thing.'

'Off the top of my head, I'm not sure.' Then a thought struck him. 'Bonnie might. She spends a lot of time out in the hills but she was saying she was ready to have a base back in The Bay; feels she's ready to get cracking in the shop, part-time at least –'

'Has she got her act together?' asked Laura dubiously.

'Oh God, yes. Amber has helped her a lot. Since Erica died Bonnie seems to have found some sort of focus and strength.'

'You'd think it would be the other way around. I'd lose the plot if anything happened to Alice,' Laura said, suddenly sounding genuine and soft.

Eddie reached out and touched her hand. 'Laura, nothing is going to happen to Alice. You do trust me? I love her like my own.'

She squeezed his hand, unable to speak for a moment. 'Thanks. That's the best thing that's happened to us – her and you. I'm really grateful.

Maybe when she's older and I'm settled, she and I can have our time together.'

'Laura, I really wish you well. You go for it.'

'I've told Alice, we're having a girls' day out before I go. Big pizza feast, I imagine.'

Eddie couldn't resist a little laugh, and Laura joined in. It had been a long time since they had laughed together.

'Sounds good. Keep in touch.'

'Of course I will. And Eddie, I hope you sell your film.'

'I think I will. It's a doozie. So many things have happened during its making.'

'So what're you calling it?'

Eddie thought for a moment, how to braid together all the threads of the complex stories he'd been following, then it came to him. 'The Bay. I reckon that sums it up.'

Matty was minding the shop for Amber when Billy dropped in. 'You got another after-school job?'

'No, Amber had some big meeting at the uni. She went off – as my mother says – like a chook with its head chopped off.'

'Why's she in a dither? Going to do a course?' Billy was surprised she hadn't said anything to him, he liked to be up with all the news. People expected it.

'No. Said it was business.' Matty was rubbing lotion on her hands. 'Want to try her new cream? It's got apricots in it.'

He looked at the label. 'Hmm. Maybe she should add a line like "it's good enough to eat", eh? So how are things going with you? We never get a chance to gossip on Saturdays, always so busy.' Billy sat in the chair by the door and lit a cigarette.

'Why don't you give them up, Billy? It's disgusting, bad for your health. What do Paula and Hope say about it?'

'Don't you nag as well, Matty. I'm not allowed to smoke at home. That's why we live near the beach.'

'I hope you don't leave your stubs on the sand,' she admonished him. 'We have a campaign at school to clean up the cigarettes. "Get Your Butts off our Beach" is one of the slogans.'

'I get the message. In fact I'm thinking of going to hypnotherapy.'

'Bonnie knows some people in that line,' said Matty helpfully. 'Amber says she is doing well at kicking the habit.'

'Well, if Bonnie successfully kicks the habit, or more correctly, habits, then I might just follow up on that. But for the present, please excuse my weakness,' he said with a smile. 'You had a go at fags yet?'

The question took Matty by surprise, but it was asked so casually and uncritically that she found it easy to respond with honesty. 'Yeah, of course. Everyone has a go once they get to high school.'

'Rite of passage stuff, eh? I can remember

having my first drag down behind the toilets one lunchtime. When did you first light up?'

Now the conversation was starting to hurt and Matty fussed with a display of cosmetics to mask her feelings. The sudden recall of that moment with Erica at their headland hideaway was more painful than she expected. She was close to tears when Billy sensed the tension and changed the subject.

'How's the horsey caper going?'

Matty took a deep breath and forced a bright response. 'Fine. Alice sure knows a lot and she's a good teacher. She's got me interested in doing dressage. At least learning about it. I don't know that we'll be able to afford the dressage gear, but that doesn't matter, we're having a lot of fun.'

'That's one of the nice things about living here, it's so easy to explore new interests. Good to know that Alice has settled in so smoothly with Eddie.'

'She thinks he's a bit keen on Tina. An item,' said Matty without prompting.

Billy tried not to laugh. 'An item? As in the gossip columns of *The Beacon Bugle*?'

'Don't laugh. Alice was scared it might mean she'd be on the move again, shoved off back to her mother. But her mum's excited about starting her new job. Alice and me might go to an island resort in the holidays.'

'Woo! Lucky duckies, let's hope.'

'What's happening? Who's lucky?' Amber waltzed into the salon.

'So what have you been up to? You look like the cat that swallowed the cream,' said Billy.

'Do I have news for you!' she declared. 'I can't believe it. Now you must not say anything just yet . . .' she looked at them both.

'Scout's honour, my lips are sealed.'

'Can I tell my mum and dad?'

'Okay, Matty, but I don't want too many people to know until, well it's all official and the money is in the bank.'

'Money?' Billy gave a huge grin. 'Come on, spill the beans.'

Amber sat down and kicked off her shoes. 'Several months ago some guys from the new research centre at the uni here took some of my products home from the markets and their wives tried them, and then their friends. Then they did research in the R & D section and found my products are superb for the skin and very healing, and being free of any chemicals, very safe.'

'We've always known that,' said Billy. 'No false advertising claims for Chaste. So are they going to pay you squillions for your secret formula?'

'Something like that. Well not quite . . .'

Matty squealed and jumped up and down and Billy looked dumbfounded. 'Are you serious?'

Amber took a breath and smiled. 'Well the sequence is this – they are developing a huge industry in this region dedicated to growing herbs and plants for medicinal and therapeutic products. You know how big alternative medicines are up here – Chinese herbs, health foods like ocean minerals, barley and wheat grass juice.'

'So are they going to manufacture your stuff? Buy you out? What?' asked Billy impatient for the details.

'I am more interested in working with them, developing products which I haven't been able to afford to do. Some of the products cross over from making you feel and look good and healthy in a natural way, to being healing and medicinal.'

'So how is that going to work? Do you hang out in a lab in a white coat, or dig in the lavender garden, or flog your stuff in a department store?' Billy asked.

'Are you going to be rich?' asked Matty.

'Probably yes to all those questions. But it's all long term. I have to get a lawyer to draw up a contract so I understand things. Chaste will be a line of natural skin-care products and I'll work with them in developing other things. They think I'm the right type to be the face of Chaste, so to speak,' said Amber, grinning.

'I can see that,' agreed Billy, looking at the attractive, healthy redhead opposite him.

'When can we tell people? This is so exciting, Amber, no more cooking up stuff in your kitchen. Will you have a factory?' asked Matty.

'Oh something like that is a long way away. I don't want my products to get big and impersonal and have to put preservatives in them. We'll see,' she said. 'We want lots of other people to come in on this too.'

'This will be good for The Bay,' enthused Billy.

'Yep. They're encouraging people to start herb

and special farms to supply the research and development people as well as the manufacturers who need the plants for their oils.'

'You should tell Eddie,' Matty said. 'Maybe someone could get his avocado farm going again and grow herbs.'

'That's a great idea!' said Amber. 'They're going to need suppliers because the uni wants all the big natural health companies to base themselves up here too.'

'This is big vision stuff,' said Billy shaking his head. 'You're really in on the ground floor, Amber. This could be huge. Really. You'll make a million or more by the time you're thirty!'

Holly rang Sid Wainwright to tell him about Tor's arrival and the documents he had brought with him. Sid was immediately intrigued and wanted to go through them at once.

'There's one especially grand photograph. I'm going to use it in my ads. Mr and Mrs Nilsen standing outside Richmond House. It's just lovely.'

'I'd like a copy of that. Better give copies of it all to Tina for her archives. Have you been through all her stuff yet, Holly?'

'Oh, Sid, I've had so much to do here. But I will one day. Tor has letters . . . none of it has sunk in yet. I'm so delighted to have this missing link in the story of the house.'

'Hmm, I'll be very interested to see it all. Would the young man like to come around and see my stuff? Give him an idea of what it was like when his family first landed here.'

'I'm sure he would. Thanks, Sid.'

Kimberley had been working late at night and early in the morning, digging, ferreting, steadily stitching together clues and information from council records, uncovering pieces of the Mighty Beach puzzle. She was putting her notes in a folder to take to the Sundowners meeting when Councillor Tricia Rich popped into her small office. 'Kim, you might be interested to know that someone from Sydney has been making inquiries about the history of that land parcel at Mighty Beach. No name was given.'

Kimberley raised an eyebrow. 'Hmm. I wonder why?'

'Don't know. Obviously not a reporter or someone official or they would have left a number. He was most interested to find out if we knew anything about a company called Eureka Developments. Before my time, I'm afraid. By the way,' she paused and lowered her voice, 'I'm not voting for rezoning. People everywhere are talking about it. How's the protest march coming along?'

'Going to be bigger than Ben Hur,' said Kimberley. 'But whether that's going to change the votes in here is another matter. Thanks for the news, Tricia.' Kimberley deliberately didn't mention that the file in her hand contained notes connecting a company named Eureka Development to the land at Mighty

Beach before ownership was moved to Beacon. She had learned since working for the council that discretion could pay big dividends.

'Sam, it's Jimmy.'

'Why're you sounding so worried? It's a lovely afternoon for a round of golf.'

'Seems to be a lot to worry about these days, Sam. The staff tell me they've been getting quite a few phone calls asking about Beacon Land Holdings.'

'So what, it's making news.'

'Yeah, but these are calls from Sydney, not your usual curious or angry ratepayer. They're also asking what we have on file about Eureka Developments and its connection with the land.'

'Shit.'

'Sam, are you still there?'

'Yeah. Anything else?'

'A few of the councillors are getting nervy about the rezoning caper. Staff're dragging their heels on this one, as expected. What's this Eureka business all about, Sam?'

'Forget it, Jimmy. Thanks for the call. Keep in touch. Golf's off.'

Mac took Tor to Sid's old house where he had morning tea set out alongside piles of photographs, newspapers and scrapbooks of clippings going back decades.

'Still living in organised chaos, I see,' observed Mac with a wink to Tor. 'Impressive chaos nonetheless.'

'You can joke about it, but I know where everything is. Those piles mean something to me, even if it looks like a mess to you,' said Sid defensively but in good humour. 'She's like most women, wants everything neat and tidy.'

Tor laughed, delighted with the way Australians seemed so relaxed about sending each other up. 'I'm not buying into the argument,' he announced. Then he added diplomatically, 'The delicious smell coming from whatever is under that cover is far more interesting.'

Sid took a corner of the red chequered tea towel covering the plate and with a flourish flicked it aside. 'Pumpkin scones,' he trumpeted with pride. 'Home made.'

'You've just met the best scone maker in town,' said Mac. 'Let's indulge in something you can write home about.'

After demolishing the scones covered with home-made jam and cream, they began passing around a selection of old photographs of the beaches and whaling station that were the focus of the local branch of the Nilsen family almost a hundred years ago. Tor was amazed at the amount of work Sid had put into recording the local history.

'Yep, I'm a sort of one-man local hysterical society. People bring me stuff when the oldies die, or things turn up at farm sales. Few years back I started taping talks with some of the old-timers before they drop off the perch.'

'The old people in town trust Sid, they've known him for so long,' Mac explained.

'Trust me so much they even let the family skeletons out of the cupboard a few times,' laughed Sid. 'Here, take a look at these pictures.' He handed Tor a selection of large photographs, all browned with age.

They presented a wonderful sense of what life had been like back in the era of his relatives. He now had a sense of the vibrancy of the town in the old days, the pioneers in the Big Scrub, people at picnics, swimming, galas in town. He tried to imagine Hannah and Lars living here, and peered at photographs of crowds wondering if they might have been among the blurred faces in the old prints. He was also fascinated by a more recent photo of the central beach in which the surf club and pub were the only buildings. 'Look at how the beach is level with the road, the sand came right up to the main street,' he exclaimed. 'Now it is further back, what happened?'

'Sand mining,' said Sid bitterly. 'Bloody disaster that was. Though it was big business at the time. Mining the dunes for minerals, mainly rutile. After extracting the rutile they used the sand for some of the streets and to fill in lots to build on in town.' Sid looked at Mac. 'I have my theories about the tailings, just like they filled in the cattle dips. Where do you suppose all the chemicals and poison went?'

'I know what you're saying. I bet if you ran a

geiger counter over parts of town it'd go off the scale,' Mac said. 'Wouldn't get away with it today. Contamination issues would have the mobs out in the streets, to say nothing of health issues and the environmental destruction. We're sitting on a time bomb in parts of this town, only the newcomers don't know it.'

'Reckon we'll have the mobs out soon anyway,' said Sid. 'Mighty Beach is becoming a mighty issue. C'mon, let's take Tor to his great-great-grandmother.'

The drive took them past a property filled with gardens growing all manner of plants, trees and vegetables.

'Is that a farm?' Tor asked.

'Seed Savers, a great idea. They network with people from all over the world who save the seeds they grow and then share them to keep the pure old-fashioned lines growing,' said Mac.

'They also train people from developing countries in permaculture and agriculture principles that they can use in villages and not have to rely so much on technology and globalisation,' Sid added. 'There's always a bunch of nice kids from somewhere in the world working and learning in those gardens. Typical of the passion in this part of the world for doing things differently and encouraging alternative thinking. Dunno what the wheeler dealers in New York would make of it,' he said with a chuckle.

It was a beautiful spring day and as they walked among palm trees at the entrance to the cemetery Tor felt glad that Hannah was resting in such a peaceful place. He had been to the flower shop and bought a bunch of daffodils. He liked the cheerful colour and they were a familiar bloom.

They found her grave, a simple headstone in a far corner with the words, '*Hannah Nilsen. Born 1-11-1875. Departed 16-6-1965 to join her beloved husband Lars, sons Sven and Erik in Heaven, at peace.*'

Tor knelt down and touched the neglected grave, overwhelmed that here rested a woman who was connected to him by sons and time and distance. He felt moved and saddened that Hannah had lived so much of her life alone, perhaps always hoping she might be reunited with her family.

Mac had brought a vase and bottle of water, and she knelt beside him and helped arrange the daffodils while Sid wandered off to pick a spray of wattle. Mac put a hand gently on the boy's shoulder as he shut his eyes and silently prayed. When they stood up Sid was waiting nearby.

'Wattle, perfect partner for the daffs,' he said, handing it to Tor. 'It's an Aussie spring and summer flower, mate. I bet she loved it. There are a lot of wattle trees on the hill near the old house.'

Tor nodded his thanks, admiring the clusters of fluffy gold balls. 'She lived so long. Ninety years old. She was alone so many years.'

'She was known as a bit of a recluse, alone in

that house for so many years. She finally went into the Anglican nursing home,' said Sid.

'And she never knew that Erik survived,' sighed Tor.

'What was the story there?' Sid asked. 'What did the family in Norway tell her? Why didn't they send the boy back?'

'Ah, families, complex and emotional. I cannot make excuses for what happened, but my grandmother has put the story together from letters and diaries,' Tor said. 'Lars fell out with his parents over the girl he wished to marry. So he sailed away and became a whaling captain. He married Hannah in Australia, had the two sons and over the years they exchanged just a few letters with the family in Norway.'

'But he did take the sons back to visit. Trying to patch things up, no doubt,' said Mac as they walked slowly between the gravestones. 'Tragic loss. A storm you said.'

'Erik survived, and was sent to his grandparents in Norway. Lars's mother could not give him up, she had lost her only son when he ran away to sea. So they sent word to Australia that both sons had perished.'

Sid shook his head. 'And what about the lad, surely he asked about his mother back in Australia?'

'Hannah stayed behind because she was expecting a child. They told Erik she'd died in childbirth. A sorry story, yes?'

'Bloody dreadful. Still, you're here. And I reckon Hannah knows you're here,' said the old man.

Mac linked her arm through Tor's. 'I believe she knows you have come back. It will put her soul at peace. She has been lost and lonely for a long time. Trapped in that house.'

'I saw her,' said Tor quietly. 'Holly knew she was there.'

'She is released now. The circle is complete. But then you knew that when you encountered the whale, didn't you?'

Tor nodded. 'I felt a release. I never understood why all my life I have felt such pain and guilt over whaling when Norway is, you know . . . still whaling. And knowing my ancestors were whalers.'

'Now you can acknowledge and celebrate the fact the whales are here, that we are learning more about them. And you can contribute to that,' said Mac. 'While you're here, doing your post-graduate work.'

'I have such a strange feeling I will stay here. I think I knew that when I left,' he paused. 'I think my mother knew it too, which is why she gave me my grandmother's material that she'd compiled about Hannah and Lars.'

'Life here will be a bit of a change from back over there,' commented Sid, who hadn't quite grasped their talk about spirits.

'Don't worry about change, Tor,' Mac said. 'It's something that can happen so very beautifully around here, and often in ways you hadn't expected. You just wait and see.'

534

Eddie peered through the viewfinder at Tor on the track up to the lighthouse, lifted his arm and signalled to him to begin walking towards the camera. He had decided Tor made a perfect peg for his doco, which had been lacking a clear focus in terms of a central figure. With whatever came out of the protest rally, the council, and what the girls would be piecing together at their Sundowners meeting this afternoon, he knew he had the ingredients for a hot and colourful story.

By the time Tor had finished looking around the lighthouse, Tina had spread out Hannah's diary, some pages marked with notated tags, photographs and logbooks from the *Lady Richmond*. Then she left him to enter the distant world of his Australian-based ancestors. She knew it was going to be an emotional journey back in time.

Two hours later she and Eddie spotted Tor standing at the parapet of the lighthouse looking over The Bay. In his mind's eye he was seeing how it might have been when Hannah and Lars had first sailed in, and when Lars sailed out on that fateful voyage in 1908. He wiped away another tear, took a deep breath and waved to them.

When he came down he hugged Tina and shook Eddie's hand. 'I can't thank you enough for what you've done to make this day such a memorable one. I'm sure Hannah and Lars thank you as well.'

'It's not over yet. We've been invited to the Sundowners meeting. Let's go,' said Tina picking up Hannah's diary. 'Apparently Kimberley has some big news.'

'Is it too early for champers?' asked Nola, pulling the bottle from the ice bucket anyway. 'Eddie, as we have gentlemen here today, you can do the honours. Stolle, pass the glasses.'

'Shouldn't we wait for Holly?' said Lynn.

'She'll be here soon,' said Mac. 'What's your news, Kimberley?'

Kimberley stood up. 'Well, first of all let's make a toast to welcome Tor.'

Nola recognised her oversight and resumed command. 'Indeed, a very special guest. Welcome to The Bay, Tor.'

Mac gave him a special smile. 'Welcome home.'

It was taken up by everyone. 'Welcome home, Tor.'

Tor rose to his feet in acknowledgment. 'Thank you all so very much for making me welcome. Today has been one of the most memorable in my life. Thank you again.'

As he sat down Holly bustled in and gave him a kiss and hug. 'I've brought your family letters and papers,' she whispered and handed him the envelope.

Kimberley reached for her folder and suddenly everyone was attentive. 'I've gone through all the records and paperwork that's available at this point. In summary, the Richmond Whaling

Company was owned by an American group and managed here for a number of years by Lars Nilsen. Now, according to documents Buck got from the Registrar General's Office and the Lands Department in Sydney, at some stage early this century the ownership of the company passed to Lars and Hannah Nilsen; they acquired all the shares. With the ownership of the company went the ownership of Mighty Beach.'

There was a chorus of gasps and everyone started talking at once. Nola clinked a teaspoon on her champagne glass. 'Order, please. Order. Go on, Kimberley.'

'To avoid any confusion, I should point out that Richmond House was on a separate title and has changed hands several times since Hannah died. No problems there,' Kimberley said. 'Hannah eventually sold the total shareholding of Richmond Whaling Company to Eureka Developments, a Bay-based company set up by Sam Mann. And with the deal went the land.'

This time there was a stunned silence. She went on: 'Eureka took title of the land, and a year later sold it to Beacon Land Holdings. The Richmond Whaling Company went out of existence as a company with no assets.'

Holly rose immediately. 'A question please. From what you've seen of the documents from Sydney and at council, is there any question about the legality of all of this?'

'It looks completely kosher. All the legal work was done by the late Gordon Sweetman, an old mate of Sam's, apparently, and father of local solicitor Letitia Sweetman. Letitia is associated with both Sam and Beacon in the current Mighty Beach project.'

'Are there any others?' Holly asked.

Tor had been leafing through the papers Holly had given him and comparing them with documents Kimberley had put on the table. 'According to the paperwork you have here,' he said, 'the ownership of the land passed from Hannah to Eureka in early 1966. Right?'

Kimberley checked her notes. 'Yes. Correct.'

'Well, that is very odd, because this morning I went to Hannah's grave and the headstone records her death as June 1965.'

Nola spoke what was in everyone's mind. 'Oh dear. Hanky-panky.'

Eddie decided it was time to say something. 'For some months now Tina and I have been going through the diaries and logbooks stored at the lighthouse, most of them related to the Nilsen family. Some time ago we found an entry in Hannah's diary that recorded Lars being given shares in the company as a bonus for a good year's production of whale oil. We didn't think anything more about it until now, but that entry certainly confirms the family had a strong financial interest in the company, and the land. It makes sense that later Lars would take up more shares, if he got the opportunity. What do you think, Tina?'

'Well, I've read every entry Hannah wrote in those diaries,' she said. 'Hannah and Lars clearly developed a great love of this place and had faith in the future of the whaling industry. They could never imagine the very different situation today. Yes, buying out the American owners would certainly make sense. What I can't understand is how the title deeds got into the hands of Sam Mann, after Hannah died. If that is what happened.'

The key documents were passed around, and Mac and Tor found themselves sharing views on what they were reading. He was surprised when Mac gave an involuntary shudder. 'Something wrong, Mac?'

'Yes, there is. The writing, Hannah's signature on the copy of the land title when it was transferred to Eureka, it's giving me bad vibes.' He glanced at her a little puzzled, then looked again at the signature. Without saying anything he went back through his family papers.

'These are letters from Hannah to our family after she first arrived here. They somehow got handed down through the family and were eventually given to me. Have a look,' Tor said.

Mac took them, glanced through the content, and then studied the signature at the end of each letter. 'Totally consistent signatures,' she said. Then she very carefully compared them with the signature on the deeds. 'Different,' she announced. 'Not by the same hand. A forgery, I'd say.'

A press of people clustered around the table, each studying the various signatures, each noting real or imagined differences. It was Holly who took the initiative and got the attention of everyone.

'Friends, a little bit of quiet please,' she called. 'We can all see what this is suggesting and it doesn't look good for certain people. On the face of it we have a forged signature on a transaction made with a dead person. We need to get a legal opinion before taking another step. We should not go public with this information until getting that opinion. Agreed?'

There was a murmur of assent, then Nola took over. 'I believe this is going to be a sunset to remember,' she said waving a glass at the light show on the horizon. 'Please help yourself to another champers and let's pray our luck continues.'

'Luck?' said Mac quietly to Holly. 'More than that, I'm sure.'

Holly nodded in agreement and their glasses touched in salute. 'To Hannah,' they both said.

Street stalls were set up outside shops, market stalls were trading under umbrellas and canvas awnings were strung along the grassy verge of Beach Road. Busy Friday morning shoppers and tourists fossicked through the heaps of home-made gifts, clothes, food and knick-knacks. A chocolate wheel and raffles by local services clubs raising money for charities added to the atmosphere.

Lynn and Stolle had set up their stall and were pleased with how the morning sales were going. As it was a 'townie' market they hadn't set out bulky antiques and furniture but limited their offerings to two long tables of old china, linen, books, silver, and a few ornaments and cushion covers. They were next to a stall selling honey and beeswax products and Lynn was talking to the stallholder about the medicinal virtues of jellybush honey.

Stolle leaned back in his chair thinking he might tackle a surf later in the day. Maybe Tor would like to go with him.

A heavy-set man who obviously worked out, judging by his bulging muscles and well-proportioned physique, strolled up to browse. He interested Stolle who fancied himself as a bit of a people watcher. This man didn't look like a tourist, he wasn't casually dressed nor was he a local. Definitely a city slicker – the mobile phone on his belt, the fancy watch, gold chain. Someone a bit different, Stolle concluded.

'Howdy. You're new in town, on holidays?'

The man shrugged and studied the selection of ornaments. 'Just passing through. Wouldn't mind hanging about, nice place. Bit quiet.'

'Not if you know where the action is. We make our own fun. Do you want to know what's happening in town? Bands? Pubs? The tourist info people are down the road.' Stolle indicated the direction.

'Ah no, thanks. You got any Disney characters?'

'You mean like, Mickey Mouses, Goofy? Look over there where the toys are.'

A smile broke out on the man's face as he picked up a plastic Minnie Mouse in a spotted frock and big red shoes. 'I'll take this.'

Stolle was surprised. 'Gift for your daughter?'

'Nah. Me. I collect 'em.'

'Oh, righto. There you go, five bucks.'

The man looked pleased with his purchase and the price. You can't always pick 'em, Stolle decided, turning his attention to two backpackers.

Tor had wandered among the market stalls, then went down to see Billy. He wanted his long blond hair trimmed. 'I am starting to feel like a local,' he said.

'That's good. Doesn't take long to make friends in this town. Hop into this chair, got a slack time so you're in luck. So when are you off to uni?' asked Billy.

'I have another month before I start. Tina at the lighthouse introduced me to the Southern Cross Centre for Whale Research. It interests me very much so I might do some volunteer work with them, help monitor the whales and record their songs – most fascinating.'

'Yeah. We all love the big 'uns, wonderful creatures. But I tell you what, if that International Whaling Commission doesn't do the right thing, we can kiss the whales goodbye. It's nothing but a bloody fishing club.'

'What do you mean?' Tor asked.

'They're scrapping the South Pacific Whale Sanctuary which goes from here right across the Pacific. Soon it will be back to the bad old days of wholesale whale slaughter.'

'That would be terrible,' exclaimed Tor.

'It's greed. When the whales are gone they'll eat the dolphins. And if we can't save the whales and dolphins how can we fight for environmental issues that aren't so obvious?'

'Well, I will raise my voice as best I can,' Tor said in a very decisive tone.

'You sound like you've just declared war,' joked Billy. 'That short enough on the top?'

Tor grinned and nodded approval. He had indeed made a decision – that he would use his skills and knowledge in marine studies to concentrate on cetacean research and the preservation of whales in the Southern Hemisphere. A brief stop in the hairdressing shop in The Bay had shown him his path for the rest of his life.

Letitia left her office to walk along Beach Street for a quiet lunch at her favourite cafe; it was a routine she followed most days. She was cutting through a carpark when someone called.

'Letitia. A word.'

She stopped, surprised to see Sam getting out of his red Mercedes.

'I thought you would be headed this way. The office tipped me off when I phoned. Hop in for a minute. Fairly important.' He opened the passenger door for her.

'Sure, Sam.'

'I'll make this brief. We've never talked much about the past, like when you were a kid, but as you know your father and I were old mates. We both came to town about the same time, bright, young and ambitious. We weren't even thirty. I was a builder, keen to get on council, your dad a smart new solicitor. We were a good team.' Sam nervously lit up a cigarette. 'You don't mind, do you?'

'Just put the windows down and I'll survive. What's the point you want to make?'

'Well, it's about the little Eureka enterprise we set up way back then. I was wondering if old Gordon left the files around. Eureka only lasted a year or so.'

'Oddly enough, I came across them only the other day,' she said calmly but noting his surprise, then added, 'quite by accident. Anyway, I glanced through them and everything is okay. Professional habit, I suppose.'

Sam took a deep drag on the cigarette then twisted in his seat to face her and lowered his voice. 'Get rid of that file. In the wrong hands it might damage us all and stuff up the Mighty Beach deal.'

'Sam, who decided to set up Eureka? You? Or my father?'

'Like I said, we were a team.'

'You scratch my back, I'll scratch yours,' said Letitia. 'Why are you so worried? I don't want to see this deal fall over.'

'Good girl. Like father, like daughter.' He stubbed out the cigarette and put on his gold-rimmed sunglasses. 'Thanks, Letitia. I'm off to my golf game. Enjoy lunch.'

She didn't. The conversation had forced disturbing images into her mind, images from the Eureka file, particularly several enigmatic notes written in her father's hand and attached to some vital documents.

Sam declared it had been the worst round of golf he'd ever played, and his usual golfing companions heartily agreed with the assessment.

'Your mind must be on other things, Sam,' said one of them back at the clubhouse bar.

'Yeah. That's the understatement of the year.'

To ease the pain he had a few more drinks than usual with the Friday-special lunch. On Fridays his wife would be at bowls by the time he got home, so he could sleep off the over-indulgence before she returned.

It therefore came as a surprise when he arrived home to find a car parked outside. He didn't recognise the white Commodore, but hoped Freda hadn't come in early and brought some bowlers along. He garaged the car and walked out to the sunroom but stopped in his tracks as he opened the French doors. A complete stranger sat in his chair. A big man, and he was twiddling a Disney toy, a Minnie Mouse.

'Hello, Sam. I let myself in.'

'Who the hell are you and what are you doing in my house?'

'The General sent me, Sam. I'm Tony.'

Sam did a double take. 'The General? Oh, the General. Oh, right. You gave me a fright for a moment.' He held out his hand in greeting, but the big man ignored it.

'Have a good round of golf?'

'Lousy. Care for a drink?'

'Already poured myself one from your bar, thanks,' he said, casually indicating a large scotch and ice on the desk.

The visitor showed no indication of getting out of the big lounge chair so Sam pulled up an office chair from the other side of his desk. 'What can I do for you, and the General, then?'

'Ah, now that is a really good question, Sam. Let's start by you telling me all about a little outfit called Eureka. Every little detail, please. The General has had some high-priced people doing research on this in Sydney, and he is very anxious to check out the details with your version.'

'Oh, everything was above board, I can assure you,' Sam said trying to stay calm, but he felt betrayed by a nervous twitching of one eye.

'I certainly hope that's right, because the General doesn't take kindly to his name being publicly associated with enterprises that attract the law and suggest that he is not a man of good character. The buzz around town is that documents have come to light that may well do just that.'

Sam's jaw dropped and he sat in stunned silence. Tony reached into his sports coat and pulled out an automatic pistol and put it on the desk beside his glass. 'Talk, Sam.'

Early the next morning Andrew's bedside telephone rang and woke him. He looked at the clock.

It was 2 am. 'Bloody hell, who is ringing at this absurd hour,' he mumbled.

'Hello.'

'Andrew, sorry to bother you, but it is a matter that cannot wait.'

Andrew recognised the voice instantly. 'Hello, General. Sorry, I was sound asleep when the phone rang.'

'Pity, but inconvenience plagues all our lives from time to time. Now listen carefully. A friend of Tony's will call on you tomorrow morning. Please give him the money you received. You know what I'm talking about. The full amount, please. He will explain what needs to be explained. And, Andrew, be very discreet in answering any questions from anyone. Goodbye.' The line went dead before he could respond.

'Jesus,' muttered Andrew to himself. 'What the fuck has gone wrong?'

Chapter Eighteen

EVERYONE WAS THRILLED FOR AMBER AS NEWS OF the university offer became public. It had the potential for delivering so much to individuals and the community in terms of lifestyle and economics. At a congratulatory gathering of friends at the Caffe Latte Nola had proclaimed, 'Absolutely wonderful, Amber. Your perseverance looks like paying big dividends. That's what makes this place so interesting. It's bubbling with ideas, but not many as good as this one.'

Tina had then raised the idea of Eddie getting on board the herbal bandwagon and rejuvenating his farm. So a week later they picked up Amber, Ross Hammond from the University Valley Health Project and Nola, who insisted on being included to hear more about the concept.

'Lovely up here. Why was the farm let go?' she asked as they approached the property in Tina's four-wheel drive.

'Access to the creek is on the land next door. There was some council problem; it was not for sale,' Eddie said. 'But I did find out it'd be worth putting a bore down.'

'Even better if you added that land and the creek to this,' said Nola. 'Great for a few organic plots of comfrey, lavender, calendula, wouldn't you say, Amber?'

'I don't know anything about growing that stuff,' said Eddie.

'That's where we come in,' said Ross, as they parked the car and piled out. 'If we certify you as a supplier then we provide advice and people to oversee the development right through to harvesting.'

'There you go,' said Nola. 'Learn as you grow.'

'And you can still buzz off and make your films,' said Tina. 'I think it sounds great. It's silly to not use all these acres.'

'I just like looking at it, knowing the girls can ride about, hear a cow moo.'

'You can do all of that too. Nothing wrong with looking at a paddock of lavender. I'd love to do that,' mused Nola, leaning on a fence and taking in a vista of grassed flats and low rolling hills fringed by forest regrowth. 'Yes, it would be nice to come out here and smell a field of lavender at harvest time.'

The remark surprised Amber. It was a soft side of Nola that was at odds with her high-society background and the extravagant, rather materialistic lifestyle that had given her a measure of fame among bemused locals.

Ross Hammond began his briefing, pointing out the prime pieces of land for the various herbs, estimating production costs and potential income, and declaring the farm a definite goer, so long as the water supply could be guaranteed.

'That needs money I don't have,' said Eddie. 'The bloke next door will probably sell me access to the creek, but I'm up to my neck with the bank already.'

Nola joined in. 'Get a partner with money, Eddie. Simple.'

'And where do I go to find them? To Centrelink?' The absurdity of his despairing remark set them all laughing.

'Well, darlings,' said Nola as they began walking back to the farmhouse for morning tea, 'I rather like the idea of getting dividends from a field of lavender, as well as good vibes.'

It took a moment for her seemingly casual remark to sink in, and it was Amber who first responded. 'Nola, are you saying you'd invest? Actually put money into this?'

Everyone stopped walking and looked at Nola, who simply smiled.

'You can't just decide like that! I mean, it'd be fantastic but . . . surely you have to get more advice, or something?'

'I've done a bit of homework since this all made news in the *Bugle*. Don't worry,' said Nola with some seriousness. 'I'm not losing my marbles. It's a great idea, I want to see it happen, I can afford it and, as I said,' she smiled and resumed as the Nola they all knew, 'I like lavender.'

'Really, Nola, it's a dream, a miracle.' Eddie felt quite overcome.

'Ah, miracles do happen, Eddie. Particularly up here. But I suppose it's too much to expect champers to celebrate my move into farming,' she laughed.

'A pot of tea or instant coffee and some Anzac biscuits, that's it,' replied Eddie.

'How very rural,' said Nola, and they hugged each other.

'It'll be a lot of hard work too,' said Nola cheerfully. 'And the house needs work as well. We'd have to add an office, set up an oil extraction plant – don't you think the pressing should be done as soon as the plants are picked?' she asked Ross who nodded in agreement and before he could elaborate, Nola went on. 'Mitchell can come up with some ideas and do some of the work perhaps.'

'Holly will miss having Mitchell around, won't she?' said Amber.

'I think he'll find a reason to keep visiting,' Tina said with a grin.

'Yeah, their dogs love each other,' said Eddie. 'Gives them an excuse to walk on the beach every day.' He leaned across Amber to ask Tina, 'What say we get a new dog?'

'Alice would love that,' she replied.

'I was thinking if I got a dog, it'd give me a reason to walk it to the lighthouse every day.'

'National Park, dogs aren't allowed,' said Tina.

'I might get special privileges. Otherwise, you'll have to spend more time here,' he said.

The chorus of birds in the garden provided an appropriate background for Holly as she worked on the final draft of her publicity brochure for Richmond House. She calculated that everything would be in place for her to open the doors to customers within a fortnight. The advertising campaign had been mapped out, and with Stolle's help she had drawn up an impressive publicity campaign in local, regional and interstate media.

The crunching of car tyres on the newly gravelled driveway disrupted the birds and Holly's train of thought. She strolled around the verandah to see who had dropped in and was taken aback to see Letitia Sweetman collecting a file from the back seat of her convertible. She tensed as Letitia strode purposefully up the path.

'Good afternoon, Mrs Jamieson. I apologise for not telephoning but I won't take much of your time.'

Holly forced herself to stay calm and polite. 'No trouble, Letitia. Please call me Holly. Really, there isn't much call for formality in this town, is there? Let's sit here on the verandah.'

'Thank you. You may think I've come to talk about Andrew. I haven't. There is something more important that needs addressing. Well, that might be disputed, but too bad.' She opened the file and pulled out a document. 'It's about Mighty Beach and my father's involvement with it in the 1960s.'

Practically lost for words, Holly simply said, 'Go on.'

'My father's professional files on that period still exist and are quite safe, despite suggestions made to me in the last few days that they should be destroyed.'

Holly gasped. This confessional session seemed to have no end of shocks.

'I did not know of the Nilsen file and its content until a few days ago. Professional privacy obligations restrict what I can release, but this is a copy of one document that you could say fell off the back of a truck.' She handed it to Holly, who saw instantly that it was a photocopy of Hannah Nilsen's will. 'You'll find it interesting, given what transpired at the recent meeting of your little sunset group. Yes, I think I'm aware of most of what was said there concerning Sam Mann and my father. Most of the people here couldn't keep a secret even if their lives depended on it. Gossip travels fast.'

'So I'm discovering,' said Holly, anxious for Letitia to keep talking.

'The will left the land to the community to be held in trust as a permanent nature reserve. At the time of her death, my father was handling her affairs. He was very close to Sam Mann in those days. I don't think I need to say anything more. I guess you already know that Beacon Land Holdings, fronted by Maxwell Hamilton in Sydney, is actually owned by Sam. He had good reason to be hiding his connection. Had good reasons ever since the mid sixties. He was waiting for the right time to cash in.'

Holly scanned the two pages of the will, seeing the words but not taking in the details as her mind was spinning in emotional confusion. 'Thank you,' was all she managed to mumble.

Letitia stood up to leave. 'I am very distressed at what this sad affair says about my father, but I know that I have done nothing wrong in my role as a solicitor. However, I am leaving The Bay soon and moving to Melbourne or Brisbane, maybe Sydney. That's where the action is, that's where I stand a better chance of getting what I want out of life. And I'll leave all this sorry mess behind me.' She turned and walked swiftly to her car and drove off without another word.

Freda Mann came home from bowls and checked the sunroom. She expected to find her husband, but he wasn't there. She put a chair back in its right spot, collected a glass from the desk and took it to the kitchen, where she began preparing the evening meal. It was dark before she began ringing around her husband's haunts trying to find him. He usually left a note or telephoned if he was not going to be home for dinner. She was still telephoning when the front doorbell rang.

'Good evening, Mrs Mann,' said the police officer standing on the verandah with another officer behind him. 'Sorry to bother you, but is Sam around?'

'No. I've been on the phone for an hour trying to track him down. Why?'

The two officers exchanged glances. 'A short while ago we found his car abandoned on a lonely beach track south of The Bay. Keys were still in it.'

'Well, I know he came home from golf, and I know he had a drink in the sunroom. Oddly enough, the spare office chair was in the wrong place, as if someone had moved it to talk with him. He always sat in the leather swivel chair. Can't imagine what he would have been doing down a remote beach track.'

'Okay, Mrs Mann, thanks for that. Get Sam to give the station a ring when he gets in. We locked the car. Here are the keys.'

When they reached their car they checked in with the duty officer at the station and briefed him on the situation at the Mann household.

But the police station didn't get a call from Sam. He never came home.

Letitia's secretary put Andrew through immediately.

'Hi baby. Listen, what the hell is going on with Sam? I've had a very unpleasant phone call from the General.'

'Well I'd say that was your problem.'

'You don't sound very concerned. We're in this together. You made the introduction after all.'

'I'm out, Andrew. Of everything. It's not going to happen and I'm afraid I don't like being associated with dud deals. I'm off.'

'What are you talking about?' His voice had risen.

'I'm sorry. I've decided to move on. From this project, from you. When it's appropriate, I'm out of The Bay.' She sounded tired and resigned. She was over the disappointment.

'What the hell? Why? For God's sake tell me what is going on.'

'Keep your hair on. This whole project was flawed from the start. I have documents showing Sam owns Beacon, has for years. And was probably involved in illegal acts.'

'Jesus! Like what?'

'Like forgery for starters.'

'What's he forged? What are you talking about?'

'Like forging a dead woman's signature. You win some, you lose some. Goodbye, Andrew.'

She hung up and buzzed her secretary and asked her not to put through any further calls from Andrew Jamieson.

'Perfect morning for a march,' Mitchell said as Holly climbed into his car.

'I was in a quandary about what to wear to a

demo,' she laughed. 'Seeing as the nation's media is on our doorstep!'

'I seem to remember you looked very cute at the dog rally. And you're right, the media is certainly onto this, you've all done a fantastic job.'

'I can't believe how this has fired people up. I suppose it shows The Bay is at crunch time. If ever a beachfront development like this one were approved, The Bay as we know it would be lost forever. I know it looks like we're going to win this one without the rezoning ever being put to a vote at council. Lawyers are going to sort it out in the end.'

'The march today is still needed,' said Mitchell, 'even if it is almost a victory demo rather than a protest demo. It will boost community spirit. Got your speech ready?'

Holly pulled some notes out of her shoulder bag. 'I've rehearsed it, but I'm still nervous.'

'I'm not surprised. This is more emotional than walking through town with a bunch of dogs and their owners.'

Holly grinned. 'Ah yes, my baptism as a demonstrator.'

Her nervousness increased as they drove along the road to the dunes above Mighty Beach. Cars and vans and motorbikes were parked everywhere. People were heading towards the small park that had been unnamed for so long. She baulked a little at the sight of the placards, banners and the swarm of reporters, camera crews and photographers. Then she saw so many familiar smiling faces, the

Sundowners, Buck Hagen, old Sid, Billy with his daughter on his shoulders. A wave came from Frankie the Snakeman, then smiles from a group of Aboriginal people from the district. It brought home to her again that she was part of a community that cared, a community that was determined not to surrender its values to the contemporary pressures of self-centred individualism.

Buck was at her side. 'I suggest we all walk to the beach and you speak with the ocean as a backdrop. There's a sandhill just clear of the dunes that can serve as a stage.'

Holly turned to the crowd now gathering around her. 'Come and see what is one of the most beautiful places in the world, a place that has to be preserved!'

With a cheer, they linked arms and began walking in ragged rows behind the lead group of Nola, Billy, Mitchell, Holly, Kimberley, Ashok and Matty, Tor and Amber. The camera crews dashed ahead to get shots as the marchers came through the shrubbery that bordered the trail, and out onto the broad stretch of sand. Among the crowd teenagers started the chant that was picked up by other protestors, 'Save Mighty Beach. Save Mighty Beach.'

At the top of the sandhill, with the expanse of pristine beach behind them, Holly was handed a microphone plugged into a battery-operated speaker.

She called for attention, her voice a little shaky but she quickly gained confidence as Tor moved forward and stood at her side. 'Friends of The Bay.' She paused to allow a ragged cheer. 'We are standing on land that symbolises all that is good about Beacon Bay. This is a beautiful piece of coastline. It was once exploited, but recovered, and for a long time the community believed it would always be like this – a haven of natural pleasure for everyone to share. Then came the shock of the rezoning application.'

After a scatter of boos, she went on. 'I have some good news. That rezoning application is dead in the water, dead because this land was stolen from the people of this town. Now lawyers are working to give it back to us.' There was a huge roar of approval, even though very few of those present really understood how this miracle could occur. 'To make the situation clearer, I would like to introduce this young man to you all,' said Holly as she turned and asked Tor to take a step forward. 'He is Tor Nilsen, a direct descendant of the Nilsens who helped this area get on its feet a century ago. His family once owned practically all of Mighty Beach.' Applause and cheers welcomed him. 'Tor has been visiting us only a short while, but in that time much has happened and I would like him to say a few words.'

Tor took the microphone and looked around the crowd before lifting it to speak. 'Thank you all for coming out here today. I am sure the spirits of Lars and Hannah Nilsen are looking on this wonderful happening with gratitude. They loved this land, this place. Hannah particularly recorded the strength of that love in her diaries, which are still here in The Bay and which I have had the great pleasure of reading. It is not appropriate to go into all the details now, but when she died, Hannah Nilsen in her will left all this land, Mighty Beach, to the people of The Bay. She had one modest request, that part of it becomes a parkland reserve named in memory of her husband, Lars.'

There was a roar from the crowd at this bombshell.

'Legal documents have come to light that suggest the Beacon Land company has *no right* to Mighty Beach. As Holly has told you, lawyers are going to have to sort it all out, but in my view, today is a day for celebration.'

Applause, cheers, and a brief chorus of 'Why was He Born so Beautiful' from a section of the crowd delighted Tor, and he gave an exaggerated bow of acknowledgment.

'Done in true Bay style,' announced Holly when the crowd calmed down. 'Thanks, Tor. Friends, it may take some time for this fiasco to be sorted out, but I'm sure the *Bugle* will trumpet the news to us as it happens. Thanks again for coming. Now we can all go and celebrate.'

Family and friends rallied around Freda Mann in true Bay fashion when word of her husband's disappearance began circulating. An unexpected visitor to arrive with a bunch of flowers was

Bonnie Bitternden. Freda had been an occasional customer at Bonnie's shop and had felt sorry for her when the local paper reported details of the death of her daughter.

When Freda answered the door her surprise at seeing Bonnie obviously showed, but on being handed the flowers, she invited her inside. 'It's very kind of you, very kind indeed,' said Freda as she put them with others on a table where several framed photographs of her husband and the two of them together were on display. 'He was such a good husband, and he didn't give a hint that anything was wrong. Terrible things are being said all over town, but I know he isn't dead, Bonnie. Oh, no. He staged this disappearance so he could go away and do all the things he dreamed about doing when he retired. I've always just wanted to sit here and enjoy the life we've got. But not Sam. Oh no,' she said a little bitterly, then wiped away a small tear.

Bonnie sighed in sympathy and patted Freda's arm. It was a shock to hear such a far-fetched explanation of Sam's sudden disappearance. Whether it was true or not didn't matter. If that was how Freda wanted to see it, then so be it. At least for the time being. Bonnie had been through an emotional trauma and knew what was needed.

'Well, Freda, you're here where you want to be, and you're not alone. You have friends, lots of us, in The Bay and we'll help you over the rough spots ahead.'

'Oh, I know that,' said Freda. 'Comforting, isn't it? That's why I never wanted to leave.'

Back at Richmond House, Mitchell and Holly sat together on a shaded garden seat and sipped champagne in a little celebration of their own.

'You did well, Holly. It was a brilliant idea to brief Tor and give him the chance to reveal details of the will. You ought to go into politics.'

'You've got to be joking.'

'I was.'

'Oh, in that case you can stay, even have another drink. You know what I liked most about today and the events leading up to it? Just how much people power can achieve if ordinary people unite for the common good and refuse to be pushed around.'

'You're right,' said Mitchell, 'but it can be a tough call for many folk. Look at the price you've had to pay.'

Holly knew he was referring to the collapse of her marriage and for a minute or two neither said anything, but sat listening to the birds and the distant surf.

'Yes, we pay for everything in the end,' she said, breaking the reverie, 'but if we listen to what life is teaching us, we get some great rewards as well.'

Mitchell put his arm around her shoulders. 'That's true. How well we both know that,' he said softly as their eyes met. He leaned over and kissed her. There was no need to say any more, do anything, think or make plans. The spirit of The Bay would take care of the future.

Dawn, New Year's Day

Tiny Bay Beach looked like an impressionist painting in pinks and lavender, and a glow on the distant horizon signalled that soon the sun would rise. Holly was the only person on the beach, but didn't feel alone as she strolled to a favourite rock where she often sat. Curly and Romany bounded back from a little run to settle beside her, as if sensing that this sunrise merited complete attention. A sand castle with dribbled sand spires and cupolas was still intact, windows lit by long-burning candles inside the miniature rooms. Soon enough it would melt away, but the mysterious sand sculptor, the Sand Man, would return and build another.

She thought back on what a great evening it had been – an unforgettable New Year's Eve party at Richmond House with friends, resident guests and her children, Melanie and Marcus. Mitchell came with his son Tom, and Tor was down from Townsville, staying in the attic room which Holly had made his base whenever he came to The Bay. The younger set had left after midnight for a gig in town, and eventually Richmond House became quiet and peaceful again.

Inevitably, she recalled the same time a year

ago when she and her husband had watched the sunrise from a parked car on a hill overlooking The Bay after a long night's drive from Sydney. Had it been only a year? It felt longer.

Holly leaned down to pat Curly and scooped up a handful of sand. She let it trickle slowly through her fingers and reflected on just how much in her life had changed. She had found many new friends, there had been sadness, challenges and great joys, and a new and wonderful sense of personal worth. She had begun to discover herself. Yes, that was what made it a year to remember.

She closed her eyes and said a short prayer of thanks. And when she opened them, the first rays of the sun had splashed the ocean with fresh colours to herald the start of another day, another year, at The Bay.

THE END

My Journey to
The Bay

YOU CAN TAKE CERTAIN STEPS IN LIFE THAT, AS
happens, set you on a path you hadn't planned, to
a place you had never before considered.

At the start of the 1990s I was walking
through the days with a heavy heart, an unhappy
woman. I had dropped out of television to achieve
my childhood dream of writing books. But the key
to my dreams had been handed to me at a low ebb
in my life. By a series of fortuitous circumstances I
had a contract for a novel. I also had a deadline
far away in impossible mists. After years of talking about writing a novel I now had to do it. It
was a struggle as I tried to write of great love in
the dying throes of a mad second marriage.

My children were at high school in India with

their dad. They had urged me to break free of this marriage and do what I'd always wanted. It wasn't easy. There were setbacks as pages of the novel were discarded, criticised, and re-written again and again. Good friends stepped in to encourage me and smooth the way. I spent time on a distant property researching, finding inspiration in the outback, meeting physical challenges and trusting my instincts.

Returning to Sydney's trendy Northern Beaches the work came slowly. I was too close to my old home, divided friendships and my husband's new girlfriend. I made the hero in my novel everything I felt my second husband wasn't, creating the man of my dreams on paper.

I took a break to go and see family in Los Angeles. While I was there I met a group of Australians making a film. They were from some place called Byron Bay. Never having been a hippy or a surfie I hadn't heard of it. I confided to them my troubles in writing, in settling, in finding ways to calm my heart and soul.

In unison they chorused, 'You must go to Byron Bay.'

As soon as I got back to Australia my son visited and I announced we were going north to Byron Bay, the most easterly point on the mainland. I discovered that our former neighbours, Brenda and Jim, had retired there. They told me it was difficult to find a place to rent year round at Byron because in the holiday season the owners wanted high rents or to use the houses themselves.

But they knew of one place that was available all year.

A high-powered executive friend who'd had a place in Byron (he lost it in his divorce) told me to speak to Tom, the famed local publican, as he would know what was going on around town.

Jim and Judy, my dear friends from the bush, were concerned at this plan to 'run away', so they came to the coast with me to check it out. With my son Nick we drove to Byron and stayed at a motel opposite the beach. Together we went and looked at the house that Brenda and Jim had told me about, and my heart sank. Near the railway line, it was old with claustrophobic dark rooms and a flecked pink laminex kitchen. Nick tried to be encouraging. 'It's got a mango tree in the back, Mom.'

We walked down the road to the Railway Pub and sat at an outside table. I was disheartened. I wanted light, air, sunny rooms, near water. But I had very little money, the advance for the book was modest and my share from the heavily mortgaged marital home had disappeared in paying off a bank loan and the costs of developing a film with Ken Russell. I was told to dream on!

I went into the bar to buy a round and a cheerful bloke dressed in shorts and T-shirt with a large schooner in his hand asked me if I was on holidays. No, looking for somewhere to live, I explained. What did I do? he asked.

For the first time the words fell from my mouth. 'I'm a writer.' They hung in the air and suddenly I felt terrific. 'I'm writing a book. I have a contract with a big publisher and I need peace and quiet. I'm looking for somewhere to live – just me. I can't afford much.'

'I might have a place,' he said. 'Come back tomorrow morning.' He was Tom, the publican I'd been told to look up. That's how things happen in The Bay.

I walked out with the drinks and said to everyone, 'I think I've found somewhere to live.'

Tom's wife Catherine hadn't been too impressed with his offer. They had been living in a cabin at the bottom of their five acres while building their new home, and they had no intention of renting it. But she took us to see it anyway.

We roared down the lethal driveway to the little hideaway house. It was a log cabin with floor to ceiling glass doors and a deck overlooking a big dam festooned with blue water lilies. Sunny, airy, private, near water – just as I wanted.

My bush mates gasped and said I wouldn't last six months. It was too quiet, I didn't know anyone in the area except for Brenda and Jim, there would be a zillion brown snakes around the dam and billions of cane toads. With the cabin surrounded by dense bush I couldn't see or hear another living soul.

I took it regardless. The deal was done with a handshake. I was told the cabin had been built as a temporary home revamped from Mexican Mick's old house. It was basic but the ambience was friendly, inviting and romantic.

My retired friends Brenda and Jim offered to give me any help I needed when I moved in. We celebrated with an Indian feast and Jim and Judy drove us back to Sydney as Nick was returning to India. I phoned my daughter Gabrielle, who was heading to university in California, and broke the news.

When I was ready to drive north I decided to leave Sydney at 5 am and get to Byron before dark. What bits of furniture I had would arrive a few days later. I'd never driven much. I quivered at the thought of driving over the Sydney Harbour Bridge from the North Shore. So a seven hundred kilometre drive with my goods and chattels and darling dog Sheila seemed a huge step.

Mum got up early and made me breakfast at four o'clock. There was a howling thunderstorm but I wouldn't be talked out of delaying. I felt a sense of urgency to get to my new home. Mum kissed me goodbye and I promised to find a phone box and call whenever I stopped.

Sheila the schnauzer sat in the back wincing at the thunder and lightning. My thirtieth birthday present of a 300-year-old Imari platter (we were living in Japan at the time) was wrapped in a blanket wedged next to a spinning wheel and every pair of shoes I owned. Before I'd gone two blocks I came across electrical wires blown down, snaking sparks across the road, so I drove across broken branches on the footpath. After Hornsby I hit fog on the freeway. The dawn was dismal.

At midday I stopped at McDonald's and

ordered lunch for Sheila and me at the drive thru. We picnicked in clearing showers and I was elated. This was a huge achievement for me. By the time I saw the sign announcing Byron Bay, the weather was clear – balmy – a stunning sunset. I crested a hill and there below were the twinkling lights of a township clinging to the crescent bay and a headland where the lighthouse beam suddenly flashed a greeting.

I drove to Brenda and Jim's house and the door swung open and Brenda stood with a glass of champagne at the ready. 'Welcome home,' she said.

Concerned that I might feel afraid in the lonely, empty cabin they invited Sheila and me to stay with them, but I decided to camp at my place. That night I curled up on the floor with Sheila burrowed beside me, listening to the night noises – rustling trees, snuffling animals and the creaks of the wood. For a moment I was teary. Then I decided I would cast a mental charmed circle around the house and I would be protected. And for the nine years I lived there, I was.

I came to terms with coping on my own. I had to deal with a carpet snake on the bed in the middle of the night and various other wildlife intrusions, a fox attacking my chickens, a near cyclone, and worries about money. I lived on avocados, mangoes and other fruit that grew on the property and my endless supply of eggs. Brenda invited me over for Sunday lunch and sent me home with leftovers that lasted till Wednesday.

I walked for miles on the beach and I kept to myself. For the first time in my life I was alone and I learned to like my own company. I made a garden, and made new friends – good women friends. I was told Byron Bay was a healing place for women and I grew in many ways. And I wrote and wrote.

My first book, *Heart of the Dreaming*, was a success, and each Christmas after that I produced a new one. Tom in the big house seemed quite chuffed to be able to tell his friends there was a sheila down by the chooks writing books. Every couple of months he and Catherine would share a bottle or three from their cellar with me and it was an interesting trip back down the hill in the dark, often in bare feet, to my bottom acre.

If ever I hit a rough patch I stepped outside the door and scolded myself, thinking, look where you live. How dare you whinge. Then one day I decided to stop waiting for Mr Wonderful on his white charger to sweep me off to his palace. It seemed I was here to stay, claimed by The Bay. So two years ago I bought my own house, moved the chooks and the ducks and Sheila's ashes – she had been with me for seventeen years. I was ready to share my life. And, along came an old friend. It happens like that in The Bay.

The Bay has changed since I arrived, though not as much for me as for the oldtimers. It is a special place and most people living in Byron believe we are led here. It has taught me many lessons. I love feeling part of a unique community. My mother moved nearby, my children stay as often and as long as they can. And I'm about to start my twelfth book. Frankly, I'm afraid to move away. I believe there is magic caught here in the cusp of the Cape, Mount Warning and the hinterland.

It's taken me eleven years to feel ready to write about this place. I hope I got it right. I hope one day you will share it too.

Di Morrissey
Byron Bay
7 September 2001

Heart of the Dreaming

The book that launched Di Morrissey as Australia's most popular female novelist.

At 21, Queenie Hanlon has the world at her feet and the love of handsome bushman TR Hamilton. Beautiful, wealthy and intelligent she is the only daughter of Tingulla Station, the famed outback property in the wilds of western Queensland.

At 22, her life lies in ruins. A series of disasters has robbed her of everything she ever loved. Everything except Tingulla – her ancestral home and her spirit's Dreaming place . . .

And now she is about to lose that too . . .

An extraordinary story of thwarted love and heroic struggle, *HEART OF THE DREAMING* is the tale of one woman's courage and her determination to take on the world and win.

Follow the Morning Star

Queenie and TR return in this sequel to the bestselling *HEART OF THE DREAMING*.

Queenie Hanlon has a perfect life. She's the mother of two adoring children, the wealthy owner of a thriving station property and the wife of TR Hamilton.

Then one day, Queenie's perfect life comes crashing down . . .

Her bitter and vengeful brother returns from Italy to lay claim to his inheritance. Her precious daughter is seduced by her uncle into giving up all that Queenie's strived for. And her beloved TR, injured in a riding accident, can no longer recall the life they once shared.

FOLLOW THE MORNING STAR is a triumphant story of courage and a rare love that endures the test of time.

Scatter the Stars

Larrikin Australian actor Randy Storm had it all. Swept up by Hollywood, he had the looks, charm and talent to take on the world.

But that was the 1950s. In the '90s he's forgotten, burned out after a life of excess and wild living.

When TV producer Michael Matthews bumps into Randy, he is surprised to find a man who is at peace with himself. He and researcher Janie Callendar set out to discover the source of this inner peace. One person not surprised by Randy's contentment is his agent, Ariel Margoles, who has always stuck by him. When she is called by world-acclaimed film director Patricia Jordan who is making the hottest Hollywood film of the year – Ariel sees the chance for Randy to be a star once more.

Just as he is about to reach his pinnacle, a secret from his past threatens to bring down his greatest triumph . . .

SCATTER THE STARS is a story of glamour, greed, loss and one man's life that charts the path for all of us.

When the Singing Stops

The journey that changes her life . . .

A young Australian woman leaves Sydney for a new world – Guyana, South America.

Captivated by Guyana's wild, unspoilt beauty, Madison Wright joins the native Amerindians struggling to preserve their culture against corporate exploitation. But her new-found commitment soon plunges Madison into a mire of murder, drug smuggling and political corruption. And finally, an unexpected love that pits her heart against her beliefs.

From Sydney's sparkling harbour to the lush rainforests of South America, *WHEN THE SINGING STOPS* is a triumph of storytelling.

'Morrissey is a gifted storyteller . . . well researched and evocatively written'
AUSTRALIAN BOOKSELLER & PUBLISHER

Tears of the Moon

Broome, Australia 1893
It's the wild passionate heyday of the pearling industry, and when young English bride Olivia Hennessy meets the dashing pearling master, Captain Tyndall, their lives are destined to be linked by the mysterious power of the pearl.

Sydney 1995
Lily Barton embarks on a search for her family roots which leads her to Broome. But her quest for identity reveals more than she could ever have imagined . . .

TEARS OF THE MOON is the spellbinding bestseller from Australia's most popular female novelist.

'Morrissey's research into the pearl industry and the history of Broome is formidable . . . she tells a good story'
SYDNEY MORNING HERALD

The Last Rose of Summer

A compelling story of two beautiful and remarkable women connected across the decades by the men who love them . . . and the magic of a place called Zanana.

KATE, a strong willed heiress determined to defy Edwardian convention, but she must pay the ultimate price to keep the home she loves so much . . .

ODETTE, an independent and idealistic young journalist caught in a fierce battle to save Zanana from ruthless developers . . .

Years apart yet inextricably linked by Zanana, the mansion they both love, these two women prove they are not afraid to fight for what they believe in.

From turn-of-the-century India to contemporary Sydney, *THE LAST ROSE OF SUMMER* is an epic story of love, possession and intrigue.

The Last Mile Home

A classic love story . . .

It is 1953 in a small Australian country town, a time of postwar prosperity and hope.

The Holtens are wealthy yet austere graziers who have lived on the land for generations. The McBrides are a large and loving shearer's family who are new arrivals to the district.

When the McBrides' eldest daughter falls in love with the Holtens' only son and heir, it seems impossible that they can have a future together.

As conflict and tragedy confront them, it is only with great determination that their love can survive.

THE LAST MILE HOME is an unforgettable story of the power of enduring love.

The Songmaster

A timely and profound novel that entrances and entertains.

In Melbourne, a baby is found abandoned in the Victorian Art Gallery. She is wrapped in a shawl decorated with a motif that links her to ancient rock paintings in the Kimberley . . .

In Los Angeles, a movie producer's dying daughter is haunted by nightmares after visiting the Kimberley . . .

And it is to the Kimberley that ex-nun Beth Van Horton brings a disparate group of travellers whose lives will be changed forever.

The Kimberley – a land that cradles Australia's ancient treasures – is also home to a people whose powerful secrets could unlock the future for modern mankind.

'It's daring, it's controversial, it's a great story and it's unputdownable . . . what more can I say about *The Songmaster* other than I wish I'd written it.'
BRYCE COURTENAY